Be wary, young sailor,
   Of wind and high water.
The sea has a secret,
   The sea has a daughter.

She'll swim along starboard,
   And capture your hea~~rt~~
With a flip of her tail-f~~in~~
   Underwater, d~~~~

MERMAIDS!

EDITED BY
JACK DANN & GARDNER DOZOIS

ACE FANTASY BOOKS
NEW YORK

MERMAIDS!

An Ace Fantasy Book/published by arrangement with
the editors

PRINTING HISTORY
Ace Fantasy edition/January 1986

ISBN: 0-441-52567-9

Ace Fantasy Books are published by
The Berkley Publishing Group,
200 Madison Avenue, New York, New York 10016.
PRINTED IN THE UNITED STATES OF AMERICA

Acknowledgment is made for permission to print the following material:

"The Prevalence of Mermaids" by Avram Davidson. Copyright © 1986 by Avram Davidson. Reprinted by permission of the author and the author's agent, John Silbersack.

"Nothing in the Rules" by L. Sprague de Camp. Copyright © 1939 by Street & Smith Publications, Inc.; © 1966 by L. Sprague de Camp. First published in *Unknown*, July 1939. Reprinted by permission of the author.

"She Sells Sea Shells" by Paul Darcy Boles. Copyright © 1983 by TZ Publications. First published in *The Twilight Zone Magazine*, Dec. 1983. Reprinted by permission of the author and the author's agent, Russell and Volkening, Inc.

"The Soul Cages" by T. Crofton Croker. From *Fairy Legends and Traditions of the South of Ireland*, by T. Crofton Croker, 1825.

"Sweetly the Waves Call to Me" by Pat Murphy. Copyright © 1981 by Pat Murphy. First published in *Elsewhere* (Ace). Reprinted by permission of the author.

"Driftglass" by Samuel R. Delany. Copyright © 1967 by Galaxy Publishing Corporation. First published in *Worlds of IF*, June 1967. Reprinted by permission of the author and the author's agent, Henry Morrison, Inc.

"Mrs. Pigafetta Swims Well" by Reginald Bretnor. Copyright © 1963 by Mercury Press, Inc. First published in *The Magazine of Fantasy & Science Fiction*, May 1963. Reprinted by permission of the author.

"The Nebraskan and the Nereid" by Gene Wolfe. Copyright © 1985 by Gene Wolfe. First published in *Isaac Asimov's Science Fiction Magazine*, December 1985. Reprinted by permission of the author and the author's agent, Virginia Kidd.

For George R. R. Martin
—*because He Is There.*

The editors would like to thank the following people for their help and support:

Trina King, Jane Yolen, Michael Swanwick, Susan Casper, Jeanne Dann, Bob Walters, Janet and Ricky Kagan, Virginia Kidd, Perry Knowlton, Avram Davidson, John Silbersack, Art Saha, John Kessel, Stuart Schiff, Gene Wolfe, Howard Waldrop, Lewis Shiner, Bob Frazier, Bruce Sterling, Jeff Levin, Christine Pasanen Morris, Edward Ferman, Pat Lo-Brutto, Kirby McCauley, Tom Whitehead of the Special Collections Department of the Paley Library at Temple University (and his staff, especially John Betancourt and Connie King), Brian Perry and Tawna Lewis of Fat Cat Books (263 Main Street, Johnson City, New York 13790), Barry Malzberg, David Whalen, the staff at the Sir Speedy Printing Center in Philadelphia (especially Lisa), and special thanks to our own editors, Ginjer Buchanan and Susan Allison.

CONTENTS

ADVENTURES IN UNHISTORY
The Prevalence of Mermaids

by

Avram Davidson

For many years now, Avram Davidson has been one of the most eloquent and individual voices in science fiction and fantasy, and there are few writers in any literary field who can hope to match his wit, his erudition, or the stylish elegance of his prose. His recent series of stories about the bizarre exploits of Doctor Engelbert Eszterhazy (collected in his World Fantasy Award-winning The Enquiries of Doctor Eszterhazy) *and the strange adventures of Jack Limekiller (as yet uncollected, alas), for instance, are Davidson at the very height of his considerable powers, and rank among the best work of the seventies. Davidson has won the Hugo, the Edgar, and the World Fantasy Award. His books include the renowned* The Phoenix and the Mirror, Masters of the Maze, Rogue Dragon, Peregrine: Primus, Rork!, Clash of Star Kings, *and the collections* The Best of Avram Davidson, Or All the Seas With Oysters, *and* The Redward Edward Papers. *His most recent books are* Peregrine: Secundus, *a novel,* Collected Fantasies, *a collection, and, as editor, the anthology* Magic For Sale.

Here, in an essay published for the first time in this anthology—one of a series of "Adventures in Unhistory" that Davidson has been writing for the past few years, examining curious and little-known areas of history and folklore—Davidson follows the watery trail of the most beautiful and seductive of all supernatural creatures: the mermaid.

* * *

*My father was the keeper of the Eddystone Light
And he slept with a mermaid one fine night;*

1

The offspring of this strange union were three:
A porpoise, and a porgy, and the third was me.
—*Old Sea Shanty*

NORMAN DOUGLAS CALLED THEM "PROVOCATIVE CITIZENS OF the deep..." And indeed they are provocative. We all know about the mermaid, "the most pleasing myth of all," as she has been called. Today we perhaps know a little less about her than our ancestors did. To us she is merely the woman who sits on a rock or bobs up in the waves; she carries a mirror in one hand and a comb in another, both for use when she arranges her long green hair; her long green hair is all the cover she has; and she is a woman to the hips and below that she is a nonspecific breed of fish, and she has scales on the fishy part of her. And that is about that.

Formerly there was more. Much more.
Most of which, it seems, is gone.

Mermaids, some of you will be faintly surprised to hear, did not belong exclusively to tales one's grandfather told ("See, my boy? That is a mermaid! And I want you to remember it, because there's no such thing!"), but also belonged to a school of mystical literature; surely you know De la Motte Fouqué's *Undine*... You don't? *Oh* well...

Even before the Age of Reason, we had come to feel a need to anchor the items of the imagination firmly between the rocks of reality, a natural explanation has been sought for every element of legend. Sought for... and, sometimes, found. The dragon has been traced to the crocodile, the werewolf to the rabid dog or to a human bitten by one, the mandrake to an alkaloid, the vampire to a psychosis... and so on. The mermaid, we might as well say, has been traced to the manatee, or sea cow... but, somehow, she doesn't stay traced. I think that the mermaid's tail, or trail, lies elsewhere. It is true that I, in collaboration with Randall Garrett, once wrote and published a story based on the possibility that, while the manatee may not look much like a mermaid, the mermaid might look much like a manatee. We had her speaking English with a strong Austrīlian accent, and she wound up as the first cook in a seafood restaurant somewhere on the coast of California.

It was lots of fun writing it, and, besides the fact that we had mixed up the manatee, or Atlantic Ocean sea cow, with the dugong, or Indian Ocean sea cow, it really was no answer.

Here are some few other items from the grab bag. Gary and Warmington, in their book *The Ancient Explorers,* say that Nearchus, the pilot-scout of Alexander the Great, heard that "the enchanted Mermaiden's Island of . . . Astola," "sacred to the Sun" in the Indian Ocean, "was once inhabited by one of the Nereids who made love to all who landed, turned them into fish, and threw them into the sea. But the Sun in pity and anger made them men once more." And a Nereid is defined as "any one of the sea-nymphs held to be the daughters of the sea-god Nereus." *Nereus?* What happened to Poseidon? Perhaps Nereus was senior in the position, for, we are told, Poseidon was originally a horse-god; and when the ancestors of the ancient Greeks came riding down from the sealess interior they were so impressed by the resemblance the white-maned waves bore to their horses that, thinking the thunder of the waves was caused by horses beneath the sea, they considered the sea to be Poseidon's realm as well. In which case . . . were the mermaids originally horse-maids? Enough, sir, enough. Onward.

It does seem that the earliest mermaid we have record of was actually a mer*man,* and his picture was even provided for us by the artists of ancient Babylon: he has a full beard, and his name was *On*—or *Oannes.* Yes. And he came out of the sea, splashing his fishytail, and he taught the proto-Babylonians the arts of agriculture, handicraft, metallurgy, writing and religion. By day. Day by day. For each night he returned beneath the sea. And if Mr. Von Daniken or his numerous imitators haven't explained to us that *On* or *Oannes* was really an ancient astronaut who happened to live in a yellow submarine, why not? Perhaps because the system of writing he taught, that of cuneiform, was probably the worst system of writing ever devised by any god or man. And yet there are those who say that *On/Oannes* was the origin of mermaids! The fools! Just because he had his picture taken in a bathing suit . . .

But let us hear what the Reverend Mr. S. Baring-Gould has to say—for he was one of those incredible Victorian clergymen who seemed to have what to say about everything. He says that the wise one, the giver of benefits, who came out of the sea each day and went back into it each night, was none other than the sun itself. "As On, the sun-god, rising and setting in the sea, was supplied with a corresponding moon-goddess, Atergatis . . . so the fiery Moloch, 'the great lord,' was supplied with his Mylitta, 'the birth-producer.' Moloch was the fierce flame-god, and Mylitta the goddess of moisture. Their worship was closely united. *The priests of Moloch wore female attire, the priestesses of Mylitta were dressed like men."* I think that's significant. I'm not sure *why* I think that's significant, but I do. Probably because it *sounds* significant. As a matter-of-fact, it sounds like Polk Street on Saturday night, is what it sounds like.

The Rev. Mr. Baring-Gould shows us that this worship had made its way, via, I suppose, Phoenicia, to Carthage and elsewhere in North Africa; doubtless, too, to ancient Greece. And thence? He says that "The prevalence of mermaids"—say, there's a good title! *The Prevalance of Mermaids!*—"The prevalence of mermaids among Celtic populations indicates these water-nymphs as having been originally deities of these peoples; and I cannot but believe that the circular mirror they are usually represented as holding is a moon-disk." Robert Graves goes him one better; the comb they are usually represented as holding, Graves cannot but believe, represents the plectrum, or pick, with which they used to play their lyre. Remember the sirens' song? It had instrumental accompaniment.

The name Mylitta, goddess of moisture, reminds one of the Greek word *thalatta,* the sea . . . which is, certainly, moist . . . but as the Greeks (who had a word for everything) had *two* words for the sea,* the other being *thalassa;* one is reminded also of the Greek word *Melissa,* or *bee.*

However, as for the mermaids' mirror, listen: "In China magical mirrors were used to foretell the future . . ." One of the magical powers of mermaids was that of prophecy. So, unless someone can come up real quickly with a reference to the moon-disk's being used to foretell the future, maybe it's back to the mirror, after all . . . though, of course, in a way, they are both reflective. . . .

How nice, "to meet a mermaid washing her silken sark by the stream" in the words of the learned L. C. Wimberly, author of *Folklore in the English and Scottish Ballads.* He says this was "evidently common experience; no special artifice was needed to get such a story believed." In which case no special

*Well, *ac*tually, they had a third word (*pelagi*): but who counts?

credit would have been obtained by telling it. In which case no special reason was needed to make it up. How's that for remorseless logic? And has anyone ever spoken of remorseful logic? Don't answer that. Washing her silken sark by the stream: ever such a lovely alliteration; remember the bear-sarks? Who went berserk? Serk or sark, then, means skin . . . or garment . . . and, by extension, skirt: to which it is obviously related; and shirt, just a bit less obviously. A cutty sark, in small letters, is a short garment, and, by extension, either a loose woman or a cut-down sail. *The Cutty Sark* was a famous sailing vessel, and a brand of whiskey is named after it. I was once, like the wedding guest in *The Rhime of the Ancient Mariner,* seized hold of, in England, by a very old man who proceeded to tell me that one of his cousins had been the last second mate on the ship *Cutty Sark* and that another of his cousins had shot the last man killed in a duel in England. It would have been even more interesting and to the point had he himself been an ancient mariner, but he was actually an ancient dentist. From time to time, though, I have had a mental image of a sailor, clad in a cutty sark, having had a drink of Cutty Sark, sent aft (or would it be forward?) to trim the cutty sark of the *Cutty Sark.* Whilst so engaged he espies a woman a-washing her cutty sark; "A mermaid!" he cries. Says the second mate, "No, she is only a cutty sark." Ah well.

Here is old Jacob Grimm, in his *Teutonic Mythology,* telling us that "Morolt [Who he? Go thou and learn: *Grimm:* Tute. Myth. Page 434, *genuk.*] Morolt also has an aunt a *merminne* who . . . rules over dwarfs . . . they dwell on a mountain by the sea, in an ever-blooming land . . . a precisely corresponding male being, the taciturn prophetic . . . marmendill . . . coral is named [marmendill's smithery], he cunningly wrought it in the sea. [the mersay] . . . and the Fair Melusina . . . precisely the fairy being that had previously been called *merrimenni.*"

Listen, I don't want any complaints, Grimm will drive you *crazy,* no he never read The Chicago Style Manual; and oh God does he need an up-to-date editor! Shall we try to untangle this knotted mass of sea-wrack? There is an under-water creature called *merminni* and/or marmendill, also called a merfay, shall we say "sea-fairy"? Gad, we'd better.——of which one is the Fair Melusina; one of the many such creatures who deceitfully marry humans and get away with the masquerade until one night he espies her fish-tail, and——But for now:

enough. Also, says Jacob, called merrimenni. Merrimenni.

It seems a curious thing that the *merimenni*, when they crossed the English Channel, were transmogrified into *merry-maidens*. Evidently the etymological connection of *mer* with *sea* had been lost; the *minne*, *menni* were seen to be masculine and thus in need of feminization; and the *mer* became *merry*, as in jovial. However. One never knows, and a quick trip to my dictionary tells me that *merry*, as in jolly, relates to an old word, *murg*, meaning short. In other words, cutty. As in cutty sark. Odd.

But there is obviously a form missing between *merimenni* and *merrymaidens*, and we find it in the title of Robert Louis Stevenson's *The Merry Men*. If you have read it, you will follow; if you haven't read it, go and read it. What a shame he felt obliged to end it so hastily. It is a mere cutty sark of a book; good, though.

Well, well, the merrymen. The singular of men is man, which will lead me easily to the word manatee, with which there is of course no connection... grammatically, that is... but with this Adventure there is a connection. It is a commonplace to say, "The manatee, or sea cow, nursing its calf crooked in a fore-flipper above the surface gave rise to the legend of the mermaid." As it happens, alas, the manatee (we are told) nurses its calf *below* the surface: so, so much for that. It is also a commonplace to backtrack, and express wonder as to "How the manatee, or sea cow, with its huge almost shapeless head, and whiskers, could have given rise to the legend of the mermaid." And, with a few coarse digs in the ribs about the overheated imagination of sailors too long at sea, the matter is rather quickly dropped. Leaving it for me to pick it up and dust it off. Having dallied with the manatee, the practice is to go on and dally with the seal: the seal, it is pointed out to us, has a much more humanoid face, and so on. Well, heaven knows how often in hunting season human beings are shot by mistake for deer, and yet an upright biped does not look very much like a quadruped, does it? Before hunters used to wear dayglow jackets in orange and red they commonly wore khakies. There's a story that a countryman, accidentally shot by a city hunter who said that he "mistook him for a deer," went and had a hunting outfit made by the local awning maker: green and white stripes. And was shot by a city hunter; excuse? "I mistook him for a zebra." I can remember coming back with a flock of sheep in Galilee and being asked by a visiting girl from Chicago if I had left one of my sheep "back there"— looking "back there" I observed a perfectly normal-looking camel. So let us not be too hard if some people long ago thought that a seal was a human. It could have happened.

One wonders, though, how often it could have happened. How, for example, in such seal-rich regions as the coasts of Ireland, Scotland, Cornwall—regions rife with mermaid legends—could people *not* tell the difference between humans and seals? The answer is, they can tell the difference very well. And they say that sometimes the seals turn into people, and/ or the people into seals. Often. And so that's *one* explanation. ... An old Scotch word for seal is "silkie," and aficionados of folk-songs will at once recollect the haunting old song made popular by Joan Baez: *I am a man upon the land. I am a silkie on the sea* ... Shades of Shapeshifters and Skinchangers, what, what? And so, without warning, I mention the name of *sirens*. And with that, the legend changes.

Faithful old Webster's Collegiate lists four meanings for the word, but it's chiefly the first which fits our needs here as follows: *"One of a group of creatures in Greek mythology having the heads and sometimes the breasts and arms of women but otherwise the forms of birds that lured mariners to destruction by their singing."* To which most of us would echo, *Birds?* Originally, that is. The evidence is there on more than one surviving Greek urn or pickle plate. Ulysses is tied to the mast, the sailors are rowing away and we know that their ears are plugged: and there, swooping overhead are the birdies, with sure enough the heads and faces of women. Only later on did the sirens get, somehow, changed in form so that they seemed more as we think of mermaids.

But if, as for example E. M. Forster and many others say, the sirens were simply seals, then "what song the sirens sang" was merely the ooping and yerping which most of us, probably, have heard either along a sea-coast or in a circus, aquarium, or zoo. Interesting. Hardly romantic, though. But *why* was their song so deadly? I search in vain the accounts of the legends for a rational explanation, and perhaps I am wrong to do so: in more recent times we read that merpeople are sometimes the souls of the dead, particularly the drowned-dead: *there* is a reason: as you are now, so once was I; as I am now, so you must be: come into Drownlandia and join me.... But what may the reason have been in the beginning? I have a theory. Hearken on. Look at detailed maps of whatsoever waters of whatsoever countries which have coasts, and sooner or later you will see for certain, next to very small dots, the immemorial words, *Seal Rocks*. Not once and again, but again and again.

And again and again and again.

In other words, if as you sailed along uncharted waters and uncharted shores in those days before charts and were close enough to hear the seals, well, sonny, you were too close. Much too close. And even as we accept that before the sirens were seals, or some sort of sea-creatures, they were bird-women, the principles of navigation remain the same: birds, seabirds, often frequent offshore rocks and inshore crags, rocky seacliffs; and if you are close enough to hear them "singing," say, you are too close: your vessel may strike those rocks. *"And the angry rocks they gored her sides, like the horns of an angry bull."* And then it will be a case of *"Going down. My God. Going down!"*

These are facts, and the rest is embroidery.

It is, or course, a fairly gorgeous embroidery.

This thought occurred to me: "Mermaid sightings were the UFO sightings of times past." However, I don't want to follow that thought to its logical confusion. However, I do want to give a partial listing of what I might term "major mermaid sightings" throughout a period of hundreds of years, because it might be useful. When I say "major mermaid sightings," really, I mean, those which were for one thing written down, and for another, were reported in the very good book *Sea Enchantress: The Tale of the Mermaid and Her Kin,* by Mr. Owen Benwell and Sir Arthur Waugh, and published by The Citadel Press, N.Y., in 1965. (The authors are described as "both prominent members of the British Folk-Lore Society— Sir Arthur has been its President—and have devoted several years to collecting mer-legends of all times and places." I don't know if Sir Arthur is any relation to Evelyn Waugh, whose father was also named Arthur, but who was not a knight and who died many years ago.) I have collected these sightings out of the book and arranged them for this Adventure and sometimes abbreviated the language of the book. And, following these listings, I shall list others. Surely you will all see why.

Some time in the first half century of the Christian Era,

Pliny the Elder cites as his "authors," i.e. authorities, "divers knights of Rome, right worshipfull persons and of good credite, who testifie that in the coast of the Spanish Ocean neere unto Gades [Cadiz], they have seene a Mereman, in every respect resembling a man in all parts of the bodie as might bee."— This last sounds ambiguous; but such is the report.

Here's one from an old Irish, that is, Gaelic, MS: "In the year 558 was taken the Mermaid, i.e. Liban, the daughter of Eochaidh, the son of Murieadh, on the strand of Ollarbha, in the net of Beoan, son of Inli, the fisherman of Comhgall of Beannchair."—The fact that the geneology of the mermaid is known so nicely, is here passed by without comment.

Another from the Irish. In the years 887 "a mermaid was cast ashore by the sea in the country of Alba . . . she was whiter than the swan all over."

The year 1018: "Another wonderful tale from Ireland: a mermaid was taken by the fisherman of the Weir of Lisarglinn in Ossory, and another at Port-Lairge."

Year 1147: Knights going to the Second Crusade were in the Bay of Biscay, "'annoyed' by sirens, 'who made a horrible noise of wailing, laughing and jeering, like the clamour of insolent men in a camp.' . . . it is recorded that the Crusaders became penitent."

The 12th century, that is, the same as the previous two: "A monster was seen near Greenland . . . 'approximated' in all respects to a human being down to the waist, thereafter she resembled a fish. The hands seem . . . to be long, and the fingers . . . united like a web like that on the feet of water-birds . . ."— This in turn reminds us of the story that Charlemagne's grandmother had webbed feet, *la reine pedauque;* she was sometimes called Big-footed Bertha. Some say only that she had hairy feet. The consensus must be, she had funny feet. It is true that sometimes babies are born with some sort of webbing between two of more toes, this may be merely ontology recapitulating ichthyology, or whatever; it may be the origin of a fairly common tradition in many places that certain human families are descended from mermaids.

The year 1197: ". . . at Oreford in Suffolk . . . a fish was taken by fishers in their nets . . . resembling in shape a wild or savage man . . ." Nothing is said in the description, which is very detailed, of his having a fish-tail. He did eat fish both raw and cooked and he "would not or could not utter any

speech." Eventually he escaped back to sea. A logical explanation might be simply that he was either a mute, or a nut who
liked to swim a whole hell of a lot: *but:* he was caught in
fishnets, therefore he was a fish. Figures . . . don't it . . . in a
way? "All fish swim, Fred swims, therefore Fred is a fish."

The year 1403. The scene Holland. The event a great storm.
Alas, no brave little Dutch boy was around to stick his finger
into the leak in the dike, and the dikes broke and flooded "the
vicinity of Edam," where the cheese comes from. "A mermaid
floated in" but could not float out, and was taken up by kindly
Dutch homemakers who fed her and clothed her and taught her
to spin and to "kneel down . . . before the crucifix, she never
spake, but lived dumbe and continued alive . . . fifteen years;
then she died."—It may be that all strange mutes found near
water were retroactively legendized into mer-folk. Eh? And
worse things could have happened to them, considering.

1523: " 'the third day of November, there was seen at Rome
this sea-monster, the bignesse of a child of five yeeres old, like
to a man even to the navell, except the ears; in the other parts
it resembled a fish.' "—the source here is a famous and respected Ambrose Paré, the Surgeon-General of France, and a
pioneer in treating wounds and wounded.

1550. Orefund, Denmark: A creature taken from the sea
was brought, either dying or already dead, to the king, and "its
head 'resembled that of a human creature with cropped
hair . . .' "—This differs from the usual traditional description
of very long hair.

1560. "The report of the netting, in one draught, of seven
mermen and mermaids off the coast of Mandar, Ceylon . . .
must have carried conviction to those who heard it, supported
as it was by the testimony of several Jesuits and by one Bosquez, physician to the Viceroy of Goa. Bosquez, his profes-
sional instincts thoroughly aroused, dissected the seven luckless
sea-creatures. His report (which was taken seriously enough to
be included in the *Histoire de la Compagnie de Jesus,* No.
276) stated that, both externally and internally, the mermen
and mermaids were exactly similar to human beings."—Can it
be that they *were* human beings? What, then, made them sea-
creatures? Answer: They were found in the sea.

About the same date: " . . . a work by the French historian
and traveller, André Thevet [mentions] . . . sea-monsters in human shape . . . seen off the coast of Africa . . . 'that the floud

had left on the shore, the which was heard to cry. In like case the female came with the next floud, crying aloud and sorrowing . . . By this may be knowen, that the Sea doeth nourishe and bring forth divers, and strange kind of monsters, as well as the land.'"——To which one may only reply, indeed it doeth.

1565. "The 18th of November we came to Thora, which Citie is on the shoare of the Red Sea, of no lustre; the Haven small, in which ships laden with Spices out of Arabia, Abassia, and India resort. In this citie we saw a mermaids skin taken there . . . which in the lower part ends Fish-fashion: of the upper part, onely the Navill and Breasts remaine; the arms and head being lost."——So no report about the hair.

We now enter the 17th century; date: 1608, chronicler Hendrik Hudson, on his second voyage: "The 15th of June all day and night cleere sunshine . . . latitude . . . 75 deg. 7 minutes . . . One of our companie . . . saw a Mermaid . . . From the Navill upward, her backe and breasts were like a woman's . . . her body as big as one of us; her skin very white; and long haire hanging down behinde, of colour blacke; in their going downe they saw her tayle, which was like the tayle of a Porposse, and speckled like a Macrell. Their names that saw her were Thomas Hilles and Robert Raynar." Benwell and Waugh quote the comments of Philip Gosse. "Seals and walruses must have been as familiar to these polar sailors as cows to a milkmaid. Unless the whole story was a concocted lie between the two men, reasonless and objectless, and the worthy old navigator doubtless knew the character of his men, they must have seen some form of being as yet unrecognized."

Same year: 1608. One Captain Whitbourne relates, ". . . of a morning early as I was standing by the waterside in the Harbour of St. Johns [Newfoundland] . . . I espied verie swiftly . . . swimming towards me, looking cheerfully, as it had beene a woman, by the Face, Eyes, Nose, Mouth, Chine, Eares, Necke and Forehead: It seemed to be so beautiful and in those parts so well proportioned . . . the shoulders and backe downe to the middle, to be as square, white and smooth as the back of a man, and from the middle to the hinder part, pointing in proportion like a broad hooked Arrow . . . whether it were a Mermaide or no, I know not; I leave it to others to judge . . ."

1614. Captain John Smith, the same whose adventures with Pocahontas excited us in the first grade, seemed like the actions of a familiar friend in the second, and had begun to bore us by the third; Captain John Smith, a-sailing in the West Indies, saw something "swimming with all possible grace near the shore. The upper part of her body resembled that of a woman . . . she had large eyes, rather too round, a finely-shaped nose (a little too short), well-formed ears, rather too long,"—picky, picky Captain Smith!—". . . and her green hair imparted to her an original character by no means unattractive . . . [but] from below the waist the woman gave way to the fish."

1619. A merman is captured off the coast of Norway by two senators, names Ulf Rosensparre and Christian Hollh, and then released. Perhaps he could vote.

1670. Here is the account of the Rev. Lucas Debes, Provost of the Lutheran churches in the Faroes Islands of Denmark. "There was seen . . . by many of the inhabitants . . . a Mer-maid close to the shore . . . She had long hair on her head, which hung down to the surface of the water all round about her. She held a fish . . . in her right hand."

Really, the reported sightings are too numerous to relate without fatigue, so from the 1700's I now mention only one. In 1739, as reported in the distinguished publication *The Gentleman's Magazine*, "some fisherman near the City of Exeter drawing their nets ashore, a Creature leap'd out, and run away very swiftly; not being able to overtake it, they knock'd it down by throwing sticks after it. At their coming up to it, it was dying, having groan'd like a human Creature: Its Feet were webb'd like a Duck's, it had Eyes, Nose and Mouth resembling those of a man, only the Nose somewhat depress'd; a Tail not unlike a Salmon's, turning up towards its Back, and is 4 Feet high. It was publickly shewn here."

And so we come to the 19th century.

Mr. William Munro, a Scotch schoolteacher (and a schoolteacher in Scotland was traditionally expected to be of superior qualifications and was held in great respect, until at least recently being called the *dominie*, from the Latin, *lord*), writes a letter to a Dr. Torrance in Glasgow; letter being published in *The Times* of London on Sept. 8, 1809.

"About 12 years ago . . . when I was Parochial Schoolmaster at Reay, in the course of my walking on the shore of Sandside Bay . . . my attention was arrested by the appearance of a figure resembling an unclothed human female, sitting upon a rock extending into the sea, and apparently in the action of combing its hair, which flowed around its shoulders, and of a light brown colour. The resemblance which the figure bore to its prototype in all its visible parts was so striking, that had not the rock on which it was sitting been dangerous for bathing, I would have been constrained to have regarded it as really an human form, and to an eye unaccustomed to the situation, it must have undoubtedly appeared as such . . . the forehead round, the face plump, the cheeks ruddy, the eyes blue, the mouth and lips of a natural form . . . the breasts and abdomen, the arms and fingers, from the action in which the hands were employed, did not appear to be webbed, but as to this I am not positive. It remained on the rock three of four minutes after I observed it . . . combing its hair . . . and then dropped into the sea . . . whence it did not reappear to me. I had a distinct view of its features, being at no great distance on an eminence above the rock where it was sitting, and the sun brightly shining.

"Immediately before its getting into its natural element it seemed to have observed me . . . It may be necessary to remark, that previous to the period I beheld this object, I had heard it frequently reported by several persons, and some of them persons whose veracity I never heard disputed, that they had seen such a phenomenon as I have described, though then, like many others, I was not disposed to credit their testimony . . . I can say of a truth, that it was only by seeing the phenomenon, I was perfectly convinced of its existence.

"If the above narrative can in any degree be subservient towards establishing the existence of a phenomenon hitherto almost incredible to naturalists, or to remove the skepticism of others, who are ready to dispute everything which they cannot fully comprehend, you are welcome to it, from,

"Dear Sir,
"Your most obliged and most humble servant,
"William Munro."

I have quoted from this at length, and I am not disposed to doubt that Mr. Munro saw exactly what he said he saw. I am disposed only to ask, What on earth persuaded him that he had seen a mermaid? He says he did not think her fingers were webbed; he says he was close enough to see that her eyes were blue; he certainly saw no tail or else he would certainly have said so: Why did he think he saw a mermaid? As he is not available to ask, I must answer for myself. As follows: (1) She was by the sea, or *mer*. (2) She was mother-naked. (3) She sat on a rock which was "dangerous for bathing." (4) She was combing her hair, an action traditional for mermaids. (5) She dived into the sea, and did not reappear to him. And that is all.

To me the matter in no way enters the realm of the unnatural, the supernatural, the supranatural, preternatural, or even the mysterious. A Scotch woman, in good health, and tired of all those long, long (and mostly woolen) clothes, decides to go skinny-dipping; there being no facilities for such at that time and in that place, other than the sea itself, into the sea she goes. Coming oot, there being also no bathing caps in them days, she sits herself doon upon a rock, and she cambs her hair and spreads it oot to dry. One would think she might have been private there, but no: alang comes some silly old dominie, and gapes at her: so into the sea she dives again . . . nae doot hiding under a shelving she knows of till the gowk has passed—

But to guid Mr. Munro, it was so much less likely that a woman in Scotland during the reign of George III would go barebottomed in the level daylight, and upon a rock he deemed too dangerous for bathing: it was infinitely likelier that she was a meremaid. He was, after all, a schoolteacher and a parochial one, and the parish was of the Kirk of Scotland.—But who knows how often this may have happened?

The next sighting is not long later, and in the same country: It does seem that either Scotland was partial to mermaids, or they to her.

1811. "In Campbelltown, 29th of October . . . In presence of Duncan Campbell, Esq., Sheriff-substitute of Kintyre, appeared John McIsaac, tenant [-farmer] . . . solemnly sworn and examined depones . . . That having taken a walk towards the seashore, he came to the edge of a precipice . . . from which he saw something white upon a black rock . . . the upper half of it was white, and of the shape of a human body, and the other half towards the tail of a brindled reddish-grey colour apparently covered with long hair; and as the wind blew . . . it sometimes raised the hair over the creature's head, and every time . . . the animal would lean towards one side, and taking up the opposite hand, would stroke the hair backwards, and then leaning upon the other side of its head in the same manner. That at the same time . . . it would also spread or extend its tail like a fan . . . and while so extended, the tail continued in tremulous motion . . . That the animal . . . was between four and five feet long, as near as he could judge. That it had a head, hair, arms and body, down to the middle like a human being, only that the arms were short in proportion to the body which appeared to be about the thickness of that of a young lad, and tapering gradually to the point of the tail . . . he cannot say if [the fingers] were webbed or not. [. . .] That after the sea had . . . [ebbed] . . . the animal . . . then tumbled clumsily into the sea . . . he saw its face . . . which to him had all the appearance of the face of a human being, with very hollow eyes . . . the animal was constantly . . . stroking and washing its breast . . . he cannot say if the bosom was formed like a woman's or not . . . All which he declares to be truth as he shall answer to God . . .

"Duncan Campbell, Sheriff-substitute."

Appended to this affidavit is another and briefer one: "We the Rev. Doctor George Robinson and Mr. Norman MacLeod, minister of Campbelltown, and James Maxwell, Esq., Chamberlain [i.e. J.P.] of Mull, do hereby certify that we were present when . . . John McIsaac delivered his testimony . . . That we know of no reason why his veracity should be called in question; and that from the manner in which he delivered his evidence, we are satisfied that he was impressed with a perfect belief, that the appearance of the animal he has described was such as he has represented it to be."

This seems to knock my rationalizations into a cocked hat . . . or a Highland bonnet. And only a few days later, on Nov. 2nd, Sheriff Campbell is to take another deposition, this one from Katherine Loynachan, age not given, "who . . . was herding cattle for her father about three weeks ago [so, actually, *before* John McIsaac, on Sunday the 18th of Oct., saw his Animal] at the seaside . . . [when] she observed some creature sliding on its belly off one of the rocks . . . into the sea; . . . this creature had a head covered with long hair of a darkish color, the shoulders and back white, with the rest of the body tapering like a fish and . . . of a darkish brown color . . . it disappeared under water, but . . . immediately . . . came above water again . . . and . . . laid one hand, which was like a boy's hand, upon another rock . . . That . . . the fact of it . . . had all the appearance of a child and as white, and at this time the animal was constantly rubbing or washing its breast with one hand, the fingers being close together . . . [Notice this inexplicable gesture . . . again.]

"Duncan Campbell, Sheriff-substitute."

Sheriff Campbell's conclusions, after these two incidents, would be very interesting indeed, but we don't have them. What we have next, though, is another sighting, also in Scotland, but about twenty years later, on the island of Benbecula, between the two larger islands (as Benwell and Waugh don't tell you, I shall) of North Uist and South Uist, in the Outer Hebrides: Gaelic in speech and Roman Catholic in religion. In that region where, about ninety years earlier Bonnie Prince Charley had made his romantic and ill-fated entrance into Scotland, some people had gone to cut seaweed. There was a splash, a cry, and those who ran to see what the cause, saw "a creature 'in the form of a woman in miniature,' some few feet away in the sea." The creature, whatever she was, was having fun in the water, tumbling about, evading attempts to catch her, when the inevitable rascal boy threw stones. "She was next heard of a few days later, but, alas, then she was dead; her body was washed ashore, about two miles from where she was first seen. A detailed examination followed . . . 'the upper part of the creature was about the size of a well-fed child of three or four years of age, with an abnormally developed breast. The hair was long, dark and glossy, while the skin was white, soft, and tender. The lower part of the body was like a salmon, but without scales.'

"The lifeless body . . . attracted crowds to the beach where she lay, and the . . . spectators were convinced that they had gazed upon a mermaid at last.

"But the story does not end there. Mr. Duncan Shaw, factor (land agent) for Clanranald [the Clan Clanranald's head], baron-baillie and sheriff of the district, after seeing the corpse, gave orders that a coffin and shroud be made for the mermaid, and in the presence of many people she was buried"—not in churchyard or graveyard, but—"a little distance above the shore where she was found. This action of the factor [say Benwell and Waugh] is more eloquent than any signed testimony. A man who held his office was unlikely to be credulous, and that he ordered a coffin and shroud for the strange little creature cast upon his shores suggested that he thought she was at least partly human."

Indeed it did. One might add that "a man who held his office" was not likely to be generous, either. Not without extremely good reason.

• • •

The next listings are somewhat different. For lack of space here, I will cut them to the bone and number them, and—I warn you—am leaving out, for the time being, a most important piece of information. Chronologically they pick up where the others left off. Thus:

1) "In the month of February, 1849, two soldiers saw a boy come out of the jungle and go down to the stream to drink. They caught him, and gave him to a poor cultivator's widow. She could never get him to speak." 2) c. 1850. "A trooper was passing along the bank of a river when he saw a little boy on all fours who went down to the stream and drank. The trooper secured the boy and tried to make him speak, but could get nothing from him. Captain Nicholetts made the boy over to the charge of his servants, who take great care of him, but can never get him to speak a word." 3) c. late 1840's. "A trooper on the left bank of the _____River saw a boy drinking in the stream. He had a man with him on foot, and they managed to seize the boy. He could never be heard to utter more than one articulate sound . . . could not understand or utter a word . . ." 4) "In 1860 the police brought in a male child, who moved by hops something like a monkey. He gave vent to snarls and sounds, something between a bark and a grunt." 5) c. same date. ". . . could never be taught to speak . . ." 6) Date unknown. "He was to all appearance about twenty years of age, was mute, but able to show signs of pleasure or anger by sounds . . ." 7) 1867-1894. "He was eventually tamed, but always had a wild look about him. He lived to be between thirty and forty, but never spoke."

"Sightings" 5 and 6 are not precisely dated, but please keep clear that these seven reports refer to *seven different beings!* I could give more, but perhaps these will suffice. Perhaps, too, in reading these mid-19th century reports you will be reminded of the one dated 1197. "At Oreford, in Suffolk," something called "a fish," although "resembling in shape a wild or savage man," was taken in a fishnet, and *"he would not or could not utter any speech . . ."* And perhaps, too, you recalled at once the incident at Edam in 1403, when the dike broke. "A mermaid floated in . . . *she never spake, but lived dumbe for fifteen years; then she died."* I had suggested that perhaps these two, and perhaps others, were what are usually termed deaf-mutes (I believe that a term preferred today is, "deaf people who cannot speak"). They might also have been suffering from another form of speechlessness, not congenitally so; "mute by the visitation of God," but perhaps through shock (shipwreck, for example). Do I suggest the same for the seven I cite from the 19th century? It is time for me to reveal my source for these seven; it is the book called *Wolf-Children and Feral Man;* printed in 1942 by the University of Denver, and "Reprinted 1966 in an Unaltered and Unabridged Edition [by Archon Books] With Permission of Harper and Row, Inc." It is two books in one. The first part entitled *The Diary of the Wolf-Children of Midnapore (India),* by the Reverend J.A.L. Singh / Missionary S.P.G. [Society for the Propagation of the Gospel] Mission and the Rector / The Orphanage, Midnapore / Bengal, India / with a Preface by / The Right Reverend H. Pakenham-Walsh (Bishop) / Christa Ishya Ashram, Tadagam, P.O. Coimbatore, India / *and* / *Appendix, Chronology of the Wolf-Children;* the second part is called *Feral Man and Cases of Extreme Isolation of Individuals,* by Robert M. Zingg, Ph.D. / University of Denver / *Author of the Huichols: Primitive Artists* / Forewords / Professor R. Ruggles Gates, Ph.D., D.Sc., LL. D., F.R.S. / King's College, University of London, Chairman, Human Heredity Bureau, London / Professor Arnold Gesell, M.D., Director / Clinic of Child Development, The School of Medicine / Yale University, New Haven, Connecticut / Author of *Wolf Child and Human Child* / Professor Frances N. Maxfield, Ph.D. / Director of Psychological Clinic / Ohio State University, Columbus, Ohio / Professor Kingsley Davis, Ph.D. / Associate Professor of Sociology / The Pennsylvania State College . . .

I have copied the entire subtitle page, unusually long for a modern book, on purpose in order to make it clear that whatever else it may or may not be, *Wolf-Children and Feral Man* is not a mere rip-off from some volume of forgotten lore, and neither are its authors and foreworders loonies or zanies. If a more respectable group sacred and secular can be found . . . well. . . .

Stories of human children raised by animals are as ancient as Romulus and Remus and more modern than Tarzan. All seven reports cited here from the 19th century are from India, and all refer to alleged "wolf-children." There are, as I say, more. Sources include two rajahs, and Gen. Sir William Sleeman, best known for his successful campaign to suppress thuggee. He and the rajahs were believers. Skeptics included Dr.

John Whishaw of the Lucknow (India) Lunatic Asylum, who bluntly wrote in 1874, "The majority of wolf-boys are idiots, taken by their parents and left near some distant police station." Even this skeptical statement avoids absolute finality with the words, *The majority.* I take no sides. The matter is immense, and immensely complex. Read the book.

The Rev. Mr. Singh's part of the book refers to two girl-children he said he and jungle villagers rescued from a wolf's den in Bengal in 1920, and which he and his wife certainly raised and cared for; one died young, the other lived about nine years; and was (with infinite patience) taught to walk on two feet, to speak about 40 words, an otherwise to behave as a human being, albeit always a strange one. Prof. Zingg's part of the book covers the whole field of wild men, wild women, wild children, "feral man," and people raised in isolation from others; is there one word in the whole book regarding, specifically, *mermaids?*—not a single one, as far as I could see: why, then, am I writing of it in this connection?

Serendipity enters, yet again. Looking for data in connection with my hypothesis that at least some of the "mermaids" or "mermen" found and cared for might really have been human beings unable to speak and/or hear, I sought a few specific books on the treatment and education of the deaf and the mute. None of them were on the library shelves, but near to where they would have been was the book *Wolf-Children and Feral Man*. I took it down, I opened it, I read a few words, I took it out. . . .

I learned a lot.

We observe in five of these reports, from Europe and Asia, that the strange beings had this in common: *they were found by water:* and *they could not speak.* I acknowledge that in none of the four cases was mention made of a tail, fish-like or otherwise. I would hasten to point out that the Encyclopedia Britannica emphasizes that in a very large number of mermaid legends the merperson *has* no tail* . . . but I do not exactly hasten, because in these legends he or she invariably *does* speak. And one of the things which, usually, *she* says is, in effect, "Very well, I will marry you, but on condition that you do not watch me" do this or that: in Chinese and Japanese

---

*"They could, however, assume human shape occasionally, and in some forms of the tradition, they were without tails."

werefox-witch stories the act forbidden to be watched is eating, in Western European mermaid stories it is bathing. A very old variation on this is the non-Scriptural story that the Queen of Sheba had (a) hairy feet, or (b) webbed feet (this latter pops up again with *la reine pedauque* as the ancestress of Charlemagne), or (c) hooved feet. As she never lifted her long skirts at all, King Solomon took her to a part of the palace where the floor was of polished blue marble: *"Water!"* cried the Sheban queen, hoisting her hems to avoid wetting them. Thus showing all. It is entirely possible that a person afflicted with an abnormality of the feet might not wish them to be seen even by a spouse; and the aspect of the legend wherein the "mortal" spouse eventually peeks and sees the fishy-tail, whereupon the mer-spouse dives into the moat and vanishes, may rest upon just such a circumstance. A fishy-tail, though more abnormal, is more dramatic than a clubfoot. (The fox-witch-woman, on the other hand, reveals her true self by dining on a single grain of rice: an economical but, under the circumstances, undesirable trait.)

Clear across the Old World, from England to Japan, rivers were worshiped . . . and feared. Sometimes they demanded human sacrifice; sometimes they got them. Suppose, then, a strange person, unable to speak and to "give an account of oneself," being found near a river . . . near any water, for that matter . . . why, he or she would almost of necessity be subsumed into that awe of the sacred and the terrible. I leave this to be considered, and I pass on.

Professor Zingg writes: "The term and concept of feral man (L. ferus, "wild") was first taken from the realm of myth and history into organized science by the great scientific systematizer, Carl Linnaeus (b. 1707, d. 1778). He included *Homo sapiens ferus* in the tenth and subsequent editions of his early and great work, *Systema Naturae*, 1758. He considers *Homo ferus* (generally given elsewhere as *Homo sapiens ferus*) as a subdivision of *Homo sapiens* in the order of the primates, which includes man and the apes . . ."

The examples of *Wild Wise Man* listed by Linnaeus were nine, and ranged from *Juv. ursinus Lithuanus* [The Lithuanian bear-boy] *1661* to *Johannes Leodicensis* [Jean of Liège, "a poor case," says Zingg; no date give.] Perhaps the one most germane to us is that of the *Puella Campanica* [The Girl of Champagne] *1731*—but all had in common that they had been found in woods and wildernesses in a state considered wild, brutish, and other than normally human: *Did* they represent another order of mankind, a sort of modern Neanderthal? No, of course they didn't; *we* know better than *that,* you dumb Squarehead! (We also know how to make lots more things which will kill us than Linnaeus did—and we go right on making them, too; don't we? Yes we do.) All these Wild Boys and Wild Girls, then, represented the then-equivalent of the Sasquatch, Yeti, and Bigfoot, with the addition of being *found:* quite an addition.

Puella Campanica. She came in from the woods to a village (Songi) in Champagne, in France, at dusk, one September day in 1701. Zingg writes, "As instances of the other pole of idiocy, *dementia ex separatione,* of those whose mental functions remain intact or able to develop despite the influence of long-continued isolation, Rauber cites the wild-girl of Songi." So will I.

> . . . a girl of nine or ten years . . . Her feet were naked, her body was covered with rags and skins of animals, [. . . .] She carried a club . . . she saw a [raw] fowl . . . and began immediately to eat it. She strangled a little rabbit . . . and ate it . . . her thumbs were very large . . . the result of climbing trees . . . swinging from one tree to another . . . She was just as agile in diving and catching fish . . . swimming and diving . . . Even after two years after her capture she still had not lost the tendency to jump into water to catch fish. In this manner she once escaped from the Castle of Songi through an open door which led to a pond. She jumped into it completely dressed, swam through it and landed on a small island. . . .

Later, after she had been taught to speak French, she told the good people at the convent which housed her that *"She . . . believed that she preserved a . . . memory of the sea or a river and a large water-animal."*

I have no hesitation in saying that in an earlier age she would have been declared a mermaid, tail or no tail. There are one or two things about her which I find rather humanly endearing: *"She liked macaroons, and gin, which she called, 'burn-stomach.'"* For reasons apparent if one reads her story

carefully and in full, I believe that *Puella Campanica* was a bit
of a faker, just a bit; but what the hell. An abandoned child,
life handed her a lemon. And she made lemonade. *I* would a
lot rather have macaroons and gin than raw frogs *any* day, Jean
Jacques Rousseau, even if *you* wouldn't—"Burn-stomach!"
Whoopee!

As for the once-famous Peter the Wild Boy of Hanover,
Linnaeus' *Juv. Hannoveranus 1724*, who became and remained
a favorite of Royalty for almost forty years, mostly in England—alas for all theories that he was a sort of junior grade
Noble Savage, hatched from an acorn or something—the evidence subsequently discovered seems to prove rather plainly
that Wild Peter was (a) severely tongue-tied, (b) severely retarded, and (c) driven from home by his peasant-father and
stepmother, figures straight out of the fairy tales of their countryman, Grimm. *Sailors had seen at different times a naked
child on the banks of the river* . . . But go read it. What kept
poor speechless Peterkin alive was a pension from George II
of England and Hanover: The only nice thing I have ever heard
about that sullen, hard-bitten, red-faced little monarch (to his
Queen, on her deathbed: "I won't marry again. I'll just have
mistresses.") . . . *Sehst, Peterchen, 's'is' geworen besser bei
uns in England. . . .*
Notice, though, once again, the two items, *Noticed near
the water*, and *Could not talk*. Am I really the first person to
have noticed all this?
Well. So. Notice some more. Here is Wild Peter, "when he
particularly liked anything [given him to eat, as green beans,
etc.], he indicated his satisfaction by *striking repeatedly on his
chest.*" And the official deposition made in Scotland on October
29, 1811, of the mermaid on the rock, which *"was constantly
stroking and washing its breast* . . ."—how that is echoed by
the other deposition made in Scotland, on November 2nd of
the same year, about a "creature" which was *"constantly rubbing or wishing its breast with one hand* . . ." Notice this gesture. And let us go back to one of the *Juvenes ursini Lithuani
1657* cited by Linnaeus. Writes a contemporary, ". . . in the
woods of Lithuania a boy was found among bears and captured
. . . With much care he was taught to go erect, but . . . the *voice
was lacking* . . . He could not be taught to make the sign of the

cross. *He reached his hand to me that I should make the sign
of the cross on his breast.*"

Had someone once tried to teach Wild Peter to "make the
sign of the cross on his breast" before eating?—a gesture (particularly if ill-done) likely not to have been understood in Prot-
estant England? Was *that* what the unidentified "creatures" in
Scotland were doing? . . . or attempting? *Was* that what the Lithuanian bear-boy really wanted done? Have these four habits
really anything in common? If so, what? What can it mean?
Does it mean anything? I wish I knew. I wish I knew.

The so-called Wild Men or Wild Children may or may not
have anything to do with mermaids; I think they may, but I
leave the matter loose. That any of them may at any time have
actually lived with animals I do not insist; the matter is still
much disputed. That some of them were children in a state of
severe mental retardation seems beyond dispute. What remains
uncertain is this: of those who were so afflicted, were all so
from their birth, or were not anyway some of them "retarded"
as a result of what old Rauber termed *dementia ex separatione*
. . . demented as a result of having been separated . . . separated,
that is, from other human company? Rauber was a pioneer
psychologist in the early 19th century: but everything learned
since substantiates that children raised in isolation suffer severe
mental damage . . . sometimes irreparable damage: regardless
of whether they had been isolated from a human home and
lived in the woods for long, or if they had been isolated *at*
home. "The idiot kept in the closet" is, alas, alas, by no means
a thing of the past. And, even worse, the child "in the closet"
has not always been an idiot; sometimes the child has been
illegitimate; sometimes the isolating parent or parents have been
themselves mentally unstable.

To carry the matter further lies beyond my space and scope.

Now we come to, or come back to, that more-than-man-
sized (and -woman-sized) mammal, the sea cow, so often said—
along with, or instead of, the seal—to be the real origin of the
mermaid myth. If the story of the mermaid had an origin in
the manatee, how are we to account for these so-called sightings
in places where there were no manatees; and if they were

inspired by seals, how to account for the sightings in places where there were no seals? Or how to account for them where seals were too well-known? Some, no doubt—say, even, certainly—had their origins in the minds of alleged witnesses whose imaginations had been stirred by already-existent stories, of whatsoever origin. Others, it seemed to me, did not . . . at least, not entirely. I believe that in days gone by, any naked and shipwrecked person washed ashore in an insular or isolated region where his or her language was not known was likely to be assumed to be a mermaid, a merman, or a sea-monster of some sort and not alone in Europe. There is a record from the East Indies (now Indonesia) from the 1500's, of the finding of "a great white sea-ape." This creature was prudently chained to a wall in the local king's garden, and stayed chained there until it died. We are entitled to disbelieve that it was really "a great white sea-ape," not only because there are no such things, but because on the wall to which it was chained it left graffiti in several languages including Latin and Dutch. In other words, it was a human being, of a race strange to the natives, speaking languages equally strange—and, as it lived chained up there for 34 years, one must only hope that it was at least a very long chain.—This finding has not that I know of ever been applied to the mermaid legend. But I think it very worthy of such application.

Because, besides the legend of the *mer-* or *mere*, i.e., *sea-*, maid, there is the legend of the undine or ondine, a sort of river- or lake-dwelling equivalent, I have a theory that this may have preceded the mermaid one. Perhaps certain inland tribes (my theory goes) who not only could not swim but had never heard of people who could, coming upon, in their wanderings, a strange river, lake, or pool, and seeing a human form performing in the water after the manner of a water-creature—a fish—had no explanation for such a brief (we may assume) sighting other than that the creature in the water, though human-shaped, was at least part fish. To try and take it back further in history is beyond my task.

Returning, for a while, to the manatee, or sea-cow: far from this poor beast being "the origin of the mermaid legend," it was attached to it fairly late in the day, and I don't really see how it could have been involved in it much earlier. The Atlantic sea cow, the manatee, is in the Old World not found farther north than the Gulf of Guinea in Africa, far off of the way for early European or Asian travelers. Even if one or two voyages out of Carthage did cruise those waters briefly, not only is there nothing in their accounts to show that they encountered any manatees, but it was to be almost 2000 years before Europeans came that far. The earliest reference to them in this connection, found in Benwell and Waugh, dates from early in the 18th century: I mean, the earliest reference of anyone saying, "No, it was not a mermaid, it was a manatee." The manatee may not look much like a cow, "sea cow" named or not; it looks about as much like a woman as a cow looks like a woman: only bigger; though, like a woman and unlike a cow, its teats are pectoral, i.e., on the chest.

But what about the Indian Ocean sea cow, or dugong? There are reports from both sides of the Indian Ocean, Somalia on the west and Indonesia in the east. Beginning with expectedly coarse jests, the matter soon become serious: "We don't dare tell our wives," the sailors and fisherman say, "that we have even *seen* a dugong. They would neither talk with us nor sleep with us for weeks . . ." Their wives, it seems, incline to believe the worst. In some places the mention of the word dugong brings the frowing comment, "It is bad luck to talk of that." But talk of that we must.

The earliest mermaid or merman account, that of *On* or *Oannes*, as I have said, does come out of the greater Indian Ocean area, to wit the Persian Gulf. Old *On*, with his long beard and his funny hat and his fish-tail, does not seem very dugongish to me, but listen to a quotation from a naturalist, H.A.F. Gohar, at one time "the Director of the Marine Biological Station at A Ghardaqa at the entrance to the Gulf of Suez," which disembogues into the Red Sea, which disembogues into the Indian Ocean (which *used* to be called the Erythraean, or Red, Sea). The quotation is from *In Search of Mermaids*, by Dr. Colin Bertram, the zoologist; his book is mostly about manatees and Guyana, but—but enough. Listen:

"Gohar interestingly refers to the mermaid legend which he would firmly attribute, if at all, to the dugong and not the manatee. He may be quoted thus:

"'In the dugong, the oval face of the relatively small head, of light colour and roughly the same size as a human face, also the fatty chin and the protruding nose-like alveolus of the upper jaw, lying over a small mouth, all these are characters that enhanced the resemblance to a human face. The flat ventral surface of the muzzle gives the impression of a woman hanging a veil over her face to below the eyes.

"*'It has also been claimed* [italics in this quote are mine: AD] that the mother has been seen, in shallow water, holding her large-size young with one or both flippers and standing waist-high out of the water; while suckling the young at its well-developed pectoral breasts. *At all events* [italics in this quote are mine: AD], it is imperative that the mother should, during suckling, maintain her own as well as her infant's nostrils above the water for aerial respiration. The resemblance to a woman carrying her child has been accentuated by the great shyness of dugongs, which made it impossible to watch them except at a great distance, and often only in the darker nights. At the sight of an approaching object or person, they dived and the appearance of the tail beating the surface of the water aroused the curiosity and served to enliven and perpetuate the sea-man's faith in such mythical creatures.'

"*'The stories of mermaids* were especially told by voyagers in the south-eastern seas, where only dugongs occurred. Furthermore, it is of special interest to remember, in this connection, *the many stories* told of marriages taking place between mermaids and men. Marriages which—*the stories often went on to relate*—resulted in an offspring that talked the languages of both the father and the mother, etc. Although *such stories are extremely imaginative*, yet they cannot be passed over without some meditation, as they must have some meaning which may lead us to the clue of the problem we are confronted with. At the same time, due consideration should be given to the following facts: 1) The great resemblance between the genitalia of dugongs and those of man; 2) That dugongs are warm-blooded animals and, on account of their blubber, will retain the high temperature of their bodies for some hours after death, especially in the hot climate of the regions in which they occur; 3) That they are docile and inoffensive creatures; 4) That in old times voyages took very long and men were for months and even years away from their homes and families, at sea or in places or islands completely devoid of human inhabitants. Considering these facts together, it is not difficult to understand, under such abnormal conditions, how much femininity a thing like a female dugong may suggest and how much the seizure or even the sight of one may mean. It may be remembered, in this respect, man has not completely raised himself above the rank of animals.'"

Well. There is a great deal suggested in this quotation, most of it not at all nice, and we will not be at all disposed to linger.

Moving on, although perhaps not a million miles, we encounter—or rather, you encounter, I have already encountered—in my own notes for a series of novels based on the medieval Vergil Magus Legend—we encounter, I say, somewhat perhaps to our surprise, the names of Dante and of Dorothy L. Sayers. What is the connection? This. Miss Sayers, best known as the author of the Lord Peter Whimsey detective stories, was also the translator of and commentator on *The Divine Comedy* of Dante. And Dante's guide through the Inferno and Purgatory was Vergil. Here we go.

"Vergil (11,58-9) calls the Siren 'that ancient witch' because of whose beguilements the souls do penance . . . She is at first sight unattractive, she only acquires strength and beauty from Dante's own gaze. She is, therefore, the projection upon the outer world of something in the mind: the soul, falling in love with itself, perceives other people and things, not as they are, but as wish-fulfillments of its own, i.e., its love for them is not love for a 'true other' (cf. XVIII, 22-6 and note), but a devouring egotistical fantasy, by absorption in which the personality rots away into illusion. The Siren is, in fact, the 'ancient witch,' Lillith, the fabled first wife of Adam, who was not a real woman of flesh and blood, but a magical *imago*, begotten of Samael, the Evil One, to be a fantasm of Adam's own desires . . . In later legends, the magical fantasm of man's own desire is the demon lover called the succubus (or, in the case of the woman, the incubus), intercourse with which saps the strength and destroys the life."

Let me tell you something which may perhaps surprise you but which scarcely surprises me at all. I had never seen Dr. Bertram's book, *In Search of Mermaids*, before I began to prepare this Adventure. I had never heard of the Director of the Marine Biological Station on the Red Sea, H.A.F. Gohar, whose "meditation" on the mermaid legend and the dugong I quoted a page or so before. The quotations from Dorothy L. Sayers' notes on Dante have been in my notebooks for years and I gave them no thought in connection with this Adventure:

but just after finishing my extract from Gohar I pulled out the card on *Sirens* from my Virgil Magus file, and the first reference on it was to that passage from Sayers' note on Dante which I have just quoted. You see how well, how almost perfectly, it fits in. Although I had certainly heard of the phenomena of "feral children," it never had occurred to me that there might be a conceivable connection with the mermaid legend: until I "accidently picked up" the Sing-Zingg book. I would be surprised . . . if this had not happened to me a thousand times.

I tell you, very sincerely, very simply, very humbly: these things are made by magic. The net which caught the siren mermaid does catch us all. It is Indra's net, a net of almost infinite dimensions, and where any two cords of it come together, there come together a line of time and a line of space, until every moment in time and every line in space are connected.

And each connection, it is said, shines and glitters, like a jewel.

Nothing in the Rules

by

L. Sprague de Camp

Born in 1907, L. Sprague de Camp is a seminal figure in the development of modern fantasy and science fiction, one whose career as writer, critic, and anthologist spans almost fifty years. De Camp began writing for John W. Campbell's Astounding *during the Campbellian "Golden Age" of the late thirties and the forties, but it was in* Astounding's *sister fantasy magazine,* Unknown, *that de Camp's talent really blossomed, and where he produced some of the best short fantasies ever written, including "The Wheels of If," "Divide and Rule," and "The Gnarly Man." De Camp's most famous book is probably* The Complete Enchanter, *an omnibus of the "Harold Shea" stories he wrote with Fletcher Pratt, although his* Lest Darkness Fall *is considered by many critics to be one of the three or four best "alternate worlds" novels ever written. De Camp's other novels include* Rogue Queen, The Land of Unreason *(with Fletcher Pratt),* The Glory That Was, The Search for Zei/The Hand of Zei, The Tower of Zanid, *and* The Hostage of Zir, *as well as several fine historical novels. His short fiction has been collected in* The Best of L. Sprague de Camp, The Reluctant Shaman, *and* The Purple Pterodactyls. *As an anthologist, de Camp is largely responsible for the revitalization of the once-languishing sub-genre of "sword & sorcery" or "heroic fantasy," and, as writer and editor, also played a large part in launching the big* Conan *boom of the sixties and seventies. He has also written some of the major critical books about fantasy, notably* Literary Swordsmen and Sorcerers *and the definitive* Lovecraft: A Biography. *His most recent books are the novels* The Unbeheaded King *and (with Catherine Crook de Camp)* The Bones of Zora, *and* Dark Valley Destiny *(with Catherine Crook de Camp and Jane Whittington Griffin), a biography of Conan's creator, Robert E. Howard.*

In the forties, de Camp was the mainstay of Unknown *with wry, funny, and sprightly stories like the one that follows, in which sportsmen in search of a winning "edge" in an athletic competition resort not to steroids or amphetamines, but instead to something numinal and strange.*

* * *

NOT MANY SPECTATORS TURN OUT FOR A MEET BETWEEN TWO minor women's swimming clubs, and this one was no exception. Louis Connaught, looking up at the balcony, thought casually that the single row of seats around it was about half-full, mostly with the usual bored-looking assortment of husbands and boy friends, and some of the Hotel Creston's guests who had wandered in for want of anything better to do. One of the bellboys was asking an evening-gowned female not to smoke, and she was showing irritation. Mr. Santalucia and the little Santalucias were there as usual to see mamma perform. They waved down at Connaught.

Connaught—a dark devilish-looking little man—glanced over to the other side of the pool. The girls were coming out of the shower rooms, and their shrill conversation was blurred by the acoustics of the pool room into a continuous buzz. The air was faintly steamy. The stout party in white duck pants was Laird, coach of the Knickerbockers and Connaught's arch rival. He saw Connaught and boomed: "Hi, Louie!" The words rattled from wall to wall with a sound like a stick being drawn swiftly along a picket fence. Wambach of the A.A.U. Committee, who was refereeing, came in with his overcoat still on and greeted Laird, but the booming reverberations drowned his words before they got over to Connaught.

Then somebody else came through the door; or rather, a knot of people crowded through it all at once, facing inward, some in bathing suits and some in street clothes. It was a few seconds before Coach Connaught saw what they were looking at. He blinked and looked more closely, standing with his mouth half-open.

But not for long. *"Hey!"* he yelled in a voice that made the pool room sound like the inside of a snare drum in use. "Protest! PROTEST! *You can't do that!"*

It had been the preceding evening when Herbert Laird opened his front door and shouted, "H'lo, Mark, come on in." The chill March wind was making a good deal of racket but not so much as all that. Laird was given to shouting on general principles. He was stocky and bald.

Mark Vining came in and deposited his brief case. He was younger than Laird—just thirty, in fact—with octagonal glasses and rather thin severe features, which made him look more serious than he was.

"Glad you could come, Mark," said Laird. "Listen, can you make our meet with the Crestons tomorrow night?"

Vining pursed his lips thoughtfully. "I guess so. Loomis decided not to appeal, so I don't have to work nights for a few days anyhow. Is something special up?"

Laird looked sly. "Maybe. Listen, you know that Mrs. Santalucia that Louis Connaught has been cleaning up with for the past couple of years? I think I've got that fixed. But I want you along to think up legal reasons why my scheme's okay."

"Why," said Vining cautiously, "what's you scheme?"

"Can't tell you now. I promised not to. But if Louie can win by entering a freak—a woman with webbed fingers—"

"Oh, look here, Herb, you know those webs don't really help her—"

"Yes, yes, I know all the arguments. You've already got more water resistance to your arms than you've got muscle to overcome it with, and so forth. But I know Mrs. Santalucia has webbed fingers, and I know she's the best damned woman swimmer in New York. And I don't like it. It's bad for my prestige as a coach." He turned and shouted into the gloom: "Iantha!"

"Yes?"

"Come here, will you please? I want you to meet my friend Mr. Vining. Here, we need some light."

The light showed the living room as usual buried under disorderly piles of boxes of bathing suits and other swimming equipment, the sale of which furnished Herbert Laird with most of his income. It also showed a young woman coming in in a wheelchair.

One look gave Vining a feeling that, he knew, boded no good for him. He was unfortunate in being a pushover for any reasonably attractive girl and at the same time being cursed with an almost pathological shyness where women were concerned. The fact that both he and Laird were bachelors and took their swimming seriously were the main ties between them.

This girl was more than reasonably attractive. She was,

thought the dazzled Vining, a wow, a ten-strike, a direct sixteen-inch hit. Her smooth, rather flat features and high cheekbones had a hint of Asian or American Indian and went oddly with her light-gold hair, which, Vining could have sworn, had a faint greenish tinge. A blanket was wrapped around her legs.

He came out of his trance as Laird introduced the exquisite creature as "Miss Delfoiros."

Miss Delfoiros did not seem exactly overcome. As she extended her hand, she said with a noticeable accent: "You are not from the newspapers, Mr. Vining?"

"No," said Vining. "Just a lawyer, I specialize in wills and probates and things. Not thinking of drawing up yours, are you?"

She relaxed visibly and laughed. "No. I 'ope I shall not need one for a long, long time."

"Still," said Vining seriously, "you never know—"

Laird bellowed: "Wonder what's keeping that sister of mine. Dinner ought to be ready. *Martha!*" He marched out, and Vining heard Miss Laird's voice, something about "—but Herb, I had to let those things cool down—"

Vining wondered with a great wonder what he should say to Miss Delfoiros. Finally he said, "Smoke?"

"Oh, no, thank you very much. I do not do it."

"Mind if I do?"

"No, not at all."

"Whereabouts do you hail from?" Vining thought the questions sounded both brusque and silly. He never did get the hang of talking easily under these circumstances.

"Oh, I am from Kip—Cyprus, I mean. You know, the island."

"Will you be at this swimming meet?"

"Yes, I think so."

"You don't"—he lowered his voice—"know what scheme Herb's got up his sleeve to beat La Santalucia?"

"Yes . . . no . . . I do not . . . what I mean is, I must not tell."

More mystery, thought Vining. What he really wanted to know was why she was confined to a wheelchair; whether the cause was temporary or permanent. But you couldn't ask a person right out, and he was still trying to concoct a leading question when Laird's bellow wafted in: "All right, folks, soup's on!" Vining would have pushed the wheelchair in, but before he had a chance, the girl had spun the chair around and was halfway to the dining room.

Vining said: "Hello, Martha, how's the schoolteaching business?" But he was not really paying much attention to Laird's capable spinster sister. He was gauping at Miss Delfoiros, who was quite calmly emptying a teaspoonful of salt into her water glass and stirring.

"What . . . what?" he gulped.

"I 'ave to," she said. "Fresh water makes me—like what you call drunk."

"Listen, Mark!" roared his friend. "Are you sure you can be there on time tomorrow night? There are some questions of eligibility to be cleared up, and I'm likely to need you badly."

"Will Miss Delfoiros be there?" Vining grinned, feeling very foolish inside.

"Oh, sure. Iantha's our . . . say, listen, you know that little eighteen-year-old Clara Havranek? She did the hundred in one-oh-five yesterday. She's championship material. We'll clean the Creston Club yet—" He went on, loud and fast, about what he was going to do to Louie Connaught's girls. The while, Mark Vining tried to concentrate on his own food, which was good, and on Iantha Delfoiros, who was charming but evasive.

There seemed to be something special about Miss Delfoiros' food, to judge by the way Martha Laird had served it. Vining looked closely and saw that it had the peculiarly dead and clammy look that a dinner once hot but now cold has. He asked about it.

"Yes," she said, "I like it cold."

"You mean you don't eat *anything* hot?"

She made a face. "'Ot food? No, I do not like it. To us it is—"

"Listen, Mark! I hear the W.S.A. is going to throw a post-season meet in April for novices only—"

Vining's dessert lay before him a full minute before he noticed it. He was too busy thinking how delightful Miss Delfoiros' accent was.

When dinner was over, Laird said, "Listen, Mark, you know something about these laws against owning gold? Well, look here—" He led the way to a candy box on a table in the living room. The box contained, not candy, but gold and silver coins. Laird handed the lawyer several of them. The first one he examined was a silver crown, bearing the inscription "Carolus II Dei Gra" encircling the head of England's Merry Monarch with a wreath in his hair—or, more probably, in his wig. The second was an eighteenth-century Spanish dollar. The third was a Louis d'Or.

"I didn't know you went in for coin collecting, Herb," said Vining. "I suppose these are all genuine?"

"They're genuine all right. But I'm not collecting 'em. You might say I'm taking 'em in trade. I have a chance to sell ten thousand bathing caps, if I can take payment in those things."

"I shouldn't think the U. S. Rubber Company would like the idea much."

"That's just the point. What'll I do with 'em after I get 'em? Will the government put me in jail for having 'em?"

"You needn't worry about that. I don't think the law covers old coins, though I'll look it up to make sure. Better call up the American Numismatic Society—they're in the 'phone book—and they can tell you how to dispose of them. But look here, what the devil is this? Ten thousand bathing caps to be paid for in pieces-of-eight? I never heard of such a thing."

"That's it exactly. Just ask the little lady here." Laird turned to Iantha, who was nervously trying to signal him to keep quiet. "The deal's her doing."

"I did . . . did—" She looked as if she were going to cry. "'Erbert, you should not have said that. You see," she said to Vining, "we do not like to 'ave a lot to do with people. Always it causes us troubles."

"Who," asked Vining, "do you mean by 'we'?"

She shut her mouth obstinately. Vining almost melted, but his legal instincts came to the surface. If you don't get a grip on yourself, he thought, you'll be in love with her in another five minutes, and that might be a disaster. He said firmly:

"Herb, the more I see of this business, the crazier it looks. Whatever's going on, you seem to be trying to get me into it. But I'm damned if I'll let you unless I know what it's all about."

"Might as well tell him, Iantha," said Laird. "He'll know when he sees you swim tomorrow, anyhow,"

She said: "You will not tell the newspaper men, Mr. Vining?"

"No, I won't say anything to anybody."

"You promise?"

"Of course. You can depend on a lawyer to keep things under his hat."

"Under his—I suppose you mean not to tell. So, look." She reached down and pulled up the lower end of the blanket.

Vining looked. Where he expected to see feet, there was a pair of horizontal flukes, like those of a porpoise.

Louis Connaught's having kittens, when he saw what his rival coach had sprung on him, can thus be easily explained. First he doubted his own senses; then he doubted whether there was any justice in the world.

Meanwhile, Mark Vining proudly pushed Iantha's wheel-chair in among the cluster of judges and timekeepers at the starting end of the pool. Iantha herself, in a bright green bathing cap, held her blanket around her shoulders, but the slate-gray tail with its flukes was plain for all to see. The skin of the tail was smooth and the flukes were horizontal; artists who show mermaids with scales and a vertical tail fin, like a fish's, simply do not know their zoölogy.

"All right, all right," bellowed Laird. "Don't crowd around. Everybody get back to where they belong. Everybody, please."

One of the spectators, leaning over the rail of the balcony to see, dropped a fountain pen into the pool. One of Connaught's girls, a Miss Black, dove in after it.

Ogden Wambach, the referee, poked a finger at the skin of the tail. He was a well-groomed, gray-haired man.

"Laird," he said, "is this a joke?"

"Not at all. She's entered in the back stroke and all the free styles, just like any other club member. She's even registered with the A.A.U."

"But . . . but . . . I mean, is it alive? Is it real?"

Iantha spoke up. "Why do you not ask me those questions, Mr. . . . Mr. . . . I do not know you—"

"Good grief," said Wambach. "It talks! I'm the referee, Miss—"

"Delfoiros. Iantha Delfoiros."

"My word. Upon my word. That means—let's see—Violet Porpoise-tail, doesn't it? *Delphis* plus *oura*—"

"You know Greek? Oh, 'ow nice!" She broke into a string of *dimotiki*.

Wambach gulped a little. "Too fast for me, I'm afraid. And that's *modern* Greek, isn't it?"

"Why, yes. I am modern, am I not?"

"Dear me. I suppose so. But is that tail really real? I mean, it's not just a piece of costumery?"

"Oh, but yes." Iantha threw off the blanket and waved her flukes. Everyone in the pool seemed to have turned into a pair of eyeballs to which a body and a pair of legs was vaguely attached.

"Dear me," said Ogden Wambach. "Where are my glasses? You understand, I just want to make sure there's nothing spurious about this."

Mrs. Santalucia, a muscular-looking lady with a visible mustache and fingers webbed down to the first joint, said, "You mean I gotta swim against *her?*"

Louis Connaught had been sizzling like a dynamite fuse. "You can't do it!" he shrilled. "This is a woman's meet! I protest!"

"So what?" said Laird.

"But you can't enter a fish in a woman's swimming meet! Can you, Mr. Wambach?"

Mark Vining spoke up. He had just taken a bunch of papers clipped together out of his pocket, and was running through them.

"Miss Delfoiros," he asserted, "is not a fish. She's a mammal."

"How do you figure that?" yelled Connaught.

"Look at her."

"Um-m-m," said Ogden Wambach. "I see what you mean."

"But," howled Connaught, "she still ain't human!"

"There is a question about that, Mr. Vining," said Wambach.

"No question at all. There's nothing in the rules against entering a mermaid, and there's nothing that says the competitors have to be human."

Connaught was hopping about like an overwrought cricket. He was now waving a copy of the current A.A.U. swimming, diving, and water polo rules. "I still protest! Look here! All through here it only talks about two kinds of meets, men's and women's. She ain't a woman, and she certainly ain't a man. If the Union had wanted to have meets for mermaids they'd have said so."

"Not a woman?" asked Vining in a manner that juries learned meant a rapier thrust at an opponent. "I beg your pardon, Mr. Connaught. I looked the question up." He frowned at his sheaf of papers. "Webster's International Dictionary, Second Edition, defines a woman as 'any female person.' And it further defines 'person' as 'a being characterized by conscious apprehension, rationality, and a moral sense.'" He turned to Wambach. "Sir, I think you'll agree that Miss Delfoiros has exhibited conscious apprehension and rationality during her conversation with you, won't you?"

"My word ... I really don't know what to say, Mr. Vining ... I suppose she has, but I couldn't say—"

Horwitz, the scorekeeper, spoke up. "You might ask her to give the multiplication table." Nobody paid him any attention.

Connaught exhibited symptoms of apoplexy. "But you can't—What the hell you talking about—conscious ap-ap—"

"Please, Mr.Connaught!" said Wambach. "When you shout that way I can't understand you because of the echoes."

Connaught mastered himself with a visible effort. Then he looked crafty. "How do I know she's got a moral sense?"

Vining turned to Iantha. "Have you ever been in jail, Iantha?"

Iantha laughed. "What a funny question, Mark! But of course, I have not."

"That's what *she* says," sneered Connaught. "How you gonna prove it?"

"We don't have to," said Vining loftily. "The burden of proof is on the accuser, and the accused is legally innocent until proved guilty. That principle was well established by the time of King Edward the First."

"Oh, damn King Edward the First," cried Connaught. "That wasn't the kind of moral sense I meant anyway. How about what they call moral turp-turp—You know what I mean."

"Hey," growled Laird, "what's the idea? Are you trying to cast—What's the word, Mark?"

"Aspersions?"

"—cast aspersions on one of my swimmers? You watch out, Louie. If I hear you be—What's the word, Mark?"

"Besmirching her fair name?"

"—besmirching her fair name, I'll drown you in your own tank."

"And after that," said Vining, "we'll slap a suit on you for slander."

"Gentlemen! Gentlemen!" said Wambach. "Let's not have any more personalities, please. This is a swimming meet, not a lawsuit. Let's get to the point."

"We've made ours," said Vining with dignity. "We've shown that Iantha Delfoiros is a woman, and Mr. Connaught has stated, himself, that this is a woman's meet. Therefore, Miss Delfoiros is eligible. Q.E.D."

"Ahem," said Wambach. "I don't quite know—I never had a case like this to decide before."

Louis Connaught almost had tears in his eyes; at least he sounded as if he did. "Mr. Wambach, you can't let Herb Laird do this to me. I'll be a laughingstock."

Laird snorted. "How about your beating me with your Mrs. Santalucia? I didn't get any sympathy from you when people laughed at me on account of that. And how much good did it do me to protest against her fingers?"

"But," wailed Connaught, "if he can enter this Miss Delfoiros, what's to stop somebody from entering a trained sea lion or something? Do you want to make competitive swimming into a circus?"

Laird grinned. "Go ahead, Louie. Nobody's stopping you from entering anything you like. How about it, Ogden? Is she a woman?"

"Well . . . really . . . oh, dear—"

"Please!" Iantha Delfoiros rolled her violet-blue eyes at the bewildered referee. "I should so like to swim in this nice pool with all these nice people!"

Wambach sighed. "All right, my dear, you shall!"

"Whoopee!" cried Laird, the cry being taken up by Vining, the members of the Knickerbocker Swimming Club, the other officials, and lastly the spectators. The noise in the inclosed space made sensitive eardrums wince.

"Wait a minute," yelped Connaught when the echoes had died. "Look here, page 19 of the rules. 'Regulation Costume, Women: Suits must be of dark color, with skirt attached. Leg is to reach—' and so forth. Right here it says it. She can't swim the way she is, not in a sanctioned meet."

"That's true," said Wambach. "Let's see—"

Horwitz looked up from his little score-sheet littered table. "Maybe one of the girls has a halter she could borrow," he suggested. "That would be something."

"Halter, phooey!" snapped Connaught. "This means a regular suit with legs and a skirt, and everybody knows it."

"But she hasn't got any legs!" cried Laird. "How could she get into—"

"That's just the point! If she can't wear a suit with legs, and the rules say you gotta have legs, she can't wear the regulation suit, and she can't compete! I gotcha that time! Ha-ha, I'm sneering!"

"I'm afraid not, Louie," said Vining, thumbing his own copy of the rule-book. He held it up to the light and read: "'Note.—These rules are approximate, the idea being to bar costumes which are immodest, or will attract undue attention and comment. The referee shall have the power'—et cetera, et cetera. If we cut the legs out of a regular suit, and she pulled the rest of it on over her head, that would be modest enough for all practical purposes. Wouldn't it, Mr. Wambach?"

"Dear me—I don't know—I suppose it would."

Laird hissed to one of his pupils, "Hey, listen, Miss Havranek! You know where my suitcase is? Well, you get one of the extra suits out of it, and there's a pair of scissors in with the first-aid things. You fix that suit up so Iantha can wear it."

Connaught subsided. "I see now," he said bitterly, "why you guys wanted to finish with a 300-yard free style instead of a relay. If I'd 'a known what you were planning—and, you, Mark Vining, if I ever get in a jam, I'll go to jail before I hire you for a lawyer, so help me!"

Mrs. Santalucia had been glowering at Iantha Delfoiros. Suddenly she turned to Connaught. "Thissa no fair. I swim against people. I no-gotta swim against mermaids."

"Please, Maria, don't *you* desert me," wailed Connaught.

"I no swim tonight."

Connaught looked up appealingly to the balcony. Mr. Santalucia and the little Santalucias, guessing what was happening, burst into a chorus of: "Go on, mamma! You show them, mamma!"

"Aw right. I swim one, maybe two races. If I see I no got a chance, I no swim no more."

"That's better, Maria. It wouldn't really count if she beat you anyway." Connaught headed for the door, saying something about "telephone" on the way.

Despite the delays in starting the meet, nobody left the pool room through boredom. In fact, the empty seats in the balcony were full by this time and people were standing up behind them. Word had gotten around the Hotel Creston that something was up.

By the time Louis Connaught returned, Laird and Vining were pulling the altered bathing suit on over Iantha's head. It did not reach quite so far as they expected, having been designed for a slightly slimmer swimmer. Not that Iantha was fat. But her human part, if not exactly plump, was at least comfortably upholstered, so that no bones showed. Iantha squirmed around in the suit a good deal and threw a laughing remark in Greek to Wambach, whose expression showed that he hoped it did not mean what he suspected it did.

Laird said, "Now listen, Iantha, remember not to move till the gun goes off. And remember that you swim directly over the black line on the bottom, not between two lines."

"Are they going to shoot a gun? Oh, I am afraid of shooting!"

"It's nothing to be afraid of; just blank cartridges. They don't hurt anybody. And it won't be so loud inside that cap."

"Herb," said Vining, "won't she lose time getting off, not being able to make a flat dive like the others?"

"She will. But it won't matter. She can swim a mile in *four* minutes, without really trying."

Ritchey, the starter, announced the fifty-yard free style. He called: "All right, everybody, line up."

Iantha slithered off her chair and crawled over to the starting platform. The other girls were all standing with feet together, bodies bent forward at the hips and arms pointing backward. Iantha got into a curious position of her own, with her tail bent under her and her weight resting on her hand and flukes.

"Hey! Protest!" shouted Connaught. "The rules say that all races, except back strokes, are started with dives. What kind of a dive do you call that?"

"Oh, dear," said Wambach. "What—"

"That," said Vining urbanely, "is a mermaid dive. You couldn't expect her to stand upright on her tail."

"But that's just it!" cried Connaught. "First you enter a non-regulation swimmer. Then you put a non-regulation suit on her. Then you start her off with a non-regulation dive. Ain't there anything you guys do like other people?"

"But," said Vining, looking through the rule book, "it doesn't say—here it is. 'The start in all races shall be made with a dive.' But there's nothing in the rules about what kind of dive shall be used. And the dictionary defines a dive simply as 'a plunge into water.' So if you jump in feet first holding your nose, that's a dive for the purpose of the discussion. And in my years of watching swimming meets, I've seen some funnier starting dives than Miss Delfoiros.'"

"I suppose he's right," said Wambach.

"Okay, okay," snarled Connaught. "But the next time I have to meet with you and Herb, I bring a lawyer along too, see?"

Ritchey's gun went off. Vining noticed that Iantha flinched a little at the report and was perhaps slowed down a trifle in getting off by it. The other girls' bodies shot out horizontally to smack the water loudly, but Iantha slipped in with the smooth, unhurried motion of a diving seal. Lacking the advantage of feet to push off with, she was several yards behind the other swimmers before she really got started. Mrs. Santalucia had taken her usual lead, foaming along with the slow strokes of her webbed hands.

Iantha did not bother to come to the surface except at the turn, where she had been specifically ordered to come up so that the judge of the turns would not raise arguments as to whether she had touched the end, and at the finish. She hardly used her arms at all, except for an occasional flip of her trailing hands to steer her. The swift up-and-down flutter of the powerful tail flukes sent her through the water like a torpedo, her wake appearing on the surface six or eight feet behind her. As she shot through the as yet unruffled waters at the far end of the pool on the first leg, Vining, who had gone around to the side to watch, noticed that she had the power of closing her nostrils tightly under water, like a seal or a hippopotamus.

Mrs. Santalucia finished the race in the very creditable time of 29.8 seconds. But Iantha Delfoiros arrived, not merely first, but in the time of 8.0 seconds. At the finish she did not reach up to touch the starting platform and then hoist herself out by her arms the way human swimmers do. She simply angled up sharply, left the water like a leaping trout, and came down with a moist smack on the concrete, almost bowling over a time-keeper. By the time the other contestants had completed the turn she was sitting on the platform with her tail curled under her. As the girls foamed laboriously down the final leg, she smiled dazzlingly at Vining, who had had to run to be in at the finish.

"That," she said, "was much fun, Mark. I am so glad you and 'Erbert put me in these races."

Mrs. Santalucia climbed out and walked over to Horwitz's table. That young man was staring in disbelief at the figures he had just written.

"Yes," he said, "that's what it says. Miss Iantha Delfoiros, 8.0; Mrs. Maria Santalucia, 29.8. Please don't drip on my score sheets, lady. Say, Wambach, isn't this a world's record or something?"

"My word!" said Wambach. "It's less than half the existing short-course record. Less than a third, maybe; I'd have to check it. Dear me! I'll have to take it up with the Committee. I don't know whether they'd allow it; I don't think they will, even though there isn't any specific rule against mermaids."

Vining spoke up. "I think we've complied with all the requirements to have records recognized, Mr. Wambach. Miss Delfoiros was entered in advance like all the others."

"Yes, yes, Mr. Vining, but don't you see, a record's a serious matter? No ordinary human being could ever come near a time like that."

"Unless he used an outboard motor," said Connaught. "If you allow contestants to use tail fins like Miss Delfoiros, you oughta let 'em use propellers. I don't see why these guys should be the only ones to be let bust rules all over the place, and then think up lawyer arguments why it's okay. I'm gonna get me a lawyer, too."

"That's all right, Odgen," said Laird. "You take it up with the Committee, but we don't really care much about the records anyway, so long as we can lick Louie here." He smiled indulgently at Connaught, who sputtered with fury.

"I no swim," announced Mrs. Santalucia. "This is all crazy business. I no got a chance."

"Now, Maria," said Connaught, taking her aside, "just once more, won't you please? My reputation—" The rest of his words were drowned in the general reverberation of the pool room. But at the end of them the redoubtable female appeared to have given in to his entreaties.

The hundred-yard free style started in much the same manner as the fifty-yard. Iantha did not flinch at the gun this time and got off to a good start. She skimmed along just below the surface, raising a wake like a tuna clipper. These waves confused the swimmer in the adjacent lane, who happened to be Mrs. Breitenfeld of the Creston Club. As a result, on her first return leg, Iantha met Miss Breitenfeld swimming athwart her—Iantha's—lane, and rammed the unfortunate girl amidships. Miss Breitenfeld went down without even a gurgle, spewing bubbles.

Connaught shrieked: "Foul! Foul!" although in the general uproar it sounded like "Wow! Wow!" Several swimmers who were not racing dove in to the rescue, and the race came to a stop in general confusion and pandemonium. When Miss Breitenfeld was hauled out, it was found that she had merely had the wind knocked out of her and had swallowed considerable water.

Mark Vining, looking around for Iantha, found her holding on to the edge of the pool and shaking her head. Presently she crawled out, crying:

"Is she 'urt? Is she 'urt? Oh, I am so sorree! I did not think there would be anybody in my lane, so I did not look ahead."

"See?" yelled Connaught. "See, Wambach? See what happens? They ain't satisfied to walk away with the races with their fish-woman. No, they gotta try to cripple my swimmers by butting their slats in. Herb," he went on nastily, "why dontcha get a pet swordfish? Then when you rammed one of my poor girls she'd be out of competition for good!"

"Oh," said Iantha, "I did not mean—it was an accident!"

"Accident my foot!"

"But it was. Mr. Referee, I do not want to bump people. My 'ead 'urts, and my neck also. You think I try to break my neck on purpose?" Iantha's altered suit had crawled up under her armpits, but nobody noticed particularly.

"Sure it was an accident," bellowed Laird. "Anybody could see that. And listen, if anybody was fouled it was Miss Delfoiros."

"Certainly," chimed in Vining. "She was in her own lane, and the other girl wasn't."

"Oh dear me," said Wambach. "I suppose they're right again. This'll have to be re-swum anyway. Does Miss Breitenfeld want to compete?"

Miss Breitenfeld did not, but the others lined up again. This time the race went off without untoward incident. Iantha again made a spectacular leaping finish, just as the other three swimmers were halfway down the second of their four legs.

When Mrs. Santalucia emerged this time, she said to Connaught: "I no swim no more. That is final."

"Oh, but Maria—" It got him nowhere. Finally he said, "Will you swim in the races that she don't enter?"

"Is there any?"

"I think so. Hey, Horwitz, Miss Delfoiros ain't entered in the breast stroke, is she?"

Horwitz looked. "No, she isn't," he said.

"That's something. Say, Herb, how come you didn't put your fish-woman in the breast stroke?"

Vining answered for Laird. "Look at your rules, Louie. 'The feet shall be drawn up simultaneously, the knees bent and open,' et cetera. The rules for back stroke and free style don't say anything about how the legs shall be used, but those for breast stroke do. So no legs, no breast stroke. We aren't giving you a chance to make any legitimate protests."

"Legitimate protests!" Connaught turned away, sputtering.

While the dives were being run off, Vining, watching, became aware of an ethereal melody. First he thought it was in his head. Then he was sure it was coming from one of the spectators. He finally located the source; it was Iantha Delfoiros, sitting in her wheelchair and singing softly. By leaning nearer he could make out the words:

> *"Die schoenste Jungfrau sitzet*
> *Dort ober wunderbar;*
> *Ihr goldnes Geschmeide blitzet;*
> *Sie kaemmt ihr goldenes Haar."*

Vining went over quietly. "Iantha," he said. "Pull your bathing suit down, and don't sing."

She complied, looking up at him with a giggle. "But that is a nice song! I learn it from a wrecked German sailor. It is about one of my people."

"I know, but it'll distract the judges. They have to watch the dives closely, and the place is too noisy as it is."

"Such a nice man you are, Mark, but so serious!" She giggled again.

Vining wondered at the subtle change in the mermaid's manner. Then a horrible thought struck him.

"Herb!" he whispered. "Didn't she say something last night about getting drunk on fresh water?"

Laird looked up. "Yes. She—My God, the water in the pool's fresh! I never thought of that. Is she showing signs?"

"I think she is."

"Listen, Mark, what'll we do?"

"I don't know. She's entered in two more events, isn't she?

Back stroke and 300-yard free style?"

"Yes."

"Well, why not withdraw her from the back stroke, and give her a chance to sober up before the final event?"

"Can't. Even with all her firsts, we aren't going to win by any big margin. Louie has the edge on us in the dives, and Mrs. Santalucia'll win the breast stroke. In the events Iantha's in, if she takes first and Louie's girls take second and third, that means five points for us but four for him, so we have an advantage of only one point. And her world's record time don't give us any more points."

"Guess we'll have to keep her in and take a chance," said Vining glumly.

Iantha's demeanor was sober enough in lining up for the back stroke. Again she lost a fraction of a second in getting started by not having feet to push off with. But once she got started, the contest was even more one-sided than the free-style races had been. The human part of her body was practically out of water, skimming the surface like the front half of a speedboat. She made paddling motions with her arms, but that was merely for technical reasons; the power was all furnished by the flukes. She did not jump out on to the starting-platform this time; for a flash Vining's heart almost stopped as the emerald-green bathing cap seemed about to crash into the tiles at the end of the pool. But Iantha had judged the distance to a fraction of an inch, and braked to a stop with her flukes just before striking.

The breast stroke was won easily by Mrs. Santalucia, although her slow, plodding stroke was less spectacular than the butterfly of her competitors. The shrill cheers of the little Santalucias could be heard over the general hubbub. When the winner climbed out, she glowered at Iantha and said to Connaught:

"Louie, if you ever put me in a meet wit' mermaids again, I no swim for you again, never. Now I go home." With which she marched off to the shower room.

Ritchey was just about to announce the final event, the 300-yard free style, when Connaught plucked his sleeve. "Jack," he said, "wait a second. One of my swimmers is gonna be delayed a coupla minutes." He went out a door.

Laird said to Vining: "Wonder what Louie's grinning about.

He's got something nasty, I bet. He was 'phoning earlier, you remember."

"We'll soon see—What's that?" A hoarse bark wafted in from somewhere and rebounded from the walls.

Connaught reappeared carrying two buckets. Behind him was a little round man in three sweaters. Behind the little round man gallumped a glossy California sea lion. At the sight of the gently rippling, jade-green pool, the animal barked joyously and skidded into the water, swam swiftly about, and popped out on the landing platform, barking. The bark had a peculiarly nerve-racking effect in the echoing pool room.

Ogden Wambach seized two handfuls of his sleek gray hair and tugged. "Connaught!" he shouted. "What is that?"

"Oh, that's just one of my swimmers, Mr. Wambach."

"Hey, listen!" rumbled Laird. "We're going to protest this time. Miss Delfoiros is at least a woman, even if she's a kind of peculiar one. But you can't call *that* a woman."

Connaught grinned like Satan looking over a new shipment of sinners. "Didn't you just say to go ahead and enter a sea lion if I wanted to?"

"I don't remember saying—"

"Yes, Herbert," said Wambach, looking haggard. "You did say it. There didn't used to be any trouble in deciding whether a swimmer was a woman or not. But now that you've brought in Miss Delfoiros, there doesn't seem to be any place we can draw a line."

"But look here, Ogden, there is such a thing as going too far—"

"That's just what I said about you!" shrilled Connaught.

Wambach took a deep breath. "Let's not shout, please. Herbert, technically you may have an argument. But after we allowed Miss Delfoiros to enter, I think it would be only sporting to let Louie have his seal. Especially after you told him to get one if he could."

Vining spoke up. "Oh, we're always glad to do the sporting thing. But I'm afraid the sea lion wasn't entered at the beginning of the meet as is required by the rules. We don't want to catch hell from the Committee—"

"Oh, yes, she was," said Connaught. "See!" He pointed to one of Horwitz's sheets. "Her name's Alice Black, and here it is."

"But," protested Vining, "I thought *that* was Alice Black."

He pointed to a slim dark girl in a bathing suit who was sitting on a window ledge.

"It is," grinned Connaught. "It's just a coincidence that they both got the same name."

"You don't expect us to believe *that?*"

"I don't care whether you believe or not. It's so. Ain't the sea lion's name Alice Black?" He turned to the little fat man, who nodded.

"Let it pass," moaned Wambach. "We can't take time off to get this animal's birth certificate."

"Well, then," said Vining, "how about the regulation suit? Maybe you'd like to try to put a suit on your sea lion?"

"Don't have to. She's got one already. It grows on her. Yah, yah, yah, gotcha that time."

"I suppose," said Wambach, "that you *could* consider a natural sealskin pelt as equivalent to a bathing suit."

"Sure you could. That's the point. Anyway, the idea of suits is to be modest, and nobody gives a damn about a seal lion's modesty."

Vining made a final point. "You refer to the animal as 'her,' but how do we know it's a female? Even Mr. Wambach wouldn't let you enter a male sea lion in a women's meet."

Wambach spoke: "How do you tell on a sea lion?"

Connaught looked at the little fat man. "Well, maybe we had better not go into that here. How would it be if I put up a ten-dollar bond that Alice is a female, and you checked on her sex later?"

"That seems fair," said Wambach.

Vining and Laird looked at each other. "Shall we let 'em get away with that, Mark?" asked the latter.

Vining rocked on his heels for a few seconds. Then he said, "I think we might as well. Can I see you outside a minute. Herb? You people don't mind holding up the race a couple of minutes more, do you? We'll be right back."

Connaught started to protest about further delay but thought better of it. Laird presently reappeared, looking unwontedly cheerful.

"'Erbert!" said Iantha.

"Yes?" he put his head down.

"I'm afraid—"

"You're afraid Alice might bite you in the water? Well, I wouldn't want that—"

"Oh, no, not afraid that way. Alice, poof! If she gets nasty I give her one with the tail. But I am afraid she can swim faster than me."

"Listen, Iantha, you just go ahead and swim the best you can. Twelve legs, remember. And don't be surprised, no matter what happens."

"What you two saying?" asked Connaught suspiciously.

"None of your business, Louie. Whatcha got in that pail? *Fish?* I see how you're going to work this. Wanta give up and concede the meet now?"

Connaught merely snorted.

The only competitors in the 300-yard free-style race were Iantha Delfoiros and the sea lion, allegedly named Alice. The normal members of both clubs declared that nothing would induce them to get into the pool with the animal. Not even the importance of collecting a third-place point would move them.

Iantha got into her usual starting position. Beside her, the little round man maneuvered Alice, holding her by an improvised leash made of a length of rope. At the far end, Connaught had placed himself and one of the buckets.

Ritchey fired his gun; the little man slipped the leash and said: "Go get 'em, Alice!" Connaught took a fish out of his bucket and waved it. But Alice, frightened by the shot, set up a furious barking and stayed where she was. Not till Iantha had almost reached the far end of the pool did Alice sight the fish at the other end. Then she slid off and shot down the water like a streak. Those who have seen sea lions merely loafing about a pool in a zoo or aquarium have no conception of how fast they can go when they try. Fast as the mermaid was, the sea lion was faster. She made two bucking jumps out of water before she arrived and oozed out onto the concrete. One gulp and the fish had vanished.

Alice spotted the bucket and tried to get her head into it. Connaught fended her off as best he could with his feet. At the starting end, the little round man had taken a fish out of the other bucket and was waving, it, calling: "Here Alice!"

Alice did not get the idea until Iantha had finished her second leg. Then she made up for lost time.

The same trouble occurred at the starting end of the pool; Alice failed to see why she should swim twenty-five yards for a fish when there were plenty of them a few feet away. The result was that, at the halfway-mark, Iantha was two legs ahead. But then Alice caught on. She caught up with and passed Iantha in the middle of her eighth leg, droozling out of the water at each end long enough to gulp a fish and then speeding down to the other end. In the middle of the tenth leg, she was ten yards ahead of the mermaid.

At that point, Mark Vining appeared through the door, running. In each hand he held a bowl of goldfish by the edge. Behind him came Miss Havranek and Miss Tufts, also of the Knickerbockers, both similarly burdened. The guests of the Hotel Creston had been mildly curious when a dark, severe-looking young man and two girls in bathing suits had dashed into the lobby and made off with the six bowls. But they had been too well-bred to inquire directly about the rape of the goldfish.

Vining ran down the side of the pool to a point near the far end. There he extended his arms and inverted the bowls. Water and fish cascaded into the pool. Miss Havranek and Miss Tufts did likewise at other points along the edge of the pool.

Results were immediate. The bowls had been large, and each had contained about six or eight fair-sized goldfish. The forty-odd bright-colored fish, terrified by their rough handling, darted hither and thither about the pool, or at least went as fast as their inefficient build would permit them.

Alice, in the middle of her ninth leg, angled off sharply. Nobody saw her snatch the fish; one second it was there, and the next it was not. Alice doubled with a swirl of flippers and shot diagonally across the pool. Another fish vanished. Forgotten were her master and Louis Connaught and their buckets. This was much more fun. Meanwhile, Iantha finished her race, narrowly avoiding a collision with the sea lion on her last leg.

Connaught hurled the fish he was holding as far as he could. Alice snapped it up and went on hunting. Connaught ran toward the starting-platform, yelling: "Foul! Foul! Protest! Protest! Foul! Foul!"

He arrived to find the timekeepers comparing watches on Iantha's swim, Laird and Vining doing a kind of war dance, and Ogden Wambach looking like the March Hare on the twenty-eighth of February.

"Stop!" cried the referee. "Stop, Louie! If you shout like

that you'll drive me mad! I'm almost mad now! I know what you're going to say."

"Well . . . well . . . why don't you do something, then? Why don't you tell these crooks where to head in? Why don't you have 'em expelled from the Union? Why don't you—"

"Relax, Louie," said Vining. "We haven't done anything illegal."

"What?" Why, you dirty—"

"Easy, easy." Vining looked speculatively at his fist. The little man followed his glance and quieted somewhat. "There's nothing in the rules about putting fish into a pool. Intelligent swimmers, like Miss Delfoiros, know enough to ignore them when they're swimming a race."

"But—what—why you—"

Vining walked off, leaving the two coaches and the referee to fight it out. He looked for Iantha. She was sitting on the edge of the pool, paddling in the water with her flukes. Beside her were four feebly flopping goldfish laid out in a row on the tiles. As he approached, she picked one up and put the front end of it in her mouth. There was a flash of pearly teeth and a spasmodic flutter of the fish's tail, and the front half of the fish was gone. The other half followed immediately.

At that instant Alice spotted the three remaining fish. The sea lion had cleaned out the pool and was now slithering around on the concrete, barking and looking for more prey. She gallumped past Vining toward the mermaid.

Iantha saw her coming. The mermaid hoisted her tail out of the water, pivoted where she sat, swung the tail up in a curve, and brought the flukes down on the sea lion's head with a loud *spat*. Vining, who was twenty feet off, could have sworn he felt the wind of the blow.

Alice gave a squawk of pain and astonishment and slithered away, shaking her head. She darted past Vining again, and for reasons best known to herself hobbled over to the center of argument and bit Ogden Wambach in the leg. The referee screeched and climbed up on Horwitz's table.

"Hey," said the scorekeeper, "You're scattering my papers!"

"I still say they're publicity-hunting crooks!" yelled Connaught, waving his copy of the rule book at Wambach.

"Bunk!" bellowed Laird. "He's just sore because we can think up more stunts than he can. He started it, with his web-fingered woman."

"Damn your complaints!" screamed Wambach. "Damn your sea lions! Damn your papers! Damn your mermaids! Damn your web-fingered women! Damn your swimming clubs! Damn all of you! I'm going mad! You hear? Mad, mad, mad! One more word out of either of you and I'll have you suspended from the Union!"

"*Ow, ow, ow!*" barked Alice.

Iantha had finished her fish. She started to pull the bathing suit down again; changed her mind, pulled it off over her head, rolled it up, and threw it across the pool. Halfway across it unfolded and floated down onto the water. The mermaid then cleared her throat, took a deep breath, and, in a clear ringing soprano, launched into the heart-wrenching strains of:

> "*Rheingold!*
> *Reines Gold,*
> *Wie lauter und hell*
> *Leuchtest hold du uns!*
> *Um dich, du klares—*"

"*Iantha!*"

"What is it, Markee?" she giggled.

"I said, it's getting time to go home!"

"Oh, but I do not want to go home. I am having much fun."

> "*Nun wir klagen!*
> *Gebt uns das Gold—*"

"No, really, Iantha, we've got to go." He laid a hand on her shoulder. The touch made his blood tingle. At the same time, it was plain that the remains of Iantha's carefully husbanded sobriety had gone. That last race in fresh water had been like three oversized Manhattans. Through Vining's head ran a paraphrase of an old song:

> "*What shall we do with a drunken mermaid*
> *At three o'clock in the morning?*"

"Oh, Markee, always you are so serious when people are 'aving fun. But if you say please I will come."

"Very well, please come. Here, put your arm around my

neck, and I'll carry you to your chair."

Such, indeed was Mark Vining's intention. He got one hand around her waist and another under her tail. Then he tried to straighten up. He had forgotten that Iantha's tail was a good deal heavier than it looked. In fact, that long and powerful structure of bone, muscle, and cartilage ran the mermaid's total weight up to the surprising figure of over two hundred and fifty pounds. The result of his attempt was to send himself and his burden headlong into the pool. To the spectators it looked as though he had picked Iantha up and then deliberately dived in with her.

He came up and shook the water out of his head. Iantha popped up in front of him.

"So!" she gurgled. "You are 'aving fun with Iantha! I think you are serious, but you want to play games! All right, I show you!" She brought her palm down smartly, filling Vining's mouth and nose with water. He struck out blindly for the edge of the pool. He was a powerful swimmer, but his street clothes hampered him. Another splash cascaded over his luckless head. He got his eyes clear in time to see Iantha's head go down and her flukes up.

"Markeeee!" The voice was behind him. He turned, and saw Iantha holding a large black block of soft rubber. This object was a plaything for users of the Hotel Creston's pool, and it had been left lying on the bottom during the meet.

"Catch!" cried Iantha gaily, and let drive. The block took Vining neatly between the eyes.

The next thing he knew, he was lying on the wet concrete. He sat up and sneezed. His head seemed to be full of ammonia. Louis Connaught put away the smelling-salts bottle, and Laird shoved a glass containing a snort of whiskey at him. Beside him was Iantha, sitting on her curled tail. She was actually crying.

"Oh, Markee, you are not dead? You are all right? Oh, I am so sorry! I did not mean to 'it you."

"I'm all right, I guess," he said thickly. "Just an accident. Don't worry."

"Oh, I am so glad!" She grabbed his neck and gave it a hug that made its vertebrae creak alarmingly.

"Now," he said, "if I could dry out my clothes. Louie, could you—uh—"

"Sure," said Connaught, helping him up. "We'll put your clothes on the radiator in the men's shower room, and I can lend you a pair of pants and a sweatshirt while they're drying."

When Vining came out in his borrowed garments, he had to push his way through the throng that crowded the starting end of the pool room. He was relieved to note that Alice had disappeared. In the crowd, Iantha was holding court in her wheelchair. In front of her stood a large man in a dinner jacket and a black cloak, with his back to the pool.

"Permit me," he was saying. "I am Joseph Clement. Under my management, nothing you wished in the way of a dramatic or musical career would be beyond you. I heard you sing, and I know that with but little training, even the doors of the Metropolitan would fly open at your approach."

"No, Mr. Clement. It would be nice, but tomorrow I 'ave to leave for 'ome." She giggled.

"But my dear Miss Delfoiros—where is your home, if I may presume to ask?"

"Cyprus."

"Cyprus? Hm-m-m—let's see, where's that?"

"You do not know where Cyprus is? You are not a nice man. I do not like you. Go away."

"Oh, but my dear, dear Miss Del—"

"Go away, I said. Scram."

"But—"

Iantha's tail came up and lashed out, catching the cloaked man in the solar plexus.

Little Miss Havranek looked at her teammate Miss Tufts, as she prepared to make her third rescue of the evening. "Poisonally," she said, "I am getting damn sick of pulling dopes out of this pool."

The sky was just turning gray the next morning when Laird drove his huge old limousine out into the driveway of his house in the Bronx. The wind was driving a heavy rain almost horizontally.

He got out and helped Vining carry Iantha into the car. Vining got in the back with the mermaid. He spoke into the voice tube: "Jones Beach, Chauncey."

"Aye, aye, sir," came the reply. "Listen, Mark, you sure we remembered everything?"

"I made a list and checked it." He yawned. "I could have done with some more sleep last night. Are you sure you won't fall asleep at the wheel?"

"Listen, Mark, with all the coffee I got sloshing around in me, I won't get to sleep for a week."

"We certainly picked a nice time to leave."

"I know we did. In a coupla hours, the place'll be covered six deep with reporters. If it weren't for the weather, they might be arriving now. When they do, they'll find the horse has stolen the stable door—that isn't what I mean, but you get the idea. Listen, you better pull down some of those curtains until we get out on Long Island."

"Righto, Herb."

Iantha spoke up in a small voice. "Was I very bad last night when I was drunk, Mark?"

"Not very. At least, not worse than I'd be if I went swimming in a tank of sherry."

"I am so sorry—always I try to be nice, but the fresh water gets me out of my head. And that poor Mr. Clement, that I pushed in the water—"

"Oh, he's used to temperamental people. That's his business. But I don't know that it was such a good idea on the way home to stick your tail out of the car and biff that cop under the chin with it."

She giggled. "But he looked so surprised!"

"I'll say he did! But a surprised cop is sometimes a tough customer."

"Will that make trouble for you?"

"I don't think so. If he's a wise cop, he won't report it at all. You know how the report would read? 'Attacked by mermaid at corner Broadway and Ninety-eighth Street, 11:45 P.M.' And *where* did you learn the unexpurgated version of 'Barnacle Bill the Sailor'?"

"A Greek sponge diver I met in Florida told me. 'E is a friend of us mer-folk, and he taught me my first English. 'E used to joke me about my Cypriot accent when we talked Greek. It is a pretty song, is it not?"

"I don't think 'pretty' is exactly the word I'd use."

"'Oo won the meet? I never did 'ear."

"Oh, Louie and Herb talked it over, and decided they'd both get so much publicity out of it that it didn't much matter. They're leaving it up to the A.A.U., who will get a first-class headache. For instance, we'll claim we didn't foul Alice, because Louie had already disqualified her by his calling and fish-waving. You see that's coaching, and coaching a competitor during an event is illegal.

"But look here, Iantha, why do you have to leave so abruptly?"

She shrugged. "My business with 'Erbert is over, and I promised to be back to Cyprus for my sister's baby being born."

"You don't lay eggs? But of course you don't. Didn't I just prove last night you are mammals?"

"Markee, what an idea! Anyway, I do not want to stay around. I like you and I like 'Erbert, but I do not like living on land. You just imagine living in water for yourself, and you get an idea. And if I stay, the newspapers come, and soon all New York knows about me. We mer-folk do not believe in letting the land men know about us."

"Why?"

"We used to be friends with them sometimes, and always it made trouble. And now they 'ave guns and go around shooting things a mile away, to collect them, my great-uncle was shot in the tail last year by some aviator man who thought he was a porpoise or something. We don't like being collected. So when we see a boat or an airplane coming, we duck down and swim away quick."

"I suppose," said Vining slowly, "that that's why there were plenty of reports of mer-folk up to a few centuries ago, and then they stopped, so that now people don't believe they exist."

"Yes. We are smart, and we can see as far as the land men can. So you do not catch us very often. That is why this business with 'Erbert, to buy ten thousand bathing caps for the mer-folk, 'as to be secret. Not even his company will know about it. But they will not care if they get their money. And we shall not 'ave to sit on rocks drying our 'air so much. Maybe later we can arrange to buy some good knives and spears the same way. They would be better than the shell things we use now."

"I suppose you get all these old coins out of wrecks?"

"Yes. I know of one just off—no, I must not tell you. If the land men know about a wreck, they come with divers. Of course, the very deep ones we do not care about, because we cannot dive down that far. We 'ave to come up for air, like a whale."

"How did Herb happen to suck you in on that swimming meet?"

"Oh, I promised him when he asked—when I did not know

'ow much what-you-call-it fuss there would be. When I found
out, he would not let me go back on my promise. I think he
'as a conscience about that, and that is why he gave me that
nice fish spear."

"Do you ever expect to get back this way?"

"No, I do not think so. We 'ad a committee to see about
the caps, and they chose me to represent them. But now that
is arranged, and there is no more reason for me going out on
land again."

He was silent for a while. Then he burst out: "Damn it all,
Iantha, I just can't believe that you're starting off this morning
to swim the Atlantic, and I'll never see you again."

She patted his hand. "Maybe you cannot, but that is so.
Remember, friendships between my folk and yours always make
people un'appy. I shall remember you a long time, but that is
all there will ever be to it."

He growled something in his throat, looking straight in front
of him.

She said: "Mark, you know I like you, and I think you like
me. 'Erbert 'as a moving-picture machine in his house, and he
showed me some pictures of 'ow the land folk live.

"These pictures showed a custom of the people in this country, when they like each other. It is called—kissing, I think.
I should like to learn that custom."

"Huh? You mean *me?*" To a man of Vining's temperament,
the shock was almost physically painful. But her arms were
already sliding around his neck. Presently twenty firecrackers,
six Roman candles, and a skyrocket seemed to go off inside
him.

"Here we are, folks," called Laird. Getting no response, he
repeated the statement more loudly. A faint and unenthusiastic
"Yeah" came through the voice tube.

Jones Beach was bleak under the lowering March clouds.
The wind drove the rain against the car windows.

They drove down the beach road a way, till the tall tower
was lost in the rain. Nobody was in sight.

The men carried Iantha down on the beach and brought the
things she was taking. These consisted of a boxful of cans of
sardines, with a strap to go over the shoulders; a similar but
smaller container with her personal belongings, and the fish
spear, with which she might be able to pick up lunch on the
way.

Iantha peeled off her land-woman's clothes and pulled on the emerald bathing cap. Vining, watching her with the skirt of his overcoat whipping about his legs, felt as if his heart was running out of his damp shoes onto the sand.

They shook hands, and Iantha kissed them both. She squirmed down the sand and into the water. Then she was gone. Vining thought he saw her wave back from the crest of a wave, but in that visibility he couldn't be sure.

They walked back to the car, squinting against the drops. Laird said: "Listen, Mark, you look as if you'd just taken a right to the button."

Vining merely grunted. He had gotten in front with Laird and was drying his glasses with his handkerchief, as if that were an important and delicate operation.

"Don't tell me you're hooked?"

"So what?"

"Well, I suppose you know there's absolutely nothing you can do about it."

"Herb!" Vining snapped angrily. "Do you have to point out the obvious?"

Laird, sympathizing with his friend's feelings, did not take offense. After they had driven a while, Vining spoke on his own initiative. "That," he said, "is the only woman I've ever known that made me feel at ease. I could talk to her."

Later, he said, "I never felt so damn mixed up in my life. I doubt whether anybody else ever did, either. Maybe I ought to feel relieved it's over. But I don't."

Pause. Then: "You'll drop me in Manhattan on your way back, won't you?"

"Sure, anywhere you say. Your apartment?"

"Anywhere near Times Square will do. There's a bar there I like."

So, thought Laird, at least the normal male's instincts were functioning correctly in the crisis.

She Sells Sea Shells

by
Paul Darcy Boles

Humans seem to be nature's xenophobes, hell-bent on conquest, ravaging the land and everything growing and living on it in order to "possess" it. We destroy and conquer out of fear ...fear of anyone or anything unlike ourselves. Not satisfied with destroying the land, we are now hard at work trying to ruin the sea as well, dumping radioactive wastes and millions of tons of lethal chemical sludge into it, poisoning its inhabitants (and slaughtering those we don't poison), befouling it with massive oil-slicks that spread through the living water like huge black cancers....

And yet, throughout history there have always been those who have a gift for living in sympathy with nature, those who are the friends of the earth ... and of the sea. For them, for those wise enough to see with their hearts, the sea can bring gifts of life, and love.

For the others, for the ravagers and despoilers, the sea has a cold gift of quite another sort.... •

The late Paul Darcy Boles was an internationally-known author with eleven books to his credit, including Limner, Parton's Island, Night Watch, *and the collection* I Thought You Were a Unicorn and Other Stories.

His most recent novel was Glory Day.

* * *

SHE WAS A QUIET WOMAN, THE BEST KIND. UP AROUND THE rocks nobody much goes in after Labor Day. But there she was, here into October, stroking in as if the water wasn't fit to chill a lobster. Naked, far as I could see, but for what looked like a shell necklace. Clean arms, with the shine of silver along them in the twilight and her legs scissoring nice and smooth, and no strain to it at all. A wonderful swimmer. Quiet, as I said.

Sun was just going out of sight out at Bradford Point, hanging behind the old lighthouse and making it look like a black candle in the middle of the afterglow. It's a time when I always liked to be by myself on shore. The summer people—the "straphangers" we call them, and you can figure out why—are gone and the pines and the rocks just sort of turn into themselves again. The boards of the docks look bleaker and quieter. The ring of green weed around the dock pilings gets a gentle, lost light in the evening. Molly's Fish House down the line gets its shabby contented look back again. It seems to be about to fall into the sea but it never does. The smell of the water is stronger and like iodine around a scratch. Some places on the island you can stand still and hear a moose drinking from one of the creeks. It's a near-to-wintering time when the sun feels better than it will again all year.

When she got in under the shadow of the steepest rocks I said, "Evening," and heard her stand up in the shallows. Then she looked around and up at me, just her face showing in a little spotlight of last sun. It was a searching face, like a seal's, and smooth as brown stone under the water-shine. Her hair hung down to her backbone, wet and heavy and looking like dripping amber in that light. The eyes were the color of the periwinkles you see growing in some of the inland gardens where the wind doesn't reach enough to tear them out of the ground. They were wide and a little surprised to see me there. With her two hands she lifted the hair from her back and stroked the water off in a downflowing motion. Then she said, "It's darkening fast. Will you walk me back to my place?"

I nodded that I would. I guessed she trusted my looks. I didn't know her from Adam's off ox, but she didn't look like leftover summer people to me. They have a different shine, as if they're already on their way to somewhere else in their heads. She seemed as if she belonged. And she didn't look as though she fooled around with paint and canvas, bothering the lobstermen by sketching them or parking herself on the rocks and making a common buoy and some gulls come out like daubs. Or writing poems about the coastline and how the fog makes her think of her lost childhood. I waited while she dressed under the overhang of the rock. It was nearly good dark when she came around up the path. Her feet were bare and she walked

like she swam, neat and quick. She carried a little old tote bag
she'd kept her dress in. The dress was just any old wrapping.

We headed up the shoreline toward Molly's. With some
people you have to make talk. You could wait for her to make
it. After a while when she thought it was time to say something,
in her own good pace, she said, "There are whales out past
the Point."

By now it was dark along the sand and the water had a
steadier sound as it lapped. The light at the Point was sweeping
across out there, picking out pieces of the cove and then letting
them go like a sliding eye. It touched the side of her face and
let it go.

I said, "If you got that far out you're some navigator. That's
about five nautical miles, where the whales hang out. Stand a
good chance of letting yourself get caught in a tide rip."

The light came around again and this time when it touched
her I could see she was smiling. "I don't mind a little tide.
I've fought them before." She looked ahead to where the lights
of Molly's were starting to show the outlines of the fishnet
draped over the windows. "It's only when I come back that I
get frightened. There are too many murderers on shore."

She happened to lean against me and I took her arm. It was
cool as wet sand and lean and hard but round too, with the
pump of blood I could feel under my fingertips.

I said, "I'm Jeb Malifee. Portygee on my mama's side and
green apple saltwater on my old man's. They've both been
gone awhile. I've got the little black shack you see crosswise
from the Point. But you can't see it after dark or get there
unless you know the path."

I waited for her to tell me something about where she sprang
from. She took her time about that. Neither of us were in any
chattering hurry.

"Marna," she said after a spell. She sort of walked around
the name and caressed it like a woman will try a ribbon on for
color and effect in a mirror. "Marna," she said again, as if she
liked it all right. "I come from not far off."

I like anybody who doesn't care to tell too much about
themselves. There's a decent mystery in that. She appeared
and felt old enough to me to have been married and rid of
whatever man had bogged her down and maybe even to have
had kids. But they'd need to be little kids; she wasn't that old.
I kept holding her arm and didn't mind it a whit. Neither did

she. She gave off that clean smell of the salt that soaks into your pores and seems to touch your bones when you've been swimming a time.

I said, "I take supper at Molly's most evenings. Before I walk you home maybe you'd like to join me. The chowder's not bad, and she sets good greens."

We were inside the light that came out through the fishnet windows now. There were a couple of local cars. Bigbee's truck and such, parked in the yard. A first wind had come up and was shaking the yard grass some. I could see her eyes clearer. They were pretty close to mine. The Point light didn't reach us here because of the breakwater slabs. But it touched the slabs in its swing and made the tip ends of her drying hair shine brighter when it passed over. I said, "I'd think you'd be sharp-set from swimming. I've got some handyman's pay in my pocket. My treat."

She said in a low voice. "Yes, I'm hungry."

I don't know how it happened then. But she swung in against me. And I took her shoulders and then I was covering her mouth up good. It was like tasting bright brine on a sunned morning when you're a kid. With a lot of heat at the center. It was like applejack too, with the rindy kick you get that wakes you up like blowing weather.

I held her close and then let her go. Just holding her arm again now. But it was different for both of us. We went on into Molly's. She was doing all the parlor serving herself, her summer waitresses gone back to school or wherever. She's a big woman with a front like a bosomy tree full of russets, and hair that goes springier every year she dyes it more. She took us to a window table where we could look out through the holes of the nets and see the grass pushing in the wind, and past that, her husband Jack's dory where it was left after he drowned. It was all clogged with sand up to the flat keel around the bow. She told me, "I'll need some shoring up soon, the timbers on the east wall, Jeb. Before real winter."

I said, "I'll bring my tool bag over tomorrow."

I lit the candle in its cup on the table. Marna gazed across at me, nodding when I asked if I could order. I ordered plenty of chowder and all the greens going and a side order of cod for both of us. The candle flame made her eyes turn up at the corners like a cat's. When Molly'd gone I said, "You don't have to fret about murder on the island. The only thing kills anybody is the water. Coming from around here you should know that."

She was listening, looking right at me. From over at his table Ed Bigbee and his boys let up some laughs. I figured they might be laughing at me for picking up a woman they didn't know and walking in here bold as cooters. I didn't care about that.

I lifted a saltshaker and laid it on its side like it was a man lying down. "Ten men in the last month of summer," I said. "Every one done in by the water. Jack Meliorot was the first." I nodded out to the bleaching dory. "Flat calm, but the dory came in without him. He wasn't a steady drunk. Just some tanking on weekends." I picked up the shaker and laid it down on its flank again. "All like that. Island people and people with God-sense about the water." I looked up. "So you can see what could happen to a one-woman swimmer without even a boat. Going way beyond the limit and finding whales."

Her eyes stayed so blue they hurt on mine.

"They come up dark as glory and then beside you," she said. "Their eyes looking at you and their power shared with you. They smile in their bellies and roll like churches in a storm. They make me full of wonder and charged with joy."

She reached and touched my hand. It was like touching cool fire. "There were fishermen, trying to harpoon them. But they go deep, when they feel that. They speak in the deep. They sing about the narrowness of the land and the tininess of men. About what'll happen when the world changes and they walk on land again."

I kept her hand firm in mine. "Sure," I said. "The only trouble is they don't have thumbs. If they had thumbs like monkeys and could learn to walk they'd be pretty big beans. Nothing wrong with their brains. But it won't work if they're planning a takeover. Don't you know in the Writ where it says, 'There shall be no more sea?'"

She saw then I was laughing a little inside me without showing it. She pulled her hand out of mine like a fin going small and slipping the bight.

She stared at me with the eyes afire in the middle of the blue and then started to get up.

I said, "Sit down. I'm sorry. I won't talk so again. When you look like that I'd swear you can see in the dark."

She settled back. I took out my pipe and lit it. While I got it going she reached in a pocket of that wadded do-nothing dress and pulled out a shell. Not the kind you see washed in by the thousands, but gold-tipped with the whorls in it creamy and a perfect nacre moonlight on the outside. I figured it for one of those I'd seen in the necklace when she'd come swimming in. It caught the light and sent back a kind of light itself.

I said, "That's a different animal."

"From the floor of the sea," she said.

"Well, how?" I said. I blew a cloud. "You can't go that far down, you wouldn't be here. A suited diver can't make it five miles out. I'll show you cartographic soundings sometime, if you want."

She said, "The whales bring them for me."

I had sense enough to keep my lips tight.

"I sell them to a shop, a store in Boston. They sell to museums, collectors."

"That makes sense," I said.

After a time her hand came back. I held it like it was a quiet child I'd saved from a beating.

Molly came with our orders. I'd been wondering if hunger for this woman meant hunger in the way of appetite for food. I needn't have worried about that. She ate with her head low and nothing before her but the eating. It should have been something you wanted to look away from, but it wasn't. Just like an animal with health in it, and that fierceness. It excited me some. She didn't need any of Molly's bibs. It all went down without a scrap left but the peeled cod bones.

When we got outside again in the dark, Bigbee's truck was just leaving with his boys and some bottles waving back, and the rest of the cars were gone. She'd put the valuable shell back in her tote bag. I put an arm around her and felt her lean into it. I said, "If you don't want to show me your place inside, you don't have to. No obligation. But give me a general idea which way it lies."

She'd put up a hand and she rubbed the hair at the nape of my neck. "It's past your shack, to leeward. Under the dune there, beside the inlet. It's not a house. It's a cave."

I said, "I know the place. I haven't been there in a time. Some of us island kids used to root around there summers, before we had to make ourselves a living. It will get cold as Billy B. Hell when the snows come."

She said, "I won't be there then. I'm moving in with you."

"So be it," I said. Her hand stayed in my nape hair while we walked on. We passed my shack, black clapboard with salt caked on the seaward boards and my own dory upended on tubs in the yard and my toolshed unlocked in case anybody wanted to borrow—whoever did would leave a note—and went right on to the dune. The inshore breeze was pestering the sea oats, making them lean like stiff wheat. The dune shoulder loomed up high and the tide was in and the surf starting to make. She let go of me and cut a little ahead. I followed her over the dune and down to where the cave is: an old granite deposit with walls like carved fleece. She hunkered down to go in, and for a minute it was dark, then she found a match and struck it to the binnacle lamp set on the cave floor. The wick widened with fire.

While she gathered shells, a good many of them, all strange and different, and stuffed them in a gunnysack on top of dried seaweed, I kept looking at the lamp. It was old as whaling days. Had worm holes in the elm strapping, thick wavy glass. I said, "Pete Chalorous had a lamp like this. Got it from his father, carried it in his dory. When Pete and his son washed up, the dory came in a day later. Nobody ever found the lamp."

His back was turned. Her hair was dry as moss now. Shining like something fed by the half dark. Falling deep to her shoulders when she faced me. "I found the dory afloat before it came in. I thought it had gone adrift. I took the lamp for my own."

"Nobody needs it," I said. "Pete's wife's gone to live with relatives at Bangor."

I helped her carry the lamp and the sack full of weed-cradled shells and her little bag. That was about all she seemed to have. Travel light and stay clam pure; it didn't seem to be a bad life, if lonesome. Maybe she knew what I was thinking. Because when we mounted the dune again, breeze at our backs and the surf talking, she said over hair floating from her shoulders, "I send the money from the shells to a wildlife group. They're trying to save the whales."

"Yes," I said. "Everybody's trying to save something."

At the shack I went in first to light the stove and lay some wood in the fireplace. That was all I usually needed to see by at night. She put her shells out where they could catch the light around the sill beams. When I had the pine and birch logs drawing I stood up and wheeled around and then just stood. She'd stripped her dress. She lifted her arms as if she might be going to dance or make a dive.

When I took her she arched back as if she didn't have any bones, making a singing noise in the back of her throat that seemed to get in my head and stay there. It stayed even after the first time, while we were just lying in the firelight. I had her head across my chest, her hair like a fine seine I could just see shadows through. It smelled of kelp and clean salt. The song kept on. I thought it must be coming from the whole body, not just the throat. The way a cat does from the inside out. With one hand I spread the hair back from her ears, and ran a finger down an earlobe and along in back of the cord of the throat there, but she rolled over and crouched and spread herself above me, and I forgot about anything else.

By morning the half-easterly had blown itself out, and while I made coffee and fried bacon and dipped bread in egg batter I said, "I'll be at Molly's about till noon. Then I've got to go to Abel Masterson's, he needs some plastering. His store's next to the P.O. If you've got some shells to ship you could do them up now and I'll post them."

She was combing her hair with an old ivory-toothed comb that had been my grandmother's. Malifees hardly ever throw away anything. Her hair was like a buried walnut gun stock when you've rubbed it with the heel of your hand about a century. She shook her head. "I want to gather a few more before I send what I have. There aren't many good days for it left this year."

I couldn't argue with that. She was so set in her mind she'd have made a good selectman. But I told her not to try that five-mile jaunt again. "The weather stations do what they can. But a squall line can come up so fast it's around you before you can see it's there."

She looked at me like she knew more than generations of seagoing Malifees had ever fathomed. She said, soft, "You are a good man. Born here among the cruel men in this place."

When I left with my tool bag and the plastering gear, she waved till I was past the blueberry brambles. Then I couldn't see her any longer, though she stayed in my mind all morning, while I shored Molly's and went on to middle-island where the stores were and where people like Abel Masterson were breathing slower after the summer rush. The usual bunch of old islanders were gathered like numbers circling a clock dial around the octagon bench under the maple in front of Abel's place, cutting up their neighbors and gently spitting.

I was working on Abel's entrance wall, with the door open, when Ed Bigbee's truck roared up and his big-bellied self and his sons poured out.

I suppose as I listened to him—you could hear him half the block—he was what she meant by a cruel man. He wasn't that, though. Just crafty and stupid, the usual mix. I knew he'd wanted to get those whales for a long time, and now here it was; he and some of his buddies were grabbing the full advantage of no outlanders being left on the island, no ecology and wildlife champions. I stepped to the door in time to hear him boom it out: "We got her all rented and set for morning, boys! Cutter like a Coast Guard's, with a sharper bow. This crew knows what they're doing, and they'll split the meat with us. All we do is pay for the time and trouble. Hell, they done it before, plenty of times—maybe a ton of equipment on board with these depth-propelled harpoons like a torpedo. Sneak up on Mister Leviathan and jab him in the giblets."

Bailee Bigbee, Ed's oldest son, caught my eye. His own glistened. "You comin', Jeb? We're just trustin' people from here who can keep their mouths shut. This ever got out, those fancy straphangers'd nail us to the wall. All we got to do is go out to meet 'em and watch the fun. They ain't even coming in the cove. Just cruising straight to the feeding grounds."

"Yeah, join us, Jeb," Ed said. "We're goin' in my dory. Give you a whaleburger later. Save you puttin' your own dory back in the water."

I said something that made no promises. Then I finished up the plastering, ate half a lead-heavy egg sandwich at the drugstore, and walked by myself through reams of Indian summer light to the rocks. I took my shirt off there and stretched out. With the sun on my eyelids I thought about Marna, if that was her name, and I didn't care if it was or wasn't. I thought about her claim that the whales brought up special seashells for her. I thought about the high average of people who'd been drowned when they'd bothered those whales this past year, too. When I dropped off to sleep I had a drowning dream—which happens sometimes if you're island-born and have seen enough men washed in.

I woke up at dusk, the rock under me cooling.

At first I didn't see her coming in. It could have been a sleek piece of driftwood. Then just as the Bradford Point light came on I could make out her arms and legs slicing along, no tiredness in them. When she reached the shallows and waded in I could see three new shells, the strange kind, draped around her neck on a rope of what looked like seaweed. They showed like odd diamonds under and across her breasts.

I went down off the rocks and took her free hand and walked her into the rock chink where she'd left her dress and bag. She took off the shells and stood back and shook herself, then slid into the dress, and I didn't say a word. I didn't want to break the spell she held around her. Then she moved to me, still wet, the dress sponging, and when I kissed her I thought I'd go on keeping quiet.

She clung close on the way back to the shack. As if the sand and trees and rocks happened to be alien and the shadows threats. When we passed Molly's windows I could see Ed Bigbee's jutting head as he tipped a beer toward somebody and explained how smart he was to revive the sport and business of whale-killing in this Year of our Lord.

In the shack you could see the fog creeping up outside. And feel it. You could almost taste it. Our lovemaking was so fierce it was like hitting each other, or being in a nor'easter, and behind her eyes I could see the faces of all the men I'd known who'd been lost in the deep. The Davy Jones men. They were all there, from this past summer and way back, my relatives among them.

About midnight I got up and went outside. The fog was a pea-souper. By the time I had my dory off the tubs and on rollers and to the inlet creek my hair and pants were soaked. It wasn't an ice chill but it was winter waiting. Inside, I rubbed down and folded myself beside her. I could hear that secret singing of hers. I could feel it through my hands like a harp.

In the morning the fog was still there, hanging on but starting to lift a little. Which it would do when the sun played through. I didn't make breakfast, just told her, "Take me where the whales are."

She fixed my eyes with hers a second, and nodded. Then we had the dory worked out in the cove. The sun started coming through when we hit the open water. I could hear others setting off behind us now. A lot of happy shouting with that shut-in

sound it gets across the water. There were soft swells now and
where the light patched the patches were blue as a robin's egg.
I started my dory engine and gave her the gun. Marna stooped
at my shoulder and guided my hand on the engine tiller for
direction. It was warming now with the sun as far as you could
look and the last fog wisps traveling up into the sky. Now and
then when I looked back I could see just the specks of other
island-craft coming, and I hoped to God my engine would hold
out and not blow from all I was giving it. I kept squinting back
through the spray. Then she said, calling above the engine's
racket, "Here." I cut the engine and we wallowed ahead a few
seconds and then were alone in near silence. Except for the
lap of water on the strake-boards.

When I held to the gunwale with my knuckles going white
and looked down, I could see the first of the whales. It was a
gray-blue shape far below, coming up through brightening layers of light, getting so big you felt when it broke the surface
it would shut out the world. Around it in its upward passage
silver green fire flew. Behind it came eight more, all the same,
all rising and looking up to Marna who'd cast off her dress
and stood in the bow. Then the first one checked just under
the dory. It made a curving wave that rippled the dory-length
and seemed to hold it like a chip on a bubble. They were all
just a few feet under and around us now, not sounding, just
waiting, in wonderful islands with their darkness solid and
glistening and their tiny port-wine-colored eyes holding the
sun. The understanding was what reached upward, more important than the size. One rolled a little to see Marna better.
Weed wrapped its flanks like a green lace shawl. Marna was
calling now, and they were answering. The noises were high
and clean above the water. Below, they must have been heard
for fathoms.

I raised my head when Marna pointed. I saw the hired
whaleboat coming directly over us. It had a high flat bow with
a knife-shaped pitch, and behind it, off in the blaze of daylight,
lighter craft were bobbing like waterbugs against the blue. Its
hull was battleship gray, and guns were bearing down on us
from the foredeck. Its rigging cut the sun in tight black lines.

Marna dived. She curved into the water beside the nearest
whale, her arm caressing it as she came up, her flesh and the
whale's looking like one easy body, then she held to the gunwale and kissed me, lips salt and cool and eyes wild as a hawk's

and sad as Time. "Good-bye. If you fools of men would accept and keep what you have, it would be enough!" Her hair was swept back. I could see the gill on that side of her throat, a pale rose color, still pulsing as it had done underwater.

Every part of me wanted to dive with her. But she was gone again so quick I couldn't follow. Sinking with bubbles trailing her and her legs moving like a single fin, then getting small as the whales went down with her. All the whales behind her made one deep sweep as if led by her command. Then they were gone from that place and from all land.

After that I had to hang to a thwart to keep from going over while the blue-cold steel skin of the whaler passed so close the wash came creaming and tumbling into the dory and tried to suck me with it. Then I was half swamped and bailing with an old bucket. Somebody, one of the friendly island sportsmen—I was gagging too much to tell who—was hauling me into another dory then and cussing me for fifty kinds of fool. Telling me the Goddamned whales were gone and saying maybe I'd been the one to spook them. I didn't care much if he threw me overboard. It seemed kind of silly to still be breathing.

But maybe, I told myself afterward when I got calmer, I ought to stay around to do something about those shells she'd left behind.

There were a good many chancy stories about that morning. Ed Bigbee stayed so plagued and mad he wouldn't talk to me—kind of a wonderful relief—for two months, not until he knocked a hole in his living room floor trying to shoot a deer from his window and needed a good reasonable repairman to carpenter it. There were a lot of tales about whales having naturally vengeful natures, some saying they'd seen the lead mammal swallow the girl. I made "ee-yah" noises to that, it being the safest sort of sound to make around foolishness.

When all the to-do was dead and it was cold winter, with people dragging out the family pung for a turn around the back roads, and ice on Cherry Pond, I went down to the P.O. to call on Miss Orvington, who's held the postmistressing job forever, and asked her about a box a woman named Marna might've taken out some time back.

Miss Orvington fiddled with her stacks of paper—she has records of when Vice President Dawes, who sort of assisted Coolidge, summered here and took a box in the twenties—and came up with a slip for paid box rent. Signed, Marna something. Paid in U.S. cash. So I put a few more questions, knowing Miss Orvington's feeling for detail, and got out of her that Marna had sent boxes to this shop in Boston, and received checks from them for the contents of same. And I got from Miss Orvington the adjacent news that Marna—"same woman, a dress you wouldn't give an orphans' rummage sale"—had sent money orders to the Save the Sea Mammals Society, in Delaware. Then I plodded home and made up a seaweed-packed box of the shells and sent them along to Boston, and when I got their check sent it along to the Society.

I felt better after, but only a little. Still had the megrims, which hard work doesn't cure any more than not working does, and didn't feel kindly disposed to anybody. The straphangers came down in force in the summer, like blackflies with spending money. We all lived through that, and when they were gone counted our blessings and their money. Then the good days came. October with that autumn-nut kindness, a time of opening up, of hoping.

I was leaning on the rocks in the evening looking across to the Bradford Point light when Bailee Bigbee came up behind and leaned into my pipe smoke. He said, "The whales come back, but they didn't linger. Me and Papa was trawling last night and seen 'em. Gone now though. Swam off most while we watched."

"Shows their basic common sense," I said.

"That ain't all. Somebody left a package on your shack doorstep."

I thought with the way luck had run all year it would be a stack of summonses for city jury duty and such. But it wasn't. When I opened the basket and peeled back the blue cover, here was this spit-and-image of her, with a dash of me around the nose. About three months old and a hale specimen. Bawling his head off, but when I took him over to Molly's she knew what to do and instructed me in the essentials, and warmed up milk and so forth.

Time being, I keep these knitted hats snugged tight around his head. And he plays with the handsome exotic shell he brought with him—it was lying on his naked chest when I first saw him—but he has plenty of other toys for when he outgrows it. His hair's starting to come out fine, thick as a raccoon's. When it's long enough it will cover the gills, and then we'll throw away the hats. The gills are interesting but nothing you could explain to a preacher at baptizing time.

Merman Malifee's not a bad name. It has a kind of quiet ring to it.

The Soul Cages

by

T. Crofton Croker

The Irish version of the mermaid is the Merrow. Female Merrows are usually portrayed as intoxicatingly beautiful, but the male Merrows are startlingly ugly, with, in W. B. Yeats's words, "green teeth, green hair, pig's eyes, and red noses." In spite of their ugliness, though, Merrow-men are generally jovial and affable, and, in the great Irish tradition, like nothing better than to swap songs and stories over a tasty bite of dinner and a good shellful of brandy.

In the wry and lively story that follows, we meet the venerable Merrow Coomara, who, it turns out, keeps spirits even more precious than brandy in his fine, dry cellars on the bottom of the sea. . . .

Born in Cork in 1798, folklorist T. Crofton Croker traveled throughout Ireland in the early nineteenth century to collect the tall tales and legends of the country people at first hand. They were published in 1825 in his Fairy Legends and Traditions of the South of Ireland, *one of the cornerstone books of Irish folklore.*

* * *

JACK DOGHERTY LIVED ON THE COAST OF THE COUNTY CLARE. Jack was a fisherman, as his father and grandfather before him had been. Like them, too, he lived all alone (but for the wife), and just in the same spot. People used to wonder why the Dogherty family were so fond of that wild situation, so far away from all human kind, and in the midst of huge shattered rocks, with nothing but the wide ocean to look upon. But they had their own good reasons for it.

The place was just the only spot on that part of the coast

72

where anybody could well live. There was a neat little creek, where a boat might lie as snug as a puffin in her nest, and out from this creek a ledge of sunken rocks ran into the sea. Now when the Atlantic, according to custom, was raging with a storm, and a good westerly wind was blowing strong on the coast, many a richly-laden ship went to pieces on these rocks; and then the fine bales of cotton and tobacco, and such like things, and the pipes of wine and the puncheons of rum, and the casks of brandy, and the kegs of Hollands that used to come ashore! Dunbeg Bay was just like a little estate to the Dogh-ertys.

Not but they were kind and humane to a distressed sailor, if ever one had the good luck to get to land; and many a time indeed did Jack put out in his little *corrahg* (which, though not quite equal to honest Andrew Hennessy's canvas life-boat would breast the billows like any gannet), to lend a hand towards bringing off the crew from a wreck. But when the ship had gone to pieces, and the crew were all lost, who would blame Jack for picking up all he could find?

"And who is the worse of it?" said he. "For as to the king, God bless him! everybody knows he's rich enough already without getting what's floating in the sea."

Jack, though such a hermit, was a good-natured, jolly fel-low. No other, sure, could ever have coaxed Biddy Mahony to quit her father's snug and warm house in the middle of the town of Ennis, and to go so many miles off to live among the rocks, with the seals and sea-gulls for next-door neighbours. But Biddy knew that Jack was the man for a woman who wished to be comfortable and happy; for to say nothing of the fish, Jack had the supplying of half the gentlemen's houses of the country with the *Godsends* that came into the bay. And she was right in her choice; for no woman ate, drank, or slept better, or made a prouder appearance at chapel on Sundays, than Mrs Dogherty.

Many a strange sight, it may well be supposed, did Jack see, and many a strange sound did he hear, but nothing daunted him. So far was he from being afraid of Merrows, or such beings, that the very first wish of his heart was to fairly meet with one. Jack had heard that they were mighty like Christians, and that luck had always come out of an acquaintance with them. Never, therefore, did he dimly discern the Merrows mov-ing along the face of the waters in their robes of mist, but he made direct for them; and many a scolding did Biddy, in her own quiet way, bestow upon Jack for spending his whole day out at sea, and bringing home no fish. Little did poor Biddy know the fish Jack was after!

It was rather annoying to Jack that, though living in a place where the Merrows were as plenty as lobsters, he never could get a right view of one. What vexed him more was that both his father and grandfather had often and often seen them; and he even remembered hearing, when a child, how his grandfather, who was the first of the family that had settled down at the creek, had been so intimate with a Merrow that, only for fear of vexing the priest, he would have had him stand for one of his children. This, however, Jack did not well know how to believe.

Fortune at length began to think that it was only right that Jack should know as much as his father and grandfather did. Accordingly, one day when he had strolled a little farther than usual along the coast to the northward, just as he turned a point, he saw something, like to nothing he had ever seen before, perched upon a rock at a little distance out to sea. It looked green in the body, as well as he could discern at that distance, and he would have sworn, only the thing was impossible, that it had a cocked hat in its hand. Jack stood for a good half-hour straining his eyes, and wondering at it, and all the time the thing did not stir hand or foot. At last Jack's patience was quite worn out, and he gave a loud whistle and a hail, when the Merrow (for such it was) started up, put the cocked hat on its head, and dived down, head foremost, from the rock.

Jack's curiosity was now excited, and he constantly directed his steps towards the point; still he could never get a glimpse of the sea-gentleman with the cocked hat; and with thinking and thinking about the matter, he began at last to fancy he had been only dreaming. One very rough day, however, when the sea was running mountains high, Jack Dogherty determined to give a look at the Merrow's rock (for he had always chosen a fine day before), and then he saw the strange thing cutting capers upon the top of the rock, and then diving down, and then coming up, and then diving down again.

Jack had now only to choose his time (that is, a good blowing day), and he might see the man of the sea as often as he pleased. All this, however, did not satisfy him—"much will have more";

he wished now to get acquainted with the Merrow, and even in this he succeeded. One tremendous blustering day, before he got to the point whence he had a view of the Merrow's rock, the storm came on so furiously that Jack was obliged to take shelter in one of the caves which are so numerous along the coast; and there, to his astonishment, he saw sitting before him a thing with green hair, long green teeth, a red nose, and pig's eyes. It had a fish's tail, legs with scales on them, and short arms like fins. It wore no clothes, but had the cocked hat under its arm, and seemed engaged thinking very seriously about something.

Jack, with all his courage, was a little daunted; but now or never, thought he; so up he went boldly to the cogitating fish-man, took off his hat, and made his best bow.

"Your servant, sir," said Jack.

"Your servant, kindly, Jack Dogherty," answered the Merrow.

"To be sure, then, how well your honour knows my name!" said Jack.

"Is it I not know your name, Jack Dogherty? Why man, I knew your grandfather long before he was married to Judy Regan, your grandmother! Ah, Jack, Jack, I was fond of that grandfather of yours; he was a mighty worthy man in his time: I never met his match above or below, before or since, for sucking in a shellful of brandy. I hope, my boy," said the old fellow, with a merry twinkle in his eyes, "I hope you're his own grandson!"

"Never fear me for that," said Jack; "if my mother had only reared me on brandy, 'tis myself that would be a sucking infant to this hour!"

"Well, I like to hear you talk so manly; you and I must be better acquainted, if it were only for your grandfather's sake. But, Jack, that father of yours was not the thing! he had no head at all."

"I'm sure," said Jack, "since your honour lives down under the water, you must be obliged to drink a power to keep any heat in you in such a cruel, damp, *could* place. Well, I've often heard of Christians drinking like fishes; and might I be so bold as ask where you get the spirits?"

"Where do you get them yourself, Jack?" said the Merrow, twitching his red nose between his forefinger and thumb.

"Hubbubboo," cries Jack "now I see how it is; but I suppose, sir, your honour has got a fine dry cellar below to keep them in."

"Let me alone for the cellar," said the Merrow, with a knowing wink of his left eye.

"I'm sure," continued Jack, "it must be mighty well worth the looking at."

"You may say that, Jack," said the Merrow; "and if you meet me here next Monday, just at this time of the day, we will have a little more talk with one another about the matter."

Jack and the Merrow parted the best friends in the world. On Monday they met, and Jack was not a little surprised to see that the Merrow had two cocked hats with him, one under each arm.

"Might I take the liberty to ask, sir," said Jack, "why your honour has brought the two hats with you today? You would not, sure, be going to give me one of them, to keep for the *curiosity* of the thing?"

"No, no, Jack," said he, "I don't get my hats so easily, to part with them that way; but I want you to come down and dine with me, and I brought you that hat to dive with."

"Lord bless and preserve us!" cried Jack, in amazement, "would you want me to go down to the bottom of the salt sea ocean? Sure, I'd be smothered and choked up with the water, to say nothing of being drowned! And what would poor Biddy do for me, and what would she say?"

"And what matter what she says, you *pinkeen?* Who cares for Biddy's squalling? It's long before your grandfather would have talked in that way. Many's the time he stuck that same hat on his head, and dived down boldly after me; and many's the snug bit of dinner and good shellful of brandy he and I have had together below, under the water."

"Is it really, sir, and no joke?" said Jack; "why, then, sorrow from me for ever and a day after, if I'll be a bit worse man nor my grandfather was! Here goes—but play me fair now. Here's neck or nothing!" cried Jack.

"That's your grandfather all over," said the old fellow; "so come along, then, and do as I do."

They both left the cave, walked into the sea, and then swam a piece until they got to the rock. The Merrow climbed to the top of it, and Jack followed him. On the far side it was as straight as the wall of a house, and the sea beneath looked so deep that Jack was almost cowed.

"Now, do you see, Jack," said the Merrow: "just put this hat on your head, and mind to keep your eyes wide open. Take hold of my tail, and follow after me, and you'll see what you'll see."

In he dashed, and in dashed Jack after him boldly. They went and they went, and Jack thought they'd never stop going. Many a time did he wish himself sitting at home by the fireside with Biddy. Yet where was the use of wishing now, when he was so many miles, as he thought, below the waves of the Atlantic? Still he held hard by the Merrow's tail, slippery as it was; and, at last, to Jack's great surprise, they got out of the water, and he actually found himself on dry land at the bottom of the sea. They landed just in front of a nice house that was slated very neatly with oyster shells! and the Merrow, turning about to Jack, welcomed him down.

Jack could hardly speak, what with wonder, and what with being out of breath with travelling so fast through the water. He looked about him and could see no living things, barring crabs and lobsters, of which there were plenty walking leisurely about on the sand. Overhead was the sea like a sky, and the fishes like birds swimming about in it.

"Why don't you speak, man?" said the Merrow: "I dare say you had no notion that I had such a snug little concern here as this? Are you smothered, or choked, or drowned, or are you fretting after Biddy, eh?"

"Oh! not myself indeed," said Jack, showing his teeth with a good-humoured grin; "but who in the world would ever have thought of seeing such a thing?"

"Well, come along, and let's see what they've got for us to eat?"

Jack really was hungry, and it gave him no small pleasure to perceive a fine column of smoke rising from the chimney, announcing what was going on within. Into the house he followed the Merrow, and there he saw a good kitchen, right well provided with everything. There was a noble dresser, and plenty of pots and pans, with two young Merrows cooking. His host then led him into the room, which was furnished shabbily enough. Not a table or a chair was there in it; nothing but planks and logs of wood to sit on, and eat off.There was, however, a good fire blazing upon the hearth—a comfortable sight to Jack.

"Come now, and I'll show you where I keep—you know what," said the Merrow, with a sly look; and opening a little door, he led Jack into a fine cellar, well filled with pipes, and kegs, and hogsheads, and barrels.

"What do you say to that, Jack Dogherty? Eh! may be a body can't live snug under the water?"

"Never the doubt of that," said Jack, with a convincing smack of his upper lip, that he really thought what he said.

They went back to the room, and found dinner laid. There was no tablecloth, to be sure—but what matter? It was not always Jack had one at home. The dinner would have been no discredit to the first house of the country on a fast day. The choicest of fish, and no wonder, was there. Turbots, and sturgeons, and soles, and lobsters, and oysters, and twenty other kinds, were on the planks at once, and plenty of the best of foreign spirits. The wines, the old fellow said, were too cold for his stomach.

Jack ate and drank till he could eat no more: then taking up a shell of brandy, "Here's to your honour's good health, sir," said he; "though, begging your pardon, it's mighty odd that as long as we've been acquainted I don't know your name yet."

"That's true, Jack," replied he; "I never thought of it before, but better late than never. My name's Coomara."

"And a mighty decent name it is," cried Jack, taking another shellfull: "here's to your good health, Coomara, and may ye live these fifty years to come!"

"Fifty years!" repeated Coomara; "I'm obliged to you, indeed! If you had said five hundred, it would have been something worth the wishing."

"By the laws, sir," cried Jack, *"youz* lived to a powerful age here under the water! You knew my grandfather, and he's dead and gone better than these sixty years. I'm sure it must be a healthy place to live in."

"No doubt of it; but come, Jack, keep the liquor stirring."

Shell after shell did they empty, and to Jack's exceeding surprise, he found the drink never got into his head, owing, I suppose, to the sea being over them, which kept their noddles cool.

Old Coomara got exceedingly comfortable, and sung several songs; but Jack, if his life had depended on it, never could remember more than

> *"Rum fum boodle boo,*
>   *Ripple dipple nitty dob;*
> *Dumdoo doodle coo,*
>   *Raffle taffle chittiboo!"*

It was the chorus to one of them; and, to say the truth, nobody that I know has ever been able to pick any particular meaning out of it; but that, to be sure, is the case with many a song nowadays.

At length said he to Jack, "Now, my dear boy, if you follow me, I'll show you my *curiosities!*" He opened a little door, and led Jack into a large room, where Jack saw a great many odds and ends that Coomara had picked up at one time or another. What chiefly took his attention, however, were things like lobster-pots ranged on the ground along the wall.

"Well, Jack, how do you like my *curiosities?*" said old Coo.

"Upon my *sowkins,** sir," said Jack, "they're mighty well worth the looking at; but might I make so bold as to ask what these things like lobster-pots are?"

"Oh! the Soul Cages, is it?"

"The what? sir!"

"These things here that I keep the souls in."

"*Arrah!* what souls, sir?" said Jack, in amazement; "sure the fish have no souls in them?"

"Oh! no," replied Coo, quite coolly, "that they have not; but these are the souls of drowned sailors."

"The Lord preserve us from all harm!" muttered Jack, "how in the world did you get them?"

"Easily enough: I've only, when I see a good storm coming on, to set a couple of dozen of these, and then, when the sailors are drowned and the souls get out of them under the water, the poor things are almost perished to death, not being used to the cold; so they make into my pots for shelter, and then I have them snug, and fetch them home, and is it not well for them, poor souls, to get into such good quarters?"

Jack was so thunderstruck he did not know what to say, so he said nothing. They went back into the dining room, and had a little more brandy, which was excellent, and then, as Jack knew that it must be getting late, and as Biddy might be uneasy,

---

*Sowkins, diminutive of soul.

he stood up, and said he thought it was time for him to be on the road.

"Just as you like, Jack," said Coo, "but take a *duc an durrus*†
before you go; you've a cold journey before you."

Jack knew better manners than to refuse the parting glass.

"I wonder," said he, "will I be able to make out my way
home?"

"What should ail you," said Coo, "when I'll show you the
way?"

Out they went before the house, and Coomara took one of
the cocked hats, and put it upon Jack's head the wrong way,
and then lifted him up on his shoulder that he might launch
him up into the water.

"Now," says he, giving him a heave, "you'll come up just
in the same spot you came down in; and, Jack, mind and throw
me back the hat."

He canted Jack off his shoulder, and up he shot like a
bubble—whirr, whirr, whiz—away he went up through the
water, till he came to the very rock he had jumped off where
he found a landing-place, and then in he threw the hat, which
sunk like a stone.

The sun was just going down in the beautiful sky of a calm
summer's evening. *Feascor* was seen dimly twinkling in the
cloudless heaven, a solitary star, and the waves of the Atlantic
flashed in a golden flood of light. So Jack, perceiving it was
late, set off home; but when he got there, not a word did he
say to Biddy of where he had spent his day.

The state of the poor souls cooped up in the lobster-pots
gave Jack a great deal of trouble, and how to release them cost
him a great deal of thought. He at first had a mind to speak to
the priest about the matter. But what could the priest do, and
what did Coo care for the priest? Besides, Coo was a good
sort of an old fellow, and did not think he was doing any harm.
Jack had a regard for him, too, and it also might not be much
to his own credit if it were known that he used to go dine with
Merrows. On the whole, he thought his best plan would be to
ask Coo to dinner, and to make him drunk, if he was able, and
then to take the hat and go down and turn up the pots. It was,
first of all, necessary, however, to get Biddy out of the way;

†*Rectè, doech án dorrus*—door-drink or stirrup-cup.

for Jack was prudent enough, as she was a woman, to wish to keep the thing secret from her.

Accordingly, Jack grew mighty pious all of a sudden, and said to Biddy that he thought it would be for the good of both their souls if she was to go and take her rounds at Saint John's Well, near Ennis. Biddy thought so too, and accordingly off she set one fine morning at day-dawn, giving Jack a strict charge to have an eye to the place. The coast being clear, away went Jack to the rock to give the appointed signal to Coomara, which was throwing a big stone into the water. Jack threw, and up sprang Coo!

"Good morning, Jack," said he; "what do you want with me?"

"Just nothing at all to speak about, sir," returned Jack, "only to come and take a bit of dinner with me, if I might make so free as to ask you, and sure I'm now after doing so."

"It's quite agreeable, Jack, I assure you; what's your hour?"

"Any time that's most convenient to you, sir—say one o'clock, that you may go home, if you wish, with the daylight."

"I'll be with you," said Coo, "never fear me."

Jack went home, and dressed a noble fish dinner, and got out plenty of his best foreign spirits, enough, for that matter, to make twenty men drunk. Just to the minute came Coo, with his cocked hat under his arm. Dinner was ready, they sat down, and ate and drank away manfully. Jack, thinking of the poor souls below in the pots, plied old Coo well with brandy, and encouraged him to sing, hoping to put him under the table, but poor Jack forgot that he had not the sea over his head to keep it cool. The brandy got into it, and did its business for him, and Coo reeled off home, leaving his entertainer as dumb as a haddock on a Good Friday.

Jack never woke till the next morning, and then he was in a sad way. "'Tis to no use for me thinking to make that old Rapparee drunk," said Jack, "and how in this world can I help the poor souls out of the lobster-pots?" After ruminating nearly the whole day, a thought struck him. "I have it," says he, slapping his knee; "I'll be sworn that Coo never saw a drop of *poteen*, as old as he is, and that's the *thing* to settle him! Oh! then, is not it well that Biddy will not be home these two days yet; I can have another twist at him."

Jack asked Coo again, and Coo laughed at him for having

no better head, telling him he'd never come up to his grand-father.

"Well, but try me again," said Jack, "and I'll be bail to drink you drunk and sober, and drunk again."

"Anything in my power," said Coo, "to oblige you."

At this dinner Jack took care to have his own liquor well watered, and to give the strongest brandy he had to Coo. At last says he, "Pray, sir, did you ever drink any poteen?—any real mountain dew?"

"No," says Coo; "what's that, and where does it come from?"

"Oh, that's a secret," said Jack, "but it's the right stuff—never believe me again, if 'tis not fifty times as good as brandy or rum either. Biddy's brother just sent me a present of a little drop, in exchange for some brandy, and as you're an old friend of the family, I kept it to treat you with."

"Well, let's see what sort of thing it is," said Coomara.

The *poteen* was the right sort. It was first-rate, and had the real smack upon it. Coo was delighted: he drank and he sung *Rum bum boodle boo* over and over again; and he laughed and he danced, till he fell on the floor fast asleep. Then Jack, who had taken good care to keep himself sober, snapt up the cocked hat—ran off to the rock—leaped, and soon arrived at Coo's habitation.

All was as still as a churchyard at midnight—not a Merrow, old or young, was there. In he went and turned up the pots, but nothing did he see, only he heard a sort of a little whistle or chirp as he raised each of them. At this he was surprised, till he recollected what the priests had often said, that nobody living could see the soul, no more than they could see the wind or the air. Having now done all that he could for them, he set the pots as they were before, and sent a blessing after the poor souls to speed them on their journey wherever they were going. Jack now began to think of returning; he put the hat on, as was right, the wrong way; but when he got out he found the water so high over his head that he had no hopes of ever getting up into it, now that he had not old Coomara to give him a lift. He walked about looking for a ladder, but not one could he find, and not a rock was there in sight. At last he saw a spot where the sea hung rather lower than anywhere else, so he resolved to try there. Just as he came to it, a big cod happened to put down his tail. Jack made a jump and caught hold of it, and the cod, all in amazement, gave a bounce and pulled Jack up. The minute the hat touched the water away Jack was whisked, and up he shot like a cork, dragging the poor cod, that he forgot to let go, up with him tail foremost. He got to the rock in no time and without a moment's delay hurried home, rejoicing in the good deed he had done.

But, meanwhile, there was fine work at home; for our friend Jack had hardly left the house on his soul-freeing expedition, when back came Biddy from her soul-saving one to the well. When she entered the house and saw the things lying *thrie-na-helah** on the table before her—"Here's a pretty job!" said she; "that blackguard of mine—what ill-luck I had ever to marry him! He has picked up some vagabond or other, while I was praying for the good of his soul, and they've been drinking all the *poteen* that my own brother gave him, and all the spirits, to be sure, that he was to have sold to his honour." Then hearing an outlandish kind of grunt, she looked down, and saw Coomara lying under the table. "The Blessed Virgin help me," shouted she, "if he has not made a real beast of himself! Well, well, I've often heard of a man making a beast of himself with drink! Oh hone, oh hone!—Jack, honey, what will I do with you, or what will I do without you? How can any decent woman ever think of living with a beast?"

With such like lamentations Biddy rushed out of the house, and was going she knew not where, when she heard the well-known voice of Jack singing a merry tune. Glad enough was Biddy to find him safe and sound, and not turned into a thing that was like neither fish nor flesh. Jack was obliged to tell her all, and Biddy, though she had half a mind to be angry with him for not telling her before, owned that he had done a great service to the poor souls. Back they both went most lovingly to the house, and Jack wakened up Coomara; and, perceiving the old fellow to be rather dull, he bid him not to be cast down, for 'twas many a good man's case; said it all came of his not being used to the *poteen*, and recommended him, by way of cure, to swallow a hair of the dog that bit him. Coo, however, seemed to think he had had quite enough. He got up, quite out of sorts, and without having the manners to say one word in the way of civility, he sneaked off to cool himself by a jaunt through the salt water.

Coomara never missed the souls. He and Jack continued

**Trí-na-cheile, literally through other*—i.e., higgledy-piggledy.

the best friends in the world, and no one, perhaps, ever equalled Jack for freeing souls from purgatory; for he contrived fifty excuses for getting into the house below the sea, unknown to the old fellow, and then turning up the pots and letting out the souls. It vexed him, to be sure, that he could never see them; but as he knew the thing to be impossible, he was obliged to be satisfied.

Their intercourse continued for several years. However, one morning, on Jack's throwing in a stone as usual, he got no answer. He flung another, and another, still there was no reply. He went away, and returned the following morning, but it was to no purpose. As he was without the hat, he could not go down to see what had become of old Coo, but his belief was, that the old man, or the old fish, or whatever he was, had either died, or had removed from that part of the country.

Sweetly the Waves
Call to Me

by

Pat Murphy

*Selkies (or silkies, or selchies, as they are sometimes called)
have been associated with mermaids for hundreds of years. A
tale from Shetland describes how a mermaid once sacrificed
her life for a selkie, and how for this reason the selkies have
done all that they can to help the mermaids and warn them of
danger, often risking their own lives to save them. Both selkies
and mermaids are fond of posing upon seaside rocks, both are
credited with the gift of prophecy, both sing in the most haunting
and melodious of voices. And both mermaids and selkies are
the most abundant along the same stony gray coasts: the Or-
kneys, the Shetlands, the Hebrides, the West Coast of Ireland,
the rugged coast of Cornwall. .*

*A selkie is nothing more or less than a were-seal . . . al-
though unlike the unhappy werewolf of popular conception
(sad-faced Larry Talbot, for instance), its transformation is
not necessarily tied to the phases of the moon, and is usually
not involuntary. In the words of the haunting old Childe ballad:*

> *"I am a man upon the land*
> *I am a selkie in the sea . . ."*

*Like their soi-disant cousins, the mermaids—and, in fact,
like most of the various kinds of Merfolk who have been scattered throughout the seas of the world by the human imagination—selkies have a curious predilection for taking human
lovers . . . and although the eloquent and melancholy tale that
follows takes place in modern-day California, it has all the
ingredients of the classic selkie story: a lonely woman in an
isolated house along an empty and desolate strand of beach,*

*a moonlit night, the dark and restless immensity of the sea,
and the eyes that may or may not be human silently watching
from the waves. . . .*

*Pat Murphy lives in San Francisco, where she works for a
science museum, the Exploratorium, and edits their quarterly
magazine. Her elegant and incisive stories have been turning
up for the past few years in* Isaac Asimov's Science Fiction
Magazine, Elsewhere, Amazing, Universe, Shadows, Galaxy,
Chrysalis, *and other places. Her first novel,* The Shadow Hunter,
*was published in 1982. She is currently at work on a new
novel, set in Yucatan, tentatively entitled* Ancient Voices.

* * *

THE HARBOR SEAL LAY JUST BEYOND THE REACH OF THE
waves—its dark eyes open in death. The surf had rolled and
battered the body; the mottled gray fur was dusted with white
sand. Gulls had been pecking at a wound in the animal's head.

Kate shifted her weight uneasily as she stared down at the
body. She was alone; Michael, her lover, was still asleep at
the cottage. Kate had come walking on the beach to escape the
restless feeling left by a melancholy dream. She could not
remember the dream; it had retreated like a wave on the beach,
leaving behind feelings of loneliness and abandonment.

She raised one hand to touch the ivory pendant that dangled
from a chain around her neck, a circle etched with the likeness
of a seal. Michael had given her the pendant the night before—
as a peace offering, she thought.

Michael had come to visit for the weekend to apologize and
to forgive her—managing the seemingly contradictory acts
with the competence that he brought to every task. Kate had
left Santa Cruz and Michael to live for a summer in her parents'
old cottage; she had needed the solitude to finish her thesis on
the folklore of the sea. Michael had brought her the scrimshaw
pendant to apologize for accusing her of using her thesis as an
excuse for leaving him.

She did not think that she was using the thesis as an excuse.
But sometimes, in the dim light of early morning when the
gulls cried overhead, she was not sure. She knew that sometimes she needed him. She knew that he was solid and he was
strong.

She could hear the distant roar of a truck traveling down
Highway One. The cottage was halfway between Davenport

and Pescadero—south of nowhere in particular, north of no place special. A lonely place.

Looking down at the dead body of the seal, Kate had the uneasy feeling that she was being watched. She looked up at the cliff face, then out to sea where the waves crashed. Just past the breakers, a dark head bobbed in the water—a curious harbor seal. As she stared back, he ducked beneath a wave.

She hurried back to the cottage, scrambling up the sandstone slope, following the narrow path that was little better than a wash eroded by the last rain.

The cottage was perched at the top of the bluff. The waves that pounded against the cliff threatened to claim the ramshackle building someday. The sea fog had begun a slow offensive against the cottage: the white paint was chipped and weathered; the porch sagged at one corner where a supporting post had rotted through; the windchimes that hung from the low eaves were tarnished green.

"Bad news," Kate said as she stepped in the kitchen door. "There's a dead seal on the beach."

The kitchen was warm and bright. Michael was making coffee. "Why's that bad news?"

"Bad luck for the person who shot it," she said. "It could have been a silkie, a seal person who could change shape and become human on land. If a person kills a silkie, the sea turns against him."

Michael was watching her with an expression that had become familiar during the time that they had lived together—he did not know how seriously to take her. "You've been working on that thesis too long," he said, and poured her a cup of coffee.

She laughed and slipped an arm around his waist, leaning up against him and feeling the warmth of his body. Almost like old times. "Huh," she said, "There speaks the scientist."

"It'll be simple enough to get rid of any bad luck," he added. "I'll call the University of Santa Cruz. There's a class that recovers stranded marine mammals for dissection."

Kate released him, and sat down in one of the two wooden kitchen chairs. The cup of coffee warmed her hands, still cold from the fog. "They don't need to get it. It'll wash out to sea at high tide tonight."

Michael frowned. "They'll want it. This is the only way that they can get specimens."

"Oh." She sipped the hot coffee. Far out at sea, over the crash of the waves, she could hear a sea lion barking. "It doesn't feel right," she said. "It seems like the body should go back to sea." Then, before he could laugh or call her foolish, she shrugged. "But I suppose it doesn't matter. In the interest of science and all."

Michael called the University and arranged to have a crew of students come to pick up the seal that afternoon, explaining that Kate would meet them, that he would be gone.

He looked at her when he hung up the phone and said, inexplicably, "Is that all right?"

"Of course, of course, it's all right," she said irritably. And when he came around the table to hug her, she realized that he had meant that he was leaving, and was that all right? She had been thinking of the seal.

When Kate stood alone on the porch, waving goodbye, she felt uneasy again, unsettled. The fog smelled of salt spray and dying kelp. Michael lifted a hand in farewell and she listened to the crunch of wheels on gravel and watched the sedan until it vanished into the fog. The engine changed in pitch when he stopped at the end of the drive, turned onto the highway, and picked up speed.

Kate realized that one hand was clinging to the pendant around her neck, and she released it. A gull shrieked in the fog and she retreated into the kitchen to work.

The papers that she spread on the kitchen table were the result of months of collecting the stories told in the Santa Cruz fishing community. There were so many stories—and so many warnings—about how one should behave around the sea.

She remembered sitting in the sun on the fishing dock while an old man mended a net and advised her: "If you cut yourself near the sea, never let the blood touch the water. Blood calls to blood. If the sea has your blood, you belong to the sea." She remembered a Scottish fisherman's widow, a sturdy old woman with bright blue eyes, had served her tea and warned: "You must not take the sea lightly. Those who take from the sea lay themselves open to the powers of the sea. And many dark creatures dwell beneath the waves."

The sea dwellers of legend were tricky. The kelpies or water horses could take human form to entice mortals into the water to drown. Mermaids and mermen could raise storms to sink ships.

But the silkies, the seal people that Kate's thoughts kept returning to, were a gentle folk. Kate leafed through one of her notebooks and found the widow's account of a young salmon fisherman who had shot a seal feeding near his boat, and had died in a storm the next month. The old widow had said that the silkies were tolerant of humans and angered only by the death of their own kind. They came ashore on moonlit nights to dance on the beach in human form. Fishermen had captured silkie maidens for wives by stealing the skin they used in their seal form; silkie men had been known to take human lovers.

Kate began listing the elements that the widow's tale had in common with traditional tales of silkies. Just before lunch, she was interrupted by the sound of tires on the gravel drive. She picked up her sweatshirt and stepped onto the porch.

Three students—two men and a woman—climbed down from the cab of the ancient pickup truck parked in the drive. "I guess you came to pick up the seal," Kate said hesitantly. With Michael gone, her uneasiness about the seal had returned. But she could not turn the students away. "I'll take you down," she said.

The day was still overcast and the wind from the sea was cold. Kate hauled her sweatshirt over her head. The cloth caught on the chain of her pendant and she yanked at the sweatshirt impatiently—too hard. The chain broke and she caught the pendant as it fell. "Damn," she muttered. Aware of the eyes of the students upon her, she stuffed the pendant and chain into her pocket. "I'll take you right down," she repeated.

The students unloaded a stretcher from the back of the truck and followed Kate down the narrow path. They had to scramble over the jumble of rocks that extended from the base of the cliff to the water. At high tide, the waves crashed against the cliff, making the broad beach where the seal lay inaccessible from the path. When the moon was full and the tides reached full height, the sea swallowed both the tiny beach at the bottom of the path and the broad beach to the north.

Kate felt ill at ease with the students, unwilling to introduce herself or ask their names. These people did not belong on her beach. She stood several yards away as the two men squatted by the seal and positioned the stretcher so that they could roll the seal onto it. The woman stood at the animal's head. She shifted her weight uneasily, glanced out to sea, then back at the seal. Kate crossed her arms and hugged her sweatshirt tighter around her, suddenly cold. The woman shivered, though she was dressed more warmly than Kate.

She stepped toward Kate and caught her eye. "You must be half seal yourself to go in swimming this time of year."

Kate frowned. "Why do you figure I've been in swimming?"

The woman pointed to a set of footprints, left by bare feet, leading along the edge of the sea toward the body. The prints were almost obscured by bird tracks and boot prints.

"Not me," Kate said. "But that's odd. Those weren't here this morning. And I'm the only one who lives near here."

The woman shrugged. "Probably just a hitchhiker who stopped off the highway to walk on the beach." She looked out to sea, where the gray waves crashed against the rocks.

Kate nodded. "I suppose so." She squatted beside the footprints and peered at them closely. Just footprints in the sand; nothing unusual.

"Come on," one of the men called. The two men had picked up the stretcher and started back in the direction of the path. Kate and the woman walked in silence. Over the sound of the surf, they could hear the men talking and laughing.

"I don't see how those guys can joke about picking up bodies," the woman said. "I always feel like a grave robber."

"Yeah?" Kate glanced at the woman's face. "That's how I feel. My boyfriend called the University. I would have just as soon let the body wash back out to sea. I don't know why."

The woman nodded sympathetically. "It must be something about the ocean. And the fog. And the time of year—we're almost to the shortest day."

"The winter solstice," Kate murmured. "A bad time to mess with the ocean."

"Yeah?" The woman shot Kate a curious glance. "Why's that?"

Kate shrugged. "According to folk stories, the winter solstice is when the powers of darkness are at their strongest. It's a dangerous time."

The woman hugged her jacket closer around her, hunching her shoulders against the cold wind that blew from the sea. "You almost sound serious about that."

"I'm studying folklore and the old stories kind of get to you after a while." Kate hesitated. "It's not that I believe them. It's more like I respect them. This is old stuff. Strong stuff." She shrugged again, then fell silent.

The men lifted the stretcher into the back of the truck and the dead eyes of the seal gazed mournfully at the rusty metal of the tailgate. The woman paused before she climbed after the men into the cab. She laid a hand on Kate's arm. "Take care of yourself," she said. She hesitated as if she wanted to say more, then climbed into the cab.

The tires crunched on the gravel drive; Kate lifted a hand in farewell. She turned her back on the highway and listened to the truck shift gears when it reached the end of the drive, but she did not watch it drive away.

The fog had lifted but the sky was overcast. The horizon was marked by an almost imperceptible difference in shading between the gray-blue of the ocean and the blue-gray of the sky. The ocean was calm. A gray beast waiting at the foot of the cliff, not impatient for an end, but certain that an end would come. The setting sun was a hazy circle behind the clouds on the horizon.

Kate shifted her feet and the gravel made grinding noises. To reach the beach, a hitchhiker would have had to follow the drive to the path. If anyone had passed the cottage, she would have heard him walking in the gravel. But there had been footprints on the beach.

The sun sank out of sight. A night breeze ruffled Kate's hair and she shivered, then retreated to the cottage.

After dinner, when the warmth of the cottage had chased away thoughts of silkies and solitude, she stepped out on the porch to watch the moon rise. The lights of the kitchen glowed cheerfully through the curtains behind her. The moon would be full the following night, full and round like the ivory circle of her pendant.

She dug in her pocket to touch the smooth ivory. Her pocket was empty. Her fingers found a hole in the cloth and she cursed herself for carelessness. She must have dropped it on the path or on the beach.

No gleam of ivory rewarded her search of the path. She walked toward the broad beach, searching the sand with no luck. The tide was rising. A breaking wave washed among the rocks at the base of the cliff. When the wave retreated, she hurried across.

The dry sand of the broad beach just above where the wave

had reached was marked by footprints. Bare feet. The prints led away from the path, toward the spot where she had found the seal's body.

"Hello," Kate shouted. "Is anyone out there?" No answer.

She looked back toward the jumble of rocks that separated her from the footpath. The tide was rising and the water lapped higher with each wave. Kate broke into a run, following the footprints. She took long strides and when the waves hissed under her feet she ignored the spray that splashed up to wet her jeans. Beside the rocky outcropping where she had found the seal, she stopped and scanned the beach.

There. In the shadow of the cliff at the end of the beach she saw a flickering light and a moving shadow. The light was too pale and too bright to be a campfire. A flashlight beam, perhaps.

"Hey!" Kate called. "The tide's coming in. Hey, you!"

The light remained where it was. Kate raced toward it, shouting, then saved her breath for running. When the light moved, she could see the outline of the person holding it.

She was a hundred feet away when a wave crashed against the cliff and sent an arc of spray over the flickering light. The shadowy figure moved, a darting movement too quick and graceful to be human. Like a cat. Like a sea otter. Like a seal in the water. And the light vanished.

Kate's momentum carried her three more steps. She stared at the cliff, which suddenly seemed clearly lit by moonlight. There was no one standing beneath the cliff. There was no flashlight beam. There was no nook, no cranny, no crevice where a person could hide. Just moonlight and water and a tall black cliff. Just a vanishing light and a fleet shadow.

Over the hiss of a retreating wave, Kate thought she heard a sound—a long sigh like a seal taking a breath of air after a long dive. The moonlight gleamed on a white circle on the sand before her. Her pendant. Here, far from where she had walked. She stepped forward and reached for it, aware of eyes upon her. A wave rushed in to snatch the circle of ivory away before she could touch it. She groped after it in the surf, but it slipped away, lost in the foam and the moonlight.

Kate turned and ran for the path. She passed the rocky crag—her heart pounding, her breath rasping through a dry throat. The waves splashed high against the cliff and even in retreat left no dry rocks. Moonlight glistened on the swells.

A wave washed among the rocks and Kate plunged into the water, hoping to cross before another broke. The icy water sucked at her legs, dragging on her jeans. Beneath her boots, the rocks were slick with kelp and eel grass. The water was knee-deep, waist-deep. The ocean tugged at her legs, another wave broke, and a rock shifted beneath her boot. She slipped and floundered in the water, her ankle caught between two rocks. She wrenched the foot free and stood, sputtering through a curtain of wet hair. She struggled forward, hampered by wet jeans, crippled by an ankle that gave beneath her. Stumbling again, but recovering. She limped through water that was waist-deep, knee-deep. Onto a sandy bottom. Onto a tiny beach.

She collapsed on the dry sand and drew in a long shuddering breath. And another. Only when she lifted her right hand to brush the wet hair from her face did she realize that she was bleeding from a ragged gash across her palm. Cut on a rock. She staggered to her feet, and her ankle throbbed with dull persistent pain. The waves hissed in the sand, leaving an innocent line of foam.

Droplets of blood fell from her clenched fist to stain the foam.

A shadow moved beyond the breakers. A flicker of pale white light. A will-o'-the-wisp. The eyes were still upon her; she could feel them. And the loneliness that had touched her that morning had returned.

"Not me," she called hoarsely to the light. "I didn't kill her. Not me." The light dipped out of sight beneath the crest of a wave.

Kate turned away to stagger home to the sanity of a warm kitchen, a cup of tea, a hot shower. But the rush of water from the showerhead rattling against the metal walls of the shower did not cover the sound of the surf. Even as Kate washed sand from the cut on her hand, she could hear the rhythmic crashing of the waves, gentle and steady. While she was heating water for tea, a storm began with the soft touch of rain against the windows, a persistent whispering like many soft voices speaking so quietly that she could not understand them. When she caught herself listening for words in the soft rainfall, she turned on the radio.

The storm picked up in force, competing with the wailing of pop rock. The wind howled across the chimneytop. The rain lashed against the windows and blew in through the bathroom window, which was warped partly open. Kate stuffed news-paper into the gap and the paper soaked up the rain. Once soaked, the paper dripped on the floor, beating a steady coun-terpoint to the pealing of the wind chimes—high and furious—outside the window.

Kate paced within the kitchen, trapped but unable to sit still. Once, when the wind rattled the door, Kate thought she felt the cottage shake and she thought of mudslides and collapsing cliffs. The silkies, like the mermaids, could raise storms to shatter ships. A storm could also shatter the timbers of an old beach cottage.

The cut on her hand throbbed; her ankle ached, but she paced. She picked up the phone to call Michael, but the phone was dead. No doubt the lines were down on the highway. And if she had been able to get through, what could she have told him? That she feared for her life in a storm that the silkies had raised.

So she paced, reminding herself that the seal people were a gentle folk—not like the mermaids, not like the kelpie. She had done nothing to harm the silkies, really.

At midnight, the wind lessened and the rain eased to a gentle rhythm. As Kate lay in bed, trying to ignore the twin pains in her ankle and hand, she heard a sea lion barking from the rocks below the cliffs. It sounded much closer.

She slept uneasily and woke shivering when the wind chimes rang lightly. The rain had stopped and the sea fog had crept up the cliff to wrap itself around the cottage. She had dreamed again, though the memory of the dream was not clear. She remembered an overpowering loneliness, a fierce yearning, a hunger for something unattainable.

Kate hugged the blanket closer around her, but the chill of the fog had seeped into the cottage and into her bones. Reluc-tantly, she left her bed to get another blanket, crossing the cold kitchen floor to the linen cupboard and pulling a quilted com-forter from the stack on the shelf.

The wind chimes jingled again, and Kate thought she heard another sound—a long sigh that could have been the wind. But it did not sound quite like the wind. The floorboards creaked beneath her as she stepped toward the door. She hesitated with her hand on the doorknob.

What did she fear, she wondered. Her mind formed an image

in answer: she feared a slender manshape, standing on the porch with the fog swirling around his waist and hiding his webbed feet. The fingers of the hand that she imagined to be resting on the porch rail were joined by a thin skin. From his other hand, her pendant dangled. He smelled of the sea and a strand of eel grass clung to his shoulder. When she reached out to take the pendant, she touched his hand. It was cold—as cold as the sea.

Kate stopped with her hand on the doorknob, only half aware that she was listening for the sound of breathing. Then she twisted the knob and jerked the door open.

Shadows of the fenceposts shifted and moved in the moonlight and drifting fog. The posts teetered this way and that, barely supporting the single strand of rusty wire that was all that remained of the fence. Nothing to hold back the sea.

The porch was empty. No webbed hand rested on the porch rail, but at the spot where she had imagined his hand lay a circle of white. With fingers that were suddenly as cold as the fog, she picked up the pendant by the chain and held it in her bandaged hand. The breeze stirred the mist and the wind chimes jingled faintly. She backed away, retreating into the kitchen, and from the doorway, she noticed a single strand of eel grass trailing across the top step. She locked the door behind her.

She did not sleep after that. With the kitchen lights blazing, she wrapped herself in the comforter and made hot chocolate. She worked on her paper and tried to ignore the ringing of the wind chimes and the crash of the waves.

In the light of dawn, with a cup of coffee in her hand, she opened the door and peered out onto the porch. The strand of eel grass still lay on the top step, and she told herself that it must have fallen from her boot when she staggered into the cottage. Just as she must have put the pendant on the railing when she broke the chain rather than into her pocket.

She called Michael from a pay phone at a gas station, saying only that she had twisted her ankle and was coming to town to see a doctor. She arranged to meet him for dinner.

In the restaurant that evening, the traffic noises ebbed and surged like the sound of the waves. The sound distracted Kate and disrupted her thoughts as she told Michael of the storm. She did not mention her vision of the silkie, but talked of mudslides and her feeling that the cottage could collapse into the sea. Even so, she felt like a fool. In the warm café that smelled of coffee and pastry, the crashing terror of the storm seemed far away.

He gently took her bandaged hand in his hand. "Something really has you worried, doesn't it?" he asked.

She shrugged. "The ocean gets to me when I'm out at the cottage, that's all," she said. "The fog and the waves and the sea lions barking . . ." And the madness that lingers at the ocean's edge, she thought.

"I told you it was a lonely spot," he said.

"Not lonely so much as . . ." She hesitated. "I never feel quite alone anymore. And I get to imagining things. The other night, I thought I saw a light, dancing on the waves just beyond the breakers. I don't know; I guess my eyes were just playing tricks."

Michael grinned and stroked her hand. "Don't worry about your eyes," he said. "You probably did see a light. Have you ever heard of bio-luminescence? There are microorganisms that glow . . ."

Michael explained it all—talking about red tides and marine chemistry. Kate let the reassuring words wash over her. Michael never had time for the vague, ill-defined feelings that plagued her. She listened to him, and when he was done, she managed a smile.

"You've been working on that project much too hard," he said. "Why don't you just stay in town tonight and spend the night with me?"

She stared at her coffee in silence.

"Don't be afraid to come back to me," he said softly. "You can if you want to."

She did not know what she wanted. "I have to go back tonight," she said. "I have work to do."

"Why tonight?" he asked. "Why not wait until tomorrow?"

The answer came to her mind, but she did not voice it: the moon would be full that night.

She freed her hand from Michael's grasp and held her coffee cup between her palms. "I have work to do," she repeated.

She drove back that night, speeding around the curves in the twisting road that led from Santa Cruz to her little patch of nowhere. The old Beatles song on the tape deck drowned out the whisper of the waves: "I'd like to be under the sea in an octopus's garden with you."

The full moon hung in the sky over the cottage as she rolled up the drive. She turned her key. The music stopped. And the crash of the surf filled the car.

Kate walked to the edge of the cliff. Below her, the sea shimmered in the moonlight, the swells rising and falling in a rhythm as steady as breathing. She felt eyes watching her from the ocean below.

She slipped three times as she descended the path. The third time she caught herself with her wounded hand and the cut flared with a bright new pain. Her ankle throbbed but she continued to pick her way down the slope.

The waves had not yet reached the bottom of the path. The tiny beach was a silver thread in the moonlight, extending away in either direction in a shimmering line. She stood on the silver strand and gazed out to sea.

A light danced on the wave. Loneliness swept over her as a wave swept over the sand, touching the toes of her boots with foam. Involuntarily, she took a step to follow the retreating water. The next wave lapped around her ankles and a fierce pain touched her wounded hand so that she longed to soothe it by touching it to the cold water. Somewhere in the back of her mind, she heard the echo of a voice saying: "Blood calls to blood." She took another step forward and the water lapped at her knees, dragging on the legs of her jeans.

The light danced—out of reach. The water was cold against her ankle. It eased the pain. The water could ease the stinging in her hand. If only she waded out further.

With her bandaged hand, she gripped the pendant that hung around her neck. Michael would not believe that there was a watcher in the water. But the light was there. And the loneliness was with her. She watched the dancing light and thought about the glowing microorganisms that Michael had described. The water tugged at her legs.

"No," she said softly to the water and the light. Then louder, "No." The water tugged at her, urging, insisting. "No."

She could feel eyes on her as she trudged up the path. Turning her back on wonder. No, turning her back on cold gray waters that would beat her against the rocks.

There was no storm that night. But she heard the sound of the waves against the cliffs—calling, calling. She slept uneasily and she dreamed of a lover: a salt-sea lover with hands like ice and the face of a prince. Between his fingers, webbing stretched; his teeth were pointed; he carried with him the scent of the sea. He loved her with a steady rocking as rhythmic as the sea, and he held her when she cried out—was it in pleasure or pain?—at the chill of his touch. She stroked his dark hair, sleek as the fur of a seal. He came to her for comfort, this silent lover whose kisses tasted of salt. He came to her to make a truce.

She woke to the scent of the sea and the sound of a gentle thumping. Half-awake, she fumbled uselessly for the pendant at her neck. It was not there, though she could not remember taking it off the night before. She left her bed, wrapping the quilt around her and stepping into the kitchen.

The door to the porch swung wide open, moving slightly in the breeze and bumping gently against the kitchen wall. She picked up her pendant from where it lay on the porch railing. She did not put it on. She did not need it. No fear was left in her.

The single wire of the old fence was strung with drops of dew, one drop on each rusty barb. The old fence should come down, she thought. It served no purpose anymore.

The waves washed against the base of the cliff; the ocean moved in its endless rhythm. Drops of her blood ebbed and surged with those waters. And the strength of the sea surged in her.

Far away, a sea lion barked. And the bright sunlight of early morning glinted on the two strands of eel grass that lay across the steps.

Driftglass

by
Samuel R. Delany

It is not surprising that humans are fascinated by the sea—we came from the sea, after all, as did all life, and our bodies, which are more than ninety percent water, respond to the moon's phases with the same rhythm as the tides. For thousands of years, people have lived near the sea, and on the sea, and taken their living from the sea . . . and dreamed of what it would be like to live beneath the sea as well. In the brilliant and evocative story that follows, we are taken to a future world where this age-old dream has been fulfilled by sophisticated medical technology, and surgically-created merfolk are renouncing the land for the mystery and danger and endless bountiful promise of the sea. . . .

Samuel R. Delany was widely acknowledged during the sixties as one of the two most important and influential American SF writers of that decade (the other was Roger Zelazny). By 1969, critic Algis Budrys was calling Delany "the best science-fiction writer in the world," and he is still regarded by many critics as one of the genre's greatest living authors. He has won four Nebula Awards and a Hugo Award. His books include The Einstein Intersection, Babel-17, Nova, The Fall of the Towers, Triton, *the controversial bestseller* Dhalgren, *and the landmark collection* Driftglass. *His most recent books are* Tales of Neveryon, *and the novel* Stars In My Pocket Like Grains of Sand.

* * *

I

SOMETIMES I GO DOWN TO THE PORT, SPLASHING SAND WITH my stiff foot at the end of my stiff leg locked in my stiff hip, with the useless arm a-swinging, to get wet all over again, drink in the dives with old cronies ashore, feeling old, broken, sorry for myself, laughing louder and louder. The third of my face that was burned away in the accident was patched with skin grafts from my chest, so what's left of my mouth distorts all loud sounds; sloppy sartorial reconstruction. Also I have a hairy chest. Chest hair does not look like beard hair, and it grows all up under my right eye. And: my beard is red, my chest hair brown, while the thatch curling down over neck and ears is sun-streaked to white here, darkened to bronze there, 'midst general blondness.

By reason of my being a walking (I suppose my gait could be called headlong limping) horror show, plus a general inclination to sulk, I spend most of the time up in the wood and glass and aluminum house on the surf-sloughed point that the Aquatic Corp gave me along with my pension. Rugs from Turkey there, copper pots, my tenor recorder which I can no longer play, and my books.

But sometimes, when the gold fog blurs the morning, I go down to the beach and tromp barefoot in the wet edging of the sea, searching for driftglass.

It was foggy that morning, and the sun across the water moiled the mists like a brass ladle. I lurched to the top of the rocks, looked down through the tall grasses into the frothing inlet where she lay, and blinked.

She sat up, long gills closing down her neck and the secondary slits along her back just visible at their tips because of much hair, wet and curling copper, falling there. She saw me. "What are you doing here, huh?" She narrowed blue eyes.

"Looking for driftglass."

"What?"

"There's a piece." I pointed near her and came down the rocks like a crab with one stiff leg.

"Where?" She turned over, half in, half out of the water, the webs of her fingers cupping nodules of black stone.

While the water made cold overtures between my toes, I picked up the milky fragment by her elbow where she wasn't looking. She jumped, because she obviously had thought it was somewhere else.

"See?"

"What . . . what is it?" She raised her cool hand to mine.

For a moment the light through the milky gem and the pale film of my own webs pearled the screen of her palms. (Details like that. Yes, they are the important things, the points from which we suspend later pain.) A moment later wet fingers closed to the back of mine.

"Driftglass," I said. "You know all the Coca-Cola bottles and cut crystal punch bowls and industrial silicon slag that goes into the sea?"

"I know the Coca-Cola bottles."

"They break, and the tide pulls the pieces back and forth over the sandy bottom, wearing the edges, changing their shape. Sometimes chemicals in the glass react with chemicals in the ocean to change the color. Sometimes veins work their way through a piece in patterns like snowflakes, regular and geometric; others, irregular and angled like coral. When the pieces dry they're milky. Put them in water and they become transparent again."

"Ohhh!" She breathed as though the beauty of the blunted triangular fragment in my palm assailed her like perfume. Then she looked at my face, blinking the third, aqueous-filled lid that we use as a correction lens for underwater vision.

She watched the ruin calmly.

Then her hand went to my foot where the webs had been torn back in the accident. She began to take in who I was. I looked for horror, but saw only a little sadness.

The insignia on her buckle—her stomach was making little jerks the way you always do during the first few minutes when you go from breathing water to air—told me she was a Biological Technician. (Back up at the house there was a similar uniform of simulated scales folded in the bottom drawer of the dresser and the belt insignia said Depth Gauger.) I was wearing some very frayed jeans and a red cotton shirt with no buttons.

She reached up to my neck, pushed my collar back from my shoulders and touched the tender slits of my gills, outlining them with cool fingers. "Who are you?" Finally.

"Cal Svenson."

She slid back down in the water. "You're the one who had the terrible—but that was years ago. They still talk about it, down—" She stopped.

As the sea softens the surface of a piece of glass, so it blurs the souls and sensibilities of the people who toil beneath her. And according to the last report of the Marine Reclamation

Division there are to date seven hundred and fifty thousand who have been given gills and webs and sent under the foam where there are no storms, up and down the American coast.

"You live on shore? I mean around here? But so long ago . . ."

"How old are you?"

"Sixteen."

"I was two years older than you when the accident happened."

"You were eighteen?"

"I'm twice that now. Which means it happened almost twenty years ago. It is a long time."

"They still talk about it."

"I've almost forgotten," I said. "I really have. Say, do you play the recorder?"

"I used to."

"Good! Come up to my place and look at my tenor recorder. And I'll make some tea. Perhaps you can stay for lunch—"

"I have to report back to Marine Headquarters by three. Tork is going over the briefing to lay the cable for the big dive, with Jonni and the crew." She paused, smiled. "But I can catch the undertow and be there in half an hour if I leave by two-thirty."

On the walk up I learned her name was Ariel. She thought the patio was charming, and the mosaic evoked, "Oh, look!" and "Did you do this yourself?" a half-dozen times. (I had done it, in the first lonely years.) She picked out the squid and the whale in battle, the wounded shark and the diver. She told me she didn't get time to read much, but she was impressed by all the books. She listened to me reminisce. She talked a lot to me about her work, husbanding the deep-down creatures they were scaring up. Then she sat on the kitchen stool, playing a Lukas Foss serenade on my recorder, while I put rock salt in the bottom of the broiler tray for two dozen oysters Rockefeller, and the tea water whistled. I'm a comparatively lonely guy. I like being followed by beautiful young girls.

II

"Hey, João!" I bawled across the jetty.

He nodded to me from the center of his nets, sun glistening on polished shoulders, sun lost in rough hair. I walked across to where he sat, sewing like a spider. He pulled another section up over his horny toes, then grinned at me with his mosaic smile: gold, white, black gap below, crooked yellow; white, gold, white. Shoving my bad leg in front, I squatted.

"I fished out over the coral where you told me." He filled his cheek with his tongue and nodded. "You come up to the house for a drink, eh?"

"Fine."

"Now—a moment more."

There's a certain sort of Brazilian you find along the shore in the fishing villages, old, yet ageless. See one of their men and you think he could be fifty, he could be sixty—will probably look the same when he's eighty-five. Such was João. We once figured it out. He's seven hours older than I am.

We became friends sometime before the accident when I got tangled in his nets working high lines in the Vorea Current. A lot of guys would have taken their knife and hacked their way out of the situation, ruining fifty-five, sixty dollars' worth of nets. That's an average fisherman's monthly income down here. But I surfaced and sat around in his boat while we untied me. Then we came in and got plastered. Since I cost him a day's fishing, I've been giving him hints on where to fish ever since. He buys me drinks when I come up with something.

This has been going on for twenty years. During that time my life has been smashed up and land-bound. In the same time João has married off his five sisters, got married himself and has two children. (Oh, those *bolinhos* and *carne assada* that Amalia of the oiled braid and laughing breasts would make for Sunday dinner/supper/Monday breakfast.) I rode with them in the ambulance 'copter all the way into Brasilia and in the hospital hall João and I stood together, both still barefoot, he tattered with fish scales in his hair, me just tattered, and I held him while he cried and I tried to explain to him how a world that could take a prepubescent child and with a week of operations make an amphibious creature that can exist for a month on either side of the sea's-foam-fraught surface could still be helpless before certain general endocrine cancers coupled with massive renal deterioration. João and I returned to the village alone, by bus, three days before our birthday—back when I was twenty-three and João was twenty-three and seven hours old.

* * *

"This morning," João said. (The shuttle danced in the web at the end of the orange line.) "I got a letter for you to read me. It's about the children. Come on, we go up and drink." The shuttle paused, back-tracked twice, and he yanked the knot tight. We walked along the port toward the square. "Do you think the letter says that the children are accepted?"

"It's from the Aquatic Corp. And they just send postcards when they reject someone. The question is, how do you feel about it?"

"You are a good man. If they grow up like you, then it will be fine."

"But you're still worried." I'd been prodding João to get the kids into the International Aquatic Corp nigh on since I became their godfather. The operations had to be performed near puberty. It would mean much time away from the village during their training period—and they might eventually be stationed in any ocean in the world. But two motherless children had not been easy on João or his sisters. The Corp would mean education, travel, interesting work, the things that make up one kind of good life. They wouldn't look twice their age when they were thirty-five; and not too many amphimen look like me.

"Worry is part of life. But the work is dangerous. Did you know there is an amphiman going to try and lay cable down in the Slash?"

I frowned. "Again?"

"Yes. And that is what you tried to do when the sea broke you to pieces and burned the parts, eh?"

"Must you be so damned picturesque?" I asked. "Who's going to beard the lion this time?"

"A young amphiman named Tork. They speak of him down at the docks as a brave man."

"Why the hell are they still trying to lay the cable there? They've gotten by this long without a line through the Slash."

"Because of the fish." João said. "You told me why twenty years ago. The fish are still there, and we fishermen who cannot go below are still here. If the children go for the operations, then there will be less fishermen. But today . . ." He shrugged. "They must either lay the line across the fish paths or down in the Slash." João shook his head.

Funny things, the great power cables the Aquatic Corp has been strewing across the ocean floor to bring power to their undersea mines and farms, to run their oil wells—and how many flaming wells have I capped down there—for their herds of whale, and chemical distillation plants. They carry two hundred sixty cycle current. Over certain sections of the ocean floor, or in sections of the water with certain mineral contents, this sets up inductance in the water itself which sometimes— and you will probably get a Nobel prize if you can detail exactly why it isn't always—drives the fish away over areas up to twenty-five and thirty miles, unless the lines are laid in the bottom of those canyons that delve into the ocean floor.

"This Tork thinks of the fishermen. He is a good man, too."

I raised my eyebrow—the one that's left, anyway—and tried to remember what my little Undine had said about him that morning. And remembered not much.

"I wish him luck," I said.

"What do you feel about this young man going down into the coral-rimmed jaws to the Slash?"

I thought for a moment. "I think I hate him."

João looked up.

"He is an image in a mirror where I look and am forced to regard what I was," I went on. "I envy him the chance to succeed where I failed, and I can come on just as quaint as you can. I hope he makes it."

João twisted his shoulders in a complicated shrug (once I could do that) which is coastal Brazilian for "I didn't know things had progressed to that point, but seeing that they have, there is little to be done."

"The sea is that sort of mirror," I said.

"Yes." João nodded.

Behind us I heard the slapping of sandals on concrete. I turned in time to catch my goddaughter in my good arm. My godson had grabbed hold of the bad one and was swinging on it.

"Tio Cal—"

"Hey, Tio Cal, what did you bring us?"

"You will pull him over," João reprimanded them. "Let go."

And, bless them, they ignored their father.

"What did you bring us?"

"What did you bring us, Tio Cal?"

"If you let me, I'll show you." So they stepped back, green-eyed and quivering. I watched João watching: brown pupils on ivory balls, and in the left eye a vein had broken in a jagged smear. He was loving his children, who would soon be as alien to him as the fish he netted. He was also looking at the terrible thing that was me and wondering what would come to his own spawn. And he was watching the world turn and grow older, clocked by the waves, reflected in that mirror.

It's impossible for me to see what the population explosion and the budding colonies on Luna and Mars and the flowering beneath the ocean really look like from the disrupted cultural mélange of a coastal fishing town. But I come closer than many others, and I know what I don't understand.

I pushed around in my pocket and fetched out the milky fragment I had brought from the beach. "Here. Do you like this one?" And they bent above my webbed and alien fingers.

In the supermarket, which is the biggest building in the village, João bought a lot of cake mixes. "That moist, delicate texture," whispered the box when you lifted it from the shelf, "with that deep flavor, deeper than chocolate."

I'd just read an article about the new vocal packaging in a U.S. magazine that had gotten down last week, so I was prepared and stayed in the fresh-vegetable section to avoid temptation. Then we went up to João's house. The letter proved to be what I'd expected. The kids had to take the bus into Brasília tomorrow. My godchildren were on their way to becoming fish.

We sat on the front steps and drank and watched the donkeys and the motorbikes, the men in baggy trousers, the women in yellow scarfs and brighter skirts with wreaths of garlic and sacks of onions. As well, a few people glittered by in the green scales of amphimen uniforms.

Finally João got tired and went in to take a nap. Most of my life has been spent on the coast of countries accustomed to siestas, but those first formative ten were passed on a Danish collective farm and the idea never really took. So I stepped over my goddaughter, who had fallen asleep on her fists on the bottom step, and walked back through the town toward the beach.

III

AT MIDNIGHT ARIEL CAME OUT OF THE SEA, CLIMBED THE rocks and clicked her nails against my glass wall so that droplets ran down, pearled by the gibbous moon.

Earlier I had stretched in front of the fireplace on the sheepskin throw to read, then dozed off. The conscientious timer had asked me if there was anything I wanted, and getting no answer had turned off the Dvořák Cello Concerto that was on its second time around, extinguished the reading lamp and stopped dropping logs onto the flame so that now, as I woke, the grate was carpeted with coals.

She clicked on the glass again, and I raised my head from the cushion. The green uniform, her amber hair—all color was lost under the silver light outside. I lurched across the rug to the glass wall, touched the button and the glass slid down into the floor. The breeze came to my face as the barrier fell.

"What do you want?" I asked. "What time is it, anyway?"

"Tork is on the beach, waiting for you."

The night was warm but windy. Below the rocks silver flakes chased each other in to shore. The tide lay full.

I rubbed my face. "The new boss man? Why didn't you bring him up to the house? What does he want to see me about?"

She touched my arm. "Come. They are all down on the beach."

"Who all?"

"Tork and the others."

She led me across the patio and to the path that wound to the sand. The sea roared in the moonlight. Down the beach people stood around a driftwood fire that whipped into the night. Ariel walked beside me.

Two of the fishermen from town were crowding each other on the bottom of an overturned washtub, playing guitars. The singing, raucous and rhythmic, jarred across the paled sand. Sharks' teeth shook on the necklace of an old woman dancing. Others were sitting on an overturned dinghy, eating.

Over one part of the fire on a skillet two feet across, oil frothed through pink islands of shrimp. One woman ladled them in, another ladled them out.

"Tio Cal!"

"Look, Tio Cal is here!"

"Hey, what are you two doing up?" I asked. "Shouldn't you be home in bed?"

"Papa João said we could come. He'll be here, too, soon."

I turned to Ariel. "Why are they all gathering?"

"Because of the laying of the cable tomorrow at dawn."

Someone was running up the beach, waving a bottle in each hand.

"They didn't want to tell you about the party. They thought that it might hurt your pride."

"My what?"

"If you knew they were making so big a thing of the job you had failed at—"

"But—"

"—and that had hurt you so in failure. They did not want you to be sad. But Tork wants to see you. I said you would not be sad. So I went to bring you down from the rocks."

"Thanks, I guess."

"Tio Cal?"

But the voice was bigger and deeper than a child's.

He sat on a log back from the fire, eating a sweet potato. The flame flickered on his dark cheekbones, in his hair, wet and black. He stood, came to me, held up his hand. I held up mine and we slapped palms. "Good." He was smiling. "Ariel told me you would come. I will lay the power line down through the Slash tomorrow." His uniform scales glittered down his arms. He was very strong. But standing still, he still moved. The light on the cloth told me that. "I . . ." He paused. I thought of a nervous, happy dancer. "I wanted to talk to you about the cable." I thought of an eagle, I thought of a shark. "And about the . . . accident. If you would."

"Sure," I said. "If there's anything I could tell you that would help."

"See, Tork," Ariel said. "I told you he would talk to you about it."

I could hear his breathing change. "It really doesn't bother you to talk about the accident?"

I shook my head and realized something about that voice. It was a boy's voice that could imitate a man's. Tork was not over nineteen.

"We're going fishing soon," Tork told me. "Will you come?"

"If I'm not in the way."

A bottle went from the woman at the shrimp crate to one of the guitarists, down to Ariel, to me, then to Tork. (The liquor, made in a cave seven miles inland, was almost rum. The too tight skin across the left side of my mouth makes the manful swig a little difficult to bring off. I got "rum" down my chin.)

He drank, wiped his mouth, passed the bottle on and put his hand on my shoulder. "Come down to the water."

We walked away from the fire. Some of the fishermen stared after us. A few of the amphimen glanced, and glanced away.

"Do all the young people of the village call you Tio Cal?"

"No. Only my godchildren. Their father and I have been friends since I was your age."

"Oh, I thought perhaps it was a nickname. That's why I called you that."

We reached wet sand where orange light cavorted at our feet. The broken shell of a lifeboat rocked in moonlight. Tork sat down on the shell's rim. I sat beside him. The water splashed to our knees.

"There's no other place to lay the power cable?" I asked. "There is no other way to take it except through the Slash?"

"I was going to ask you what you thought of the whole business. But I guess I don't really have to." He shrugged and clapped his hands together a few times. "All the projects this side of the bay have grown huge and cry for power. The new operations tax the old lines unmercifully. There was a power failure last July in Cayine down the shelf below the twilight level. The whole village was without light for two days, and twelve amphimen died of overexposure to the cold currents coming up from the depths. If we laid the cables farther up, we would chance disrupting our own fishing operations as well as those of the fishermen on shore."

I nodded.

"Cal, what happened to you in the Slash?"

Eager, scared Tork. I was remembering now, not the accident, but the midnight before, pacing the beach, guts clamped with fists of fear and anticipation. Some of the Indians back where they made the liquor still send messages by tying knots in palm fibers. One could have spread my entrails then, or Tork's tonight, to read our respective horospecs.

João's mother knew the knot language, but he and his sisters never bothered to learn because they wanted to be modern, and, as children, still confused with modernity the new ignorances, lacking modern knowledge.

"When I was a boy," Tork said, "we would dare each other to walk the boards along the edge of the ferry slip. The sun would be hot and the boards would rock in the water, and if the boats were in and you fell down between the boats and the piling, you could get killed." He shook his head. "The crazy things kids will do. That was back when I was eight or nine, before I became a waterbaby."

"Where was it?"

Tork looked up. "Oh. Manila. I'm Filipino."

The sea licked our knees, and the gunwale sagged under us.

"What happened in the Slash?"

"There's a volcanic flaw near the base of the Slash."

"I know."

"And the sea is as sensitive down there as a fifty-year-old woman with a new hairdo. We had an avalanche. The cable broke. And the sparks were so hot and bright they made gouts of foam fifty feet high on the surface, so they tell me."

"What caused the avalanche?"

I shrugged. "It could have been just a goddamned coincidence. There are rock falls down there all the time. It could have been the noise from the machines—though we masked them pretty well. It could have been something to do with the inductance from the smaller cables for the machines. Or maybe somebody just kicked out the wrong stone that was holding everything up."

One webbed hand became a fist, sank into the other and hung.

Calling: "Cal!"

I looked up. João, pants rolled to his knees, shirt sailing in the sea wind, stood in the weave of white water. The wind lifted Tork's hair from his neck; and the fire roared on the beach.

Tork looked up too.

"They're getting ready to catch a big fish!" João called.

Men were already pushing their boats out. Tork clapped my shoulder. "Come, Cal. We fish now." We stood and went back to the shore.

João caught me as I reached dry sand. "You ride in my boat, Cal!"

Someone came with the acrid flares that hissed. The water slapped around the bottom of the boats as we wobbled into the swell.

João vaulted in and took up the oars. Around us green amphimen walked into the sea, struck forward and were gone.

João pulled, leaned, pulled. The moonlight slid down his arms. The fire diminished on the beach.

Then among the boats, there was a splash, an explosion, and the red flare bloomed in the sky: the amphimen had sighted a big fish.

The flare hovered, pulsed once, twice, three times, four times (twenty, forty, sixty, eighty stone they estimated its weight to be), then fell.

Suddenly I shrugged out of my shirt, pulled at my belt buckle. "I'm going over the side, João!"

He leaned, he pulled, he leaned. "Take the rope."

"Yeah. Sure." It was tied to the back of the boat. I made a loop in the other end, slipped it around my shoulder. I swung my bad leg over the side, flung myself on the black water—

Mother-of-pearl shattered over me. That was the moon, blocked by the shadow of João's boat ten feet overhead. I turned below the rippling wounds João's oars made stroking the sea.

One hand and one foot with torn webs, I rolled over and looked down. The rope snaked to its end, and I felt João's strokes pulling me through the water.

They fanned below with underwater flares. Light undulated on their backs and heels. They circled, they closed, like those deep-sea fish who carry their own illumination. I saw the prey, glistening as it neared a flare.

You chase a fish with one spear among you. And that spear would be Tork's tonight. The rest have ropes to bind him that go up to the fishermen's boats.

There was a sudden confusion of lights below. The spear had been shot!

The fish, long as a tall and a short man together, rose through the ropes. He turned out to sea, trailing his pursuers. But others waited there, tried to loop him. Once I had flung those ropes, treated with tar and lime to dissolve the slime of the fish's body and hold to the beast. The looped ropes caught, and by the movement of the flares I saw them jerked from their paths. The fish turned, rose again, this time toward me.

He pulled around when one line ran out (and somewhere

on the surface the prow of a boat doffed deep) but turned back
and came on.

Of a sudden, amphimen were flicking about me as the fray's
center drifted by. Tork, his spear dug deep, forward and left
of the marlin's dorsal, had hauled himself astride the beast.

The fish tried to shake him, then dropped his tail and rose
straight. Everybody started pulling toward the surface. I broke
foam and grabbed João's gunwale.

Tork and the fish exploded up among the boats. They twisted
in the air, in moonlight, in froth. The fish danced across the
water on its tail, fell.

João stood up in the boat and shouted. The other fishermen
shouted too, and somebody perched on the prow of a boat flung
a rope and someone in the water caught it.

Then fish and Tork and me and a dozen amphimen all went
underwater at once.

They dropped in a corona of bubbles. The fish struck the
end of another line, and shook himself. Tork was thrown free,
but he doubled back.

Then the lines began to haul the beast up again, quivering,
whipping, quivering again.

Six lines from six boats had him. For one moment he was
still in the submarine moonlight. I could see his wound tossing
scarves of blood.

When he (and we) broke surface, he was thrashing again,
near João's boat. I was holding onto the side when suddenly
Tork, glistening, came out of the water beside me and went
over into the dinghy.

"Here you go," he said, turning to kneel at the bobbing rim,
and pulled me up while João leaned against the far side to keep
balance.

Wet rope slopped on the prow. "Hey, Cal!" Tork laughed,
grabbed it up and began to haul.

The fish prized wave from white wave in the white water.

The boats came together. The amphimen had all climbed
up. Ariel was across from us, holding a flare that drooled smoke
down her arm. She peered by the hip of the fisherman who
was standing in front of her.

João and Tork were hauling the rope. Behind them I was
coiling it with one hand as it came back to me.

The fish came up and was flopped into Ariel's boat, tail
out, head up, chewing air.

I had just finished pulling on my trousers when Tork fell down on the seat behind me and grabbed me around the shoulders with his wet arms. "Look at our fish, Tio Cal! Look!" He gasped air, laughing, his dark face diamonded beside the flares. "Look at our fish there, Cal!"

João, grinning white and gold, pulled us back in to shore. The fire, the singing, hands beating hands—and my godson had put pebbles in the empty rum bottle and was shaking them to the music. The guitars spiraled around us as we carried the fish up the sand and the men brought the spit.

"Watch it!" Tork said, grasping the pointed end of the great stick that was thicker than his wrist.

We turned the fish over.

"Here, Cal?"

He prodded two fingers into the white flesh six inches back from the bony lip.

"Fine."

Tork jammed the spit in.

We worked it through the body. By the time we carried it to the fire, they had brought more rum.

"Hey, Tork. Are you going to get some sleep before you go down in the morning?" I asked.

He shook his head. "Slept all afternoon." He pointed toward the roasting fish with his elbow. "That's my breakfast."

But when the dancing grew violent a few hours later, just before the fish was to come off the fire, and the kids were pushing the last of the sweet potatoes from the ashes with sticks, I walked back to the lifeboat shell we had sat on earlier. It was three-quarters flooded.

Curled below still water, Tork slept, fist loose before his mouth, the gills at the back of his neck pulsing rhythmically. Only his shoulder and hip made islands in the floating boat.

"Where's Tork?" Ariel asked me at the fire. They were swinging up the sizzling fish.

"Taking a nap."

"Oh, he wanted to cut the fish!"

"He's got a lot of work coming up. Sure you want to wake him up?"

"No, I'll let him sleep."

But Tork was coming up from the water, brushing his dripping hair back from his forehead.

He grinned at us, then went to carve. I remember him standing on the table, astraddle the meat, arm going up and down with the big knife (details—yes, those are the things you remember), stopping to hand down the portions, then hauling his arm back to cut again.

That night, with music and stomping on the sand and shouting back and forth over the fire, we made more noise than the sea.

IV

THE EIGHT-THIRTY BUS WAS MORE OR LESS ON TIME.

"I don't think they want to go," João's sister said. She was accompanying the children to the Aquatic Corp Headquarters in Brasília.

"They are just tired," João said. "They should not have stayed up so late last night. Get on the bus now. Say good-bye to Tio Cal."

"Good-bye."

"Good-bye."

Kids are never their most creative in that sort of situation. And I suspect that my godchildren may just have been suffering their first (or one of their first) hangovers. They had been very quiet all morning.

I bent down and gave them a clumsy hug. "When you come back on your first weekend off, I'll take you exploring down below at the point. You'll be able to gather your own coral now."

João's sister got teary, cuddled the children, cuddled me, João, then got on the bus.

Someone was shouting out the window for someone else at the bus stop not to forget something. They trundled around the square and then toward the highway. We walked back across the street where the café owners were putting out canvas chairs.

"I will miss them," he said, like a long-considered admission.

"You and me both." At the docks near the hydrofoil wharf where the submarine launches went out to the undersea cities, we saw a crowd. "I wonder if they had any trouble laying the—"

A woman screamed in the crowd. She pushed from the others, dropping eggs and onions. She began to pull her hair and shriek. (Remember the skillet of shrimp? She had been the woman ladling them out.) A few people moved to help her.

A clutch of men broke off and ran into the streets of the town. I grabbed a running amphiman, who whirled to face me.

"What in hell is going on?"

For a moment his mouth worked on his words for all the trite world like a beached fish.

"From the explosion—" he began. "They just brought them back from the explosion at the Slash!"

I grabbed his other shoulder. "What happened?"

"About two hours ago. They were just a quarter of the way through, when the whole fault gave way. They had a goddamn underwater volcano for half an hour. They're still getting seismic disturbances."

João was running toward the launch. I pushed the guy away and limped after him, struck the crowd and jostled through calico, canvas and green scales.

They were carrying the corpses out of the hatch of the submarine and laying them on a canvas spread across the dock. They still return bodies to the countries of birth for the family to decide the method of burial. When the fault had given, the hot slag that had belched into the steaming sea was mostly molten silicon.

Three of the bodies were only slightly burned here and there; from their bloated faces (one still bled from the ear) I guessed they had died from sonic concussion. But several of the bodies were almost totally encased in dull, black glass.

"Tork—" I kept asking. "Is one of them Tork?"

It took me forty-five minutes, asking first the guys who were carrying the bodies, then going into the launch and asking some guy with a clipboard, and then going back on the dock and into the office to find out that one of the more unrecognizable bodies, yes, was Tork.

João brought me a glass of buttermilk in a café on the square. He sat still a long time, then finally rubbed away his white mustache, released the chair rung with his toes, put his hands on his knees.

"What are you thinking about?"

"That it's time to go fix the nets. Tomorrow morning I will

fish." He regarded me a moment. "Where should I fish to-morrow, Cal?"

"Are you wondering about—well—sending the kids off today?"

He shrugged. "Fishermen from this village have drowned. Still it is a village of fishermen. Where should I fish?"

I finished my buttermilk. "The mineral content over the Slash should be high as the devil. Lots of algae will gather tonight. Lots of small fish down deep. Big fish hovering over."

He nodded. "Good. I will take the boat out there tomorrow."

We got up.

"See you, João."

I limped back to the beach.

V

THE FOG HAD UNSHEATHED THE SAND BY TEN. I WALKED around, poking in clumps of weeds with a stick, banging the same stick on my numb leg. When I lurched up to the top of the rocks, I stopped in the still grass. "Ariel?"

She was kneeling in the water, head down, red hair breaking over sealed gills. Her shoulders shook, stopped, shook again.

"Ariel?" I came down over the blistered stones.

She turned away to look at the ocean.

The attachments of children are so important and so brittle. "How long have you been sitting here?"

She looked at me now, the varied waters of her face stilled on drawn cheeks. And her face was exhausted. She shook her head.

Sixteen? Who was the psychologist a hundred years back, in the seventies, who decided that "adolescents" were just physical and mental adults with no useful work? "You want to come up to the house?"

The head-shaking got faster, then stopped.

After a while I said, "I guess they'll be sending Tork's body back to Manila."

"He didn't have a family," she explained. "He'll be buried here, at sea."

"Oh," I said.

And the rough volcanic glass pulled across the ocean's sands, changing shape, dulling...

"You were—you liked Tork a lot, didn't you? You kids looked like you were pretty fond of each other."

"Yes. He was an awfully nice—" Then she caught my meaning and blinked. "No," she said. "Oh, no. I was—I was engaged to Jonni . . . the brown-haired boy from California? Did you meet him at the party last night? We're both from Los Angeles, but we only met down here. And now . . . they're sending his body back this evening." Her eyes got very wide, then closed

"I'm sorry."

That's it, you clumsy cripple, step all over everybody's emotions. You look in that mirror and you're too busy looking at what might have been to see what is.

"I'm sorry, Ariel."

She opened her eyes and began to look around her.

"Come on up to the house and have an avocado. I mean, they have avocados in now, not at the supermarket. But at the old town market on the other side. And they're better than any they grow in California."

She kept looking around.

"None of the amphimen get over there. It's a shame, because soon the market will probably close, and some of their fresh foods are really great. Oil and vinegar is all you need on them." I leaned back on the rocks. "Or a cup of tea?"

"Okay." She remembered to smile. I know the poor kid didn't feel like it. "Thank you. I won't be able to stay long, though."

We walked back up the rocks toward the house, the sea on our left. Just as we reached the patio, she turned and looked back. "Cal?"

"Yes? What is it?"

"Those clouds over there, across the water. Those are the only ones in the sky. Are they from the eruption in the Slash?"

I squinted. "I think so. Come on inside."

Mrs. Pigafetta Swims Well

by

Reginald Bretnor

Throughout the ages, men have yearned for romantic liaisons with mermaids—and the mermaids usually seem more than glad to oblige. But, as the following droll little story suggests, the consequences of such a seaside affair might be just a bit more serious than you bargained for....

Born in 1911, Reginald Bretnor has been active in the SF field since 1947. He is perhaps best known for his "Papa Schimmelhorn" stories, and for the long series of punning joke vignettes known as "Feghoots" (after their continuing protagonist, Ferdinand Feghoot), which he has been publishing, under the name Grendel Briarton since 1956. The Feghoots have been collected in a book entitled (naturally enough) The Compleat Feghoot. As an editor, Bretnor has assembled three major collections of critical articles about SF: Modern Science Fiction, Its Meaning and Its Future; Science Fiction, Today and Tomorrow; *and* The Craft of Science Fiction.

* * *

MR. COASTGUARD, THIS IS WHAT HAS HAPPENED TO PIETRO Pugliese, who is captain of the fishing boat *Il Trovatore,* of Monterey. Me, Joe Tonelli, I am his engineer. I know.

It is because of Mrs. Pigafetta, from Taranto. It is her fault. Also the porpoises. It is also because Pietro has been famous—

You do not know? You have not heard how one time he is the great *tenore?* Yes, in Rome, Naples, Venice—even in La Scala in Milano. *Do, re, mi, fa*—like so, only with more beauty. Caruso, Gigli—those fellows can only make a squeak alongside Pietro, I tell you.

So what, you say? It is important. It is why Mrs. Pigafetta becomes his landlady. It is why she hides his clothes so that he cannot run away like her first husband who maybe is in Boston. It is why the porpoises—

Okay, Mr. Coastguard, okay. I will tell one thing at one time. I will begin when first I hear Pietro sing, last Tuesday night.

He calls to me when he is at the wheel. Our hold is full of fish. The sea is smooth. The moon hangs in the sky like a fine oyster. But I can see that he is still not happy. He has not been happy for two months. All the time he shakes his head. He sighs.

I am worried. I ask if maybe he has a bad stomach, but he does not reply. All at once, his head is thrown back—his mouth is open—he sings! It is from the last act of *Tosca,* in the jail. They are going to execute this guy, and he is singing good-bye to the soprano, who is his girl. You know? That is why it is sad.

I am full of surprise. Never have I heard a voice so rich— like the best *zabaglione,* made with egg yolk, sugar, sweet wine. Also it is strong, like a good foghorn. Even the mast trembles.

I listen to the end. I look at him. His face is to the moon. He weeps! Slowly, many tears roll down his cheeks. What would you do? I want him to feel good. I tell him he is great. I cry, *Bravissimo!*

At last he speaks, as from the grave. "Joe, it is as you say. It is true I am a great man. Even the angels do not have a voice like me. And now"—his chest goes up and down—"it is this voice which cooks my goose! Almost, I lose all hope. But I say, 'Joe is my good friend. Maybe he can help—'"

Then, Mr. Coastguard, I hear the story. His papa is a fisherman. Once, they come to Naples. While Pietro mends the nets, he sings. He is young, handsome. A rich *marchesa* hears him. And it is done! A year—the world is at his feet. He has a palace, a gold watch, mistresses—yes, *principessas*, girls from the ballet, the wives of millionaires! He sings. All— kings, queens, cardinals—they cry with joy. Even the English often clap their hands.

He is an innocent. He does not know the other singers burn with jealousy. He does not know the critics envy him. They plot. Always they say bad things. One day there is no place for him to sing! Ah, he is wounded to the heart. He goes away. He takes a cabin on a little ship. For two days, without a fee, he sings to the waves, the passengers, the crew. But he is betrayed! The sea has envy too. There comes a storm. Those people on the ship are stupid fools. They say it is his fault. They—they throw him overboard!

He tells me this. Again he sighs. "I cannot swim. I fight against the waves. I call aloud the names of many saints. I sink! But I am not afraid. When I come up, I sing! Again the water swallows me. Then—all is black. My friend, when I awake I think that I am dead. But I am not. I am in Mrs. Pigafetta's house."

Mr. Coastguard, it is a miracle! The ship is near Taranto. There is this island. And on it is the *penzione* of Mrs. Pigafetta, for shipwrecked sailors. She has heard the fine voice of Pietro in the storm. She has rescued him. It is nothing for Mrs. Pigafetta. She swims well.

He wakes—and she is sitting there, all wet. He is surprised to see her. He makes the sign of the cross, but she says nothing. There is love in her eyes.

And she is beautiful. Not thin, like a young girl, but plump and strong, with fine hips—wide like so. Her lips are red. Her hair is black, done up on top. It shines like it has olive oil on it. Besides, she is a woman of experience—

Still, when Pietro tells me this, he grinds his teeth. "Why do I stay with her, my friend? It is because at first I am in love. It is a madness. All night, all day—such passion. There are two sailors there, Greeks; she does not speak to them. Each month she makes them pay. But me—one month, two months, three—I get no bill. She teaches me to swim. We sit on the rocks in the sun, and we sing to each other—*La Forza del Destino, Pagliacci, Rigoletto.* My love has made me deaf. I do not notice that her contralto has the sound of brass. Imagine it!"

Then, in one moment, Pietro's eyes are opened. A day comes when Mrs. Pigafetta pushes him away. She lets him kiss her neck, her ear—that is all! He does not understand. He asks, *"Carissima,* my sweet lobster, what is wrong?"

She pushes him some more. She makes her lips thin. She says, "No, no, Pietro *mio!* We must marry in the Church."

Even as Pietro tells me this, his face is sad. "At once, all is changed. It comes to me that her voice is loud, of poor quality. Besides, I am Pietro Pugliese—there is my public. I must not stay always with one woman. I make a long face. I

ask about her first husband, Pigafetta. I ask her, 'He is dead?'
And she laughs at me. She shrugs. 'He is in Boston. It is the
same.' "

From the wheelhouse of *Il Trovatore*, Pietro looks to port,
to starboard. There is light from the moon on the waves. All
over, porpoises are playing—

"Ah, she is stubborn! She makes me afraid. I see I have a
great problem, with much trouble. Why? You ask me why?
Joe, I have one more reason I cannot marry Mrs. Pigafetta in
the Church. It is because—"

He moves his hand to show me. His voice shakes.

"—because Mrs. Pigafetta is a woman only from here up.
From here down, she is a fish!"

Okay, Mr. Coastguard, you do not believe. It is because,
like me, you have never seen a woman like Mrs. Pigafetta. A
mermaid? That is what I ask Pietro. He says no, that it is
different. Mrs. Pigafetta is a woman of experience—

The days pass. Always she pushes him away. Always she
says, "No, we must marry in the Church."

He argues. "If we are married, sometime we have a son.
You think I want my son to be a sturgeon, a big sea-bass,
perhaps a flounder? I do not know your family."

She laughs. She tells him this cannot be. She says, "Our
son can be a bosun in the navy, no worse. Even so, he must
know his papa. That is why I push you away."

Soon Pietro tries to escape. He sees a sailing boat. He shouts
at it, and runs along the shore. After that, Mrs. Pigafetta takes
his clothes. She hides them in her house, which is made in a
large cave in the rocks.

But he is brave. Twice more he tries. He swims at night.
Each time, the porpoises swim with him. They turn him back,
like dogs with a sheep. They are her friends.

When he tells this, he shakes his fist at the porpoises in the
sea. "That is when I know that I must be more smart than Mrs.
Pigafetta. Again, I sing to her. I praise her voice. And all the
time I watch. Ah, she is vain! Two, three times a day she puts
on her best hat. She sits at her mirror, She looks at herself one
way, then another. She smiles. It is a large hat, with many
feathers, much fruit on the top."

Mr. Coastguard, you ask why does she want a hat? But why
not? Where she puts the hat she is a woman, not a fish.

Okay. Pietro makes a plan. He promises that they will marry in the Church. After that, she does not say, "No, no." She does not push. But every time she asks when they will marry, he delays.

"Now? My pretty perch, my sea anemone! It is the tourist season. You will be kidnapped for your lovely silver tail—sold in the black market to rich Americans!"

For weeks it is like that. At last she loses patience. "You say we go to Rome. You promise a cathedral. You even tell me I will meet this Rossellini. *Bah!* Tomorrow you will swim with me to Taranto. The priest will marry us." She is very angry. "You say it is not safe. All right! There is a church by the water. I will bring a long dress. I will wear perfume. No one will know."

Pietro pretends that he is pleased. He kisses her. Then he looks sad: "But, *cara mia,* there is—there is one small thing." He points at it. "You cannot possibly be married in this hat."

She weeps. She tells him if he loved her he would like her hat.

He kisses her again. He protests his love. It is only that the hat is out of fashion. The women in the town will laugh at her. Besides, the sea has spoiled it. Then he tells his plan. They will swim together, but she will wait for him in the water. He will buy her a new hat.

"Joe, I am smart," Pietro says. "I know that she is mad with love. In the morning, we swim to Taranto. She gives me back my clothes. I put them on. I leave her in the water. Quickly, I take a train. Then I come to America. I buy this boat, *Il Trovatore.* I make an oath—"

Again the tears fall. "My friend, I know that if I keep this oath I will be safe. Four years, I do not sing. Then, two months ago, you go to visit your papa. While you are gone, I bring a lady on the boat. Ah, she is beautiful—the wife of an old man who has a bank. She gives me wine. And—and for one moment I forget! I sing for her. From *Don Giovanni,* from *La Traviata.* But suddenly she points her finger at the sea. I look—and my heart is dead! I see the porpoises. They, too, are listening!"

That is why there has been a sadness on Pietro's soul. The porpoises are Mrs. Pigafetta's friends. He knows that they will tell her where he is.

I say, "Have courage! Taranto is a long way. The porpoises

will not want to go so far. It will take many months for her to come."

His tears fall like rain. "No, no," he cries. "The porpoises shout to each other through the sea. Also, there is the Panama Canal. She swims well. She will be here soon!"

Mr. Coastguard, the sea is full of porpoises. They play. They leap into the air. There are more now. Also they seem more glad.

"Joe, look!" Pietro grabs my arm. "That is how they are when she is near. I tell you, she comes tonight! You must help me, Joe!"

I say to him, "Have no fear. I do not let her take you back. I will do what you want."

He embraces me. He says, "I have a plan. Maybe once more I can be more smart than Mrs. Pigafetta. You remember one week ago, when we are in San Pedro, I go ashore? Okay, I go to buy a hat. It is a fine hat, the new style, green, with bright things that hang down and a long plume from the top."

The box is in the wheelhouse. He opens it. "I have paid eighteen dollars. Maybe when you give her this fine hat she is shamed and will go away."

"Me?" I say.

"Yes, yes! We watch the porpoises so I can tell when she has come real close. We bring Nick from the galley to hold the wheel. You tie me to the mast—"

I ask, "Why must I tie you to the mast?"

He looks over his shoulder. He makes his voice low. "Because it is a smart trick, made by a Greek. You tie me to the mast with lots of rope, good and strong. You wait on deck. She calls out from the sea, Pietro *mio*, where are you? I sing a little bit. She comes more quickly. She grabs the rail. She wants to climb aboard—Joe, that is when you must think well! You must say, 'Mrs. Pigafetta, it is nice meeting you. Pietro has bought for you this hat. It is expensive. It is a token of his love. But he cannot go with you to your house.' Then you must tell her something so she goes away."

For two hours, we talk about what I must tell to Mrs. Pigafetta. Sometimes Pietro weeps. Sometimes he is angry. But at last I get a good thought. I say, "I will tell her that I tie you up because you are crazy in the head with love—that you try to jump into the sea—that you believe a fat porpoise is Mrs. Pigafetta."

It is now very late. The moon has fallen in the sky. There are more porpoises even than before. They swim around *Il Trovatore*. All the time, they look at us.

Suddenly, Pietro starts to tremble. He whispers, *"She is near!"* He crouches by the mast. We call for Nick to hold the wheel. I take the rope—

And then—crash! bang!—something hits *Il Trovatore* a great blow on the bottom. The stern lifts in the air. I fall. Pietro cries aloud.

What is it? A great fish? A whale? I do not know. Next thing, I hear my engine. It runs fast—faster, faster! It screams—

I forget Pietro! I forget all but my engine. I go to it like a mama to her child who is hurt. Nick is there too. He shouts, "What is wrong?" I shout back, "A fish has broken the propeller!" I turn the engine off.

We look to see if there is a bad leak. Maybe for five minutes we look. Then, all at once—I remember! We leap up to the deck—

The boat has stopped in the water. It rocks gently. All is still. The porpoises have gone. I guess the big fish has gone too. And Pietro? He is not there any more.

Across the deck, there is sea water. In a strip—wide like so—it is wet. Also, on the deck there is the box. Next to it is a hat. But, Mr. Coastguard, it is not the fine hat Pietro buys down in San Pedro. Here, look at it! See how it is out of fashion? See the flowers, the fruit? See how it has been spoiled by the sea?

Ah, when we see it, we are just like you. At first we have no words. Then, to port, to starboard, we shout loudly, "Pietro! Where are you, Pietro? Answer us! Come back!"

There is no answer. Only, far away, we hear this voice singing. It is strong and full of joy. But it is not Pietro's voice. It is a contralto—with the sound of brass.

No, Mr. Coastguard, I do not think that you will find Pietro. It is too late. Mrs. Pigafetta is a woman of experience. She swims well.

The Nebraskan and the Nereid

by

Gene Wolfe

*Gene Wolfe is perceived by many critics to be one of the best—
perhaps* the *best—SF and fantasy writer working today. His
tetralogy* The Book of the New Sun—*consisting of* The Shadow
of the Torturer, The Claw of the Conciliator, The Sword of the
Lictor, *and* The Citadel of the Autarch—*is being hailed as a
masterpiece, quite probably the standard against which all
subsequent science-fantasy books of the eighties will be judged;
ultimately, it may prove to be as influential as J.R.R. Tolkien's*
Lord of the Rings *or T. H. White's* The Once and Future King.
*Wolfe has won two Nebula Awards, and a World Fantasy Award.
His other books include* Peace, The Fifth Head of Cerberus,
and The Devil in a Forest. *His short fiction—including some
of the best stories of the seventies—has been collected in* The
Island of Doctor Death and Other Stories *and* Other Stories
and Gene Wolfe's Book of Days. *His most recent books are*
The Castle of the Otter, *a book about the writing of* The Book
of the New Sun, *and* The Wolfe Archipelago, *a collection.*

*Here he spins a subtle and elegant tale about a folklorist
who spends his time ranging the rural Greek countryside, collecting old legends and stories, but who certainly does not
expect to be collected himself....*

* * *

THE NEBRASKAN WAS WALKING NEAR THE SEA WHEN HE SAW
her. Two dark eyes, a rounded shoulder with a hint of breast,
and a flash of thigh; then she was gone. A moment later he
heard a faint splash—or perhaps it was only the fabled seventh
wave, the wave that is stronger than the rest, breaking on the
rocks.

Almost running, he strode to the edge of the little bluff and looked east across the sea. The blue waters of the *Saronikos Kolpos* showed whitecaps, but nothing else.

"Then felt I like some watcher of the skies," he muttered to himself, "When a new planet swims into his ken; or like stout Cortez, when with eagle eyes, he stared at the Pacific— and all his men..." He groped for a moment for the final two lines, as he studied the bluff. "Looked at each other with a wild surmise—silent, upon a peak in Darien."

"Stout Cortez" chuckled as he clambered down the bluff with his tape recorder bumping his side. He was no rock climber, but the slope was neither high enough nor sheer enough to require one. He imagined himself describing his adventure in the faculty lounge. *It was nothing.*

Nothing too was the evidence he found on the beach, in some places hardly wider than a footpath, that wound along the base of the bluff. There were a few seashells and a rusty tin that had once held British cigarettes, but that was all. No cast off bikini, no abandoned beach towel, no footprints, nothing.

He looked up to see a tall and rather angular woman with a canteen at her hip walking silently toward him along the strip of damp sand. He greeted her in his halting Greek, and she extended her right hand in a regal gesture, saying in English, "And a good morning to you, Doctor. I am Dr. Thoe Papamarkos. I am of the University of Athens. You are Dr. Cooper, and you are of an American university, but they do not know to tell me which."

"The University of Nebraska at Lincoln. Pleased to meet you, Dr. Papamarkos." The Nebraskan was Lincolnesque himself, tall and pleasantly ugly.

"And you are a folklorist. You must be, from what they report of you, that you walk about all day, ask questions of old people, make recordings of their stories."

"That's right," he said. "And you?"

She laughed softly. "Oh, no. I am not the competition, as you fear."

"Good!" He smiled.

She touched the third button of her khaki shirt. "An archaeologist, I am. Do you know of Saros?"

He shook his head. "I know this is the Saronic Gulf," he said, "and I suppose it must be named after something. Is it an island?"

"No. It was a city, a city so long ago that even in the time of Socrates there was nothing left but ruins and a temple for Poseidon. Think on it, please, Doctor. You and I, we think of that time, the Age of Pericles, as ruins. But to them, to Pericles and Plato, Themistocles and Aristeides the Just, Saros was ancient, Saros was archaeology. Now I dig, with three men from the village to work for me. About five kilometers that way. There I hear of you, stories of the folklorist, and I think we should know of each other, probably we are the only truly educated people on this part of the coast, perhaps someday we may even help each other. No?"

"Yes," he said. "Certainly." He discovered that he liked her. She was an old-maid schoolteacher, no doubt about it, with her graying hair tightly knotted in a bun. She could be Miss Twiddle from "The Katzenjammer Kids" or the Miss Minerva of *Miss Minerva and William Green Hill*. And yet—

"And you," she said. "Folklore is so interesting. What is it that you do?"

He cleared his throat as he tried to think of some way to explain. "I'm trying to trace the history of the Nereids."

"Truly?" She looked at him sidelong. "You believe they were real?"

"No, no." He shook his head. "But do you know about them, Dr. Papamarkos? Do you know who they were?"

"I, who search for the temple of Poseidon? Of course. They were the ladies, the maids in waiting at his court, under the Aegean. He was one of the oldest of all the old Greek gods. They were old too, very old, the Greek—what do you call them in English? Mermaids? Sea fairies? Tell me." She hesitated, as though embarrassed. "I understand your English much better than I speak it, you must believe me. I was three years, studying at Princeton." She unhooked the canteen from her belt and unscrewed the top.

He nodded. "I'm the same way with Greek. I understand it well enough; I couldn't do what I do if I didn't. But sometimes I can't think of the right word, or remember how it should be pronounced."

"You do not want a drink of my water, I hope. This is so very warm now, but I have a nose disease. Is that what you call it? I must take my medicine to breathe, and my medicine makes me thirsty. Do you wish for some?"

"No thanks," he said. "I'm fine."

"And did I say it correctly? Mermaids?"

"Yes, mermaids. Specifically, they were a class of nymphs, the sea nymphs, the fifty daughters of Nereus. There were mountain nymphs too, the Oreads; and there were Dryads and Meliae in the trees, Epipotamides in the rivers, and so forth. And old people, rural people particularly . . ."

She laughed again. "Still credit such things. I know, Doctor, and I am not embarrassed for my country. You have these too, but with you it is the flying saucers, the little green men. Why should not my Greece have its little green women?"

"But the fascinating part," he said, warming to his subject, "is that they've forgotten all the names except one. Modern Greeks no longer talk about nymphs, or Oreads, Dryads, or Naiades. Only of Nereids, whether they're supposed to have been seen in springs, or caves, or whatever. I'm trying to find out just how that happened."

She smiled. "Have you thought, perhaps only they still live?"

When the Nebraskan got back to his tiny inn in Nemos, he stopped its dumpy little maid of all work and mustered his uncertain Greek to ask her about Dr. Papamarkos.

"She does not live here," the maid informed him, staring at the toes of his boots. "Over there. She has a tent." She ducked through a doorway and vanished; it was not until some time afterwards that it occurred to him that the Greek word for a tent also meant stage scenery.

On the stairs, he wondered again if it might be possible. Dr. Papamarkos taking off her heavy belt, the soldierish pants and shirt. Flitting naked through the woods. He chuckled.

No. The woman he had seen—and he *had* seen a woman, he told himself—had been younger, smaller, and—um—rounder. He suddenly recalled that Schliemann, the discoverer of Troy, had married a Greek girl of nineteen at the age of forty-seven. He himself was still years short of that.

The thought returned the next time he saw her. It was at almost the same spot. (He had been frequenting that spot too much, as he kept telling himself.) He heard a noise and turned, but not quickly enough. The faint splash came again. Once more he hurried, actually running this time, to the edge of the little bluff; and this time he was rewarded. A laughing face bobbed in the waves fifty yards out, a face circled by dark and floating hair. An arm rose from the sea, waved once, and was gone.

He waited five minutes, occasionally glancing at his watch. Ten. The face did not reappear, and at last he scrambled down the bluff to stand upon the beach, staring out to sea.

"Doctor! Doctor!"

He looked around. "Hello, Dr. Papamarkos. What a pleasure to meet you again." She was coming from the other direction this time, the direction of Nemos and his inn, and she was waving something above her head. It really was a pleasure, he realized. A sympathetic ear, an older woman, no doubt with a certain amount of experience, who knew the country . . . "Good to see you!"

"And to see you, my friend. Oh, Doctor, my friend, look! Just look and see what we have found under the water."

She held it out to him, and after a moment he saw it was a glazed cup, still somewhat encrusted with marine growths.

"And it is to you that I owe, oh, everything!"

The background was red, the man's head black, his curling beard and wide, fierce eye traced in a lighter color that might originally have been white. A fish, small and crude, swam before his face.

"And on the back! See, beside the trident, the two straight scratches, the bar at the top? It is our letter π, for Poseidon. They have finer cups, oh, yes, much finer, at the museum in Athens. But this is so old! This is Mycenaean, early Mycenaean, from when we were yet copying, and badly, things from Crete."

The Nebraskan was still staring at the bearded face. It was crude, hardly more than a cartoon; and yet it burned with a deft energy, so that he felt the bearded sea god watched him, and might at any instant roar with laughter and slap him on the back. "It's wonderful," he said.

It was as though she could read his thoughts. "He was the sea god," she said. "Sailors prayed to him, and captains. Also to Nereus, the old sea-man who knew the future. Now it is to Saint Peter and Saint Mark. But it is not so different, perhaps. The fish, the beard, they are still there."

"You say you found this because of me, Dr. Papamarkos?"

"Yes! I meet with you, and we talk of the Nereids, remember? Then I walk back to my dig." She opened her canteen and took a healthy swallow. "And I kept thinking of them, girls frisking in the waves, I could almost see them. I say, 'What are you trying to tell me? Come, I am a woman like you, speak out.'

"And they wave, come, Thoe, come! Then I think, yes, Saros was a seaport, so long ago. But was the coast the same? What if the sea is higher now, what if the place where I dig was a kilometer inland then? They called it a city, a *polis*. But to us it would be only a little town—the theater open to the sky, the temple, the *agora* where one went to buy fish and wine, and a few hundred houses."

She paused, gasping for breath; and he remembered what she had said about having a "nose disease."

"I have no diving equipment, nothing. But we make a big strainer—you understand? From a fishing net. I tell my men, walk out until the sea is at your belts. Shovel sand so gently into the net. And today we find this!"

Carefully, he handed back the cup. "Congratulations. It's wonderful, and it couldn't have come to a nicer person. I mean that."

She smiled. "I knew you would be happy for me, just as I would be so happy for you, should you find—I do not know, perhaps some wondrous old story never written down."

"May I walk you back to your camp? I'd like to see it."

"Oh, no. It is so far, and the day is hot. Wait until I have something there to show you. This is all I have worth showing now." She gave him her sidelong look; and when he said nothing, she asked, "But what of you? Surely you progress. Have you nothing to tell me?"

He took a deep breath, thinking how foolish his wild surmise would sound. "I've seen a Nereid, Thoe—or somebody's trying to make me think I have."

She put her hand on his shoulder, and he could not believe her soft laugh other than friendly. "But how wonderful for you! With this, you may rate the stories you collect by their accuracy. That, I imagine, has never been done. Now tell me everything."

He did—the glimpse in the woods, the waving figure that had disappeared into the sea. "And so, when you said the Nereids you imagined had waved to you, I wondered..."

"Whether I did not know more. I understand. But I think really it is only one of our girls fooling you. We Greeks, we swim like fish, all of us. Do you know of the Battle of Salamis? The Persians lost many ships, and their crews drowned. We Greeks lost some ships too, but very few men, because when the ships were sunk, the men swam to shore. You are from America, Doctor, where some swim well and many not at all. What of you? Do you swim?"

"Pretty well," he said. "I was on the team in college; I'm a little out of practice now."

"Then you may wish to practice, and it is so hot. When we part, go back to the place where you saw this girl vanish. There are many caves along this coast with entrances that are under the water. Those who live here know of them. Possibly the Nereids know of them, too." She smiled, then grew somber. "There are many currents, also. It is they who make the caves. If you are truly a good swimmer, you know a swimmer must be wary."

The Nebraskan was used to fresh water, and it was some time before he could bring himself to hold his eyes open in the stinging surge of the Saronic Gulf. When he did, he saw the cave almost at once, a dark circle in the sharply shelving bottom. He rose to the surface, took several deep breaths, swallowed and held the last, and dove; as he entered the cave's mouth, he wondered whether it held an octopus—small ones were offered in the market at Nemos every Saturday.

Twice he panicked and turned back. On the third attempt he reached the air, just when he felt he could go no farther.

It was dark—a little light conveyed by the water from the brilliant sunshine on its waves, a little more that filtered down from chinks in the bluff. It was damp too, and full of the spumy reek of rotting seaweed. As he climbed from the water, two small arms encircled him.

Her kisses were sharp with salt, her words Greek, but spoken with a lilting accent he had never heard. When they had loved, she sang a sea song to him, a lullaby about a child safe in his little rocking boat. After a time, they loved again; and he fell asleep.

The sun had set behind the bluff when the Nebraskan waded up through the surf. He found his clothes where he had hidden them and put them on again, humming the lullaby to himself.

By the time he was halfway to his inn, he had recalled a song about a mermaid who lost her morals down among the corals. He whistled it as he walked, and he was trying to remember the part about two kelp beds and only one got mussed when he opened the door of his room and saw his own bed had not been made. He found the innkeeper's wife in the kitchen and complained, and she brought him clean sheets (he was the only guest the little inn had) and made the bed herself.

Next morning he set out along the beach, instead of the top of the bluff. He saw her while he was still some distance off, and thought at first that her body was only the sail of some unlucky fishing boat washed ashore. After another hundred steps he knew, without having to look at her face. He turned her over anyway, and tried to brush the sand from her eyes, then kicked at the little, scuttling crabs that had nibbled at her arms.

A voice behind him said, "She was the maid at your inn, Doctor."

He spun around.

"She loved you. Perhaps you do not think it possible."

"Thoe," he said. And then, "Dr. Papamarkos."

"And yet it is." The tall woman unscrewed the top from her canteen and drank. "You, I think, cannot imagine what village life is like for such a girl, who has no money, no dowry. Then a stranger comes, and he is tall and strong, rich to her, a learned man respected by everyone. She heard the questions you asked of others, and she whispered her plan to me. I promised to help her if I could. This is all the help I can give her now, to make you understand that once you were loved. When you record love stories from the lips of old people, remember it."

"I will," he said. Something he could not swallow had lodged in his throat.

"Now you must go back to the inn and tell them. Not about you and her, but only that she is dead and you have recognized her. I will remain to watch."

The path along the top of the bluff was shorter. He climbed to it, and he had gone perhaps two hundred yards along it when he realized he could not convey the news of a tragic death with any decency in his inadequate Greek. Thoe would have to tell them. He would wait until someone came.

From the top of the bluff, he saw her take off her wide belt and canteen and drop them on the sand. The khaki shirt and trousers followed. She was lean—though not so gaunt as he had imagined—when she unbound her long, dark hair and dove into the sea.

When she did not come up again, he clambered down to the beach for the last time. A sign had been traced in the wet sand beside the dead girl's body; it might have been a cross with upswept arms, or the Greek letter ψ. There was nothing in any pockets of the khaki shirt, nothing in any pocket of the khaki trousers.

The Nebraskan opened the canteen and sniffed its contents. Then he put it to his lips and tilted it until the liquid touched his tongue.

As he expected, it was brine—sea water.

The Lady and the Merman
The White Seal Maid
The Fisherman's Wife

by

Jane Yolen

One of the most distinguished of modern fantasists, Jane Yolen has been compared to writers such as Oscar Wilde and Charles Perrault, and has been called "the Hans Christian Andersen of the Twentieth Century." Primarily known for her work for children and young adults, Yolen has produced more than sixty books, including novels, collections of short stories, poetry collections, picture books, biographies, and a book of essays on folklore and fairytales. She has received the Golden Kite Award, and has been a finalist for the National Book Award. Her books include the novel The Magic Three of Solatia, *and the collections* Dream Weaver, Moon Ribbon, The Girl Who Cried Flowers, *and* The Hundredth Dove. *Her most recent work is the collection* Tales of Wonder, *her seventeenth book.*

Yolen has probably written more about mermaids and other Undersea folk than any other contemporary fantasist. The theme seems to hold a powerful fascination for her, and she has returned to it again and again throughout her career, examining the lives of the Merfolk from every conceivable angle. Many of these stories were collected in her book Neptune Rising: Songs and Tales of the Undersea Folk, *from which two of the present selections were taken.*

Here, then, is a triptych of Jane Yolen's vivid and elegant stories of the Merfolk—"The Lady and the Merman," "The White Seal Maid," and "The Fisherman's Wife"—in which we meet some strange and magical creatures indeed . . . human and otherwise.

* * *

ONCE IN A HOUSE OVERLOOKING THE COLD NORTHERN SEA A baby was born. She was so plain, her father, a sea captain, remarked on it.

"She shall be a burden," he said. "She shall be on our hands forever." Then, without another glance at the child, he sailed off on his great ship.

His wife, who had longed to please him, was so hurt by his complaint that she soon died of it. Between one voyage and the next, she was gone.

When the captain came home and found this out, he was so enraged, he never spoke of his wife again. In this way he convinced himself that her loss was nothing.

But the girl lived and grew as if to spite her father. She looked little like her dead mother but instead had the captain's face set round with mouse-brown curls. Yet as plain as her face was, her heart was not. She loved her father, but was not loved in return.

And still the captain remarked on her looks. He said at every meeting, "God must have wanted me cursed to give me such a child. No one will have her. She shall never be wed. She shall be with me forever." So he called her Borne, for she was his burden.

Borne grew into a lady, and only once gave a sign of this hurt.

"Father," she said one day when he was newly returned from the sea, "what can I do to heal this wound between us?"

He looked away from her, for he could not bear to see his own face mocked in hers, and spoke to the cold stone floor. "There is nothing between us, Daughter," he said. "But if there were, I would say, *Salt for such wounds.*"

"Salt?" Borne asked, surprised for she knew the sting of it.

"A sailor's balm," he said. "The salt of tears or the salt of sweat or the final salt of the sea." Then he turned from her and was gone next day to the farthest port he knew of, and in this way he cleansed his heart.

After this, Borne never spoke again of the hurt. Instead, she carried it silently like a dagger inside. For the salt of tears did not salve her, so she turned instead to work. She baked bread in her ovens for the poor, she nursed the sick, she held the hands of the sea widows. But always, late in the evening, she walked on the shore looking and longing for a sight of her father's sail. Only, less and less often did he return from the sea.

One evening, tired from the work of the day, Borne felt faint as she walked on the strand. Finding a rock half in and half out of the water, she climbed upon it to rest. She spread her skirts about her, and in the dusk they lay like great gray waves.

How long she sat there, still as the rock, she did not know. But a strange, pale moon came up. And as it rose, so too rose the little creatures of the deep. They leaped free for a moment of the pull of the tide. And last of all, up from the depths, came the merman.

He rose out of the crest of the waves, sea-foam crowning his green-black hair. His hands were raised high above him and the webbings of his fingers were as colorless as air. In the moonlight he seemed to stand upon his tail. Then, with a flick of it, he was gone, gone back to the deeps. He thought no one had remarked his dive.

But Borne had. So silent and still, she saw it all, his beauty and his power. She saw him and loved him, though she loved the fish half of him more. It was all she could dare.

She could not tell what she felt to a soul, for she had no one who cared about her feelings. Instead she forsook her work and walked by the sea both morning and night. Yet strange to say, she never once looked for her father's sail.

That is why her father returned one day without her knowing it. He watched her through slotted eyes as she paced the shore, for he would not look straight upon her. At last he went to her and said, "Be done with it. Whatever ails you, give it over." For even he could see *this* wound.

Borne looked up at him, her eyes shimmering with small seas. Grateful even for this attention, she answered, "Yes, Father, you are right. I must be done with it."

The captain turned and left her then, for his food was growing cold. But Borne went directly to the place where the waves were creeping onto the shore. She called out in a low voice, "Come up. Come up and be my love."

There was no answer except for the shrieking laughter of the birds as they dove into the sea.

So she took a stick and wrote the same words upon the sand for the merman to see should he ever return. Only, as she watched, the creeping tide erased her words one by one by one. Soon there was nothing left of her cry on that shining strand.

So Borne sat herself down on the rock to weep. And each tear was an ocean.

But the words were not lost. Each syllable washed from the beach was carried below, down, down, down to the deeps of the cool, inviting sea. And there, below on his coral bed, the merman saw her words and came.

He was all day swimming up to her. He was half the night seeking that particular strand. But when he came, cresting the currents, he surfaced with a mighty splash below Borne's rock.

The moon shone down on the two, she a grave shadow perched upon a stone and he all motion and light.

Borne reached down with her white hands and he caught them in his. It was the only touch she could remember. She smiled to see the webs stretched taut between his fingers. He laughed to see hers webless, thin, and small. One great pull between them and he was up by her side. Even in the dark, she could see his eyes on her under the phosphorescence of his hair.

He sat all night by her. And Borne loved the man of him as well as the fish, then, for in the silent night it was all one.

Then, before the sun could rise, she dropped her hands on his chest. "Can you love me?" she dared to ask at last.

But the merman had no tongue to tell her about the waves. He could only speak below the water with his hands, a soft murmuration. So, wordlessly, he stared into her eyes and pointed to the sea.

Then, with the sun just rising beyond the rim of the world, he turned, dove arrow-slim into a wave, and was gone.

Gathering her skirts, now heavy with ocean spray and tears, Borne stood up. She cast but one glance at the shore and her father's house beyond. Then she dove after the merman into the sea.

The sea put bubble jewels in her hair and spread her skirts about her like a scallop shell. Tiny colored fish swam in between her fingers. The water cast her face in silver and all the sea was reflected in her eyes.

She was beautiful for the first time. And for the last.

The White Seal Maid

ON THE NORTH SEA SHORE THERE WAS A FISHERMAN NAMED Merdock who lived all alone. He had neither wife nor child, nor wanted one. At least that was what he told the other men with whom he fished the haaf banks.

But truth was, Merdock was a lonely man, at ease only with the wind and waves. And each evening, when he left his companions, calling out "Fair wind!"—the sailor's leave—he knew they were going back to a warm hearth and a full bed while he went home to none. Secretly he longed for the same comfort.

One day it came to Merdock as if in a dream that he should leave off fishing that day and go down to the sea-ledge and hunt the seal. He had never done such a thing before, thinking it close to murder, for the seal had human eyes and cried with a baby's voice.

Yet though he had never done such a thing, there was such a longing within him that Merdock could not say no to it. And that longing was like a high, sweet singing, a calling. He could not rid his mind of it. So he went.

Down by a gray rock he sat, a long sharpened stick by his side. He kept his eyes fixed out on the sea, where the white birds sat on the waves like foam.

He waited through sunrise and sunset and through the long, cold night, the singing in his head. Then, when the wind went down a bit, he saw a white seal far out in the sea, coming toward him, the moon riding on its shoulder.

Merdock could scarcely breathe as he watched the seal, so shining and white was its head. It swam swiftly to the sea-ledge, and then with one quick push it was on land.

Merdock rose then in silence, the stick in his hand. He would have thrown it, too. But the white seal gave a sudden shudder and its skin sloughed off. It was a maiden cast in moonlight, with the tide about her feet.

She stepped high out of her skin, and her hair fell sleek and white about her shoulders and hid her breasts.

Merdock fell to his knees behind the rock and would have hidden his eyes, but her cold white beauty was too much for him. He could only stare. And if he made a noise then, she took no notice but turned her face to the sea and opened her arms up to the moon. Then she began to sway and call.

At first Merdock could not hear the words. Then he realized it was the very song he had heard in his head all that day:

> Come to the edge,
> Come down to the ledge
> Where the water laps the shore.

> Come to the strand,
> Seals to the sand,
> The watery time is o'er.

When the song was done, she began it again. It was as if the whole beach, the whole cove, the whole world were nothing but that one song.

And as she sang, the water began to fill up with seals. Black seals and gray seals and seals of every kind. They swam to the shore at her call and sloughed off their skins. They were as young as the white seal maid, but none so beautiful in Merdock's eyes. They swayed and turned at her singing, and joined their voices to hers. Faster and faster the seal maidens danced, in circles of twos and threes and fours. Only the white seal maid danced alone, in the center, surrounded by the castoff skins of her twirling sisters.

The moon remained high almost all the night, but at last it went down. At its setting, the seal maids stopped their singing, put on their skins again, one by one, went back into the sea again, one by one, and swam away. But the white seal maid did not go. She waited on the shore until the last of them was out of sight.

Then she turned to the watching man, as if she had always known he was there, hidden behind the gray rock. There was something strange, a kind of pleading, in her eyes.

Merdock read that pleading and thought he understood it.

He ran over to where she stood, grabbed up her sealskin, and held it high overhead.

"Now you be mine," he said.

And she had to go with him, that was the way of it. For she was a selchie, one of the seal folk. And the old tales said it: The selchie maid without her skin was no more than a lass.

They were wed within the week, Merdock and the white seal maid, because he wanted it. So she nodded her head at the priest's bidding, though she said not a word.

And Merdock had no complaint of her, his "Sel" as he called her. No complaint except this: she would not go down to the sea. She would not go down by the shore where he had found her or down to the sand to see him in his boat, though often enough she would stare from the cottage door out past the cove's end where the inlet poured out into the great wide sea.

"Will you not walk down by the water's edge with me, Sel?" Merdock would ask each morning. "Or will you not come down to greet me when I return?"

She never answered him, either "Yea" or "Nay." Indeed, if he had not heard her singing that night on the ledge, he would have thought her mute. But she was a good wife, for all that, and did what he required. If she did not smile, she did not weep. She seemed, to Merdock, strangely content.

So Merdock hung the white sealskin up over the door where Sel could see it. He kept it there in case she should want to leave him, to don the skin and go. He could have hidden it or burned it, but he did not. He hoped the sight of it, so near and easy, would keep her with him; would tell her, as he could not, how much he loved her. For he found he did love her, his seal wife. It was that simple. He loved her and did not want her to go, but he would not keep her past her willing it, so he hung the skin up over the door.

And then their sons were born. One a year, born at the ebbing of the tide. And Sel sang to them, one by one, long, longing wordless songs that carried the sound of the sea. But to Merdock she said nothing.

Seven sons they were, strong and silent, one born each year. They were born to the sea, born to swim, born to let the tide lap them head and shoulder. And though they had the dark eyes of the seal, and though they had the seal's longing for the sea, they were men and had men's names: James, John, Michael, George, William, Rob, and Tom. They helped their father fish the cove and bring home his catch from the sea.

It was seven years and seven years and seven years again that the seal wife lived with him. The oldest of their sons was just coming to his twenty-first birthday, the youngest barely a man. It was on a gray day, the wind scarcely rising, that the boys all refused to go with Merdock when he called. They gave no reason but "Nay."

"Wife," Merdock called, his voice heavy and gray as the sky. "Wife, whose sons are these? How have you raised them that they say 'Nay' to their father when he calls?" It was ever his custom to talk to Sel as if she returned him words.

To his surprise, Sel turned to him and said, "Go. My sons be staying with me this day." It was the voice of the singer on the beach, musical and low. And the shock was so great that he went at once and did not look back.

He set his boat on the sea, the great boat that usually took several men to row it. He set it out himself and got it out into the cove, put the nets over, and never once heard when his sons called out to him as he want, "Father, fair wind!"

But after a bit the shock wore thin and he began to think about it. He became angry then, at his sons and at his wife, who had long plagued him with her silence. He pulled in the nets and pulled on the oars and started toward home. "I, too, can say 'Nay' to this sea," he said out loud as he rode the swells in.

The beach was cold and empty. Even the gulls were mute.

"I do not like this," Merdock said. "It smells of a storm."

He beached the boat and walked home. The sky gathered in around him. At the cottage he hesitated but a moment, then pulled savagely on the door. He waited for the warmth to greet him. But the house was as empty and cold as the beach.

Merdock went into the house and stared at the hearth, black and silent. Then, fear riding in his heart, he turned slowly and looked over the door.

The sealskin was gone.

"Sel!" he cried then as he ran from the house, and he named his sons in a great anguished cry as he ran. Down to the sea-ledge he went, calling their names like a prayer: "James, John, Michael, George, William, Rob, Tom!"

But they were gone.

The rocks were gray, as gray as the sky. At the water's edge was a pile of clothes that lay like discarded skins. Merdock stared out far across the cove and saw a seal herd swimming. Yet not a herd. A white seal and seven strong pups.

"Sel!" he cried again. "James, John, Michael, George, William, Rob, Tom!"

For a moment, the white seal turned her head, then she looked again to the open sea and barked out seven times. The wind carried the faint sounds back to the shore. Merdock heard, as if in a dream, the seven seal names she called. They seemed harsh and jangling to his ear.

Then the whole herd dove. When they came up again they were but eight dots strung along the horizon, lingering for a moment, then disappearing into the blue edge of sea.

Merdock recited the seven seal names to himself. And in that recitation was a song, a litany to the god of the seals. The names were no longer harsh, but right. And he remembered clearly again the moonlit night when the seals had danced upon the sand. Maidens all. Not a man or boy with them. And the white seal turning and choosing him, giving herself to him that he might give the seal people life.

His anger and sadness left him then. He turned once more to look at the sea and pictured his seven strong sons on their way.

He shouted their seal names to the wind. Then he added, under his breath, as if trying out a new tongue, "Fair wind, my sons. Fair wind."

The Fisherman's Wife

JOHN MERTON WAS A FISHERMAN. HE BROUGHT UP EELS AND elvers, little finny creatures and great sharp-toothed monsters from the waves. He sold their meat at markets and made necklaces of their teeth for the fairs.

If you asked him, he would say that what he loved about the ocean was its vast silence, and wasn't that why he had married him a wife the same. Deaf she was, and mute too, but she could talk with her hands, a flowing syncopation. He would tell you that, and it would be no lie. But there were times when he would go mad with her silences, as the sea can drive men mad, and he would leave the house to seek the babble of the marketplace. As meaningful as were her finger fantasies, they brought his ear no respite from the quiet.

There was one time, though, that he left too soon, and it happened this way. It was a cold and gray morning, and he slammed the door on his wife, thinking she would not know it, forgetting there are other ways to hear. And as he walked along the shore, singing loudly to himself—so as to prime his ears—and swinging the basket of fish pies he had for the fair, he heard only the sound of his own voice. The hush of the waves might have told him something. The silence of the seabirds wheeling overhead.

"Buy my pies," he sang out in practice, his boots cutting great gashes like exclamation marks in the sand.

Then he saw something washed up on the beach ahead.

Now fishermen often find things left along the shore. The sea gives and it takes and as often gives back again. There is sometimes a profit to be turned on the gifts of the sea. But every fisherman knows that when you have dealings with the deep you leave something of yourself behind.

143

It was no flotsam lying on the sand. It was a sea-queen, beached and gasping. John Merton stood over her, and his feet were as large as her head. Her body had a pale-greenish cast to it. The scales of her fishlike tail ran up past her waist, and some small scales lay along her sides, sprinkled like shiny gray-green freckles on the paler skin. Her breasts were as smooth and golden as shells. Her supple shoulders and arms looked almost boneless. The green-brown hair that flowed from her head was the color and texture of wrackweed. There was nothing lovely about her at all, he thought, though she exerted an alien fascination. She struggled for breath and, finding it, blew it out again in clusters of large, luminescent bubbles that made a sound as of waves against the shore.

And when John Merton bent down to look at her more closely still, it was as if he had dived into her eyes. They were ocean eyes, blue-green, and with golden flecks in the iris like minnows darting about. He could not stop staring. She seemed to call to him with those eyes, a calling louder than any sound could be in the air. He thought he heard his name, and yet he knew that she could not have spoken it. And he could not ask the mermaid about it, for how could she tell him? All fishermen know that mermaids cannot speak. They have no tongues.

He bent down and picked her up and her tail wrapped around his waist, quick as an eel. He unwound it slowly, reluctantly, from his body and then, with a convulsive shudder, threw her from him back into the sea. She flipped her tail once, sang out in a low ululation, and was gone.

He thought, wished really, that that would be the end of it, though he could not stop shuddering. He fancied he could still feel the tail around him, coldly constricting. He went on to the fair, sold all his pies, drank up the profit and started for home.

He tried to convince himself that he had seen stranger things in the water. Worse—and better. Hadn't he one day brought up a shark with a man's hand in its stomach? A right hand with a ring on the third finger, a ring of tourmaline and gold that he now wore himself, vanity getting the better of superstition. He could have given it to his wife, Mair, but he kept it for himself, forgetting that the sea would have its due. And hadn't he one night seen the stars reflecting their cold brilliance on the water as if the ocean itself stared up at him with a thousand eyes? Worse—and better. He reminded himself of his years culling the tides that swept rotting boards and babies' shoes and kitchen cups to his feet. And the fish. And the eels. And the necklaces of teeth. Worse—and better.

By the time he arrived home he had convinced himself of nothing but the fact that the mermaid was the nastiest and yet most compelling thing he had yet seen in the ocean. Still, he said nothing of it to Mair, for though she was a fisherman's daughter and a fisherman's wife; since she had been deaf from birth no one had ever let her go out to sea. He did not want her to be frightened; as frightened as he was himself.

But Mair learned something of it, for that night when John Merton lay in bed with the great down quilt over him, he swam and cried and swam again in his sleep, keeping up stroke for stroke with the sea-queen. And he called out, "Cold, oh God, she's so cold," and pushed Mair away when she tried to wrap her arms around his waist for comfort. Oh, yes, she knew, even though she could not hear him, but what could she do? If he would not listen to her hands on his, there was no more help she could give.

So John Merton went out the next day with only his wife's silent prayer picked out by her fingers along his back. He did not turn for a kiss.

And when he was out no more than half a mile, pulling strongly on the oars and ignoring the spray, the sea-queen leaped like a shot across his bow. He tried to look away, but he was not surprised. He tried not to see her webbed hand on the oarlock or the fingers as sure as wrackweed that gripped his wrist. But slowly, ever so slowly, he turned and stared at her, and the little golden fish in her eyes beckoned to him. Then he heard her speak, a great hollow of sound somewhere between a sigh and a song, that came from the grotto that was her mouth.

"I will come," he answered, now sure of her question, hearing in it all he had longed to hear from his wife. It was magic, to be sure, a compulsion, and he could not have denied it had he tried. He stood up, drew off his cap and tossed it onto the waves. Then he let the oars slip away and his life on land slip away and plunged into the water near the bobbing cap just a beat behind the mermaid's flashing tail.

A small wave swamped his boat. It half sank, and the tide lugged it relentlessly back to the shore where it lay on the beach like a bloated whale.

When they found the boat, John Merton's mates thought

him drowned. And they came to the house, their eyes tight
with grief and their hands full of unsubtle mimings.

"He is gone," said their hands. "A husband to the sea." For
they never spoke of death and the ocean in the same breath,
but disguised it with words of celebration.

Mair thanked them with her fingers for the news they bore,
but she was not sure that they told her the truth. Remembering
her husband's night dreams, she as not sure at all. And as she
was a solitary person by nature, she took her own counsel.
Then she waited until sunrise and went down to the shore.

His boat was now hers by widow's right. Using a pair of
borrowed oars, she wrestled it into the sea.

She had never been away from shore, and letting go of the
land was not an easy thing. Her eyes lingered on the beach
and sought out familiar rocks, a twisted tree, the humps of
other boats that marked the shore. But at last she tired of the
landmarks that had become so unfamiliar, and turned her sights
to the sea.

Then, about half a mile out, where the sheltered bay gave
way to the open sea, she saw something bobbing on the waves.
A sodden blue knit cap. John Merton's marker.

"He sent it to me," Mair thought. And in her eagerness to
have it, she almost loosed the oars. But she calmed herself and
rowed to the cap, fishing it out with her hands. Then she shipped
the oars and stood up. Tying a great strong rope around her
waist, with one end knotted firmly through the oarlock—not
a sailor's knot but a loveknot, the kind that she might have
plaited in her hair—Mair flung herself at the ocean.

Down and down and down she went, through the seven
layers of the sea.

At first it was warm, with a cool, light-blue color hung with
crystal teardrops. Little spotted fish, green and gold, were
caught in each drop. And when she touched them, the bubbles
burst and freed the fish, which darted off and out of sight.

The next layer was cooler, an aquamarine with a fine, falling
rain of gold. In and out of these golden strings swam slower
creatures of the deep: bulging squid, ribboned sea snakes, knobby
five-fingered stars. And the strands of gold parted before her
like a curtain of beads and she could peer down into the colder,
darker layers below.

Down and down and down Mair went until she reached the
ocean floor at last. And there was a path laid out, of finely

colored sands edged round with shells, and statues made of bone. Anemones on their fleshy stalks waved at her as she passed, for her passage among them was marked with the swirlings of a strange new tide.

At last she came to a palace that was carved out of coral. The doors and windows were arched and open, and through them passed the creatures of the sea.

Mair walked into a single great hall. Ahead of her, on a small dais, was a divan made of coral, pink and gleaming. On this coral couch lay the sea-queen. Her tail and hair moved to the sway of the currents, but she was otherwise quite still. In the shadowed, filtered light of the hall, she seemed ageless and very beautiful.

Mair moved closer, little bubbles breaking from her mouth like fragments of unspoken words. Her movement set up countercurrents in the hall. And suddenly, around the edges of her sight, she saw another movement. Turning, she saw ranged around her an army of bones, the husbands of the sea. Not a shred or tatter of skin clothed them, yet every skeleton was an armature from which the bones hung, as surely connected as they had been on land. The skeletons bowed to her, one after another, but Mair could see that they moved not on their own reckoning, but danced to the tunes piped through them by the tides. And though on land they would have each looked different, without hair, without eyes, without the subtle coverings of flesh, they were all the same.

Mair covered her eyes with her hands for a moment, then she looked up. On the couch, the mermaid was smiling down at her with her tongueless mouth. She waved a supple arm at one whole wall of bone men and they moved again in the aftermath of her greeting.

"Please," said Mair, "please give me back my man." She spoke with her hands, the only pleadings she knew. And the tongueless sea-queen seemed to understand, seemed to sense a sisterhood between them and gave her back greetings with fingers that swam as swiftly as any little fish.

Then Mair knew that the mermaid was telling her to choose, choose one of the skeletons that had been men. Only they all looked alike, with their sea-filled eye sockets and their bony grins.

"I will try," she signed, and turned toward them.

Slowly she walked the line of bitter bones. The first had

yellow minnows fleeting through its hollow eyes. The second had a twining of green vines round its ribs. The third laughed a school of red fish out its mouth. The fourth had a pulsing anemone heart. And so on down the line she went, thinking with quiet irony of the identity of flesh.

But as long as she looked, she could not tell John Merton from the rest. If he was there, he was only a hanging of bones, indistinguishable from the others.

She turned back to the divan to admit defeat, when a flash of green and gold caught her eye. It was a colder color than the rest—yet warmer, too. It was alien under the sea, as alien as she, and she turned toward its moving light.

And then, on the third finger of one skeleton's hand, she saw it—the tourmaline ring which her John had so prized. Pushing through the water toward him, sending dark eddies to the walls that set the skeletons writhing in response, she took up his skeletal hand. The fingers were brittle and stiff under hers.

Quickly she untied the rope at her waist and looped it around the bones. She pulled them across her back and the white remnants of his fingers tightened around her waist.

She tried to pull the ring from his hand. But the white knucklebones resisted. And though she feared it, Mair went hand over hand, hand over hand along the rope, and pulled them both out of the sea.

She never looked back. And yet if she had looked, would she have seen the sea replace her man layer by layer? First it stuck the tatters of flesh and blue-green rivulets of veins along the bones. Then it clothed muscle and sinew with a fine covering of skin. Then hair and nails and the decorations of line. By the time they had risen through the seven strata of sea, he looked like John Merton once again.

But she, who had worked so hard to save him, could not swim, and so it was John Merton himself who untied the rope and got them back to the boat. And it was John Merton himself who pulled them aboard and rowed them both to shore.

And a time later, when Mair Merton sat up in bed ready at last to taste a bit of the broth he had cooked for her, she asked him in her own way what it was that had occurred.

"John Merton," she signed, touching his fine strong arms with their covering of tanned skin and fine golden hair. "Tell me . . ."

But he covered her hands with his, the hand that was still wearing the gold and tourmaline ring. He shook his head and the look in his eyes was enough. For she could suddenly see past the sea-green eyes to the sockets beneath, and she understood that although she had brought him home, a part of him would be left in the sea forever, for the sea takes its due.

He opened his mouth to her then, and she saw it was hollow, as dark black as the deeps, and filled with the sound of waves.

"Never mind, John Merton," she signed on his hand, on his arms around her, into his hair. "The heart can speak, though the mouth be still. I will be loving you all the same."

And, of course, she did.

Till Human Voices Wake Us

by

Lewis Shiner

Many people have spent their lives searching for a dream. Some—like the protagonist of the taut and chilling story that follows—are even unlucky enough to find *it. . . .*

Lewis Shiner is widely regarded as one of the hottest new SF writers of the eighties. His stories have appeared in The Magazine of Fantasy & Science Fiction, Omni, Oui, Isaac Asimov's Science Fiction Magazine, *and elsewhere. Shiner is the editor of a sporadically-published semi-professional SF magazine,* Modern Stories, *and served on the 1984 Nebula Award Jury. His first novel,* Frontera, *appeared in 1984.*

* * *

THEY WERE AT FORTY FEET, IN DARKNESS. INSIDE THE NARROW circle of his dive light, Campbell could see coral polyps feeding, their ragged edges transformed into predatory flowers.

If anything could have saved us, he thought, this week should have been it.

Beth's lantern wobbled as she flailed herself away from the white-petaled spines of a sea urchin. She wore nothing but a white T-shirt over her bikini, despite Campbell's warnings, and he could see gooseflesh on her thighs. Which is as much of her body, he thought, as I've seen in . . . how long? Five weeks? Six? He couldn't remember the last time they'd made love.

As he moved his light away he thought he saw a shape in the darkness. He thought: shark, and felt a quick constriction of fear in his throat. He swung the light back again and saw her.

She was frozen by the glare, like any wild animal. Her long, straight hair floated up from her shoulders and blended into the darkness; the ends of her bare breasts were eliptical and purple in the night water.

Her legs merged into a green, scaly tail.

Campbell listened to his breath rasp into the regulator. He could see the width of her cheekbones, the paleness of her eyes, the frightened tremor of the gills around her neck.

Then reflex took over and he brought up his Nikonos and fired. The flare of the strobe shocked her to life. She shuddered, flicked her crescent tail toward him, and disappeared.

A sudden, inexplicable longing overwhelmed him. He dropped the camera and swam after her, legs pumping, pulling with both arms. As he reached the edge of a hundred foot drop-off, he swept the light in an arc that picked up a final glimpse of her, heading down and to the west. Then she was gone.

He found Beth on the surface, shivering and enraged. "What the hell was the idea of leaving me alone like that? I was scared to death. You heard what that guy said about sharks. . . ."

"I saw something," Campbell said.

"Fan-fucking-tastic." She rode low in the water, and Campbell watched her catch a wave in her open mouth. She spat it out and said, "Were you taking a look, or just running away?"

"Blow up your vest," Campbell said, feeling numb, desolate, "before you drown yourself." He turned his back to her and swam for the boat.

Showered, sitting outside his cabin in the moonlight, Campbell began to doubt himself.

Beth was already cocooned in a flannel nightgown near her edge of the bed. She would lie there, Campbell knew, sometimes not even bothering to close her eyes, until he was asleep.

His recurring, obsessive daydreams were what had brought him here to the island. How could he be sure he hadn't hallucinated that creature out on the reef?

He'd told Beth that they'd been lucky to be picked for the vacation, that he'd applied for it months before. In fact, his fantasies had so utterly destroyed his concentration at work that the company had ordered him to come to the island or submit to a complete course of psych testing.

He'd been more frightened than he was willing to admit. The fantasies had progressed from the mild violence of smashing his CRT screen to a bizarre, sinister image of himself floating outside his shattered office windows, not falling the forty stories to the street, just drifting there in the whitish smog.

High above him Campbell could see the company bar, glittering like a chrome-and-steel monster just hatched from its larval stage.

He shook his head. Obviously he needed some sleep. Just one good night's rest, he told himself, and things would start getting back to normal.

In the morning Campbell went out on the dive boat while Beth slept in. He was distracted, clumsy, and bothered by shadows in his peripheral vision.

The dive master wandered over while they were changing tanks and asked him, "You nervous about something?"

"No," Campbell said. "I'm fine."

"There's no sharks on this part of the reef, you know."

"It's not that," Campbell said. "There's no problem. Really."

He read the look in the dive master's eyes: another case of shell shock. The company must turn them out by the dozens, Campbell thought. The stressed-out executives and the boardroom victims, all with the same glazed expressions.

That afternoon they dove a small wreck at the east end of the island. Beth paired off with another woman, so Campbell stayed with his partner from the morning, a balding pilot from the Cincinnati office.

The wreck was no more than a husk, an empty shell, and Campbell floated to one side as the others crawled over the rotting wood. His sense of purpose had disappeared, left him wanting only the weightlessness and lack of color of the deep water.

After dinner he followed Beth out onto the patio. He'd lost track of how long he'd been watching the clouds over the dark water, when she said, "I don't like this place."

Campbell shifted his eyes back to her. She was sleek and pristine in the white linen jacket, the sleeves pushed up to her elbows, her still-damp hair twisted into a chignon and spiked with an orchid. She had been sulking into her brandy since they'd finished dinner, and once again she'd astonished him with her ability to exist in a completely separate mental universe from his own. "Why not?"

"It's fake. Unreal. This whole island." She swirled the brandy but didn't drink any of it. "What business does an American company have owning an entire island? What happened to the people that used to live here?"

"In the first place," Campbell said, "it's a multinational company, not just American. And the people are still living here, only now they've got jobs instead of starving to death." As usual, Beth had him on the defensive, but he wasn't as thrilled with the Americanization of the island as he wanted to be. He'd imagined natives with guitars and congas, not portable stereos that blasted electronic reggae and neo-funk. The hut where he and Beth slept was some kind of geodesic dome, air-conditioned and comfortable, but he missed the sound of the ocean.

"I just don't like it," Beth said. "I don't like top secret projects that they have to keep locked up behind electric fences. I don't like the company flying people out here for vacations the way they'd throw a bone to a dog."

Or a straw to a drowning man, Campbell thought. He was as curious as anybody about the installation at the west end of the island, but of course that wasn't the point. He and Beth were walking through the steps of a dance that Campbell now saw would inevitably end in divorce. Their friends had all been divorced at least once, and an eighteen-year marriage probably seemed as anachronistic to them as a 1957 Chevy.

"Why don't you just admit it?" Campbell said. "The only thing you really don't like about the island is the fact that you're stuck here with me."

She stood up, and Campbell felt, with numbing jealousy, the stares of men all around them focus on her. "I'll see you later," she said, and heads turned to follow the clatter of her sandals.

Campbell ordered another *Salva Vida*, watching her walk downhill. The stairs were lit with Japanese lanterns and surrounded by wild purple and orange flowers. By the time she reached the sandbar and the line of cabins, she was no more than a shadow, and Campbell had finished most of the beer.

Now that she was gone, he felt drained and a little dizzy. He looked at his hands, still puckered from the long hours in the water, at the cuts and bruises of three days of physical activity. Soft hands, the hands of a company man, a desk man.

Hands that would push a pencil or type on a CRT for another twenty years, then retire to the remote control of a big-screen TV.

The thick, caramel-tasting beer was starting to catch up to him. He shook his head and got up to find the bathroom.

His reflection shimmered and melted in the warped mirror over the bathroom sink. He realized he was stalling, staying away from the chill, sterile air of the cabin as long as he could.

And then there were the dreams. They'd gotten worse since he'd come to the island, more vivid and disturbing every night. He couldn't remember details, only slow, erotic sensations along his skin, a sense of floating in thick, crystalline water, of rolling in frictionless sheets. He'd awaken from them gasping for air like a drowning fish, his penis swollen and throbbing.

He brought another beer back to his table, not really wanting it, just needing it to hold in his hands. His attention kept wandering to a table on a lower level, where a rather plain young woman sat talking with two men in glasses and dress shirts. He couldn't understand what was so familiar about her until she tilted her head in a puzzled gesture and he recognized her. The broad cheekbones, the pale eyes.

He could hear the sound of his own heart. Was it just some kind of prank, then? A woman in a costume? But what about the gill lines he'd seen on her neck? How, in God's name, had she moved so quickly?

She stood up, made apologetic gestures to her friends. Campbell's table was near the stairs, and he saw she would have to pass him on her way out. Before he could stop to think about it, he stood up, blocking her exit, and said, "Excuse me?"

"Yes?" She was not that physically attractive, he thought, but he was drawn to her anyway, in spite of the heaviness of her waist, her solid, shortish legs. Her face was older, tireder than the one he'd seen out on the reef. But similar, too close for coincidence. "I wanted to... could I buy you a drink?" Maybe, he thought, I'm just losing my mind.

She smiled, and her eyes crinkled warmly. "I'm sorry. It's really very late, and I have to be at work in the morning."

"Please," Campbell said. "Just for a minute or two." He could see her suspicion, and behind that a faint glow of flattered ego. She wasn't used to being approached by men, he realized, "I just want to talk with you."

"You're not a reporter, are you?"

"No, nothing like that." He searched for something reassuring. "I'm with the company. The Houston office."

The magic words, Campbell thought. She sat down in Beth's chair and said, "I don't know if I should have any more. I'm about half-looped as it is."

Campbell nodded, said, "You work here, then."

"That's right."

"Secretary?"

"Biologist," she said, a little sharply. "I'm Dr. Kimberly." When he didn't react to the name, she softened it by adding, "Joan Kimberly."

"I'm sorry," Campbell said. "I always thought biologists were supposed to be homely." The flirtation came easily. She had the same beauty as the creature on the reef, a sort of fierce shyness and alien sensuality, but in the woman they were more deeply buried.

My God, Campbell thought, I'm actually doing this, actually trying to seduce this woman. He glanced at the swelling of her breasts, knowing what they would look like without the blue oxford shirt she wore, and the knowledge became a warmth in his groin.

"Maybe I'd better have that drink," she said. Campbell signaled the waiter. "I can't imagine what it would be like to live here," he said. "To see this every day."

"You get used to it," she said. "I mean, it's still unbearably beautiful sometimes, but you still have your work, and your life goes on. You know?"

"Yes," Campbell said. "I know exactly what you mean."

She let Campbell walk her home. Her loneliness and vulnerability were like a heavy perfume, so strong that it repelled him at the same time that it pulled him irresistibly toward her.

She stopped at the doorway of her cabin, another geodesic, but this one set high on the hill, buried in a grove of palms and bougainvillaea. The sexual tension was so strong that Campbell could feel his shirtfront trembling.

"Thank you," she said, her voice rough. "You're very easy to talk to."

He could have turned away then, but he couldn't seem to unravel himself. He put his arms around her, and her mouth bumped against his, awkwardly. Then her lips began to move and her tongue flicked out eagerly. She fumbled the door open without moving away from him, and they nearly fell into the house.

He pushed himself up on extended arms and watched her moving beneath him. The moonlight through the trees was green and watery, falling in slow waves across the bed. Her breasts swayed heavily as she arched and twisted her back, the breath bubbling in her throat. Her eyes were clenched tight, and her legs wrapped around his and held them, like a long, forked tail.

Before dawn he slid out from under her limp right arm and got into his clothes. She was still asleep as he let himself out.

He'd meant to go back to his cabin, but instead he found himself climbing to the top of the island's rocky spine to wait for the sun to come up.

He hadn't even showered. Kimberly's perfume and musk clung to his hands and crotch like sexual stigmata. It was Campbell's first infidelity in eighteen years of marriage, a final, irreversible act.

He knew most of the jargon. Mid-life crisis and all of that. He'd probably seen Kimberly there at the bar some other night and not consciously remembered her, projected her face onto a fantasy with obvious Freudian water/rebirth connotations.

In the dim, fractionated light of the sunrise, the lagoon was gray, the line of the barrier reef a darker smudge broken by whitecaps that curved like scales on the skin of the ocean. Dry palm fronds rustled in the breeze, and the island birds began to chirp and stutter themselves awake. A shadow broke from one of the huts on the beach below and climbed toward the road, weighted down with a large suitcase and a flight bag. Above her, in the asphalt lot at the top of the stairs, a taxi coasted silently to a stop and doused its lights.

If he had run, he could have reached her, and maybe he could even have stopped her, but the hazy impulse never became strong enough to reach his legs. Instead, he sat until the sun was hot on his neck and his eyes were dazzled into blindness by the white sand and water.

On the north side of the island, facing the mainland, the village of Espejo sprawled in the mud for the use of the resort and the company. A dirt track ran down the middle of it, oily water standing in the ruts. The cinder block houses on concrete piers and the Fords rusting in the yards reminded Campbell of an American suburb in the fifties, warped by nightmare.

The locals who worked in the company's kitchens and swept the company's floors lived here, and their kids scuffled in alleys that smelled of rotting fish or lay in the shade and threw rocks at three-legged dogs. An old woman sold Saint Francis flour sack shirts from ropes tied between pilings of her house. Under an awning of corrugated green plastic, bananas lay in heaps and flies swarmed over haunches of beef, and next door was a *farmacia* with a faded yellow Kodak sign that promised "One Day Service."

Campbell blinked and found his way to the back, where a ten- or eleven-year-old boy was reading *La Novela Policiaca*. The boy set the comic on the counter and said, "Yes, sir?"

"How soon can you develop these?" Campbell asked, shoving the film cartridge toward him.

"*¿Mande?*"

Campbell gripped the edge of the counter. "Ready today?" he asked slowly.

"Tomorrow. This time."

Campbell took a twenty out of his wallet and held it face down on the scarred wood. "This afternoon?"

"*Momentito.*" The boy tapped something out on a computer terminal at his right hand. The dry clatter of the keys filled Campbell with distaste. "Tonight, O.K.?" the boy said. "*A las seis.*" He touched the dial of his watch and said, "Six."

"All right," Campbell said. For another five dollars he bought a pint of Canadian Club, and then he went back onto the street. He felt like a sheet of weakly colored glass, as if the sun shone clear through him. He was a fool, of course, to be taking this kind of chance with the film, but he needed that picture.

He had to know.

He anchored the boat as close as possible to where it had been the night before. He had two fresh tanks and about half the bottle of whiskey left.

Diving drunk and alone was against every rule anyone had ever tried to teach him, but the idea of a simple, clean death by drowning seemed ludicrous to Campbell, not even worth consideration.

His diving jeans and sweatshirt, still damp and salty from the night before, were suffocating him. He got into his tank as quickly as he could and rolled over the side.

The cool water revived him, washed him clean. He purged the air from his vest and dropped straight to the bottom. Dulled by whiskey and lack of sleep, he floundered for a moment in the sand before he could get his buoyancy neutralized.

At the edge of the drop-off he hesitated, then swam to his right, following the edge of the cliff. From his physical condition, he was burning air faster than he wanted to; going deeper would only make it worse.

The bright red of a Coke can winked at him from a coral head. He crushed it and stuck it in his belt, suddenly furious with the company and its casual rape of the island, with himself for letting them manipulate him, with Beth for leaving him, with the entire world and human race. He kicked hard, driving himself through swarms of jack and blue tang, hardly noticing the twisted, brilliantly colored landscape that moved beneath him.

Some of the drunkenness burned off in the first burst of energy, and he gradually slowed, wondering what he possibly could hope to accomplish. It was useless, he thought. He was chasing a phantom. But he didn't turn back.

He was still swimming when he hit the net.

It was nearly invisible, a web of monofilament in one-foot squares, strong enough to hold a shark or a school of porpoises. He tested it with the serrated edge of his diver's knife, with no luck.

He was close to the west end of the island, where the company kept their research facility. The net followed the line of the reef as far down as he could see, and extended out into the open water.

She was real, he thought. They built this to keep her in. But how did she get past it?

When he'd last seen her she'd been heading down. Campbell checked his seaview gauge, saw that he had less than five hundred pounds of air left. Enough to take him down to a hundred feet or so and right back up. The sensible thing to do was to return to the boat and bring a fresh tank back with him.

He went down anyway.

He could see the fine wires glinting as he swam past them.

They seemed bonded to the coral itself, by some process he could not even imagine. He kept his eyes moving between the depth gauge and the edge of the net. Much deeper than a hundred feet and he would have to worry about decompression as well as an empty tank.

At 110 feet he tripped his reserve lever. Three hundred pounds and counting. All the reds had disappeared from the coral, leaving only blues and purples. The water was noticeably darker, colder, and each breath seemed to roar into his lungs like a geiser. Ten more feet, he told himself, and at 125 he saw the rip in the net.

He snagged his backpack on the monofilament and had to back off and try again, fighting panic. He could already feel the constriction in his lungs again, as if he were trying to breathe with a sheet of plastic over his mouth. He'd seen tanks that had been sucked so dry that the sides caved in. They found them on divers trapped in rock-slides and tangled in fishing lines.

His tank slipped free and he was through, following his bubbles upward. The tiny knot of air in his lungs expanded as the pressure around him let up, but not enough to kill his need to breathe. He pulled the last of the air out of the tank and forced himself to keep exhaling, forcing the nitrogen out of his tissues.

At fifty feet he slowed and angled toward a wall of coral, turned the corner, and swam into a sheltered lagoon.

For a few endless seconds he forgot that he had no air.

The entire floor of the lagoon was laid out in squares of greenery—kelp, mosses, and something that looked like giant cabbage. A school of red snappers circled past him, herded by a metal box with a blinking light on the end of one long antenna. Submarines with spindly mechanical arms worked the ocean floor, thinning the vegetation and darkening the water with chemicals. Two or three dolphins were swimming side by side with human divers, and they seemed to be talking to each other.

His lungs straining, Campbell turned his back on them and kicked for the surface, trying to stay as close to the rocks as he could. He wanted to stop for a minute at ten feet, to give at least a nod to decompression, but it wasn't possible. His air was gone.

He broke the surface less than a hundred feet from a concrete dock. Behind him was a row of marker buoys that traced the line of the net all the way out to sea and around the far side of the lagoon.

The dock lay deserted and steaming in the sun. Without a fresh tank, Campbell had no chance of getting out the way he'd come in; if he tried to swim out on the surface, he'd be as conspicuous as a drowning man. He had to find another tank or another way out.

Hiding his gear under a sheet of plastic, he crossed the hot concrete slab to the building behind it, a wide, low warehouse full of wooden crates. A rack of diving gear was built into the left-hand wall, and Campbell was just starting for it when he heard a voice behind him.

"Hey you! Hold it!"

Campbell ducked behind a wall of crates, saw a tiled hallway opening into the back of the building, and ran for it. He didn't get more than three or four steps before a uniformed guard stepped out and pointed a .38 at his chest.

"You can leave him with me."

"Are you sure, Dr. Kimberly?"

"I'll be all right," she said. "I'll call you if there's any trouble."

Campbell collapsed in a plastic chair across from her desk. The office was strictly functional, waterproof, and mildew-resistant. A long window behind Kimberly's head showed the lagoon and the row of marker buoys.

"How much did you see?" she asked.

"I don't know. I saw what looked like farms. Some machinery."

She slid a photograph across the desk to him. It showed a creature with a woman's breasts and the tail of a fish. The face was close enough to Kimberly's to be her sisters.

Or her clone's.

Campbell suddenly realized the amount of trouble he was in.

"The boy at the *farmacia* works for us," Kimberly said.

Campbell nodded. Of course he did. Where else would he get a computer? "You can have the picture," Campbell said, blinking the sweat out of his eyes. "And the negative."

"Let's be realistic," she said, tapping the keys of her CRT and studying the screen. "Even if we let you keep your job, I don't see how we could hold your marriage together. And then you have two kids to put through college...." She shook her head. "Your brain is full of hot information. There are too many people who would pay to have it, and there's just too many ways you can be manipulated. You're not much of a risk, *Mister* Campbell." She radiated hurt and betrayal, and he wanted to slink away from her in shame.

She got up and looked out the window. "We're building the future here," she said. "A future we couldn't even imagine fifteen years ago. And that's just too valuable to let one person screw up. Plentiful food, cheap energy, access to a computer net for the price of a TV set, a whole new form of government—"

"I've seen your future," Campbell said. "Your boats have killed the reef for over a mile around the hotel. Your Coke cans are lying all over the coral beds. Your marriages don't last and your kids are on drugs and your TV is garbage. I'll pass."

"Did you see that boy in the drugstore? He's learning calculus on that computer, and his parents can't even read and write. We're testing a vaccine on human subjects that will probably cure leukemia. We've got laser surgery and transplant techniques that are revolutionary. Literally."

"Is that where *she* came from?" Campbell asked, pointing to the photograph.

Kimberly's voice dropped. "It's synergistic, don't you see? To do the transplants we had to be able to clone cells from the donor. To clone cells we had to have laser manipulation of the genes...."

"They cloned your cells? Just for practice?"

She nodded slowly. "Something happened. She grew, but she stopped developing, kept her embryonic form from the waist down. There was nothing we could do except . . . make the best of it."

Campbell took a longer look at the picture. No, not the romantic myth he had first imagined. The tail was waxy-looking in the harsh light of the strobe, the fins more clearly undeveloped legs. He stared at the photo in queasy fascination. "You could have let her die."

"No. She was mine. I don't have much, and I wouldn't give her up." Kimberly's fists clenched at her sides. "She's not happy, she knows who I am. In her own way I suppose she cares for me." She paused, looking at the floor. "I'm a lonely woman, Campbell. But of course you know that."

Campbell's throat was dry. "What about me?" he rasped, and managed to swallow. "Am I going to die?"

"No," she said. "Not you, either. . . ."

Campbell swam for the fence. His memories were cloudy and he had trouble focusing his thoughts, but he could visualize the gap in the net and the open ocean beyond it. He kicked easily down to 120 feet, the water cool and comforting on his naked skin. Then he was through, drifting gently away from the noise and stink of the island, toward some primal vision of peace and timelessness.

His gills rippled smoothly as he swam.

A Touch of Strange

by

Theodore Sturgeon

Here we are introduced to two very ordinary people who are touched by the magic and romance of the sea—and who respond to that touch of strange in a way that is anything but ordinary. . . .

One of the true giants of the field, the late Theodore Sturgeon was one of the best short-story writers ever to work in the genre; even a partial listing of his short fiction will include major stories that helped to expand the boundaries of the SF story and push it in the direction of artistic maturity: "It," "Microcosmic God," "Killdozer," "Bianca's Hands," "The Other Man," "Maturity," "The Other Celia," and the brilliant "Baby Is Three," one of the best novellas of the fifties. "Baby Is Three" was eventually expanded into Sturgeon's most famous and influential novel, More Than Human. *Sturgeon's other books include the novels* Some of Your Blood, Venus Plus X, The Dreaming Jewels, *and the collections* A Touch of Strange, Caviar, Not Without Sorcery, *and* The Worlds of Theodore Sturgeon. *His most recent book was the collection* The Golden Helix.

* * *

HE LEFT HIS CLOTHES IN THE CAR AND SLIPPED DOWN TO THE beach.

Moonrise, she'd said.

He glanced at the eastern horizon and was informed of nothing. It was a night to drink the very airglow, and the stars lay lightless like scattered talc on the blackground.

"Moonrise," he muttered.

Easy enough for her. Moonrise was something, in her cosmos, that one simply knew about. He'd had to look it up. You

163

don't realize—certainly *she'd* never realize—how hard it is, when you don't know anything about it, to find out exactly what time moonrise is supposed to be, at the dark of the moon. He still wasn't positive, so he'd come early, and would wait.

He shuffled down to the whispering water, finding it with ears and toes. "Woo." Catch m' death, he thought. But it never occurred to him to keep *her* waiting. It wasn't in her to understand human frailties.

He glanced once again at the sky, then waded in and gave himself to the sea. It was chilly, but by the time he had taken ten of the fine strong strokes which had first attracted her, he felt wonderful. He thought, oh well, by the time I've learned to breathe under water, it should be no trick at all to find moonrise without an almanac.

He struck out silently for the blackened and broken teeth of rock they call Harpy's Jaw, with their gums of foam and the floss of tide-risen weed bitten up and hung for the birds to pick. It was oily calm everywhere but by the Jaw, which mumbled and munched on every wave and spit the pieces into the air. He was therefore very close before he heard the singing. What with the surf and his concentration on flanking the Jaw without cracking a kneecap the way he had that first time, he was in deep water on the seaward side before he noticed the new quality in the singing. Delighted, he trod water and listened to be sure; and sure enough, he was right.

It sounded terrible.

"Get your flukes out of your mouth," he bellowed joyfully, "you baggy old guano-guzzler."

"You don't sound so hot yourself, chum," came the shrill falsetto answer, "and you know what type fish-gut *chum* I mean."

He swam closer. Oh, this was fine. It wasn't easy to find a for-real something like this to clobber her with. Mostly, she was so darn perfect, he had to make it up whole, like the time he told her her eyes weren't the same color. Imagine, he thought, *they* get head-colds too! And then he thought, well, why not? "You mind your big bony bottom-feeding mouth," he called cheerfully, "or I'll curry your tail with a scaling-tool." He could barely make her out, sprawled on the narrow seaward ledge— something piebald dark in the darkness. "Was that really you singin' or are you sitting on a blow-fish?"

"You creak no better'n a straight-gut skua gull in a sewer

sump," she cried raucously. "Whyn'cha swallow that sea-slug or spit it out, one?"

"Ah, go soak your head in a paddlewheel," he laughed. He got a hand on the ledge and heaved himself out of the water. Instantly there was a high-pitched squeak and a clumsy splash, and she was gone. The particolored mass of shadow-in-shade had passed him in midair too swiftly for him to determine just what it was, but he knew with a shocked certainty what it was not.

He wriggled a bare (*i.e.*, mere) buttock-clutch on the short narrow shelf of rock and leaned over as far as he could to peer into the night-stained sea. In a moment there was a feeble commotion and then a bleached oval so faint that he must avert his eyes two points to leeward like a sailor seeing a far light, to make it out at all. Again, seeing virtually nothing, he could be sure of the things it was not. That close cap of darkness, night or no night, was not the web of floating gold for which he had once bought a Florentine comb. Those two dim blotches were not the luminous, over-long, widespaced (almost side-set) green eyes which, laughing, devoured his sleep. Those hints of shoulders were not broad and fair, but slender. That salt-spasmed weak sobbing cough was unlike any sound he had heard on these rocks before; and the (by this time) unnecessary final proof was the narrow hand he reached for and grasped. It was delicate, not splayed; it was unwebbed; its smoothness was that of the plum and not the articulated magic of a fine wrought golden watchband. It was, in short, human, and for a long devastated moment their hands clung together while their minds, in panic, prepared to do battle with the truth.

At last they said in unison, "But you're not—"

And let a wave pass, and chorused, "I didn't know there was anybod—"

And opened and closed their mouths, and said together, "Y'see, I was waiting for—" "Look!" he said abruptly, because he had found something he could say that she couldn't at the moment. "Get a good grip, I'll pull you out. Ready? One, two—"

"No!" she said, outraged, and pulled back abruptly. He lost her hand, and down she went in mid-gasp, and up she came strangling. He reached down to help, and missed, though he brushed her arm. "Don't touch me!" she cried, and doggy-paddled frantically to the rock on which he sat, and got a hand on it. She hung there coughing until he stirred, whereupon: "Don't touch me!" she cried again.

"Well all right," he said in an injured tone.

She said, aloud but obviously to herself, "Oh, *dear...*"

Somehow this made him want to explain himself. "I only thought you should come out, coughing like that, I mean it's silly you should be bobbing around in the water and I'm sitting up here on the—" He started a sentence about he was only trying to be—, and another about he was *not* trying to be—, and was unable to finish either. They stared at one another, two panting sightless blots on a spume-slick rock.

"The way I was talking before, you've got to understand—"

They stopped as soon as they realized they were in chorus again. In a sudden surge of understanding he laughed—it was like relief—and said, "You mean that you're not the kind of girl who talks the way you were talking just before I got here. I believe you. . . . And I'm not the kind of guy who does it either. I thought you were a—thought you were someone else, that's all. Come on out. I won't touch you."

"Well . . ."

"I'm still waiting for the—for my friend. That's all."

"Well . . ."

A wave came and she took sudden advantage of it and surged upward, falling across the ledge on her stomach. "I'll manage, I'll manage," she said rapidly, and did. He stayed where he was. They stayed where they were in the hollow of the rock, out of the wind, four feet apart, in darkness so absolute that the red of tight-closed eyes was a lightening.

She said, "Uh . . ." and then sat silently masticating something she wanted to say, and swallowing versions of it. At last: "I'm not trying to be nosy."

"I didn't think you . . . Nosy? You haven't asked me anything."

"I mean staying here," she said primly. "I'm not just trying to be in the way, I mean. I mean, I'm waiting for someone too."

"Make yourself at home," he said expansively, and then felt like a fool. He was sure he had sounded cynical, sarcastic, and unbelieving. Her protracted silence made it worse. It became unbearable. There was only one thing he could think of to say, but he found himself unaccountably reluctant to bring out into the open the only possible explanation for her presence here. His mouth asked (as it were) while he wasn't watching it, inanely, "Is your uh friend coming out in uh a boat?"

"Is your?" she asked shyly; and suddenly they were laughing together like a brace of loons. It was one of those crazy sessions people will at times find themselves conducting, laughing explosively, achingly, without a specific punchline over which to hang the fabric of the situation. When it had spent itself, they sat quietly. They had not moved nor exchanged anything, and yet they now sat together, and not merely side by side. The understood attachment to someone—something—else had paradoxically dissolved a barrier between them.

It was she who took the plunge, exposed the Word, the code attachment by which they might grasp and handle their preoccupation. She said, dreamily, "I never saw a mermaid."

And he responded, quite as dreamily but instantly too: "Beautiful." And that was question and answer. And when he said, "I never saw a—" she said immediately, "Beautiful." And that was reciprocity. They looked at each other again in the dark and laughed, quietly this time.

After a friendly silence, she asked, "What's her name?"

He snorted in self-surprise. "Why, I don't know. I really don't. When I'm away from her I think of her as *she,* and when I'm with her she's just . . . *you.* Not you," he added with a childish giggle.

She gave him back the giggle and then sobered reflectively. "Now that's the strangest thing. I don't know *his name* either. I don't even know if they have names."

"Maybe they don't need them. She—uh—they're sort of different, if you know what I mean. I mean, they know things we don't know, sort of . . . feel them. Like if people are coming to the beach, long before they're in sight. And what the weather will be like, and where to sit behind a rock on the bottom of the sea so a fish swims right into their hands."

"And what time's moonrise."

"Yes," he said, thinking, you suppose they know each other? you think they're out there in the dark watching? you suppose *he'll* come first, and what will he say to me? Or what if *she* comes first?

"I don't think they need names," the girl was saying. "They know one person from another, or just who they're talking about, by the feel of it. What's your name?"

"John Smith," he said. "Honest to God."

She was silent, and then suddenly giggled.

He made a questioning sound.

"I bet you say 'Honest to God' like that every single time you tell anyone your name. I bet you've said it thousands and thousands of times," she said.

"Well, yes. Nobody ever noticed it before, though."

"I would. My name is Jane Dow. Dee owe doubleyou, not Doe."

"Jane Dow. Oh! and you have to spell it out like that every single time?"

"Honest to God," she said, and they laughed.

He said, "John Smith, Jane Dow. Golly. Pretty ordinary people."

"Ordinary. You and your mermaid."

He wished he could see her face. He wondered if the merpeople were as great a pressure on her as they were on him. He had never told a soul about it—who'd listen?

Who'd believe? Or, listening, believing, who would not interfere? Such a wonder . . . and had she told all her girlfriends and boyfriends and the boss and what-not? He doubted it. He could not have said why, but he doubted it.

"Ordinary," he said assertively, "yes." And he began to talk, really talk about it because he had not, because he had to. "That has a whole lot to do with it. Well, it has everything to do with it. Look, nothing ever happened in my whole entire life. Know what I mean? I mean, nothing. I never skipped a grade in school and I never got left back. I never won a prize. I never broke a bone. I was never rich and never hungry. I got a job and kept it and I won't ever go very high in the company and I won't ever get canned. You know what I mean?"

"Oh, yes."

"So then," he said exultantly, "along comes this mermaid. I mean, to *me* comes a mermaid. Not just a glimpse, no maybe I did and maybe I didn't see a mermaid: this is a real live mermaid who wants me back again, time and again, and makes dates and keeps 'em too, for all she's all the time late."

"So is *he*," she said in intense agreement.

"What I call it," he said, leaning an inch closer and lowering his voice confidentially, "is a touch of strange. A touch of strange. I mean, that's what I call it to myself, you see? I mean, a person is a person all his life, he's good to his mother, he never gets arrested, if he drinks too much he doesn't get in trouble he just gets, excuse the expression, sick to his stomach. He does a day's good work for a day's pay and nobody hates him or, for that matter, nobody likes him either. Now a man like that has no *life;* what I mean, he isn't *real*. But just take an ordinary guy-by-the-millions like that, and add a touch of strange, you see? Some little something he does, or has, or that happens to him, even once. Then for all the rest of his life he's *real*. Golly. I talk too much."

"No you don't. I think that's real nice, Mr. Smith. A touch of strange. A touch . . . you know, you just told the story of my life. Yes you did. I was born and brought up and went to school and got a job all right there in Springfield, and—"

"*Spring*field? You mean Springfield Massa*chu*setts? That's my town!" he blurted excitedly, and fell off the ledge into the sea. He came up instantly and sprang up beside her, blowing like a manatee.

"Well no," she said gently. "It was Springfield, Illinois."

"Oh," he said, deflated.

She went on, "I wasn't ever a pretty girl, what you'd call, you know, pretty. I wasn't repulsive either, I don't mean that. Well, when they had the school dances in the gymnasium, and they told all the boys to go one by one and choose a partner, I never got to be the first one. I was never the last one left either, but sometimes I was *afraid* I'd be. I got a job the day after I graduated from high school. Not a good one, but not bad, and I still work there. I like some people more than other people, but not very much, you know? . . . A touch of strange. I always knew there was a name for the thing I never had, and you gave it a good one. Thank you, Mr. Smith."

"Oh that's all right," he said shyly. "And anyway, you have it now . . . how was it you happened to meet your . . . him, I mean?"

"Oh, I was scared to *death*, I really was. It was the company picnic, and I was swimming, and I—well, to tell you the actual truth, if you'll forgive me, Mr. Smith, I had a strap on my bathing suit that was, well, slippy. Please, I don't mean too *bad*, you know, or I wouldn't ever have worn it. But I was uncomfortable about it, and I just slipped around the rocks here to fix it and . . . there he was."

"In the daytime?"

"With the sun on him. It was like . . . like . . . There's nothing it was like. He was just lying here on this very rock, out of the water. Like he was waiting for me. He didn't try to get away or look surprised or anything, just lay there smiling. Waiting. He has a beautiful soft big voice and the longest green eyes, and long golden hair."

"Yes, yes. *She* has, too."

"He was so beautiful. And then all the rest, well, I don't have to tell *you*. Shiny silver scales and the big curvy flippers."

"Oh," said John Smith.

"I was scared, oh yes. But not *afraid*. He didn't try to come near me and I sort of knew he couldn't ever hurt me . . . and then he spoke to me, and I promised to come back again, and I did, a lot, and that's the story." She touched his shoulder gently and embarrassedly snatched her hand away. "I never told anyone before. Not a single living soul," she whispered. "I'm so glad to be able to talk about it."

"Yeah." He felt insanely pleased. "Yeah."

"How did you . . ."

He laughed. "Well, I have to sort of tell something on myself. This swimming, it's the only thing I was ever any good at, only I never found out until I was grown. I mean, we had no swimming pools and all that when I went to school. So I never show off about it or anything, I just swim when there's nobody around much. And I came here one day, it was in the evening in summer when most everyone had gone home to dinner, and I swam past the reef line, way out away from the Jaw, here. And there's a place there where it's only a couple of feet deep and I hit my knee."

Jane Dow inhaled with a sharp sympathetic hiss.

Smith chuckled. "Now I'm not one for bad language. I mean I never feel right about using it. But you hear it all the time, and I guess it sticks without you knowing it. So sometimes when I'm by myself and bump my head or what-not I hear this rough talk, you know, and I suddenly realize it's me doing it. And that's what happened this day, when I hurt my knee. I mean, I really hurt it. So I sort of scrounched down holding on to my knee and I like to boil up the water for a yard around with what I said. I didn't know anyone was around or I'd never.

"And all of a sudden there she was, laughing at me. She came porpoising up out of deep water to seaward of the reef and jumped up into that sunlight, the sun was low then, and red; and she fell flat on her back loud as your tooth breaking on a cherry-pit. When she hit, the water rose up all around her, and for that one second she lay in it like something in a jewel box, you know, pink satin all around and her deep in it.

"I was that hurt and confused and startled I couldn't believe what I saw, and I remember thinking this was some la—I mean, woman, girl like you hear about, living the life and bathing in the altogether. And I turned my back on her to show her what I thought of that kind of goings-on, but looking over my shoulder to see if she got the message, and I thought then I'd made it all up, because there was nothing there but her suds where she splashed, and they disappeared before I really saw them.

"About then my knee gave another twinge and I looked down and saw it wasn't just bumped, it was cut too and bleeding all down my leg, and only when I heard her laughing louder than I was cussing did I realize what I was saying. She swam round and round me, laughing, but you know? there's a way of laughing *at* and a way of laughing *with*, and there was no bad feeling in what she was doing.

"So I forgot my knee altogether and began to swim, and I think she liked that; she stopped laughing and began to sing, and it was..." Smith was quiet for a time, and Jane Dow had nothing to say. It was as if she were listening for that singing, or to it.

"She can sing with anything that moves, if it's alive, or even if it isn't alive, if it's big enough, like a storm wind or neaptide rollers. The way she sang, it was to my arms stroking the water and my hands cutting it, and me in it, and being scared and wondering, the way I was ... and the water on me, and the blood from my knee, it was all what she was singing, and before I knew it it was all the other way round, and I was swimming to what she sang. I think I never swam in my life the way I did then, and may never again, I don't know; because there's a way of moving where every twitch and wiggle is exactly right, and does twice what it could do before; there isn't a thing in you fighting anything else of yours...." His voice trailed off.

Jane Dow sighed.

He said, "She went for the rocks like a torpedo and just where she had to bash her brains out, she churned up a fountain of white-water and shot out of the top of it and up on the rocks—right where she wanted to be and not breathing hard at all. She reached her hand into a crack without stretching and took out a big old comb and began running it through her hair, still humming that music and smiling at me like—well, just the way you said *he* did, waiting, not ready to run. I swam to the rocks and climbed up and sat down near her, the way she wanted."

Jane Dow spoke after a time, shyly, but quite obviously from a conviction that in his silence Smith had spent quite enough time on these remembered rocks. "What . . . did she want, Mr. Smith?"

Smith laughed.

"Oh," she said. "I do beg your pardon. I shouldn't have asked."

"Oh please," he said quickly, "it's all right. What I was laughing about was that she should pick on me—me of all people in the world—" He stopped again, and shook his head invisibly. No, I'm not going to tell her about that, he decided. Whatever she thinks about me is bad enough. Sitting on a rock half the night with a mermaid, teaching her to cuss . . . He said, "They have a way of getting you to do what they want."

It is possible, Smith found, even while surf whispers virtually underfoot, to detect the cessation of someone's breathing; to be curious, wondering, alarmed, then relieved as it begins again, all without hearing it or seeing anything. *What'd I say?* he thought, perplexed; but he could not recall exactly, except to be sure he had begun to describe the scene with the mermaid on the rocks, and had then decided against it and said something or other else instead. Oh. Pleasing the mermaid. "When you come right down to it," he said, "they're not hard to please. Once you understand what they want."

"Oh yes," she said in a controlled tone. "I found that out."

"You did?"

Enough silence for a nod from her.

He wondered what pleased a merman. He knew nothing about them—nothing. His mermaid liked to sing and to be listened to, to be watched, to comb her hair, and to be cussed at. "And whatever it is, it's worth doing," he added, "because when they're happy, they're happy up to the sky."

"Whatever it is," she said, disagreeably agreeing.

A strange corrosive thought drifted against his consciousness. He batted it away before he could identify it. It was

strange, and corrosive, because of his knowledge of and feeling
for his mermaid. There is a popular conception of what joy
with a mermaid might be, and he had shared it—if he had
thought of mermaids at all—with the populace . . . up until the
day he met one. You listen to mermaids, watch them, give
them little presents, cuss at them, and perhaps learn certain
dexterities unknown, or forgotten, to most of us, like breathing
under water—or, to be more accurate, storing more oxygen
than you thought you could, and finding still more (however
little) extractable from small amounts of water admitted to your
lungs and vaporized by practiced contractions of the diaphragm,
whereby some of the dissolved oxygen could be coaxed out of
the vapor. Or so Smith had theorized after practicing certain
of the mermaid's ritual exercises. And then there was fishing
to be eating, and fishing to be fishing, and hypnotizing eels,
and other innocent pleasures.

But innocent.

For your mermaid is as oviparous as a carp, though rather
more mammalian than an echidna. Her eggs are tiny, but hon-
ored mammalian precedent, and in their season are placed in
their glittering clusters (for each egg looks like a tiny pearl
embedded in a miniature moonstone) in secret, guarded grottos,
and cared for with much ritual. One of the rituals takes place
after the eggs are well rafted and have plated themselves to the
inner lip of their hidden nest; and this is the finding and courting
of a merman to come and, in the only way he can, father the
eggs.

This embryological sequence, unusual though it may be, is
hardly unique in complexity in a world which contains such
marvels as the pelagic phalange of the cephalopods and the
simultaneity of disparate appetites exhibited by certain arach-
nids. Suffice it to say, regarding mermaids, that the legendary
monosyllable of greeting used by the ribald Indian is answered
herewith; and since design follows function in such matters,
one has a guide to one's conduct with the lovely creatures, and
they, brother, with you, and with you, sister.

"So gentle," Jane Dow was saying, "but then, so rough."

"Oh?" said Smith. The corrosive thought nudged at him.
He flung it somewhere else, and it nudged him there, too. . . .
It was at one time the custom in the Old South to quiet babies
by smearing their hands liberally with molasses and giving them

a chicken feather. Smith's corrosive thought behaved like such a feather, and pass it about as he would he could not put it down.

The mer*man* now, he thought wildly..."I suppose," said Jane Dow, "I really am in no position to criticize."

Smith was too busy with his figurative feather to answer.

"The way I talked to you when I thought you were . . . when you came out here. Why, I never in my life—"

"That's all right. You heard *me*, didn't you?" Oh, he thought, suddenly disgusted with himself, it's the same way with her and her friend as it is with me and mine. Smith, you have an evil mind. This is a nice girl, this Jane Dow.

It never occurred to him to wonder what was going through her mind. Not for a moment did he imagine that she might have less information on mermaids than he had, even while he yearned for more information on mermen.

"They *make* you do it," she said. "You just have to. I admit it; I lie awake nights thinking up new nasty names to call him. It makes him so happy. And he loves to do it too. The . . . things he says. He calls me 'alligator bait.' He says I'm his squashy little bucket of roe. Isn't that awful? He says I'm a milt-and-water type. What's milt, Mr. Smith?"

"I can't say," hoarsely said Smith, who couldn't, making a silent resolution not to look it up. He found himself getting very upset. She seemed like such a nice girl. . . . He found himself getting angry. She unquestionably *had* been a nice girl.

Monster, he thought redly. "I wonder if it's moonrise yet."

Surprisingly she said, "Oh dear. Moonrise."

Smith did not know why, but for the first time since he had come to the rock, he felt cold. He looked unhappily seaward. A ragged, wistful, handled phrase blew by his consciousness: *save her from herself*. It made him feel unaccountably noble.

She said faintly, "Are you . . . have you . . . I mean, if you don't mind my asking, you don't have to tell me . . ."

"What is it?" he asked gently, moving close to her. She was huddled unhappily on the edge of the shelf. She didn't turn to him, but she didn't move away.

"Married, or anything?" she whispered.

"Oh gosh no. Never. I suppose I had hopes once or twice, but no, oh gosh no."

"Why not?"

"I never met a... well, they all... You remember what I said about a touch of strange?"

"Yes, yes..."

"Nobody had it.... Then I got it, and... put it this way, I never met a girl I could tell about the mermaid."

The remark stretched itself and lay down comfortably across their laps, warm and increasingly audible, while they sat and regarded it. When he was used to it, he bent his head and turned his face toward where he imagined hers must be, hoping for some glint of expression. He found his lips resting on hers. Not pressing, not cowering. He was still, at first from astonishment, and then in bliss. She sat up straight with her arms braced behind her and her eyes wide until his mouth slid away from hers. It was a very gentle thing.

Mermaids love to kiss. They think it excruciatingly funny. So Smith knew what it was like to kiss one. He was thinking about that while his lips lay still and sweetly on those of Jane Dow. He was thinking that the mermaid's lips were not only cold, but dry and not completely flexible, like the carapace of a soft-shell crab. The mermaid's tongue, suited to the eviction of whelk and the scything of kelp, could draw blood. (It never had, but it could.) And her breath smelt of fish.

He said, when he could, "What were you thinking?"

She answered, but he could not hear her.

"What?"

She murmured into his shoulder, "His teeth all point inwards."

Aha, he thought.

"John," she said suddenly, desperately, "there's one thing you must know now and forever more. I know just how things were between you and *her,* but what you have to understand is that it wasn't the same with me. I want you to know the truth right from the very beginning, and now we don't need to wonder about it or talk about it ever again."

"Oh you're fine," John Smith choked. "So fine.... Let's go. Let's get out of here before—before moonrise."

Strange how she fell into the wrong and would never know it (for they never discussed it again), and forgave him and drew from that a mightiness; for had she not defeated the most lawless, the loveliest of rivals?

Strange how he fell into the wrong and forgave her, and

drew from his forgiveness a lasting pride and a deep certainty of her eternal gratitude.

Strange how the moon had risen long before they left, yet the mermaid and the merman never came at all, feeling things as they strangely do.

And John swam in the dark sea slowly, solicitous, and Jane swam, and they separated on the dark beach and dressed, and met again at John's car, and went to the lights where they saw each other at last; and when it was time, they fell well and truly in love, and surely that is the strangest touch of all.

Something Rich and Strange

by

Randall Garrett

and Avram Davidson

Avram Davidson, whose "The Prevalence of Mermaids" appears elsewhere in this book, is one of SF and fantasy's most distinguished authors, and has been widely hailed as one of the finest short-story writers of our times. (For a more complete biographical sketch, see the headnote to "The Prevalence of Mermaids.")

Randall Garrett is probably best known as the author of the popular "Lord Darcy" stories, which successfully blend the mystery story with fantasy (creating a detective who uses magic as one of his criminological tools), and which are set in an alternate twentieth century world where magic works and the Plantagenet Emperor John IV rules a widespread and prosperous Anglo-French Empire upon which the sun has never set. The "Lord Darcy" series includes the well-known novel Two Many Magicians, *and the short-story collections* Murder and Magic *and* Lord Darcy Investigates. *Garrett is also the author, along with wife Vicky Ann Heydron, of the* Gandalara Cycle *series, consisting of* The Steel of Raithskar, The Glass of Dyskornis, *the* Bronze of Eddarta, *and, most recently,* The Search For Ka. *His short fiction has been collected in* The Best of Randall Garrett.

Here—in what is, as far as we know, their only collaboration—Davidson and Garrett suggest that there is sometimes a cavernous gap between the Ideal and the Actual, but also that maybe you don't really know what you're looking for until you find it....

* * *

IF JACK WILSON'S CURIOUS VOYAGE DID NOT EXACTLY REVEAL to him what song the sirens sang, it was satisfactory in other respects.

The specialist all too often finds that he has developed his taste to such a point that he is satisfied but rarely, and excited almost never. Since the recent trouble in Tibet, for example, it is impossible to get a really properly prepared yak roast. The smaller animal of the same name, from Sikkim and Nepal, is not only deficient in marbling, but is generally fibrous and watery. There are many long faces and rumbling bellies around the old Lhassa Club in Darjeeling nowadays.

Jack Wilson, however, is a seafood specialist, and for gourmets of this kidney there is a single ray of bright light shining through the foul fog of flaccid flounder fillets that are standard Friday fare throughout the country, a single escape route from curdled shrimp in greasy batter. Knowers and lovers of seafood will recognize at once that we refer to the *J & M Seafood Grotto*, a place containing not a single ketchup bottle, and whose very slices of lemon are not the coarse, ordinary sort, but the rare and delicate Otaheite variety, from a little grove somewhere in Georgia.

Pardon us; no. We will not tell you where the *J & M Grotto* is, beyond the fact that it is only a few hundred feet from the shore of the Pacific, at the aft end of a wharf somewhere between Coronado and Nootka Sound—which is enough shoreline for anyone to search. It is doubtful whether any true seafood man will tell you where it is, either, unless you are known to him, not only as a friend, but as a fellow *aficionado*.

Nor do the proprietors of the *Grotto* advertise; they do not want customers who cannot appreciate their savory wares, and they do not lack for those who do.

And no man appreciates those wares more than Jack Wilson.

He is not one of your *Guide to* gourmets. Wine-mumblers and all their arcane habble-gabble he classifies with Turkish water-tasters, tea-tipplers, and other nuts and phonies. Beer he regards as most appropriate to wash the hair of women of a certain class. Women—of all classes—he loves. Also, seafood.

Now, the love of seafood, like the love of women, can lead a man into strange situations, and Jack Wilson, who combined these loves in a very literal way, managed to get himself into a situation which . . .

It would be easier to begin at the beginning.

Jack loves the food at the *J & M Seafood Grotto* as much as, if not more than, anyone else; but ten years ago, the *Grotto* did not exist, and Jack spent a good deal of his time traveling on faërie seas and delighting in the fruits thereof. The War—in which he had done his part—had been over only slightly more than half a decade, and the world economy, insofar as pelagic goodies were concerned, had not yet returned to its prewar norm. Russian caviar, to be sure, had begun to trickle back into the world market, but, owing to the tragically unsettled conditions in Azerbaijan and the Trans-Kur, beluga fisheries in the *western* Caspian were a mere shadow of their former selves; and the good gray roe obtained from the capacious bellies of the sea-sturgeons which frequent the *eastern* reaches of that water lack, as all the world knows, a certain degree of delicacy.

There was some compensation in Jack Wilson's knowing a small, weathered shed near New Smyrna where smoked mullet—fit for gods and Texas oilmen—was to be had.

Too, ever since the Kuomintang government had lost the Mandate of Heaven (except for Formosa, Matsu, and Quemoy), the small but suavely flavored shrimp—some say they are prawns, but no matter—found only at the spot where the Gulf of Po Hai disembogues into the Yellow Sea, were no longer to be had at any price. At least, not at any price Jack Wilson was prepared to pay.

Cost was of little consequence to him; he was of what are tritely described as "independent means," which is to say he could spend much, much money without engaging in the tedious task of working for it.

So it was that, except for the thalassic victuals indigenous to the Communist-controlled areas of the world, Jack was not forced to rely on the vagaries of the export-import trade; whither went the wind and water, there went Wilson. Manga-reva knew him, and the shoals of Capricorn. The great sea-turtle's watery epithalamion enchanted him, and so did its green soup. In a tiny fishing village on the coast of Dalmatia, whose name contained seven letters, six of which were consonants, he discovered and delighted in a small, pink squid seethed in its own sepia. He found four wonderful ways of preparing the rare and tiny mauve crab of the Laccadive Islands, all of which required it to be sautéed in ghee. He learned that *baccalà*—that dried codfish which, in shape, texture, and, for that matter, flavor, is not unlike an old washboard—when prepared with *cibbolini*, sea-urchin sauce, and olive oil of the first pressing, will take the mind of even a Sicilian *signoretto* off the subject of nubile servant girls, for a short time.

And he was infinitely appreciative of that exquisite forcemeat of pike, whitefish, and carp, lovingly poached in court bouillon, which the dispersed of Minsk and Pinsk have made known to continents and archipelagoes alike as gefilte fish.

Let it not be thought, though, that Jack Wilson's entire field of endeavor to satisfy the inner man was circumscribed by his search for gustatorial novelties or staples in the seafood line. Seafood was his *specialty*. But he shared with all men those tastes in which all men worthy of the name delight. However, although Jack was well-versed in venery and found it enjoyable, invigorating and worthwhile, it presented little challenge. A man who possesses reasonable intelligence, an amiable disposition, excellent health, a pleasing countenance, and a six-figure bank balance seldom really needs to *chase* women.

That Our Jack had never married was due to nothing so juvenile as "not wanting to give up his freedom"; nor did he have any basic objection to the institution as such. He felt, with some mild degree of certitude, that he would—some day—marry, and from this prospect he had no urge to shrink. But . . . somehow . . . whatever it was that he was looking for in a wife, he had yet to find a woman who seemed to have it.

He recalled the Mexican aphorism that "one must feed the body in order that the soul may live in it"; and, hence, food—and its preparation and consumption—always seemed to him to partake of a spiritual as well as a physical and social quality. An intelligent and appreciative interest in victualry made, in Wilson's view, all the difference between dining and mere feeding. The more a woman showed a genuine interest in the food he chose for the two of them, the more genuine was his own interest in her; an extra dimension was supplied their friendship. Alas! for the ugly advance of ready-mixed, frozen, tinned, and pre-cooked rations: Jack Wilson had rarely met a woman who was his equal in the kitchen, and few who were not infinitely his inferior.

Wilson's peregrinations were usually aboard his own vessels—for, as a lover of the dolphin-torn sea itself, he possessed a diesel-powered yacht fully capable of braving a stormy At-

lantic—and it can be realized that many a weekend, and sometimes many a week, was passed with pleasure and profit on
the bosom of the deep. And the one thing he never disclosed
to any one of the fine selection of prime cuties which he had
squired over seven or eight seas was that he was looking for
something more than perfection in a woman.

As a matter of plain fact, he was looking for a mermaid.

Wilson was quite certain that the mermaid legend was no
legend at all, but simple truth. There had been too many sightings, too many reports from widely scattered spots over the
earth's seas, over too many centuries of human history, to doubt
that such beings had once swum the seas of the planet. And,
as far as Jack Wilson was concerned, they were still swimming
them. (For that matter, he had an equally unshakable faith in
the actual existence of the sea serpent—but, then, he had no
desire to *find* a sea serpent.)

It is not to be thought that Jack actually thought of marrying
a mermaid; that would perhaps have been carrying things a bit
too far, especially for a man of his fastidious tastes. He did
not even particularly desire to make love to a mermaid, although the sheer physical mechanics of the process interested
him in a semi-scientific sort of way. What Wilson was actually
pursuing was a dream of beauty. A beatific vision.

The vision was compounded partly from the stuff that dreams
are made of, but it included, as well, some of the more memorable features of some of the more memorable women whom
Wilson had known intimately. And it happened that each of
these hauntingly lovely items in his mind had likened in some
way to the treasures of the sea itself, recasting poetry to do so:

Full fathom five my true love glides ...

His true-love had, to begin, long sun-blonde hair the color
of the golden sands of Trincomalec (Merrilyn Madison, whose
tresses remained in his mind long after the grace-notes of her
body had blended pleasantly with the symphony of a score of
others.) His true-love had teeth like a perfectly matched set of
the finest Bahrein pearls (The Contessa Della Gama; he chose
to forget that those teeth had a particularly nasty bite). His
true-love's eyes were as blue as the Bay of Naples on a summer's day (Marya Amirovna, whose eyes, like the sea, shifted

to gray when a storm was gathering). Her skin was as milky white as the waters which lave the beach at Saipan (Kirsten Jonsdotter, tall, majestic, and passionate). Her bosom was magnificently bifurcate and tipped with coral (Amy, Duchess of Norchester; she of the cool manner and the hot blood). Her . . .

But enough.

Now, each of these women had been, in her own way, as nearly perfect as anything merely human can be. Yet each had failed to satisfy him for long, not because of the presence of any particular flaw, but by the absence of some indefinable quality. And so, in Wilson's mind, over a period of years, his vision of the mermaiden had come to assimilate all the perfections of the women he had known, plus that definition-defying *something*.

He did not, on an intellectual level, consider that every mermaid would resemble his vision. He reasoned that such creatures must vary, one from the other, much as non-pinniped females do. But in his secret imagining—deep, deep, down, full fathom five—he knew that *his* mermaid would be the perfect one.

Alex MacNair, captain of the *Lorelei,* Jack Wilson's yacht, neither believed nor disbelieved in mermaids. He was perfectly willing to believe—if he saw one—but, left to himself, would not have walked to the side to look. Mermaids, he felt, were, like lurlies and kelpies, out of his province. His task was to captain a seagoing vessel. The uses to which that vessel was put were the province of the owner, and Captain MacNair was quite happy with such a division of labor and responsibility. And as for any picturesque devotion to Old Scotland, he limited that to a deep fondness for Ballantine's Twelve Year Old.

He had only once made the mistake of slighting his employer's dream-hobby. It was in Portau-Prince, early in Jack's enthusiasm. "Captain MacNair! Look! A trawler off New Zealand sighted a mermaid, according to the paper!"

The captain had politely taken the proffered journal and read the item slowly, decoding the almost 18th Century elaborateness of the French prose with deliberation while Jack fidgeted at his side.

"Ah!" MacNair said finally, looking up. "Interesting. Very interesting. I tell you what it probably was, Mr. Wilson. Very likely they spotted a dugong. Or a manatee. That's what it was." And he held out the paper as the patronizing smile slowly withered on his face.

"Captain," said Jack, his tone the only chill thing that Haitian noon, "have you ever seen a dugong?"

"I have, sir."

"And your eyesight is good?"

"Twenty-twenty, Mr. Wilson."

"Then tell me: Would *you* ever mistake a dugong for a mermaid? Does a dugong look like a beautiful woman to you?"

MacNair considered his recollection of the dugong. It was somewhat larger than a grown man, and much more visibly mammalian than—say—a porpoise or a whale. From the waist down, the ichthyoid tail, with its horizontal flukes, might have some likeness to the tail of a mermaid, but—from the waist up?

The flippers could never be mistaken for arms, certainly. And that bald, bulging head, with its swollen face and deep-seated eyes and its bristly, lumpy, divided upper lip certainly did not resemble anything human at all.

"Now that I think on it, Mr. Wilson," MacNair conceded, "I do not believe that any sober person could mistake a dugong for a pretty woman."

"Exactly! Not even the most depraved sailor would, or could, make such a mistake."

MacNair was privately of the opinion that his employer had obviously not known as many depraved sailors as he, MacNair, had, but he kept his own counsel, and never again deprecated Wilson's hobby. Ahab had chased whales; Mr. Wilson, mermaids. Mermaids, on the whole, were certainly preferable, being much safer. So was seafood. "A fare day's work for a fair day's pay," was MacNair's motto.

Wilson had long employed a clipping service in New York, another in London, a third in Paris, and, after the war, a fourth in Tokyo, to supply him with mermaid data culled from the periodicals of the world. These clippings were arranged methodically in his leather-bound scrapbooks. Over a period of years, they had expanded into several volumes.

What made Jack Wilson unhappy was that he was always too late. No matter how quickly he got to an area where a mermaid had been sighted—and he had flown on several occasions—the shy creature had always decamped by the time he arrived.

There seemed to be no help for it. The big international news services do not consider mermaid sightings to be real news. Unlike, for example, axe murders and sex circle exposés, they are relegated to the Silliness Files, and are usually a week or two old before they are ever printed. Even then, the reports are used only as fillers, and the details of fact are meager, since most of the space is given over to what Jack considered the dubious wit of the reporter or rewrite man.

Still, all in all, Jack was not a dull boy nor an unhappy one. If the chase had few hazards, yet it was not without spice. More than one worthwhile episode, culinary or amatory, had resulted.

We now come—and it is about time, considering his importance to the resolution of this story—to Professor Milton Rowe. Wilson and Rowe had never been more than nodding, can-I-just-take-a-look-at-your-notes, acquaintances in their undergraduate days at Miskatonic University. In lab and office, he was conscientious, hard-working, sober-sided, and just a little bit dull. He seemed shy, drank little, and was the despair of match-making faculty wives. He was also an ichthyologist.

Jack Wilson had been threading his way, one afternoon, through the old part of Antibes and found himself face to face with a smallish, pleasant sort of man with a receding chin, a large mouth, thick and heavy glasses, and American clothes.

It was the same Rowe that Wilson had known, a decade or so older, and yet very much not the same Rowe at all. Mildly interested in the difference, Jack invited him to join the group aboard the *Lorelei*. It was an invitation for the weekend, but it lasted six weeks. The difference became discernible within six minutes of his being introduced to Michi and Josette.

Like many plain-looking men before him, the professor had discovered that a man does not need the figure of a shot-put champion nor the features of a cinema star to attract and hold the attention of a desirable woman. Charm, wit, and understanding are much more important, and—now that he was far away from the reek of the laboratory, the chalky dryness of the classroom, and the mannered respectability of faculty social life—Professor Milton Rowe could display all three qualities without restraint.

Very few men could get as much out of a vacation as he could.

The *Lorelei*'s passengers embarked for Cythera, and for six weeks they burned upon the waters of the tideless (but certainly not dolorous) midland sea. Michi, Josette, Jack, Milt, the sweet-salt air, the sea itself, a succession of small, little known, and quite charming harbors, fine cognac, golden days, and bright nights . . .

It was with the most agreeable astonishment that Miskatonic's Professor of Marine Biology realized that oceanic life-forms were not only fascinating to study they were good to eat, too!

All four of the passengers were lolling on the decks one afternoon, not fretting their skins with anything more than those bits of fabric called *le minimum,* and drinking something both cool and invigorating from a bottle in an ice bucket.

Professor Rowe, while idly proving to himself once again that the ball of his thumb fit nicely into Josette's comely navel, launched into an exposition of the pelagic peregrinations of the Chinook salmon, at the end of which Josette asked wonderingly: "but, how do you know all zese sings? How do you know where are ze fish—where zey go—so you can study zem?"

"Well, my pet, we have several ways. But we've got a new one now that can accurately predict almost exactly where a given school will be at a given time. Within certain variable limits, that is. We use one of the new electric computers."

Jack, who had been half dozing, suddenly sat up, very interested. "Predict *where* they're *going* to be? How can you, my old?"

His old waved a careless hand. "Well, I cannot give you the details mathematical. In general, it's something like this! We have information on fish migration going back for over a century in some cases. You know the sort of thing, Jack. Fishermen's log books, containing the amount of catch, the date, information on the weather, and things like that. Weather's very important in such matters. And plankton.

"Anyway, all this is converted into a sort of mathematical code and put on punched cards—date, time of day, barometric pressure, wind velocity and direction, temperature of the air and water, kinds and number of fish sighted—" He took a deep breath. "—latitude and longitude, depth of water, direction of current, type of shoreline nearby, if any.

"Oh, and the brightness of the sun and moon, too. Light

has an effect on the depths at which certain fish swim. And then there's the state of the tide, the salinity of the water, and so on and so on.

"We have thousands and thousands of cases, you see," Rowe continued enthusiastically. "We take all that data and put it through the computer, and the damned thing chews it all over and cross-correlates everything with everything else. Get it?

"So that when we want to find out just what fish will be at a given place at a given time, all we have to do is feed in the information on date, time, latitude, longitude, and so forth, and the computer mutters to itself and then goes *chuff!* and pops a card with a lot of holes punched in it. This card is run through a decoding machine, and out comes a list of the kind and number of fish to be found at that exact place and time under those circumstances.

"On the *other* hand, if we want to know where to find a particular kind of fish, the computer will tell us what conditions to look for in what places. You see?"

Jack frowned, concentrating. Josette's smile had by now begun to flag. Michi, a direct actionist, picked up a bottle of suntan oil and tendered it to Jack. He did not seem to see, nor be interested in this offer of the freedom of her gleaming body. He nodded bemusedly. The blue waves danced. He blinked. He glanced around as if suddenly remembering where he was. "Well!" he said. He smiled, and the spell was broken. Michi once again offered the flask of anointing, and this time he took it.

Although offered passage home on the *Lorelei*'s transatlantic run, Milt declined. He didn't believe, he said, in pushing his luck. He returned on a populous Greek passenger ship, growing more and more sedate with each nautical mile, and by the time he had returned to the Miskatonic campus at Arkham he looked and acted the very model of a model ichthyologist.

Wilson made himself busy, once back in New York. He and Captain MacNair had already spent much time going through the scrapbooks and putting down, in tabular form, every bit of information available from the clippings. The next step was to get more data.

Selby Research Associates was prepared to have a stab at finding out anything for anybody who was prepared to pay for it. Selby himself, a lean, scholarly-looking, bearded man, shook

Wilson's hand, waved him to a chair, and raised polite eyebrows in inquiry.

Wilson took a sheaf of papers from his briefcase. "I want some weather reports," he said. "This is a list of ships. Find the exact latitude and longitude of each ship, the date and time given. And I want to know the weather at each time—wind direction, tide conditions, temperature, barometric pressure—everything."

Selby nodded rather absently, knowing that the first thing he intended to check was Wilson's credit rating. "Anything else, Mr. Wilson?"

"Yes. Here's a list of various locations along the coast of a score or more countries. I'll want the same weather information for the dates given, and, if possible, a contour map of the pertinent territory—shore line, and so on."

Selby stroked his beard briefly. He was not a man to resist when Opportunity came to his door with a battering ram. "Did we mention a retainer, Mr. Wilson?" was all his comment.

"How much?"

Selby, who had been thinking of a figure, doubled it, added fifty percent, and said it aloud. Wilson opened his checkbook, wrote. "Begin immediately," he said, handing it over. Selby, taking the check in his two hands as if it were a piece of T'ang chinaware, assured him they would.

Jack made several phone calls with an eye toward furthering the next step in his scheme, and found it more difficult than he'd supposed. In another ten years computers would be as numerous as leaves—fallen or otherwise—in Vallambrosa, but in 1950 they were not so easy to find. Most of the big ones were still in the experimental stage, and it was difficult to find one he could rent or hire.

He was soon convinced that in order to obtain the use of a computer complex enough to do the job he would have to see Rowe.

"Well, now, Jack, I'm not sure," said Milt. "*What* 'sea creature'?"

"Not quite in your line, Milt. A mammal, I think. Relative of the porpoise, perhaps. Or of the dugong or manatee." And he babbled on convincingly, including something about Stellar's Sea Cow (believed extinct since 1715). It was heresy, coarse and rank, and it hurt him. He hoped that the means would be justified by the end he had in mind.

Wilson outlined the data he had on mermaid sightings, without, of course, admitting that it was a mermaid he sought.

Professor Rowe listened intently, but, at the end, he answered with a slow shake of his head. "I'm afraid not, Jack. I'd like to help you, believe me, but the work we're doing will have the computer tied up for the next two years. We couldn't possibly squeeze in a private project like this. After all, we're studying *fish*, not mammals. Now, if you want to give us your data, I can put it in with the rest. It will add to our total data bank. But we couldn't possibly give over time for a rare sea mammal like that."

"Oh," said Wilson, looking downhearted. "Well, that's that, then." After a moment, he brightened. "By the by, Milt, will you be coming to the lecture I'm giving at the Faculty Club?"

"I never miss a meeting of the Faculty Club," the professor said. "What sort of lecture are you giving?"

"Oh, on the sea. Just your sort of thing, really. I'm showing some eight millimeter movies."

"Movies?" Professor Rowe felt suddenly as though a stream of ice water were defying the laws of gravity and flowing *up* his back.

"Yes. You remember. The ones we took this summer."

"You—uh—edited them, of course?" the professor asked weakly.

Wilson looked innocently bland. "Why, no. Haven't had time."

The two men looked into each other's eyes for the space of a full minute.

Then Professor Rowe looked away and sighed. "If you can find time to edit those films, Jack, I believe I can find time in the computer schedule for your project. After all," he said musingly, the light of Pure Science gleaming suddenly in his eyes, "it isn't *really* out of line with the other work we're doing."

"I'm glad you see it that way," Wilson said. "But I don't see why you want to edit the films. They're just the ones we took off Capri with the underwater camera."

Professor Rowe looked at his friend's face and scanned it carefully, almost expectantly, as if examining the mouth for signs of unmelted butter.

The process took somewhat longer than Wilson had anticipated. The vast mass of data (from which he had carefully

edited any mention of the word "mermaid") had to be reduced
to mathematical form. Each one of the hundreds of data factors
had to be assigned a numerical value expressed, not in the
decimal notation of the Arabic system, but in the binary system
used by digital computers.

Then, after the data bits had been translated into numbers,
they had to be carefully encoded as holes in cards measuring
7 and 7/16 inches by 31/4 inches—hundreds and hundreds of
them.

After the first three days, Jack Wilson stopped coming around
to watch; the immediate fascination had worn off and faded
away into monotony.

Finally Professor Rowe informed him that the calculations
had been carried to completion.

The professor's desk was covered with a stack of large sheets
of tracing paper, on each of which was drawn a long, wavy
line which appeared to follow an irregular, elongated series of
dots.

"We've graphed the whole thing, including interpolations
and extrapolations," said Professor Rowe. "Naturally, in a
multidimensional problem such as this, the graphs are necessarily two-dimensional abstracts, but all the information you'll
need is there."

Before Jack could mention the fact that he was unable to
make head or tail of the squiggly lines, the professor riffled
through the pile and extracted a single sheet. As he spread it
out on the top of the pile, he said: "Here's the most important
one, as far as you're concerned. The line follows the migration
pattern chronologically, according to weighted spatial coordinates."

Jack nodded silently.

"Your mammal," the professor went on, "follows this
curve very nicely. Now, as to the extrapolation of the
curve . . . "

He took another sheet of tracing paper from the stack, walked
over to a large Mercator projection of the Earth's surface, and
thumbtacked the tracing paper carefully over the map. For the
first time, Jack Wilson found he could make sense out of the
blue lines.

"They look like shipping routes on a navigational chart,"
he said.

"Don't they, though?" agreed the professor. "The Mediter-
ranean, the Caribbean, both very well traveled up until a few

decades ago. Then the pattern shifts more strongly to the South Pacific, via the Suez Canal and the Indian Ocean. There, the pattern is strongly cyclic, as you can see.

"The animal obviously prefers warmer waters, coming northward, toward the equator, during the winter months of June, July, and August, and heading southward, toward Australia and Oceania during the summer months of December, January, and February."

The professor reached over to his desk and picked up a card, which he handed to Wilson. "Here's the latitude and longitude and dates for the next several months. As you'll see, your best bet is to search the Great Barrier Reef, just off the coast of Queensland."

Jack Wilson took the card and looked at it while visions of sea maidens danced in his head. Rowe, all unknowning, went on, "One of those little islands along there, and the adjacent waters, is where Beast X is most likely to appear."

Wilson looked up, sharply.

"Beast X?"

"That's what we call it down in the computer room," said Rowe. "After all, we had to call it *something,* and 'creature alleged to resemble members of the order *Sirenia*' is rather cumbersome, don't you think?"

And rather incorrect, too, Jack thought. "Beast X" indeed! This lovely creature of the sun-dappled waves and the blue-green depths! Oh, well, anticipation was about to become realization, and little things like this didn't matter at all.

"Milt," he said aloud, "I'm very much obliged to you. You may expect a picture postcard from Queensland . . . and, of course, you're expected to be with us on the *Lorelei* next summer."

The professor nodded abstractedly. He did, indeed, conjecture vision of Summer Past and Summer Yet to Come, void of dumpy, nosy faculty wives and adenoidally virtuous coeds alike; and, in this vision, the gray skies of Arkham were replaced by blue ones in which shone the bright, undying, unconquered Sun, in whose warmth he lay on yellow sands alongside young women with compact but yielding curves and electric fingers. But the vision, though pleasant, was a dim one; as a bear, snug in its stuffy cave of a winter, might dimly dream of fish leaping in streams and bushes heavy with ripe berries.

• • •

"I still don't see, sir," said Captain MacNair gloomily, "why you don't take the helicopter. Seems to me, if you'll pardon my saying so, sir, that it would be a good deal less dangerous."

"Possibly it would, Captain," said Wilson, "but I don't want to frighten off our quarry now that we're this close. Besides, Professor Rowe said that these figures are only approximate. She might not show up for two or three days, and I doubt we could hover that long in a 'copter. No, MacNair; we'll do it my way."

"Very well, sir." The Captain still looked gloomy. "We'll be as close as we can get within the hour, sir."

The plan, as Jack Wilson visualized it, was quite simple. The Great Barrier Reef area was not one where ships of any great draft could move with impunity, and the island which Jack Wilson sought was well within that area. Therefore, the *Lorelei* would stand down as close as possible, and, from there on in, Wilson would go it alone. He had bought a well-built outrigger sailboat for the purpose, and loaded it with provisions, a small outboard motor, and several five-gallon cans of gasoline. Wilson was taking no chances with unfriendly winds, since he had more than forty miles to go from the point where the *Lorelei* would be waiting. As an added precaution, he carried a small, waterproof, two-way radio. In case all did not go well, a call to the *Lorelei* would bring Captain MacNair in the helicopter which had been anchored to the deck of the ship.

At the rendezvous point, Captain MacNair dropped anchor, and the crew began to lower Wilson's outrigger over the side. The sea was relatively calm, and overhead the hot sun of late January poured down upon the sweating men.

"Now, remember," said Wilson finally, just before he went down the ladder to the outrigger that bobbed lazily on the blue waters, "I'll give you a call every six hours." He glanced at the sealed skin diver's wristwatch he was carrying. "If I don't call, get in that 'copter and come a-running. Got it?"

"Yes, sir; I do," said Captain MacNair.

"Good." Wilson clambered down the ladder, boarded the outrigger, and cast free. When the wind caught the sail, he aimed her for her destination, waved toward the *Lorelei*, then concentrated on his course.

Six hours later, he reported to Captain MacNair. "I'm within sight of the island group, Captain. I'll take a look around the smaller islands, but I think I'll beach the boat on the biggest one."

"Very well, sir; but you'd best hurry. Sunset in forty-five minutes."

"Will do."

Wilson felt pretty good, all things considered. He had arrived at high tide, just as he had planned, which meant that all but the highest islands of the Reef were underwater. He had already done some aerial reconnaissance earlier in the month, and found that this particular group of tiny coral islands contained the only island that was both close to the predicted coordinates and large enough to have plants growing on it. It was also a Hell of a long way from any other island of any consequence. It *must* be—it *had* to be—the island where The Mermaid would come.

Already, in his own mind, she had ceased to be simply *"A* mermaid"; she had become *The* Mermaid—with capitals.

All these things buoyed him up. But one thing depressed him. His stomach.

Well, actually, it wasn't his stomach; it was his palate that had been insulted. He had to admit that his stomach was not upset in the least; he felt no queasiness whatever. It had, after all, been more than twenty-four hours since he had eaten that horrible mess, just before the *Lorelei* had left the mainland of Australia.

It was supposed to have been baked shark's fin, and no one else in the little restaurant in Yeereemeeree had noticed anything particularly wrong with it, but to a connoisseur, it had given the impression that the shark had been dredged from the interior of a whale, along with a bumper crop of ambergris and decayed squid. Normally, Jack would have taken a single whiff and shipped the whole thing back to the kitchen by rocket express, but it had been specially selected by Donna Brennan, a lush beauty who had come all the way from Melbourne to see him. He could hardly have refused.

But his insulted taste buds still felt indignant, and that now-faint but still perceptible indignation was the only thing that took the fine edge off Wilson's glow of adventure. In fact, as he sailed around the tiny islands in the vicinity of the larger one, the surge of excitement within him almost completely drowned out the memory of that despicable shark's fin.

Maneuvering the boat required great care; even at high tide, there were places where the jagged surface of the Great Reef was only inches below the top of the water, capable of ripping the bottom out of the boat.

There wasn't a sign of anyone or anything in the area, except for the brightly-colored fish that darted about in the clear waters. The sky, now colored a brassy orange from the reddened rays of the sun as it approached the horizon, was empty. Not a single bird floated overhead. The breeze was barely perceptible, and the only sound was the wash of the waves against the coral crags.

Wilson made his way to the largest island, beached the boat, and dragged it up on the sands. Then he looked around. The island would have delighted any cartoonist. It was somewhat larger, perhaps, than the cartoonist might have liked, since it measured about fifty yards long by thirty wide, and there was a little more vegetation on it than most cartoonists portray, but it certainly showed that tiny islands with a handful of palm trees on them *did* exist.

Wilson was working on the theory that a mermaid would not be frightened by a single, unarmed man. Historical evidence indicated that they avoided big concentrations of humanity, but that a lone individual didn't bother them. At least, Jack Wilson hoped it would work that way.

By the time he had made a complete survey of the island, the last red rim of the sun had sunk beneath the horizon. There was no one there but himself. He gathered armfuls of dried driftwood, scooped out a pit in the gritty coral sand, and built himself a small fire.

His stomach was of two minds. It wanted to be filled, but the memory of that shark's fin rejected the notion of eating just yet. Jack decided to wait until he was really hungry before he put any of the tinned beef or turtle soup into it. Meanwhile, he'd be satisfied with a cup of coffee. It was a remarkable thing, painfully remarkable, how full the sea was of good things to eat and how empty the earth of people capable of cooking them.

Twenty minutes later, he was sipping a cup of hot, black, sweet coffee *à la grecque* and contentedly smoking a cigarette as he gazed into the dancing flicker of the small driftwood fire. It was the only light in a sea of blackness that surrounded him. The night was moonless, and in the clear sky only the stars rivaled the ruddy glow from the sandpit.

How long, he wondered, would it be before The Mermaid showed up? Niggling doubts about her ever showing up he dismissed as too absurd to countenance. Hadn't she been sighted time after time? Weren't her movements so regular as to . . . Just so. Exactly. She would be along. Wilson lay back on his sleeping bag and blew plumes of smoke toward the stars. *Her hair would be long and sun-blonde, her teeth like perfectly matched Bahrain pearls, her eyes as blue as the Bay of Naples on a sunny day, her skin milky white, her breasts . . .*

"Ahum!"

He jerked his head up and looked around. The noise had sounded for all the world like someone clearing his throat. Wilson found that looking at the fire had made him a bit night-blind for the moment. Until his vision cleared . . .

"Ah*hum!*" The noise came again, this time with more persistence. He located its source as being somewhat to the right, near a coral outcropping. He suddenly wished he had brought a gun.

Very cautiously, he said: "Hello?"

"'Ullo, Cocky," came a somewhat diffident voice. "Could you spare a gasper?" The voice was a sort of whiskey tenor, and by now Jack could make out a dimly-lit shape in the flickering fire. Someone was leaning across the low ridge of coral, arms folded, like a friendly bartender. Someone with a light mop of stringy hair. Someone with odd, very odd, skin coloration—great splotches of pink, black, and white, like a piebald pony.

Half-caste abo., Wilson's mind said. *Semi-albinism. Must have seen my light and paddled over creeping around in the dark . . .*

"Who is that?" he asked, trying to peer further into the gloom.

"Me nyme's Mavis." The voice pronounced it *My-vis.* "Wot's yours, Cocky?"

The voice didn't fit in with his vision at all. Not one damn bit. Nor did anything else about the figure. But Jack Wilson's mind jumped straight to one sudden, dreadful conclusion, and his heart gave a truly horrifying leap. "You're a—a *mer*maid?"

"Not 'ardly. Old Mavis eyen't been exactly wotcher might call a *myde* for, oh, ever so long. More wotcher might call a mer-*lydy*—if you tykes me meaning, Cocky." There was a rather coarse giggle. "And now wot about that gasper?"

Wilson's mind felt numb, barely capable of functioning. "Why, sure, Mavis," he heard his voice saying, "but why don't you come over by the fire? I've got some hot coffee, and..." He came to an abrupt halt as he realized how utterly ordinary his voice sounded.

Mavis needed no urging. "Now, that's wot I calls a dinky-doo gent," she said, gratified. "I 'aven't 'ad a good, 'ot cup o' coffee since that narsty little yellerfeller scragged old Joe Kelly, wot used ter fish for trepang in the Torres Straight." As she said this, she heaved herself over the ledge and propelled herself down the sand toward Wilson, fire, and coffee.

He threw on more wood, and he could see her clearly as she came.

There was no longer any doubt that she was of the sea. None. Her method of locomotion, necessitated by the muscular, horizontal-fluked tail which took the place of her legs, was a sort of humping crawl similar to that of a seal. In the flaring firelight, details became clear. Unlike the portrayals of fanciful artists, Mavis did not have a sheath of iridescent scales on her tail; it was covered with thick, tough hide, like that of a dolphin, and was marked in many places by scars.

Her hair, one might say, was blonde, as a mass of unraveled but not unsnarled hempen rope, trailed in weedy seas for countless years, might be said to be blonde. Her teeth might be compared to pearls only if one were speaking of *baroque* pearls—long, irregular, and yellow. Her eyes, it is true, were blue—but not the blue of the Bay of Naples unless the Bay of Naples is sometimes faded and bloodshot. Her breasts were like a couple of half-emptied flour bags which had been misused by dirty hands. And she was, without any possibility of doubt, a mermaid.

Or, at any rate, a mer-lydy.

She stopped near the fire, flipped her tail expertly beneath her, and relaxed into a semi-reclining position. Wilson's innate courtesy brought him partially out of his daze. He picked up the pack of cigarettes from his sleeping bag and offered her one. As she took it, he noticed that the thick, warty fingers had a small web of leathery skin between them, which didn't quite reach the lower joint.

Jack fired up his lighter and proffered the flame. Mavis looked at the cigarette. "Coo-ee! A blinkin' *Sobranie!* You *are* a toff, *you* are." She puffed it alight and smiled at him—the smile which one sees on the face of a more-than-middle-aged, unsuccessful, but ever-optimistic prostitute. It was not exactly a leer, but it was well on its way to becoming one.

Wilson snapped out the light and busied himself with the coffee pot. "Cream?" he asked bleakly.

"'F'you please," Mavis said daintily—an effect somewhat marred by an enormous burp that seemed to have all three hundred pounds of her behind it. She looked embarrassed. "Eel," she explained. "It *will* repeat, you know. Carn't stop it. Many's the time I says to me self, 'Now, Mavis, no eel!' But, then, wot's life if you've always got to be a-dieting, eh? 'A bit of wotcher fancy does yer good' is my motto. *Erp.*"

Jack winced. "Sugar?" he asked, in a low, stricken voice.

"Four spoonsful. I do like my bit of sweet, and it's seldom I gets it nowadyes, people bein' the wye they are. Why, the sea itself eyen't syfe no more—all them perishin' skin-divers! Bleedin' lot of liberty-tykers is wot *they* are!" Resentfully, she fingered a newish scar on her tail. "I used to *love* the Pacific afore all them ruddy bombs . . ."

Wilson handed her the coffee. Close up, the fish odor was even stronger. She took it with a resounding *"Ngkyew!"* and, little finger stuck out, she slurped appreciatively. "Ah, that's good! See, it's all right as long as you styes in the bleedin' water, but if you comes out of an evening, that breeze gives you summat of a chill, it does. And 'oo wants to be took sick 'ere, miles from bloody woof-woof?" Another slurp. "Ahhhhhh."

Wilson's paralyzed mind was reacting almost automatically. "Glad you liked it. I don't suppose you get much coffee."

She gave a great, gusty, fish-laden sigh. "No, myte, I don't, and that's a fact. It eyen't like it used ter be. 'Ere I am, still in me prime, and there's 'ardly nuffink to look forward to." Few females need much encouragement to talk; Mavis needed none. Her remarks were mostly of a plaintive nature, ranging from fresh-water swimming ("I styes clear o' rivers nowadyes, Cock. Orl this pollution mucking up the plyce—some of the things yer sees floatin abaht, why, it fair brings the blush to me cheeks!") to the fun she used to have riding along in the bow wave of a sailing vessel ("Carn't tyke chances like that no more; if some idjit don't tyke a shot at you wiv a bleedin' rifle, you still runs a risk of gettin' yer arse snagged in the screw!") When she finally reached the Summing Up, she had disposed of four cups of coffee and half of the Sobranies.

"No, Cocky, I tell you," she said reflectively, drawing in a mouthful of smoke with a wet, smacking sound, "mag all you wants to, but this mermyde gyme 'as 'ad it. Why, tyke Boro-Boro an' all them other bleedin' 'eathen islands: Used ter come out in wackin' big canoes, the buggers did, first full moon arfter the flippin' solstices, all chantin' an' racketin' an' wyvin' torches to welcome me. *"Gryte Sea Muvver 'Oo Fills Our Nets Wiv Fish'* and all that palaver, y'know—fling cocoanuts, yams, 'ot taros, and 'ole roasted pigs into the old briny—then back to the beach for fun and gymes and all them lewd nytive rytch-uals. But *now?"* She was torn between sarcasm and a sigh. "Not no more, myte. Flippin' missioners 'as turned their silly 'eads; got 'em singin' *'ymns* orl night long, cor stone the crows! Fit ter splitcher bloody ear-'oles, the cows! No, I tell you the stryte dinkum oil, Cocky, this mermyde graft 'as bleedin' well *'ad* it, an' I'm 'arf ready to pack it in."

Wilson felt much the same way. But how to go about it? While he was considering the problem, Mavis suddenly said: "But 'ere, Cock! I been maggin' sumfin' orful, and you 'aven't 'ad yer tucker yet!"

"I'm not very hungry," he said weakly.

But he might as well not have spoken. "You just sit right there, Cock, and I'll pop inter the wet and snaffle a couple o' nice ones, an' we'll 'ave a bit o' scoff." She propelled herself to the water's edge and slid in with scarcely a ripple.

As she vanished, the cloud that had seemed to blanket Jack's mind vanished, too. The shock of seeing (and hearing and smelling!) his dream shattered had numbed his brain.

Now the numbness had gone, to be replaced by pain.

He tried to bring back the dream, if only for a little while, but he found the task impossible. When he tried to conjure up the beatific vision, all that came was the warty, piebald face of Mavis. Perhaps no sane man could mistake a dugong for a beautiful woman, but it would be relatively easy to mistake Mavis for a dugong. He had been building his whole life around the quixotic pursuit of a dream, and now, God help him, he had found the reality. He hated himself for having had the dream, and he hated poor Mavis for having destroyed it.

Simply sitting there in the sand, staring blindly into the fire, now mostly embers and ashes, he hardly even noticed when

Mavis returned, carrying two fish of unknown name but of reassuringly familiar construction. He paid only peripheral attention as she expertly cleaned and scaled them with a piece of shell. Not a word of her chatter penetrated as she stuffed the fish with one kind of seaweed and wrapped them in another, then plunged the dripping packages into the hot ashes of the fire, amid a hissing cloud of steam, and raked glowing embers over the pile.

He was still squatting stupidly as she humped herself over into the shadows and dug about in the sand. Uttering small cries of triumph, she disinterred two round objects and, making her way back to the fire, presented him with one.

"'Ave a bit of wallop," she said invitingly.

"Eh?" He stared at the thing. "What's this?"

Mavis chuckled richly. "Why, cor bless your 'ead, you been practically sittin' smack on top o' one o' me private caches o' workin' cocoanuts! I keeps a supply ready on all these narsty little bits of islands. Wot else would bring me ashore? 'Ere—"

Expertly, then, she pulled out the plugs of twisted palm fronds which allowed the carbon dioxide to escape during fermentation, but prevented sand from sifting in. "Nah, then! 'Ave a go!"

Wilson took the cocoanut, sniffed, and tasted. That part of his mind which had not been dulled by shock had to admit that the stuff wasn't bad. He took a long swig; it went down smooth and warm.

"Ahhh!" said Mavis, licking her bristly upper lip; "that's wot myde the deacon dance!"

Jack said nothing. There was a whole night to get through, and then the rest of his life after that, and he might as well start the ordeal as drunk as possible. He took another swig of the jungle juice. Mavis moved off, then she moved back.

"Got no bib," she said gayly, "but 'ere's your tucker, Cocky."

Wilson looked down at the palm frond she had spread on the sand in front of him. He didn't move; he merely stared at the whole baked fish resting there. Then the soft sea breeze wafted a delicate scent to his educated nostrils, bringing a flow of saliva from beneath his tongue.

Almost as if it had volition of its own, his hand reached out and broke off a bit of the crisp skin and flaky flesh and popped it into his mouth. . . .

• • •

The *J & M Seafood Grotto* was opened to a select clientele only a few months later. Jack Wilson, the junior partner, still makes excursions in the *Lorelei* to procure both rare and staple oceanic delicacies for the house's table, but he rarely stays away long.

The few people who have seen his wife, the senior partner, say that she isn't much to look at, and is confined to a wheel-chair, her lower extremities covered, which is probably why she stays hidden in the kitchen most of the time. There are rumors that she and Jack often go for midnight swims in the nearby surf; and there are other rumors of various sorts, not confirmed.

What needs no confirmation is the fact that Jack seems very fond of his wife, indeed—and that her seafood simply is out of this world.

The Crest of Thirty-Six

by

Davis Grubb

The late Davis Grubb was a West Virginia author who set much of his fiction in the Ohio River valley country of West Virginia, where his family had lived for more than two hundred years. Grubb's most famous novel was probably The Night of the Hunter, *a scary and suspenseful book that was later made into a successful film starring Robert Mitchum. Grubb was also well known for his short work, which appeared mostly in horror markets such as* Shadows *and* Dark Forces. *His other novels include* The Watchman, Fool's Parade, *and* The Voices of Glory. *His last novel was the enormous and controversial* Ancient Lights, *published in 1982.*

Here Grubb takes us to his fictional town of Glory, West Virginia—in which several of his stories are set—and beguiles us with the earthy and poetic tale of Darly Pogue, a man who has reluctant knowledge of the mighty Ohio River's greatest secret, a man doomed to spend his life on the river even though he is terrified of water . . . with good reason.

* * *

I DON'T KNOW IF SHE WAS BLACK OR WHITE. MAYBE SOME OF both. Or maybe Indian—there was some around Glory, West Virginia, who said she was full Cherokee and descended from the wife of a chief who had broken loose from the March of Tears in the 1840's. Some said not descended at all—that she was that very original woman grown incredibly old. Colonel Bruce theorized that she was the last of the Adena—that vanished civilization who built our great mound here in Glory back a thousand years before Jesus.

What matter whom she was or from whence? Does a

seventeen-year-old boy question the race or origin or age of
his first true love?

You might well ask, in the first place, what ever possessed
the Glory Town Council to hire on Darly Pogue as wharfmaster?
A man whose constant, nagging, gnawing fear—a phobia they
call it in the books—whose stuff of nightmare and the theme
of at least two attacks of the heebie-jeebies or Whiskey Horrors
was the great Ohio River.

Darly feared that great stream like a wild animal fears the
forest fire.

There were reasons for that fear. It is said that, as an infant,
he had floated adrift in an old cherry-wood pie-safe for six
days and six nights of thundering, lightning river storms during
the awful flood of 1900.

I read up a lot on reincarnation in those little five-cent
Haldemann Julius Blue Books from out Kansas way.

There was one of the little books that says man doesn't
reincarnate from his body to another body to another human
and so on. It held that our existence as spiritual creatures is
divided by God between air and water and land. And we take
turns as fish or birds or animals. Or man. A lifetime as a dolphin
might be reincarnated as a tiercel to ply the fathomed heavens
in splendor and, upon death, to become again a man. Well,
somehow, some way, something whispery inside Darly Pogue
told him that the good Lord now planned that Darly's next
incarnation would, quite specifically, be as an Ohio River catfish.

You can imagine what that did to Darly, what with his phobia
of that river.

And where could such mischievous information have orig-
inated? Maybe some gypsy fortune-teller—they were always
singing and clamoring down the river road in the springtime
in their sequined head scarves and candy-colored wagons—
maybe one of them told Darly that. In my opinion it was Loll
who told him herself: she could be that mean.

And it was, of course, a prediction to rattle a man up pretty
sore. I mean, did you ever look eyeball to eyeball with an old
flat-headed, rubber-lipped, garbage-eating, mud-covered catfish?

I didn't say *eat* one—God knows that nothing out of God's
waters is any tastier rolled in cornmeal and buttermilk batter
and fried in country butter.

I said did you ever look a catfish square in the whiskers?
Try it next time. It'll shake hell out of you. There's a big,
sappy, two-hundred-million-year-old grin on that slippery
skewered mug that seems to ask: Homo sapiens, how long you
been around? The critter almost winks as much as to remind
you that you came from waters as ancient as his—and that
you'll probably be going back some day. But, pray the Lord!
you'll exclaim, not as one of your ugly horned tribe!

What sense does it make to hire on as wharfmaster a man
who fears the very river?

To position such a man twenty-four hours a day, seven days
a week in a kind of floating coffin tied with a length of break-
able, cuttable rope to the shore?

But, what if that man has ready and unique access to the
smallest and greatest of the great river's secrets. Suppose he
can locate with unerring accuracy the body of a drowned person. Suppose he can predict with scary certainty the place where
a snag is hiding in the channel or the place where a new sandbar
is going to form. Suppose he can prognosticate the arrival of
steamboats—hours before their putting in. What if he can board
one of those boats and at one sweeping glance tell to the ounce—
troy or avoirdupois—the weight of its entire cargo?

There wasnt a secret of that old Ohio—that dark, mysterious
Belle Rivière—not one that Darly Pogue didnt have instant
access to: except one. That One, of course, was the Secret he
was married to: Loll, river witch, goddess, woman, whatever—
she was the one secret of the great flowing Mistress which
Darly did not understand.

But she was, as well, the source of all the rest of the great
river's secrets.

Loll.

Dark, strange Loll.

What could possess a man to live with such a woman and
on the very breast of that river he feared like a very demon?

The business all began the morning the water first showed
sign of rising in the spring of thirty-six. Everybody around
Glory came down to the wharfboat full of questions for Darly
Pogue and asking him either to confirm or contradict the pre-
dictions now crackling in the radio speakers. Wheeling's
WWVA.

You see, I have not told you the half of Loll—what kind
of creature she really was.

Look at Loll for yourself.

Pretend that it is about ten o'clock in the morning. Wisps of fog still hover like memories above the polished, slow, dark water out in the government channel. Loll creeps . . . mumbling about the little pantry, fixed breakfast for me and Darly— cornbread and ramps with home fries and catfish. Mmmmmmm, good. But look at Loll. Her face is like an old dried apple. A little laurel-root pipe is stuck in her withered, toothless gums. Her eyes wind out of dark, leathery wrinkles like mice in an old shoe bag. Look at the hump on her back and her clawlike hands and the long shapeless dotted Swiss of her only dress. This is her—this is Darly Pogue's wife Loll.

So what keeps him with her?

Why does he stay with this old harridan on the river he so disdains? You are on board the wharfboat, in the pantry, looking at this ancient creature. Glance there on the table at the Ingersoll dollar watch with the braided rawhide cord and the watchfob whittled out of a peach pit by a man on Death Row up in Glory prison.

I said about ten o'clock.

Actually, it's five after.

In the morning.

Now turn that nickel-plated watch's hands around to twelve twice—to midnight, that is. Instantly the scene changes, alters magically. The moon appears, imprisoned in the fringes of the violet willow tree up above the brick landing. The stars fox-trot and dip in the glittering river. A sweet, faint wind stirs from the sparkling stream. Breathe in now.

What is that lovely odor?

Laburnum maybe.

Lilac mixed with spicebush and azalea.

With a pinch of cinnamon and musk.

Who is that who stands behind the bedroom door in the small, narrow companionway?

She moves out now into the light—silvered by ardent, pant-ing moonshine—seeming almost like an origin of light rather than someone lit by it. You know you are looking at the same human being you saw at ten—and you know it cannot be but that it is: that, with the coming of nightfall, this is become the most beautiful woman you have ever seen or shall ever look upon again.

Ever.

In your lifetime.

She is naked, save for a little, shimmery see-through skirt and sandals and no brassiere, no chemise, no teddy bear, nor anything else.

And she comes slipping, a little flamewoman, down the companionway, seeming to catch and drag all the moonlight and shadows along with her, and knocks shyly, lovingly, on the stateroom door of Darly Pogue.

Darly has been drinking.

At the first rumor of a flood he panicked.

Loll knocks again.

Y-yes?

It's me, lovey. I have what you've been waiting for. Open up.

Cant you tell me through the door?

But, lovey! I want your arms around me! cried Loll, the starlight seeming to catch and glitter in the lightly tinseled aureole of her nipples. I want to make love! I want to make whoopee!

You know I caint get it up whilst I'm skeert bad, sweetie! Oh, do let me in!

Aw, shucks, I got a headache, see?

All right, pouted the beautiful girl.

Well? squeaked poor Darly in a teeth-chattering voice.

Well, what, lovey?

The crest! The crest of thirty-six! cried Darly. What's it going to be? Not as bad as twenty-eight or nineteen and thirteen surely or back in awful eighteen and eighty-four. Is it? O, dont spare me. I can take it. Tell me it haint going to rise that high!

What was the crest of 1913? asked Loll, her pretty face furrowed as she thumbed through her memory. Yes, the crest of 1913 at Glory was sixty-two feet measured on the wall of the Mercantile Bank.

I think so, grunted poor Darly. Yes. That's right.

And the crest of thirty-six—it cant be any higher than that.

The crest of thirty-six, Loll said quietly, lighting a reefer, will be exactly one hundred and fifteen feet.

Darly was quiet except for an asthmatic squeak.

What? I'm losing my hearing. It sounded exactly like you said, one hundred and fifteen feet!

I did, said Loll, blowing fragrant smoke out of her slender, sensitive nostrils.

Whoooeee! screamed poor Darly, flailing out now through the open stateroom door and galloping toward the gangplank. He was wearing a gaudy pair of underwear which he had sent away for to *Ballyhoo* magazine. He disappeared somewhere under the elms up on Water Street.

That left me alone with her on the wharfboat, peering out through a crack in my own stateroom door at this vision of beauty and light and sweet-smelling womanhood. By damn, it was like standing downwind from an orchard!

She didnt look more than eighteen—about a year older than I, who hadnt ever seen a naked lady except on the backs of well-thumbed and boy-sticky cards that used to get passed around our home room in school.

Nothing at all.

There were lights on the river: boys out gigging for frogs or gathering fish in from trotlines. The gleam of the lanterns flashed on the waters and seemed to stream up through the blowing curtains and glimmer darkling on that girl.

She was so pretty.

She sensed my stare.

She turned and—to my mingled ecstasy and terror—came down the threadbare carpet of the companionway toward my door.

She came in.

A second later we were into the bunk with her wet-lipped and coughing with passion and me not much better.

Afterward she kindly sewed the tear in my shirt and the two ripped-off buttons from our getting me undressed.

Whew!

All the time we were making love I could hear poor Darly Pogue—somewhere up on Water Street reciting the story of the Flood from Genesis, at the top of his voice.

And I haint by God no Noah neither! he'd announce every few minutes, like a candidate declining to run for office. So I haint not your wharfmaster as of this by God hereby date!

Well, I groped and blundered my way into manhood amidst the beautiful limbs of that girl.

The moon fairly blushed to see the things we did.

And with her doing all the teaching.

All through it you could hear the crackle and whisper of static from the old battery Stromberg Carlson—that and the voice of poor Darly Pogue—high atop an old Water Street elm, announcing that the Bible Flood was about to come again.

Who are you? I asked the woman.

I am Loll.

I know that, I said. But I see you in the morning—while you're fixing me and him breakfast and you're *old*—

I am a prisoner of the moon, she said. My beauty waxes and wanes with her phases.

I dont care, I said. I love you. Marry me. I'll borrow for you. I'll even steal for you.

I pondered.

I wont kill for you—but I will *steal*. Will you?

No.

Do you love me at all? I asked then in a ten-year-old's voice.

I am fond of you, she said, giving me a peck of a kiss: her great fog-gray eyes misty from our loving. You are full of lovely aptitudes and you make love marvelously.

She pouted a little and shrugged.

But I do not love you, she said.

I see.

I love *him*, she said. That ridiculous little man who refuses to go with me.

Go? Go where, Loll? You're not leaving Glory are you?

I'm not leaving the river, if that's what you mean. As for Darly Pogue—I adored him in that Other. Before he went away. And now he wont go forward with me again.

Before when, Loll? Forward where?

I got no answer. Her gray eyes were fixed on a circle of streetlamp that illuminated the verdant foliage of the big river elm—and among it the bare legs of poor Darly Pogue.

And now, she said. He must be punished, of course. He has gone too far. He has resisted me long enough. This final insult has done it!

I was getting dressed and in a hurry. I could tell she was talking in other Dimensions about Things and Powers that scared me about as bad as the river did Darly Pogue. Yet I could see what her hold on him was—how she kept him living in that floating casket on top of the moving, living surface of the waters: that great river of pools and shallows, that moving cluster of little lakes, that beloved Ohio. It was her night beauty.

I eased her out of the stateroom as slick and gentle as I could, for I didnt want her passing out one of her punishments onto me.

But I knew I would never be the same.

In fact, I suddenly knew two new things: that I was going to spend my life on the river, and that I would never marry.

Because Loll had spoilt me for even the most loving of mortal caresses.

And, what's more, she sewed my buttons back on that morning. Though the hands that held my repaired garment out to me—they were gnarled and withered like the great roots of old river trees.

Well, you remember the flood of thirty-six. It was a bad one all right.

It was weird—looking down Seventh Street to the streetlight atop the telephone pole by the confectioner's and seeing that streetlight shimmering and shivering just ten inches from the dark, pulsing stream—that streetlamp like a dandelion atop a tall, shimmering stalk of light.

Beautiful.

But kind of deathly, too.

It was a bad, bad flood in the valleys. Crest of fifty-nine feet.

But then Loll had predicted more than one hundred.

Forecast it and scared poor Darly Pogue—who knew she was never wrong—into running for his life and ending up getting himself the corner room on the fifth floor of the Zadok Cramer Hotel. There was only one higher place in Glory and that was the widow's walk atop the old courthouse and this was taller even than the mound. But Darly settled for the fifth floor of the Zadok. It seemed somehow to be the place remotest from the subject of his phobia.

I was living in the hotel by now so I used to take him up his meals—all prepared by the hotel staff: Loll had gone on strike.

Darly didnt eat much.

He just sat on the edge of the painted brass bed toying with the little carved peach pit from Death Row and looking like he was the carver.

She wants me back. And by God I haint going back.

Well, Darly, you could at least go down and see her. I'll lend you my johnboat.

And go back on that wharfboat?

Well, yes, Darly.

Like hell I will, he snaps, pacing the floor in his *Ballyhoo*

underwear and walking to the window every few minutes to
stare out at block after town block merging liquidly into the
great polished expanse of river.

On the wharfboat be damned! he cried. It's farther than that
she wants me.

I felt a kind of shiver run over me as Darly seemed to shut
his mouth against the Unspeakable. I closed my eyes. All I
could see in the dark was the tawny sweet space of skin between
Loll's breasts and a tiny mole there, like an island in a golden
river.

But I'm safe from her here! he cried out suddenly, sloshing
some J. W. Dant into the tumbler from the small washbowl.
He drank the half glass of whiskey without winking. Again I
shivered.

Aint you even gonna chase it, Darly?

With what?

Well, hell—with water.

Aint got any.

I pointed to the little sink with its twin ornamental brass
spigots with the pinheaded cupids for handles.

That's for washing—not drinking. It's—

He shuddered.

—it's *river* water.

He looked miserably at the little spigots and the bowl, golden
and browned with use, like an old meerschaum.

I tried to get a room without running water, he said. I do
hate this arrangement awfully. Think of it. Those pipes run
directly down to . . .

Naturally, he could not finish.

The night of the actual crest of thirty-six I was alone in my
own room at the hotel. Since business on the wharfboat had
been discontinued during the flood there was no one aboard
but Loll. The crest—a mere fifty-nine feet—was registered
on the wall of the Purina Feed Warehouse at Seventh and
Western. That was the crest of thirty-six. And that was all.

You would think that Darly would have greeted this news
with joy.

Or at least relief.

But it sent him into a veritable frenzy against Loll. She had
deliberately lied to him. She had frightened him into making
himself a laughstock in Glory. A hundred and fifteen feet,
indeed! We shall see about such prevarications!

In his johnboat he rowed his way drunkenly down the cobbled street to where the water lapped against the eaves of the old Traders Hotel and the wharfboat tied in to its staunchstone chimney top.

Loudly Darly began again to read the story of the Flood from Genesis. He got through that and lit into Loll for fair—saying that she had mocked God with predictions of the Flood.

Loll stayed in her stateroom throughout most of these tirades and when she would stand it no more she came out and stood on the narrow little deck looking at him. She was an old crone, now, her rooty knuckles clutched round the moon-silver head of a stick of English furze. Somehow—even in this moon aspect—I felt desire for her again.

You lied, Loll! Darly cried. Damn you, you lied. And you mocked the holy Word!

I did not lie! she cried with a laugh that danced across the renegade water. O, I did not I did not I did not!

You did! screamed Darly and charged down the gangplank from the big johnboat and sprang onto the narrow deck. No one was near enough to intervene as he struck the old woman with the flat of his hand and sent her spinning back into the shadows of the companionway.

The look she cast him in that instant—I saw it.

I tell you I am glad I was never the recipient of such a look.

Darly rowed back to his hotel and went in through a third-story window of the ballroom and up to his room on the fifth.

He was never seen alive on earth again.

He went into that little room on the top of the Zadok Cramer with a hundred and twenty-six pounds of window glazer's putty and began slowly, thoroughly sealing up his room against whatever eventuality.

It was a folly that made the townfolk laugh the harder. Because if the water had risen high as that room—wouldn't it surely sweep the entire structure away?

Yet the flood stage continued to go down. It was plainly a hoax on Loll's part. Yes, the waters kept subsiding. Until by Easter Monday it was down so low that the wharfboat could again tie in onto the big old willow at the foot of Water Street.

Everything was as usual.

Or was it?

There had been a savage electric rainstorm on the last night of the flood of thirty-six. The crest of thirty-six was a grim one and it was near what Loll had warned.

And there was no way to question her about it.

Because during the storm—at some point—she disappeared (as Darly was to do) from off our land of earth.

It all came out the next week.

Toonerville Boso, the desk clerk, hadn't seen nor heard of Darly Pogue in three days and nights. An old lady in four-oh-seven reported a slight leak of brown water in the ceiling of her bedroom. Toonerville approached the sealed room on the morning of the Sunday after Easter and he, too, noted a trickle of yellow, muddy water from under the door of Darly's room. There was also a tiny sunfish flipping helplessly about on the Oriental carpet.

You remember the rest of it—

How a wall of green water and spring mud and live catfish came vomiting out of that door, sweeping poor Boso down the hall and down the winding stairs and out the hotel door and into the sidewalk.

That room had been invaded. Yes, the spigots were wide open.

Everyone in Glory, every one in the riverlands at least, knows that the ceiling of that hotel room was the real crest of thirty-six. Colonel Bruce he worked with transit and scale and plumb bob for a month afterward—measuring it—the real crest of thirty-six. It was exactly one hundred and thirteen feet.

I know, I know—there were catfish in the room and sunfish and gars and a couple of huge goldfish and they all too big to have squeezed up through the hotel plumbing, let alone through those little brass spigots. But they did. The pressure must have been enormous. And it all must have come rushing out and filling up in the space of a few seconds—before Darly Pogue could know what was happening and could scream.

The pressure of Love? I dont know. Some force unknown to us and maybe it's all explained somewhere in one of those little five-cent blue reincarnation books from out Kansas way— I guess it was one I missed. The pressure to get those fish and a few bottles and a lot of mud and water up the pipes and into that room was, as I say, considerable. But nothing compared to the pressure it must have taken to get Darly back out into the river. Out of that room. Into the green, polished, fathomless mother of waters. Love? Maybe it is the strongest force in nature. At least, the love of someone like her.

No trace of her was ever found. No trace of Darly, either—except for his rainbow-hued *Ballyhoo* shorts—they were the one part of him that didnt go through the spigot and which hung there like a beaten flag against the nozzle.

Go there now.

To the river.

When the spring moon is high.

When the lights in the skiffs on the black river look like campfires on stilts of light.

A catfish leaps—porpoising into moonshine and mist and then dipping joyously back into the deeps. Another—smaller—appears by its side. They nuzzle their flat homely faces in the starshine. Their great rubbery lips brush in ecstasy.

And then they are gone in the spring dark—off for a bit of luscious garbage—old lovers at a honeymoon breakfast.

Lucky Darly Pogue! O, lucky Darly!

The Shannon Merrow

by

Cooper McLaughlin

*Here's another story about the fabled Irish Merrow. But unlike
T. Crofton Croker's "The Soul Cages," which comes from a
nineteenth century tradition that created the stage Irishman
and "imagined the country as a humorist's Arcadia" (to quote
W. B. Yeats), "The Shannon Merrow" takes place in troubled,
war-torn modern Ireland.*

New writer Cooper McLaughlin—a frequent contributor to
The Magazine of Fantasy & Science Fiction—*takes us not to
a pastel-colored land of myths, but instead to the gray, hard-
edged, post-Vietnam world, the all-too-familiar world of drug
addiction and pollution and high-speed computers and crime,
a world where even the most beautiful of country vistas can be
stained and shadowed by a man's memory of war and mutilation
and death.*

*But magic still lives, even in such a world, waiting around
the next corner, behind the scenes, below the surface . . . magic
waiting only for a touch to set it free . . . magic strong enough
to heal the bitterest heart. . . .*

* * *

IT WAS THREE YEARS SINCE I'D BEEN IN YOUGHAL. EVEN IF
you've never been to Ireland, you've probably seen the region.
The film *Moby Dick* was shot there, and the locals still laugh
about the day the great rubber whale blew out to sea.

From the cottage which is mine since my mother's death
you can look over the reaches of the Blackwater River. Opposite
are the green rolling hills where *Barry Lyndon* was filmed.
Down to the right you can see the decaying gray stones of an
abandoned abbey, and beyond that the fire-blackened facade
of a country house, once owned by the Anglo-Irish ascendancy.

212

I stood in the doorway of the cottage. The sun was bright but a cold March wind blew up the valley. At the mouth of the river two open fishing boats pulled a string of orange floats.

I felt depressed. It was here that I'd done my first crude sketches. Later when I'd learned to paint, I rode Uncle Frank's ancient Norton motorcycle over the country roads. With a box of watercolors and a cool bottle of stout, I was free.

From the time I was nine until I went into the army, each summer I'd fly from San Francisco to Shannon to meet my Uncle Frank. Sometimes my mother would come with me but usually she was too busy making a living for the two of us.

I looked at my watch. Ten-fifteen. I had an appointment with Uncle Frank at eleven to sign the documents transferring the title of the cottage to me. I pulled the suede jacket over my nearly useless right arm. Two AK-47 rounds had shattered my shoulder and upper arm. The bones had healed but the nerves were dead—the end of my career as a painter.

I got into the rented blue Ford Escort. It's no trouble for me to drive in Ireland. My right arm is good enough to steer and I can work the left-hand shift easily. I drove down the short rutted path and through the gate. I got out and swung it shut on the rusty hinges. I looked back at the house with its shaggy rush roof, the whitewashed walls stark against the sea of green grass. "The grass of half a cow is what you have," Uncle Frank said, "half a cow at the most." True, it was not a large place, but it was filled with the fragile ghosts of happier times.

There was a warped wooden sign bolted to the gate. Uncle Frank, who, before he'd gone into law had studied archaeology, gave me the old name of the place. CNOC GRIANAN . . . The Hill of the Place of the King. My shoulder began to ache and there was a lead ball weighting my stomach. No point in trying to hang on to the past. Perhaps I should sell the place after all. I got in the car and drove down the hill. At the bottom I stopped and pulled a bottle of Paddy from the glove box. I took a long hit, letting the smooth gold whiskey run down my throat.

Youghal is not a large town, but it is old. People talk of Cromwell's troopers as if they'd been there yesterday. I turned from the High Street and up an alley to Nalley's bar. Nalley's is for serious drinkers. No bearded young men in imitation Aran sweaters blowing tin whistles and bagpipes, no jukebox blaring Chieftains' records. Just a long dim room, the bar lined with cloth-capped men, drinking black Guinness. At the far end were three rickety beer-soaked tables. Against the smoke I caught sight of Uncle Frank at one of them, sitting under the black draped portraits of Jack and Robert Kennedy which were lit by a pair of red votive candles.

He saw me and smiled, raising two fingers. I edged my way to the bar and got the curate's attention. With one hand I carefully carried the thick glasses, each with a good fistfull of whiskey, over the layer of cigarette butts which carpeted the floor.

Uncle Frank is not really my uncle. Like my mother he is a MacNeil, and in the convolutions of Gaelic lineage, counted as her cousin. After my father's death he acted as a surrogate parent. He taught me to fish and shoot and sail a boat, and to drink with dignity.

Frank was a tall man, gray-haired, with the flattened nose of a former county hurling star. He dressed like the prosperous Dublin lawyer he was. Hanging from his gold watch chain was an ancient Roman coin. "The mark of MacNeil's folly," he called it. A souvenir of his brief career as an archaeologist. "We've enough of burrowing through the old raths like rats in a cellar." He had told my mother, "The country needs developing, not digging up." So he had abandoned the life of a scholar and read the law.

"Ah . . . the O'Reilly himself." Frank smiled. "Michael, you're a saint. Another minute and I'd have perished from the thirst."

I glanced at the empty glass at his elbow. "You don't look perishing to me . . ."

"Well, now. The first one's for the mouth. This one's for the soul." He held up the glass. I knew there was no rushing the process. One more round, talking of sports, politics, the weather. Then business.

I leaned back in the rickety chair and lit a cigarette. "Grand day today, isn't it?" I began the ritual.

Two drinks later we were finished. Frank tucked the signed documents into his briefcase and snapped it shut.

"What will you do, now the place is yours?"

I could feel the whiskey popping sweat beads on my forehead. "I don't know . . . sell it maybe . . ."

"Sell it! Its been in the family for a hundred years! You'll not be a favorite around here if you peddle it to a German or an Arab..."

"Frank, I don't know. It gets me just to see the place."

He fingered his glass, "Is it money you need then?"

"No." I thumped the dead right arm on the table. "I've a government-guaranteed lifetime income right here. Not a high return on the initial investment... but I don't need much."

"What are you doing with yourself now?"

"This and that."

"What's 'this and that'? I mean *work* for God's sake."

"Nothing much. Bumming around..."

Frank touched my arm. "You've got to do something with your life, boy. You can't go on moping about."

"I thought about writing. But I don't know if I have anything to say."

"God save us! Writing!" He slammed the glass on the table. "Just what the world needs... another scribbler. It's not the drink that's the curse of the Irish... it's literacy." He jerked his head toward the bar where a young man in steel-rimmed glasses was pulling stout. "Ten pounds to a pence he's got an unfinished novel under the pumps... or chisels Gaelic verse in the Ogham..."

"Frank, if I wanted a sermon, I'd ask Father Fitz."

He drained his Paddy. "Ah, well, boy, I know. I get carried away." He fingered the worn coin on his vest. "We need men of business. Men who can make things go, not superstitious dreamers or mystical poets."

He shoved his glass toward me. "One more then." His voice was tired.

I couldn't handle any more whiskey. So I sat there playing with a half-pint of stout. Frank's face was flushed.

"Now I've an idea. There's an American firm I'm representing. They need a bright young man like you. You're American and you'll know their ways. You could live here and keep *Cnoc Grianan*... And you've the right contacts."

"Meaning you."

"Meaning me." He smiled.

"And what does this famous company do?"

"Computer softwares."

I had a sudden vision of giant disposable diapers filled with electronic turds. The room was hot. I knew Frank meant well, and I didn't want to hurt his feelings, but I needed to get out of there.

"Frank, I don't know . . . I can't think anymore . . . for the last few years my head has been totally fucked . . ."

He flinched at the crudity and glanced quickly over his shoulder to be sure Sister Mary Monica wasn't standing there, ruler at the ready.

"Michael, I'm not pressing. It's only that I want to see you make something of your life."

"I was making something of my life. Now I don't know . . . maybe I don't really care." The stout tasted like a wet ashtray.

"When must you go back to the States?"

"Tomorrow. Next week. Doesn't make a helluva lot of difference."

Frank took out a black leather appointment book. He studied it for a moment.

"Michael. I'll ask a favor. I've got a new Seamaster up at Carrick. I need it run down to Athlone. There's no hurry. You could be a week about it. Rest yourself. Do a bit of coarse fishing. Think about your life." He hesitated, looking at my right arm, "Could you . . ."

"Could I single-hand it, you mean?" I laughed. "How big is it?"

"I wouldn't be having the *Queen Mary,* would I? It's a thirty-footer. Center cockpit."

"No problem."

"You'll do it then?" He finished his drink. "That's a great favor. I've not the time these days to bring it down myself."

"Why is it up there?"

"Getting a new top and windscreen. I lent it to a client. One of the Germans. The great clod took it under the Rooskey bridge with the top up. The boat went through, but a great part of it stayed behind."

"Did he pay for it?"

"Pay for it? Three hundred pounds' damage, and I got a bloody *verziehung* from him. So I put an extra five hundred on his bill for 'services rendered.'" He winked, "Fortunate it was that my insurance made up the deficit." We both laughed.

"Okay, why not." I stood up, "I'll get my gear together and you can pick me up in the morning."

"That's grand. I'll drive you to Carrick and then I'm back to Dublin. Call me from Athlone and I'll pick you up there."

I found the boat at the fuel dock. *Manannan McLir—Athlone* in gold Gaelic script on the transom. Jimmy Dwyer, an ancient red-haired leprechaun was pumping diesel into her. He turned as I came up the dock and waved his pipe in salute. A billow of smoke issued from his mouth as a quart of fuel sloshed over his shoes.

"Michael, man, good to see you again." He looked up at the black thunderheads coming in from the north. The cold March wind raised chop on the river. "Soft day isn't it now?"

It was a new, well-fitted boat. I ducked into the forward cabin. Frank had called ahead, and the food locker and calor refrigerator were stocked. On the galley table were a case of Guinness, a bottle of Paddy, and two fresh loaves of soda bread.

I went on deck. Jimmy handed up my gear and I stowed it in the aft cabin. I checked the engine, a specially fitted 72-hp Perkins. Jimmy tucked the fuel nozzle under his arm and scratched a match across the scarred NO SMOKING sign. "There's no telling where that U-boat commander took the top off, is there?"

"Not a bit, Jimmy. You did a good job."

"Will you be off now?"

"That I will. I'm only down to Carnardoe today, but I want to get there before the weather breaks."

"I'll be casting you off then. Watch out for periscopes."

I laughed. It is heartening to know that Americans are no longer number one on the Ugly Tourist short list.

It was only an hour run to Lake Carnardoe. I knew where I wanted to go. An old stone jetty hidden in the reed beds that surround the lake. As a boy I'd spent a lot of happy solitary time there.

Now the Shannon is one of the world's most beautiful rivers. It's an easy river, but you have to be careful. Navigational aids are minimal, and there are shifting shoals and reed beds to trap a boat. In the summer you can see the tourist rent-a-boats stranded up and down the river, waiting to be pulled off. I threaded my way through the nearly hidden channel. The rain broke, a solid sheet, bending the reeds. I kept just enough speed to make way. Then I saw it, glistening gray-black stone, a rusty iron bollard at each end. The wind was hard. I shut down and jumped to the jetty, getting a line out before the boat could blow away.

Later, I sat naked in the warm aft cabin, sipping Paddy. In the west the sky turned red. For the first time in years I felt at peace. I rolled some whiskey down my throat and listened to the rain.

It was late afternoon of the third day when I found myself below Cloondara. Thunderheads were building up in the west. I decided to make the short run to Lanesboro.

I was cruising at quarter speed when the boat began to shudder. I put it in reverse and jockeyed the throttle. There was a noise aft that sounded like the stuffing box coming through the deck. The propeller was fouled. I shut down the engine.

The river was deserted. The boat was drifting toward the reed banks. In a few minutes I'd be stuck, at least for the night, maybe longer. I went forward and let loose the anchor. Taking a boathook I tried to free the screw, but whatever was fouling it wouldn't come loose. I sat in the cockpit and smoked a cigarette. There was one solution. I could go over the side with a line and try to cut it free. I looked at the cold gray water. The prospect was not appealing, but then neither was the idea of being stranded.

"Shit." I flipped the cigarette over the side and got the snorkel gear out of the locker.

The water was freezing. The nylon line cut into my chest. Through my face mask I could see the problem. A red rag was twisted around the prop.

I came up gasping. My skin was purple and showed goose-bumps like grapes. I threw the offending rag into the cockpit. Catching the gunwale, I levered one leg over and collapsed shivering on the deck. I'd had the presence of mind to hang a towel on the wheel. I rubbed myself until the purple turned red. As I turned to go below, I heard a cry. If there is a *banshee,* it was her voice. The cry echoed its agony across the water.

I dropped the towel and stared at the reed bed. The reeds swayed. I caught a glimpse of white and gold rising from the water. The scream of a mortally wounded animal struck me. I grabbed the binoculars. My hand was shaking so badly, it was hard to focus. I held the glasses tight against the neck strap, thumb pressed against my temple.

It was a woman. No hallucination. A real woman. Long blonde hair hanging wet over her back. She turned and I could see the water running down her breasts as she struggled through the reeds. Then she was gone.

"Hello!... Hey! You need help?" I shouted. To my left I saw movement. I brought the glasses up. A slim naked body scrambled up the bank and into the trees. I let the glasses drop against my chest. *No one* swims naked in Ireland. There are men here, fathers of eight children, who've never seen a woman's skin between neck and knee.

"Hey there... hey!" The boat pitched. The anchor wasn't holding. If I didn't get moving I'd be grounded for sure. I started the engine. Something cold and wet brushed against my foot. I looked down. It was the red rag.

It was nearly dark when I sighted the Lanesboro bridge. On the right, just across from the peat-fired power plant, is a narrow stone-walled channel. I pulled in. There is just enough room for two or three thirty-footers to moor. Quiet, deserted, and protected from the winds blowing off Lough Ree.

I poured myself the last half-inch of Paddy while I changed into warm clothes. What I really needed was a tightly rolled joint and a loose woman, but these are as likely to be found in Ireland as a bushel of snakes. I was ready to settle for fresh salmon and a jar or two at the Bridge Hotel.

On deck I noticed the red rag lying near the wheel. I picked it up. I felt a jolt as if from a static charge. Looking closely, I saw it was not just a piece of cloth, but something like a watch cap. There was a metallic feel to it, yet it had the give of some synthetic fabric. Amazingly there were no rips from the propeller. It was small, but it stretched easily to fit my head.

I looked around. Frank was right. A few days on the river was what I needed. The colors were bright. The cracked gray stones of the jetty showed patterns I'd never noticed before. The aching inner canker of depression was gone. From across the river came the clear sweet sound of a tin whistle playing "Julia Delaney." With the taste of good salmon already on my tongue, I made for the bridge.

When I left the hotel, my stomach was well anchored by a large salmon steak, good Irish potatoes steeped in thick cream and butter, and half a loaf of soda bread fresh from the oven. I pushed the red watch cap back on my head and headed for Devlin's Pub.

Ed Devlin is a retired New York City detective. Like many retired Irish-Americans he finds the Old Country not only congenial, but far from the prying eyes of the IRS and the Social Security Administration. He also makes the best Irish coffee in the world—an ancient Gaelic tipple invented a few years ago by Stanton Delaplane of the San Francisco *Chronicle*.

There were a dozen or so men at the bar downing pints, and one young couple at a table. I was on my second coffee when the door to my left opened. There was a sudden silence. An old woman stood in the entrance. She was dressed in a shapeless black coat. A skirt came to the tops of her high-laced boots. On her head she wore an odd black hat of Queen Mary vintage, fastened by a steel pin. She leaned on a heavy cane and surveyed the room. The silence was broken by a flurry of Gaelic greetings and much tipping of caps.

Swinging her cane, she walked the length of the bar. As she passed me she paused. I was half-turned on my stool and gave her a smile. Her blue eyes were as cold as ice. I turned back to my drink as she clumped away into the gloom at the rear.

The noise resumed. Ed began to draw a pint.

"What was that apparition?"

Ed lowered his voice. "You've not seen her before? That, my boy, is beán O'Meara. Not 'missus,' mind you, but 'beán.' She's been around since Saint Brendan set sail." He topped off the pint and carried it to the rear.

When he returned he poured us both a shot. "She must have an eye for you. She asked me who you were."

"That's a great compliment."

"Believe it, man. Even the bishop tips the biretta to that one." He began to polish a glass, "True, she's a bit strange. Lives in a cottage up by the old rath. Tutors the young ones in Irish for the Civil Service. Like an up-to-date hedge school."

I pulled the shot glass toward me, "She looks like a witch."

Ed smiled and picked up another glass to polish, "A witch, is it? No . . . she's a good old soul. Every day to Mass, and thick with the priests. There are some who say she's of the *sidhe*." He looked at me thoughtfully, "But we're modern men and don't believe in fairies and such, now do we?"

"Only the ones I've seen back home on Castro Street."

"None of them in this country." He jerked his head toward the back, "But her now, she's a National Treasure . . . knows all the old stories. Always some professor coming up from Dublin with the boot full of tape machines. 'Folklorists,' they call themselves."

Ed moved down the bar to take orders from two hard-looking types in leather-patched jackets. I lit a cigarette and thought about tomorrow. I wanted to make the run across Lough Ree, at least as far as Glassan. It's not a long trip, but there are large warning signs above the bridge discouraging private boats from going alone. The weather is unpredictable and at times the lake gets dangerously rough.

On my way in, I'd seen two boats tied up at the quay. I finished my drink. In the morning I'd see if their skippers were interested in making the run. I pulled the watch cap over my ears and moved to the door.

There was a tap on my shoulder. I turned. "Herself requests your presence." Ed gestured toward the back.

"Me? What for?"

"I wouldn't know. Maybe she fancies your curly hair. Just be civil. She's got a tongue that'll take tar off the road. Go on with you . . ." He gave me a gentle shove.

She sat like a dowager queen, black-gloved hands folded on the top of her cane. In the smoky light her wrinkled face stood out with startling luminosity.

"Sit down, boy."

I sat, feeling like a grammar school boy accused of some heinous crime by the Mother Superior.

"Have you the Irish?"

"My grandparents were from . . ."

She cut me off. "I don't mean the blood. I can see that. You've a face like Paddy's pig. I mean the language."

"A word or two, that's all."

"That's all any of them have these days. Even the politicians . . ." She lifted the pint and took a sip. "You've been badly hurt, haven't you?"

I felt my face flush. "I got hit. In Vietnam."

She moved her gloved hand to touch my right arm. I pulled back.

"I don't mean that. I mean the inside hurting."

I wanted to tell the nosy old bitch to mind her own business. I shoved back my chair. "I've got to take care of my boat. You'll excuse me..."

"Sit! You'll go when I give you leave." The force of her voice pushed me back in the chair.

She paused, then gave me a smile. "That's better. Now, suppose you tell me how you got that red hat you're wearing."

"I found it."

Her eyes were on my face. "You found it in the water, did you?"

"How did you know?"

She ignored the question. "And did you see or hear anything strange when you got it?"

I told her what happened. I didn't mention that the woman I saw had been naked.

"Give me the cap." She took it gently, held it to her breast, eyes closed. "It is. It is indeed the *cohuleen driuth.*" She opened her eyes. "The cap of the merrow... you call them mermaids." Her voice was soft.

I repressed a sigh. I don't know what I expected, but I wasn't in the mood for some old-woman-blather about mermaids or fairy folk.

She leaned forward. "Now you listen to me, boy. You've a good heart but you're green as a cabbage. What you believe doesn't change what is. This cap is from the Tir-Faoi-Thonn ... the Country Under The Waves."

She placed the cap on the table, keeping her hand on it. "When a child is conceived in that country, the mother weaves such a cap for it. When it is born, it is placed on the child's head. That is what allows the merrow to live under the water. It is made for that one person alone, and no other. If it is lost or stolen, the merrow must leave Tir-Faoi-Thonn forever... or die."

"Are you suggesting that the cap belongs to the woman I saw, that she's a mermaid... a merrow?" I tried to keep the scepticism from my voice.

"I'm not suggesting, boy... I'm telling you now."

"Look. That was an ordinary woman I saw. No tail, no scales. I saw her walk."

She sighed and leaned back. "You're like the rest, you are. You don't believe the *sidhe* exist. Still, you think leprechauns sit on toadstools, cobbling boots, and mermaids have tails like fish. They don't. They are folk like you . . . and me."

I thought if I humored her I could cut this short. "Oh. I believe you. What's this got to do with me?"

"You've the cap, haven't you? Give it back." I felt her touch again on my arm. "Think of that poor girl—condemned to walk in the world like us—never to see home or family again. Think of her loss . . ."

"What do you want me to do? Throw it back in the river?"

"That you musn't. It might be lost forever. Take it back where you got it. Wait . . . just wait. The girl won't have gone far. Without the *cohuleen driuth* her life will be a hell. She'll come for it, I know."

The moon was up and the west wind blew fresh off the lake, bringing with it a drift of turf smoke from some distant cottage. I sat in a deck chair, watching the hypnotic shimmer of silver light on the water. I touched the red cap which I'd folded in my windbreaker pocket. It felt warm.

Even by Irish standards the O'Meara woman was an eccentric. Still, her intensity got to me. Suppose it were true and the girl was condemned to a life of misery because of me?

"Oh, bullshit!" I muttered. I went below and climbed into my bunk.

That night I dreamed I was making a night jump at Fort Bragg. I stood alone in the door and then I was out. Below I could see the markers of the drop zone. I counted for the opening shock but it didn't come. In panic I looked up to see the tightly rolled canopy streaming behind me. I had no reserve 'chute.

The black ground rushed up. I closed my eyes. Then I was in water, plunging down through a warm opalescent sea, the shroud lines wrapped tightly around my legs. There was a burst of yellow light. A woman came swimming toward me, her body gold-white in the light. A cloud of platinum hair framed her face. The red mouth opened and a soundless scream filled the sea.

I woke late, with a mouth like Cromwell's boot. When I checked the quay, the other boats were gone. I debated about making the run by myself but decided against it. I had lunch at the hotel, then stopped off at Devlin's for a resupply of the booze locker.

It was midafternoon when I got back to the boat. I lay in my bunk trying to read, but I was too restless. I pulled on my jacket and went on deck. The wind was rising but the sky was clear. I stuck my hand in the pocket of my windbreaker and felt the warm cloth of the cap.

"Cohuleen driuth" . . . Nonsense. But the Irish are susceptible to nonsense, and none are more Irish than Irish-Americans. I pulled the cap from my pocket. Beán O'Meara . . . a superstitious old witch, whatever the professors from Dublin might think. I looked again at the cap. Red. Red as a rose. Red as blood. Red as the lips of the woman in my dream.

"What's to lose?" I went below and got a fresh bottle of Paddy. I ran up the engine, then cast off and headed upstream. Laughing, I jammed the cap on my hed. What's to lose indeed? No denying the blood. Mental cases, one and all of us.

Upriver I found a rotting old fishing pier close to where I'd seen the woman. I tied off to a piling. What now? I didn't really believe anything was going to happen. The day was clear and the river still as glass. I listened to the water lap against the hull. I broke out Uncle Frank's fishing gear, and with breadballs for bait, tried my luck.

The time passed quickly. I caught three small browns, which I kept, and a large fat bream, which I released. It was almost dark. In the rhythmic ritual of fishing I'd forgotten about merrows and magic caps. I cleaned and cooked the browns for dinner. Tired, but with that sense of well-being which comes from a good day on the water, I smoked a last cigarette and watched the sun slide behind the mountains. Then I went below to sleep.

The boat rocked and I woke up. The full moon flooded the cabin with soft light. I glanced at my watch. Two A.M. I sat up abruptly. Someone was coming aboard. I threw back the blankets and swung my bare feet to the deck.

The cabin door opened. A naked woman stood before me. The moon made pearls of the water glistening on her white skin. She was small and perfectly formed. No tail or scale. A beautiful young woman with long blonde hair, standing bare before me in the dead of the Shannon night.

I stood, flat-footed, staring. What do you say to a merrow? "Come in. . . ."

"Thank you, sir." She moved forward.

"You're a merrow."

She looked at me, her eyes sad. "That I was . . . and with God's grace, will be again. You've something of mine . . ."

"The *cohuleen driuth,* you mean? I've got it . . ."

"Ah, that's a gift of grace then." She laughed and the tenseness went from her body. "Where did you learn such a strange name?"

"I was told by beán O'Meara."

"The O'Meara, was it? A misfortunate woman but a good friend of many."

I realized that I too was standing there naked. Looking at her, I knew I would soon be calling attention to myself. I sat on the bunk and pulled a blanket over my lap.

She smiled. "I've seen a man before, you know. In my country we've no need to clothe ourselves."

"Uh . . . yes. . . ." What *do* you say to a naked merrow? "Uh . . . won't you sit down?"

"I'll not refuse." She sat on the opposite bunk, our bare knees almost touching in the narrow cabin.

"Do you have the cap for me then?"

The windbreaker was hanging on a peg over the bunk. I reached awkwardly behind me and pulled out the cap. She took it and held it to her breast. There were tears in her eyes.

"You've saved my life, you know."

"Not me. It was the old woman. I didn't believe her."

"But you came." Her soft, warm hand touched my knee. She brushed her hair back and put the cap on. "There. A bit comical isn't it?"

I laughed. A gold and white vision from the sea with a Christmas stocking on her head. She stood up and pulled the cap off. "I've no need of this here." She dropped it on the bunk.

Her fingers touched the scars on my arm. For once I didn't pull away. "You've been badly done there . . ."

"I can live with it."

"Can you now?" She sighed, "It's wondrous things men do to each other. God knows this island has seen enough of it."

Her breasts were disconcertingly close to my face. "It's different then in your country . . . Tir Faoi-Thonn?"

"That it's not. We are all God's creatures. There's no perfection for any of us . . . not even the angels." I could smell the faint perfume of her skin, salt wind on a warm sea.

"You came to me . . . and I came to you." Her voice was soft. "There's little enough one can do for another in this life."

She pulled my head forward. Her breasts were firm and sweet as apples.

I woke once in the night to feel her silver-shot hair spread over my chest. I moved in the narrow bunk, easing a cramped leg.

Her eyes opened. "Do you believe in the merrow now?"

I stroked the curve of her spine. "I believe. But you know, I haven't yet heard your name."

"My name, is it? God save us from what you'll be wanting next." She gave me a small sharp nip on the side. "My given name you'd not get your tongue around. But my family name you already know."

"I do?"

"Of course you do. The same as your boat. I'm of the clan McLir. That's what got me into trouble. When I saw the name I was curious. I got too close and that great machine of yours pulled the cap right off my head."

She stroked my face with her hand. There was a webbed membrane stretched between the knuckles of her fingers. I turned on my side and pulled her closer. It was the only difference I noticed, and of no significance at the time.

I woke to the slap of the hull against the piling. I sat up, alone in the bunk, then pulled my clothes on and went above. The deck was dry under a low, cloudy sky. Not a sign on the boat, no magic bit of seaweed, no wet fairy prints on the deck. The unnamed McLir was gone.

Perhaps it had been a dream, the slipping cogs of a crippled psyche. I went below and searched the cabin. The cap was gone. I came back up and sat staring over the wind-chopped water. At last, cold and depressed, I cast off and headed downstream.

There was a mist in the air when I sighted the Lanesboro bridge. I could barely see the faded letters of the warning signs. I felt a sense of lassitude, a bone-weariness. I wanted off this island and back to the States. I slammed the throttle forward. On to Glassan. In the morning I'd leave the boat at Athlone. By tomorrow evening I'd be winging out of Shannon airport and on my way home.

Distant rain squalls stitched the surface of the lake. Visibility dropped. I turned on the running lights. Whitecaps were rising and spray began to break over the bow. Loose gear crashed in the galley. Despite the cold I was sweating.

I couldn't see the shore. My chances of getting to Glassan were nil. I'd have to go back to Lanesboro. I gave it left full rudder and shoved the throttle to the stop.

The boat swung around. The engine shuddered and died. I tried to restart it as the quartering waves began to slam the boat. No luck. I dropped to my knees and tore off the hatch cover. I fumbled in the wheel-locker and found a flashlight. I braced myself and peered down. The plastic dome of the filter was jammed with weeds.

I tucked the flashlight under my right arm and tried to loosen the wing nut. It was jammed. The boat pitched and a rush of water spilled over the side. Looking up, I could see that I was beam to the waves. I needed a tool to get the wing nut off the filter pot. Another wave hit, jolting me against the wheel.

I knew I was in real trouble. If I could keep the bow into the wind, I might be able to work on the engine. The only chance was to get the anchor out. If I could find bottom, it would pull the bow into the wind.

I staggered forward. Braced against the pitch, I let go the anchor. A wave hit the bow and I lurched back. A wet blue nylon tentacle seized my legs. Above me a vision of dark boiling clouds as I was pulled from the deck. Down into the cold roiling water of Lough Ree.

Into the black water, the pull of heavy steel cutting the line into my legs. Lungs fired, I jerked at the line, the dream shrouds of a streamered 'chute. I felt the snap of bone. My oxygen-starved brain saw a burst of yellow light . . . the night fantasy of a pearl-skinned woman with rose-red mouth, screaming a soundless scream, now not screaming. Behind her, white faces, other bodies swift in the night water. Cold hands on my face.

My eyes opened to a moon-scoured sky. The pain hit me. Up the leg, lancing the brain. I screamed. A white muscular body appeared above me, pushing me down

"He's alive . . . awake. . . ." Men's voices. I shoved against a slippery wet surface. The voices faded in and out. "The Barren Swan . . . the Barren Swan. . . ." There was a sharp prick to my shoulder. Down again into a warm sea . . . floating . . . yellow lights and peace. A last vision of the moonlit hair of the woman McLir.

Yellow light again. Pressing against my eyelids, warming the skin. The sun was full on my naked body stretched out in the cockpit. At first I dared not move, remembering the pain. There was only the coarse feel of the deck beneath me.

I willed my legs to move. They moved. I rolled to push myself up, then stopped. I was pushing with my right arm. I felt for the jagged scars which ran from shoulder to elbow. There were none. I jumped to my feet. I stroked my arm. I clapped my hands . . . both of them. I shouted, arms waving. My voice sounded over the deserted lake. No answer. Before me was a small V-shaped island. The boat rocked in the gentle breeze, the bow line tied to a wisp of a rowan tree. I sat down on a locker, flexing my fingers . . . not five but all ten. And I cried.

I live now at *Cnoc Grianan*. A great advantage, for the enlightened Irish have no income tax for artists.

Uncle Frank thinks the recovery of my arm is a miracle of modern medicine. I wouldn't try to disillusion him. When I bought the boat from him, I asked him about the name.

"You are an uneducated sort, aren't you? Manannan McLir . . . that's the old sea god. The King of the 'Country Under The Waves.' "

"What do you know about the 'Barren Swan'?"

"Barren Swan? Barren Swan? Sounds like the name of a pub." He thought for a moment. "God save us from such ignorance," he laughed. "You must mean 'Bar an Suán.' That's the 'pin of slumber' in the old mythology. . . ."

A few months ago I met Ed Devlin in Dublin. We had lunch together and I asked him about beán O'Meara.

"That's a strange story. It was right after you met her. Poor old dear passed away. God rest her soul."

"What's strange about that? She might have been a hundred."

Ed paused. "I'll tell you . . . but you mustn't breathe it to another soul. There's only me and Father Fitz and the bishop who know. We all thought she was as poor as a tinker. But she left a great chest of gold coins to the parish. There was only one condition . . . that she be buried in Lough Ree."

"What's wrong with that?"

He downed his drink. "Use your head man. The authorities would not be keen about dropping bodies in the lake, would they? What would the tourists think?"

"You dropped her in the lake?"

"Me and Father Fitz. We didn't just shove her over the side you know. Poor misfortunate thing. When we put her in the coffin was the first time I'd ever seen her without her gloves."

"What do you mean?"

"The poor woman had a deformity. Webbed like a duck between her fingers. . . ."

I keep the *Manannan McLir* at Carrick-on-Shannon. Whenever I can I take her out. I've a favorite spot above Lanesboro. I tie up to some old pilings and fish. I haven't had much luck, but I keep trying. At least I haven't yet caught what I'm looking for.

Fish Story

by

Leslie Charteris

In "Driftglass," which appears elsewhere in this anthology, we saw the formidable arsenal of ultramodern high-technology being brought to bear on the problem of adapting human beings for a life in the sea. But, as the quiet but sobering story that follows suggests, perhaps if you just wanted it intensely enough, it could be accomplished more simply than that. . . .

Leslie Charteris is probably best known as the creator of "the Saint," whose suave and dashing exploits have been depicted in a long series of mystery-adventure novels, television shows, comic strips, and movies; there was even a Saint *mystery magazine. Charteris's most recent book is a collection,* The Fantastic Saint.

* * *

I USED TO SEE THE OLD MAN EVERY DAY AROUND BILL THOMPSON's place, down at Marathon, in the Florida Keys. He was almost a part of the scenery, like the mangrove islands offshore or the pelicans that wheeled lazily back and forth and sat out on the sandbar at low tide. He didn't keep much busier than they did, either. Sometimes he'd cart off a load of trash, or trundle a barrow-load of ice out to one of the boats. But mostly he'd just be standing or sitting around on the pier or beside the pool, staring into the water.

I couldn't have guessed just how old he actually was. His rather shapeless figure, in patched and faded khaki dungarees, didn't have either the corpulence or emaciation of decay, and his slouch suggested laziness or relaxation rather than decrepitude: when he had to, he could move about as well as anyone. But he could have passed for anything from 55 to 90.

He didn't talk much to anyone unless he had to. But when

I passed him I would give him a friendly time of day, and he would always respond cordially enough. Then he would go back to staring down at the water.

It's usually pretty clear in the bay, and when it's calm you can see small fish cruising about on their aimless errands, and sometimes a conch clawing its laborious way over the bottom under its heavy shell. I looked down with the old man a couple of times, but that was about all I could see.

Once I asked him if he was looking at anything special that I was missing.

"No, sir," he said pleasantly. "Just lookin' at the fish."

He didn't seem disposed to enlarge on the subject, so I left it at that. I've heard of bird watching, which has always struck me as a slightly eccentric but harmless pastime, so I figured there might be fish watchers, too.

Next time I saw him at it, I said: "How are the fish today?"

"Fine," he said imperturbably; which was as courteous a reply as you could expect to a rather silly question.

I stood beside him for a while and looked at the fish with him. After a long while he seemed to thaw out a little in the encouraging climate of my silence.

"People could learn a lot by lookin' at fish, 'stead of talkin' about 'em so much," he volunteered. "I been watchin' 'em all my life. Started when I used to fish for a living. Figured if I watched 'em enough—how they moved about, how they et, what kind of things interested 'em—I'd know better 'n anybody how to catch 'em. I did, too. Now I just watch 'em," he concluded.

Later, I was down at the cleaning table on the dock, starting to scale a nice four-pound red snapper we'd caught that afternoon, when the old man came by. A lot of the scales were flying into the water as I scraped them off, and the mullet and needlefish were having a field day, darting and leaping for them like kids in a shower of popcorn. The old man stood by my elbow and watched them for quite a while.

"That's a fair enough little fish you got," he said at last, nodding at the one I was cleaning. "How'd you take him?"

"Spinning."

"They been comin' in with the wells full all day," he said. "Kingfish, mostly. That all you got?"

"This is all we brought home," I said. "We had a lot of sport with a whole flock of kings, but they were all too big for just my wife and me to eat, so we turned 'em loose. We aren't greedy, and this one looked just right for dinner."

I could feel something transmitted from him almost like a gentle glow, a warmth quite different from the ordinary politeness.

"It's a pity more folks don't think like that," he said presently. "I've seen 'em come in with more fish than they an' all their friends could eat, and seen 'em throw it away. I've seen 'em kill tarpon, even, which nobody can eat an' which wasn't anything like big enough to try for a record, even, an' bring 'em in just to have their pictures taken with it."

"My wife and I only fish for fun," I said, being perfectly truthful but trying not to sound smug about it. "We just enjoy playing with them and eating one occasionally."

"I can eat 'em, too," he said matter-of-factly. "They're good food."

I rinsed off the fillets I had cut from the two sides of the snapper and set them aside, and I was just starting to clean off the table when he put out his hand and picked up the strips I had trimmed from the back and the belly, with the fins and the small bones in.

"May I have these?" he asked.

It hadn't occurred to me that he might be hungry, but I had never asked what he lived on.

"Here," I said, "these fillets are quite big, and we aren't big eaters. Why don't you take one of them?"

"No," he said, "I was just going to feed the bonefish."

In Bill Thompson's swimming pool, which is nothing but a big hollow blasted out of the coral rock in front of the cottages, where anybody can swim without being nervous about being mistaken for a free lunch counter by some stray barracuda, there are a lot of fish, which have been caught and dumped there live by various contributors, and which live there in a sort of natural aquarium, quite happily, since they are walled in by a ring of fill and the water changes with every tide. Among them are three bonefish, which any angler will tell you is the fastest and spookiest thing with fins; but these three have become so domesticated and used to people that they just cruise up and down the shallows along the shore and look up at you beguilingly like spoiled puppies hoping for a handout.

I walked over to the pool with the old man and watched him feed the bonefish. He broke the trimmings up with his fingers and threw them carefully, aiming them so that the fish had to keep racing for them. Sometimes he chewed a small piece himself.

"See how they swim?" he said.

"Just like fish," I said.

"That's the only way to swim," he said. "Most everybody these days thinks he can swim, but they don't know nothin' about it. Like you. You think you swim pretty good. I've watched you."

"Oh, I just get along," I said rather huffily.

"You don't know the first thing about it," he said dispassionately. "No more'n anybody else. I see 'em all splashin' about, kickin' an' thrashin' like big overgrown beetles. All the fish must look at 'em an' laugh fit to split their sides."

"Well," I said, hoisting my fillets, "I'm going to run along and have the last laugh on this one, anyway."

I went into our cottage and found Audrey already clean and shining like a schoolgirl, the way she always looks after a shower.

"I'm starved," she said. "Whatever kept you?"

"Taking a swimming lesson," I said. "The old geezer thinks I swim like a beetle. He watches fish all the time, and he knows the difference."

Picking up my mail at the office next morning, I asked Bill Thompson about him.

"Old Andrew?" Bill said with a grin. "He's quite a character. Been around here ever since anyone can remember. Used to be the best fishing guide in these parts, too, once upon a time."

"What stopped him?" I asked.

"I don't really know. They say his wife took out in a skiff once to pick up some lobster traps; somehow the boat tipped over, and she was drowned. She couldn't swim. Andrew went on a long drink and never fished again. That's one story, anyway. Maybe it did have something to do with getting him touched in the head. But he's harmless. I give him a few odd jobs, and he makes enough to live on and get drunk once or twice a week. He's happy as long as he can hang around the dock and look at the fish."

Late that afternoon, Audrey, who pampers me demoralizingly, came and put her arms around my neck and insisted that I knock off the writing I had been doing and come with her for a swim.

"The water's like glass today," she said. "Let's take the snorkels."

We have a couple of French diving masks with built-in breathing tubes, which we call snorkels and which are the latest and best thing of their kind. The mask fits over the whole face, and you breathe naturally through the nose, instead of having to hold a tube in your mouth like the contraptions most skin divers are still using. You can't go down deep with them, like with an aqualung, but you can paddle around face down on the surface indefinitely, without ever having to come up for air, and look down into the water as if into an aquarium. This is almost our favorite pastime, and in clear warm water we can spend hours at it.

The old man was standing by the pool again, and he watched us put this gear on our heads and go in. He was still watching, after however long it was, when we came out.

"Pretty fancy helmets you got there," he remarked.

"We like them," I said—perhaps a little brusquely, because I was still ridiculously peeved about his contempt for my swimming.

"I seen spear fishermen with things like that," he said calmly. "Only not so fancy. It all comes to the same thing, I guess. Just makes it easier for 'em to go in an' kill fish."

"Is that worse than catching them on a line?" I asked.

"It is," he stated. "You catch a fish on a hook, an' he gets away, or you cut him off, the hook rusts out an' he's none the worse. A fish gets away with one o' them spears in him, an' he's goin' to die, or the other fish'll kill him, an' do no good to nobody. Then they'll go down an' spear a grouper in a hole, say, an' he thrashes around an' stirs up all the spawn that may be settin' there, an' that means a lot more little fish that ain't never goin' to be born."

"We don't really spear fish," Audrey said. "They look so pretty in the water, I just hate to see him even trying to shoot at one."

"So I gave it up," I said. "I never was much good at it, anyway. And we get as much fun out of just looking at them."

Again I felt that invisible glow that seemed to come out of him when you said something that fitted in with his ideas.

"I suppose you wouldn't let me try on one o' them things?" he said.

"Sure," I said.

I put it on for him and showed him how he had to keep his head forward so that the shut-off valve wouldn't cut off his air. He stood for a minute getting the feel of it; then, without taking off even his shirt, he walked out into the water and started swimming.

We watched for a little while, and Audrey said: "Well, you've made a friend. I'm going in and get the first shower. Don't stay all night."

She went in, and I stayed and watched the old man for a long time. He swam around very slowly and cautiously, like a frog. At last he came out and took the helmet off.

"It's mighty nice," he said.

Now that I had him weakened, I couldn't resist getting in the dig I had been saving up.

"I've been thinking," I said, working up to it, "about what you said about swimming."

"You have?" he said innocently.

"Yes," I said. "How would *you* say people ought to swim?"

"They ought to look at the fish," he said. "See how a fish swims. No flailin' around. Just a little wiggle, an' it *glides* through the water. Look at the animals that really know how to swim. Look at the seals. Look at an otter. They don't swim like people. They swim like fish."

"They're also built more like a fish," I pointed out. "People have got awkward things like arms and legs, and not enough joints to wiggle with."

"All right," he said. "But they could try. Take your two arms. Make believe they're a couple of eels, an' make 'em go snakelike, like an eel swims, from your shoulders right down to your hands. An' then your legs. You could put 'em together an' try to move 'em with your body, like a fish."

I had him now.

"So," I said, trying not to make my voice too cruel, "how come you swim like a frog?"

He looked at me in silence, and I could feel he was hurt.

"You watched me," I said, "and I was watching you."

"That's why I wasn't doin' it right," he said. "I never like to swim right when anyone's watchin'."

"Oh," I said—too politely.

He went on staring at me with his clear depthless eyes.

"You don't believe me," he said. "Nobody believes me."

"Of course I do," I said uncomfortably.

He didn't have to be a clairvoyant to detect the hollowness of my words. He seemed to be fighting a great struggle within himself, but I could feel that it wasn't a struggle with ordinary indignation. He was sorry for himself, and sorry for me, and some infinitely pent-up frustration in him was stirring in what might have been a kind of death agony.

After what seemed like an age, he seemed to come to an epochal decision. He glanced around him almost furtively, as if afraid of being seen in commission of some dread misdeed. It was getting dark already, and there was no one around. He turned away from me and walked back into the water.

He waded in up to his waist and lay forward, floating like a log. Then—it's almost impossible to describe—he gave a queer sort of fishlike wiggle, all over, and disappeared.

It must have been a trick of the fading light, but he *had* looked rather like a basking fish going down. Nothing to it really, of course: any good swimmer can duck-dive something like that. I frowned at the area where he had vanished, expecting him to come up close by at any moment, and making a mental resolution to humor him more generously thereafter.

"Hey!"

I turned rather stupidly. I knew it was his voice. And there he was, his gray head bobbing above the water at the far end of the pool.

I didn't literally rub my eyes, but I felt like doing it. It seemed only a few seconds since he had gone under. I knew that my thoughts had been wool-gathering, and obviously I'd simply been unaware of the lapse of time.

"Do that again," I called to him.

He flattened out and wriggled out of sight again, and this time I counted, keeping a deliberate rhythm: *Thousand-one, thousand-two, thousand-three, thousand-four* . . .

I'd just gotten that far, meaning four seconds, when there was a swirl in the water right at my feet, and the old man stood up out of it, shaking himself like a big dog, and plodded up the crushed coral slope to face me.

"Now, you've seen it," he said. "If I die tomorrow, somebody seen it."

Without another word he trudged slowly away into the deepening twilight, dripping water; and I went slowly into the cottage.

"Did you learn anything?" Audrey asked brightly.

"Yes," I said. "I found out I need my eyes examined. Or maybe my head."

"What do you mean?"

"Oh, nothing," I said. "The old boy can see more in fish than I can. But maybe he's the one that's cracked, and not me."

"I wouldn't be too sure of that," she said mischievously; and I laughed and was glad I could turn it off, because I wasn't ready to talk about what I'd seen. Or thought I'd seen. I was afraid I actually had suffered some kind of hallucination.

It haunted me before I fell asleep, though, and again when I woke up in the morning. I could remember exactly how I'd counted the seconds, with that trick of saying "thousand" in between which helps to keep them spaced evenly: it beat in my head like a metronome. I checked it against my watch, and it came out right on the nose.

Audrey always likes to sleep a bit late when we're on vacation, so I swallowed some breakfast and went out by the pool. I knew it was a good big swimming hole, but perhaps my eye for distance was a little vague. I paced it off carefully, from the point opposite where the old man had been when he started his last swim to the place where I knew I'd been standing. Then I shook my head and paced it over again. It came out the same.

Even if I'd faced jail for perjury, I couldn't have made it any less than fifty yards.

Fifty yards in four seconds would mean a hundred yards in eight seconds, if he could keep it up. And he hadn't seemed in the least winded when he came out.

But a hundred yards in eight seconds is a second faster than the fastest human has ever *run!*

In eight seconds, a hundred yards, that's three hundred feet, that's thirty-seven-and-a-half feet a second. Sixty miles an hour is eighty-eight feet a second (I remembered that without having to work it out, from a story I'd written involving an automobile accident). Eighty-eight into thirty-seven gives you a little more than forty percent, meaning that his speed was better than twenty-four miles an hour. That's a good clip for a twin-engine express cruiser.

I've heard that porpoises have been timed at a speed up to seventy-five miles an hour. But a man—an *old man . . .*

My head was swimming a little.

The old man had come up beside me from somewhere, silently. He had a handful of shrimp heads, and he was tossing them one by one to the fish.

"You ain't dreaming," he said, without taking his eyes off them. "You saw it."

"Would you do it again?" I asked.

"No."

"Haven't you ever thought," I said, trying not to disturb him with my excitement, "you could be one of the wonders of the world. You could break every swimming record that's ever been set. They'd pay you thousands of dollars to put on exhibitions. You could revolutionize the whole sport of swimming. Athletic coaches would pay you a fortune for your secrets—"

"I don't aim to make a spectacle of myself," he said. "And the only person I ever wanted to teach how to swim, just wouldn't learn."

"I heard about that," I said gently. "But somebody else might learn, and it might save his life."

"Anybody who wants to learn bad enough, can learn," he said with the stubbornness of his years. *"You* could learn, if you wanted to, and if you didn't think you knew it all already. All you have to do is forget everything they taught you, and just watch the fish. Try to feel like a fish, an' move like a fish, 'stead of kickin' about like a drownin' cockroach, an' one day it'll just come to you, sudden an' quiet like. But I wouldn't tell nobody. Next thing you know, everybody'd be out with them gol-darned spears, swimmin' like fish an' seein' how many they could kill."

He tossed in the last shrimp head, wiped his hands on his jeans, and stood there just looking at the bonefish cruising back and forth. I wished in vain that some inspiration would tell me how to penetrate his quiet obduracy.

"You know," he said, "folks don't give fish enough credit. What do they call somebody they're contemptuous of? A poor fish. Poor fish, my eye. Fish are a lot better off than most people. They've always got something to eat, even if it's each other, an' they don't need no money or clothes or machinery. They don't even have to worry about the weather. Down there just a few feet under it's always calm even in the worst storm, it doesn't rain or blow, it doesn't get hotter or colder. Sometimes I wonder why any creatures ever wanted to crawl up out of the

water an' live on land, like evolution says they did. Sometimes
I think we'd a been a lot better off improvin' our race by stayin'
down under the sea. An' one o' these days, maybe some of
us'll go back to it."

"We're hardly fitted for that now," I said, to keep him
talking, "unless we could get our gills back."

"What about whales an' porpoises?" he said. "They breathe
air, just like we do, but they spend all their lives in the sea an'
never come up on land. How do they do it? Well, they don't
try to stay on the top all the time, an' wear theirselves out,
like human bein's do when they're scared of drownin'. They
just relax an' let 'emselves go down, an' just push 'emselves
up when they want to get a breath. A lot o' folks wouldn't get
drowned if they only did that. They could stay in the water all
day and night if they wouldn't fight it. I know. I spent two
whole summers up at Marineland, that big aquarium they got
near St. Augustine, just watchin' the porpoises through the
glass windows. I just about got the feel of it myself. Any day
now, maybe, I'll be sure I can do it like they do. An' then I'll
go out an' be with them all the time—like some other folks
have, I reckon."

It was absurd, but he was so utterly earnest that a little chill
riffled through my hair.

"Other folks?" I repeated.

"That's right," he said, almost belligerently. "You ever hear
of mermaids?"

"I never heard of one being caught."

"You ain't likely to. They're too smart. But they been seen."

"Manatees," I said. "That's what the old-time sailors saw,
perhaps with a bottle of rum to help them. They just thought
they looked human, and took it from there."

"I'm talkin' about mermaids," he said. "Not things with
fish tails, but people who learned how to be like fish or porpoises. Like I aim to do; an' it won't be so long from now."

Then I knew that his poor old brain was really adrift, even
if he had discovered some strange new trick about swimming;
and I was almost relieved to see Audrey coming across towards
us.

"Good morning," she said to him cheerfully. "Are you giving my husband some good advice?"

"I been tryin' to, ma'am," he said gravely. "But I don't
think he believes me. Maybe you'll both find out, one o' these

days. You're young, but you got the right things in your hearts. That's why I talked more to him than I ever talked to nobody yet. An' you"—he looked at me again—"bein' a writin' feller, perhaps one day you'll tell folks that old Andrew wasn't quite as crazy as they thought."

He tipped his cap and slouched unhurriedly away.

"What *is* the bee in his bonnet?" Audrey asked.

"It isn't a bee," I said. "It's a minnow."

And I told her all about it.

"Poor old guy," she said. "Losing his wife like that must have really done it to him. . . . But of course he couldn't actually have swam as fast as you thought he did. You must have lost count, or something."

"I must have," I said, and was glad to drop it there.

It was a dead-calm day, so we took a boat out to the ocean reef and went snorkeling there. I had never found fish so fascinating to watch.

We didn't see the old man again, but other people did, they said later. He was in every bar in town, making no trouble, just drinking steadily and not talking to anyone, but he could still walk straight when they last saw him. In the morning, they found his clothes and shoes and cap and an empty pint bottle on Bill Thompson's dock, and that was all. It seemed as if he must have gone swimming in the night, and then the liquor had overpowered him and he hadn't come back. The tide didn't bring him in, and the fishing boats kept a lookout for his body for days, but it was never found. Finally they figured that the barracuda or the morays had probably finished it.

Audrey and I missed him around the dock, and felt strangely depressed about the manner of his going. It seemed as if he should have had a happier ending, somehow. But how could that have been possible?

It was several days later, sunning ourselves beside the pool, that we both looked at each other suddenly with the same complete telepathic agreement. Audrey jumped up and pulled on her bathing cap.

"Come on," she said. "I'll race you the length of the pool."

Audrey is slim and utterly feminine, but she can go through the water in a way that, to my chagrin, always takes my best efforts to keep up with. I still didn't have all my heart in the race at first, and about halfway she was a length ahead of me. I put my head down and started to work.

And then, somehow, I was still thinking about the old man, and thinking about the fish I'd looked at, and I could see in my mind the funny sort of wiggle the old man had made when I watched him, and I seemed suddenly to feel it with all my body, and I was just silly enough to try it. . . .

After a moment I looked up to catch a breath and see how I was doing. This just saved me from banging my head on a rock at the end of the pool. Audrey, going like a young torpedo, was about fifteen yards behind.

When she joined me on the beach her eyes were big and round.

"Why, you old so-and-so," she sputtered. "So you've been holding out on me ever since I've known you!"

"Never," I said.

"Making believe I could almost beat you," she fumed, "when all the time you could swim like—"

"A fish," I said, and put a finger on her lips.

Sometimes we hardly seem to need to say a word to each other. It's a way two perfectly normal people can get when they've found complete harmony with each other. But she had to finalize it.

"I know it's impossible," she said, "but do you suppose . . ."

"Of course it is," I said. "But let's think it."

But we never swim like fish where anybody can see us. And very seldom even when we know we're alone. Somehow, it has us a little scared.

In the Islands

by
Pat Murphy

Half-breeds are often outcasts, misfits, unable to feel comfortable in either of their parents' worlds, not quite one thing, not quite the other....

Here's another poignant story by Pat Murphy, whose "Sweetly the Waves Call to Me" appears elsewhere in this anthology—a quietly moving story about a boy who is literally caught between two worlds, and an older man who must face a difficult decision about where his own loyalties ultimately lie....

* * *

THOUGH THE SUN WAS NEARLY SET, MORRIS WORE DARK glasses when he met Nick at the tiny dirt runway that served as the Bay Islands' only airport. Nick was flying in from Los Angeles by way of San Pedro Sula in Honduras. He peered through the cracked window of the old DC-3 as the plane bumped to a stop.

Morris stood with adolescent awkwardness by the one-room wooden building that housed Customs for the islands. Morris: dark, curly hair, red baseball cap pulled low over mirrored sunglasses, long-sleeved shirt with torn-out elbows, jeans with ragged cuffs.

A laughing horde of young boys ran out to the plane and grabbed dive bags and suitcases to carry to Customs. With the exception of Nick, the passengers were scuba divers, bound for Anthony's Cay resort on the far side of Roatan, the main island in the group.

Nick met Morris halfway to the Customs building, handed him a magazine, and said only, "Take a look at page fifty."

The article was titled "The Physiology and Ecology of a

242

New Species of Flashlight Fish," by Nicholas C. Rand and Morris Morgan.

Morris studied the article for a moment, flipping through the pages and ignoring the young boys who swarmed past, carrying suitcases almost too large for them to handle. Morris looked up at Nick and grinned—a flash of white teeth in a thin, tanned face. "Looks good," he said. His voice was a little hoarser than Nick had remembered.

"For your first publication, it's remarkable." Nick patted Morris's shoulder awkwardly. Nick looked and acted older than his thirty-five years. At the University, he treated his colleagues with distant courtesy and had no real friends. He was more comfortable with Morris than with anyone else he knew.

"Come on," Morris said. "We got to get your gear and go." He tried to sound matter-of-fact, but he betrayed his excitement by slipping into the dialect of the Islands—an archaic English spoken with a strange lilt and governed by rules all its own.

Nick tipped the youngster who had hauled his bags to Customs and waited behind the crowd of divers. The inspector looked at Nick, stamped his passport, and said, "Go on. Have a good stay." Customs inspections on the Islands tended to be perfunctory. Though the Bay Islands were governed by Honduras, the Islanders tended to follow their own rules. The Bay Islands lay off the coast of Honduras in the area of the Caribbean that had once been called the Spanish Main. The population was an odd mix: native Indians, relocated slaves called Caribs, and descendants of the English pirates who had used the Islands as home base.

The airport's runway stretched along the shore and the narrow, sandy beach formed one of its edges. Morris had beached his skiff at one end of the landing strip.

"I got a new skiff, a better one," Morris said. "If the currents be with us, we'll be in East Harbor in two hours, I bet."

They loaded Nick's gear and pushed off. Morris piloted the small boat. He pulled his cap low over his eyes to keep the wind from catching it and leaned a little into the wind. Nick noticed Morris's hand on the tiller; webbing stretched between the fingers. It seemed to Nick that the webbing extended further up each finger than it had when Nick had left the Islands four months before.

Dolphins came from nowhere to follow the boat, riding the bow wave and leaping and splashing alongside. Nick sat in the

bow and watched Morris. The boy was intent on piloting
the skiff. Behind him, dolphins played and the wake traced a
white line through the silvery water. The dolphins darted away,
back to the open sea, as the skiff approached East Harbor.

The town stretched along the shore for about a mile: a
collection of brightly painted houses on stilts, a grocery store,
a few shops. The house that Nick had rented was on the edge
of town.

Morris docked neatly at the pier near the house, and helped
Nick carry his dive bag and luggage to the house. "There's
beer in the icebox," Morris said. "Cold."

Nick got two beers. He returned to the front porch. Morris
was sitting on the railing, staring out into the street. Though
the sun was down and twilight was fading fast, Morris wore
his sunglasses still. Nick sat on the rail beside the teenager.
"So what have you been doing since I left?"

Morris grinned. He took off his sunglasses and tipped back
his cap. Nick could see his eyes—wide and dark and filled
with repressed excitement. "I'm going," Morris said. "I'm going
to sea."

Nick took a long drink from his beer and wiped his mouth.
He had known this was coming, known it for a long time.

"My dad, he came to the harbor; and we swam together.
I'll be going with him soon. Look." Morris held up one hand.
The webbing between his fingers stretched from the base almost
to the tip of each finger. The light from the overhead bulb
shone through the thin skin. "I'm changing, Nick. It's almost
time."

"What does your mother say of this?"

"My mum? Nothing." His excitement was spilling over. He
laid a hand on Nick's arm, and his touch was cold. "I'm going,
Nick."

Ten years ago, Nick had been diving at night off Middle
Cay, a small coral island not far from East Harbor. He had
been diving alone at night to study the nighttime ecology of
the reef. Even at age twenty-five, Nick had possessed a curiosity stronger than his sense of self-preservation.

The reef changed with the dying of the light. Different fishes
came out of hiding; different invertebrates prowled the surface
of the coral. Nick was particularly interested in the flashlight
fish, a small fish that glowed in the dark. Beneath each eye,

the flashlight fish had an organ filled with bioluminescent bacteria, which gave off a cold green light. They were elusive fish, living in deep waters and rising up to the reef only when the moon was new and the night was dark.

At night, sharks came in from the open sea to prowl the reef. Nick did not care to study them, but sometimes they came to study him. He carried a flashlight in one hand, a shark billy in the other. Usually, the sharks were only curious. Usually, they circled once, then swam away.

On that night ten years before, the gray reef shark that circled him twice did not seem to understand this. Nick could see the flat black eye, dispassionately watching him. The shark turned to circle again, turning with a grace that made its movement seem leisurely. It came closer; and Nick thought, even as he swam for the surface, about what an elegant machine it was. He had dissected sharks and admired the way their muscles worked so tirelessly and their teeth were arranged so efficiently.

He met the shark with a blow of the billy, a solid blow, but the explosive charge in the tip of the club failed. The charges did fail, as often as not. But worse: the shark twisted back. As he struck at it again, the billy slipped from his hand, caught in an eddy of water. He snatched at it and watched it tumble away, with the maddening slowness of objects underwater.

The shark circled wide, then came in again: elegant, efficient, deadly.

The shadow that intercepted the shark was neither elegant nor efficient. In the beam of the flashlight, Nick could see him clearly: a small boy dressed in ragged shorts and armed with a shark billy. This one exploded when he struck the shark, and the animal turned with grace and speed to cruise away, heading for the far side of the reef. The boy grinned at Nick and glided away into the darkness. Nick saw five lines on each side of the boy's body—five gill slits that opened and closed and opened and closed.

Nick hauled himself into the boat. He lay on his back and looked at the stars. At night, the world underwater often seemed unreal. He looked at the stars and told himself that over and over.

When Nick was in the Islands, Morris usually slept on the porch of whatever house Nick had rented. Nick slept on a bed inside.

Nick was tired from a long day of travel. He slept and he came upon the forbidden dreams with startling urgency and a kind of relief. It was only a dream, he told himself. Darkness covered his sins.

He dreamed that Morris lay on a dissecting table, asleep, his webbed hands quiet at his sides. Morris's eyes had no lashes; his nose was flat and broad; his face was thin and triangular—too small for his eyes. He's not human, Nick thought, not human at all.

Nick took the scalpel in his hand and drew it through the top layers of skin and muscle alongside the five gill slits on Morris's right side. There was little blood. Later, he would use the bone shears to cut through the ribs to examine the internal organs. Now, he just laid back the skin and muscle to expose the intricate structure of the gills.

Morris did not move. Nick looked at the teenager's face and realized suddenly that Morris was not asleep. He was dead. For a moment, Nick felt a tremendous sense of loss; but he pushed the feeling away. He felt hollow, but he fingered the feathery tissue of the gills and planned the rest of the dissection.

He woke to the palm fronds rattling outside his window and the warm morning breeze drying the sweat on his face. The light of dawn—already bright and strong—shone in the window.

Morris was not on the porch. His baseball cap hung from a nail beside the hammock.

Nick made breakfast from the provisions that Morris had left him: fried eggs, bread, milk. In midmorning, he strolled to town.

Morris's mother, Margarite, ran a small shop in the living room of her home, selling black-coral jewelry to tourists. The black coral came from deep waters; Morris brought it to her.

Two women—off one of the sailing yachts anchored in the harbor—were bargaining with Margarite for black-coral earrings. Nick waited for them to settle on a price and leave. They paid for the jewelry and stepped back out into the street, glancing curiously at Nick.

"Where's Morris?" he said to Margarite. He leaned on the counter and looked into her dark eyes. She was a stocky woman with skin the color of coffee with a little cream. She wore a flowered dress, hemmed modestly just below her knees.

He had wondered at times what this dark-eyed woman thought

of her son. She did not speak much, and he had sometimes suspected that she was slow-witted. He wondered how it had happened that this stocky woman had found an alien lover on a beach, had made love with such a stranger, had given birth to a son who fit nowhere at all.

"Morris—he has gone to sea," she said. "He goes to sea these days." She began rearranging the jewelry that had been jumbled by the tourists.

"When will he be back?" Nick asked.

She shrugged. "Maybe never."

"Why do you say that?" His voice was sharp, sharper than he intended. She did not look up from the tray. He reached across the counter and took her hand in a savage grip. "Look at me. Why do you say that?"

"He will be going to sea," she said softly. "He must. He belongs there."

"He will come to say good-bye," Nick said.

She twisted her hand in his grip, but he held her tightly. "His dad never said good-bye," she said softly.

Nick let her hand go. He rarely lost his temper and he knew he was not really angry with this woman, but with himself. He turned away without saying good-bye.

He strolled down the dirt lane that served as East Harbor's main street. He nodded to an old man who sat on his front porch, greeted a woman who was hanging clothes on a line. The day was hot and still.

He was a stranger here; he would always be a stranger here. He did not know what the Islanders thought of him, what they thought of Morris and Margarite. Morris had told him that they knew of the water-dwellers and kept their secret. "They live by the sea," Morris had said. "If they talk too much, their nets will rip and their boats sink. They don't tell."

Nick stopped by the grocery store on the far edge of town. A ramshackle pier jutted into the sea right beside the store.

Ten years before, the pier had been in better repair. Nick had been in town to pick up supplies. For a month, he was renting a skiff and a house on Middle Cay and studying the reef.

The sun had reached the horizon, and its light made a silver path on the water. Somewhere, far off, he could hear the laughter and shouting of small boys. At the end of the pier, a kid in a red baseball cap was staring out to sea.

Nick bought two Cokes from the grocery—cold from the icebox behind the counter. He carried them out to the pier. The old boards creaked beneath his feet, but the boy did not look up.

"Have a Coke," Nick said.

The boy's face was dirty. His dark eyes were too large for his face. He wore a red kerchief around his neck, ragged shorts, and a shirt that gaped open where the second button should have been. He accepted the Coke and took his first swig without saying anything.

Nick studied his face for a moment, comparing this face to the one that he remembered. A strange kind of calmness took hold of him. "You shouldn't go diving at night," he said. "You're too young to risk your life with sharks."

The boy grinned and took another swig of Coke.

"That was you, wasn't it?" Nick asked. He sat beside the kid on the dock, his legs dangling over the water. "That was you." His voice was steady.

"Aye." The boy looked at Nick with dark, grave eyes. "That was me."

The part of Nick's mind that examined information and accepted or rejected it took this in and accepted it. That part of him had never believed that the kid was a dream, never believed that the shark was imaginary.

"What's your name?"

"Morris."

"I'm Nick." They shook hands and Nick noticed the webbing between the boy's fingers—from the base of the finger to the first joint.

"You're a marine biologist?" asked the kid. His voice was a little too deep for him, a little rough, as if he found speaking difficult.

"Yes."

"What was you doing, diving out there at night?"

"I was watching the fish. I want to know what happens on the reef at night." He shrugged. "Sometimes I am too curious for my own good."

The boy watched him with dark, brooding eyes. "My dad, he says I should have let the shark have you. He says you will tell others."

"I haven't said anything to anyone," Nick protested.

The boy took another swig of Coke, draining the bottle. He set the bottle carefully on the dock, one hand still gripping it. He studied Nick's face. "You must promise you will never tell." He tilted back his baseball cap and continued to study Nick's face. "I will show you things you has got no chance of finding without me." The boy spoke with quiet confidence and Nick found himself nodding. "You know those little fish you want to find—the ones that glow?" He grinned when Nick looked surprised and said, "The Customs man said you were looking for them. I has been to a place where you can find them every new moon. And I has found a kind that aren't in the books."

"What do you know about what's in the books?"

Morris shrugged, a smooth, fluid motion. "I read the books. I has got to know about these things." He held out his hand for Nick to shake. "You promise?"

Nick hesitated, then put his hand in the kid's hand. "I promise." He would have promised more than that to learn about this kid.

"I has a skiff much better than that," Morris said, jerking his head contemptuously toward the skiff that Nick had been using. "I'll be at Middle Cay tomorrow."

Morris showed up at Middle Cay and took Nick to places that he never would have found. Morris read all Nick's reference books with great interest.

And the webbing between his fingers kept growing.

Nick bought a cold Coke in the grocery store and strolled back to his house. Morris was waiting on the porch, sitting on the rail and reading their article in the magazine.

"I brought lobsters for dinner," he said. Small scratching noises came from the covered wooden crate at his feet. He thumped on it with his heel, and the noises stopped for a moment, then began again.

"Where have you been?"

"Out to the Hog Islands. Fishing mostly. I spend most of the days underwater now." He looked at Nick but his eyes were concealed by the mirrored glasses. "When you left, I could only stay under for a few hours. Now, there doesn't seem to be a limit. And the sun burns me if I'm out too much."

Nick caught himself studying the way Morris was holding the magazine. The webbing between his fingers tucked neatly out of the way. It should not work, he thought. This being that is shaped like a man and swims like a fish. But bumblebees can't fly, by logical reasoning.

"What do you think of the article?" Nick asked.

"Good, as far as it goes. Could say more. I've been watching them, and they seem to signal to each other. There's different patterns for the males and females. I've got notes on it all. I'll show you. The water temperature seems to affect them too."

Nick was thinking how painful this curiosity of his was. It had always been so. He wanted to know; he wanted to understand. He had taken Morris's temperature; he had listened to Morris's heartbeat and monitored its brachycardia when Morris submerged. He had monitored the oxygen levels in the blood, observed Morris's development. But there was so much more to learn. He had been hampered by his own lack of background—he was a biologist, not a doctor. There were tests he could not perform without harming Morris. And he had not wanted to hurt Morris. No, he did not want to hurt Morris.

"I'll leave all my notes on your desk," Morris was saying. "You should take a look before I go."

Nick frowned. "You'll be able to come back," he said. "Your father comes in to see you. You'll come back and tell me what you've seen, won't you?"

Morris set the magazine on the rail beside him and pushed his cap back. The glasses hid his eyes. "The ocean will change me," he said. "I may not remember the right things to tell you. My father thinks deep, wet thoughts; and I don't always understand him." Morris shrugged. "I will change."

"I thought you wanted to be a biologist. I thought you wanted to learn. And here you are, saying that you'll change and forget all this." Nick's voice was bitter.

"I has got no choice. It's time to go." Nick could not see his eyes or interpret his tone. "I don't belong on the land anymore. I don't belong here."

Nick found that he was gripping the rail as he leaned against it. He could learn so much from Morris. So much. "Why do you think you'll belong there. You won't fit there, with your memories of the islands. You won't belong."

Morris took off his glasses and looked at Nick with dark, wet eyes. "I'll belong. I has got to belong. I'm going."

The lobsters scratched inside their box. Morris replaced his sunglasses and thumped lightly on the lid again. "We should make dinner," he said. "They're getting restless."

During the summer on Middle Cay, Nick and Morris had become friends. Nick came to rely on Morris's knowledge of the reef. Morris lived on the island and seemed to find there a security he needed. His curiosity about the sea matched Nick's.

Early each evening, just after sunset, they would sit on the beach and talk—about the reef, about life at the University, about marine biology, and—more rarely—about Morris and his father.

Morris could say very little about his father. "My dad told me legends," Morris said to Nick, "but that's all. The legends say that the water people came down from the stars. They came a long time ago." Nick was watching Morris and the boy was digging his fingers in the sand, as if searching for something to grasp.

"What do you think?" Nick asked him.

Morris shrugged. "Doesn't really matter. I think they must be native to this world or they couldn't breed with humans." He sifted the beach sand with his webbed hands. "But it doesn't much matter. I'm here. And I'm not human." He looked at Nick with dark, lonely eyes.

Nick had wanted to reach across the sand and grasp the cold hand that kept sifting the sand, digging and sifting the sand. He wanted to say something comforting. But he had remained silent, giving the boy only the comfort of his company.

Nick lay on his cot, listening to the sounds of the evening. He could hear his neighbor's chickens, settling down to rest. He could hear the evening wind in the palms. He wanted to sleep, but he did not want to dream.

Once Morris was gone, he would not come back, Nick thought. If only Nick could keep him here.

Nick started to drift to sleep and caught himself on the brink of a dream. His hands had been closing on Morris's throat. Somehow, in that moment, his hands were not his own. They were his father's hands: cool, clean, brutally competent. His father, a high school biology teacher with a desire to be more, had taught him how to pith a frog, how to hold it tight and insert the long pin at the base of the skull. "It's just a frog," his father had said. His father's hands were closing on Morris's throat and Nick was thinking, I could break his neck—quickly and painlessly. After all, he's not human.

Nick snapped awake and clasped his hands as if that might stop them from doing harm. He was shivering in the warm night. He sat up on the edge of the bed, keeping his hands locked together. He stepped out onto the porch where Morris was sleeping.

Morris was gone; the hammock was empty. Nick looked out over the empty street and let his hands relax. He returned to his bed and dozed off, but his sleep was disturbed by voices that blended with the evening wind. He could hear his former wife's bitter voice speaking over the sound of the wind. She said, "I'm going. You don't love me, you just want to analyze me. I'm going." He could hear his father, droning on about how the animal felt no pain, how it was all in the interest of science. At last he sank into a deeper sleep, but in the morning he did not want to remember his dreams.

Morris was still gone when Nick finished breakfast. He read over Morris's notes. They were thorough and carefully taken. Nick made notes for another paper on the flashlight fish, a paper on which Morris would be senior author.

Morris returned late in the afternoon. Nick looked up from his notes, looked into Morris's mirrored eyes, and thought of death. And tried not to think of death.

"I thought we could go to Middle Cay for dinner," Morris said. "I has got conch and shrimp. We can take the camp stove and fix them there."

Nick tapped his pencil against the pad nervously. "Yes. Let's do that."

Morris piloted the skiff to Middle Cay. Through the water, Nick could see the reef that ringed the island—shades of blue and green beneath the water. The reef was broken by channels here and there; Morris followed the main channel nearly to the beach, then cut the engine and let the skiff drift in.

They set up the camp stove in a level spot, sheltered by the trunk of a fallen palm tree. Morris cracked the conch and pounded it and threw it in the pan with shrimp. They drank beer while the combination cooked. They ate from tin cups, leaning side by side against the fallen palm.

"You can keep the skiff for yourself," Morris said suddenly. "I think that you can use it."

Nick looked at him, startled.

"I left my notes on your desk," Morris said. "They be as clear as I can make them."

Nick was studying his face. "I will go tonight," Morris said. "My dad will come here to meet me." The sun had set and the evening breeze was kicking up waves in the smooth water. He drained his beer and set the bottle down beside the stove.

Morris stood and took off his shirt, slipped out of his pants. The gill slits made stripes that began just below his ribcage and ended near his hips. He was more muscular than Nick remembered. He stepped toward the water.

"Wait," Nick said. "Not yet."

"Got to." Morris turned to look at Nick. "There's a mask and fins in the skiff. Come with me for a ways."

Morris swam ahead, following the channel out. Nick followed in mask and fins. The twilight had faded. The water was dark and its surface shone silver. The night did not seem real. The darkness made it dreamlike. The sound of Nick's feet breaking the water's surface was too loud. The touch of the water against his skin was too warm. Morris swam just ahead, just out of reach.

Nick wore his dive knife at his belt. He always wore his dive knife at his belt. As he swam, he noticed that he was taking his knife out and holding it ready. It was a heavy knife, designed for prying rocks apart and cracking conch. It would work best as a club, he was thinking. A club to be used for a sudden sharp blow from behind. That might be enough. If he called to Morris, then Morris would stop and Nick could catch him.

But his voice was not cooperating. Not yet. His hands held the knife ready, but he could not call out. Not yet.

He felt the change in water temperature as they passed into deeper water. He felt something—a swirl of water against his legs—as if something large were swimming past.

Morris disappeared from the water ahead of him. The water was smooth, with no sign of Morris's bobbing head. "Morris," Nick called. "Morris."

He saw them then. Dim shapes beneath the water. Morris: slim, almost human. His father: man-shaped, but different. His arms were the wrong shape; his legs were too thick and muscular.

Morris was close enough to touch, but Nick did not strike. When Morris reached out and touched Nick's hand with a cold, gentle touch, Nick realized the knife and let it fall, watched it tumble toward the bottom.

Morris's father turned in the water to look up at Nick and Nick read nothing in those inhuman eyes: cold, dark, dispassionate. Black and uncaring as the eyes of a shark. Nick saw Morris swim down and touch his father's shoulder, urging him away into the darkness.

"Morris!" Nick called, knowing Morris could not hear him. He kicked with frantic energy, not caring that his knife was gone. He did not want to stop Morris. He wanted to go with Morris and swim with the dolphins and explore the sea.

There was darkness below him—cool, deep water. He could feel the tug of the currents. He swam, not conserving his energy, not caring. His kicks grew weaker. He looked down into the world of darkness and mystery and he sank below the surface almost gladly.

He felt a cold arm around his shoulders. He coughed up water when the arm dragged him to the surface. He coughed, took a breath that was half water, half air, coughed again. Dark water surged against his mask each time the arm dragged him forward. He choked and struggled, but the arm dragged him on.

One flailing leg bumped against coral, then against sand. Sand scraped against his back as he was dragged up the beach. His mask was ripped away and he turned on his side to retch and cough up seawater.

Morris squatted beside him with one cold webbed hand still on his shoulder. Nick focused on Morris's face and on the black eyes that seemed as remote as mirrored lenses. "Good-bye, Nick," Morris said. His voice was a hoarse whisper. "Good-bye."

Morris's hand lingered on Nick's shoulder for an instant. Then the young man stood and walked back to the sea.

Nick lay on his back and looked up at the stars. After a time, he breathed more easily. He picked up Morris's cap from where it lay on the beach and turned it in his hands, in a senseless repetitive motion.

He crawled further from the water and lay his head against the fallen log. He gazed at the stars and the sea, and thought about how he could write down his observations of Morris's departure and Morris's father. No. He could not write it down, could not pin it down with words. He did not need to write it down.

He put on the red baseball cap and pulled it low over his eyes. When he slept, with his head propped against the log, he dreamed only of the deep night that lay beneath the silver surface of the sea.

Recommended Reading List

BOOKS

Poul Anderson, *The Merman's Children*, (novel—Berkley, 1979)

Jane Yolen, *Neptune Rising: Songs & Tales of the Undersea Folk*, (collection—Philomel Books, 1982)

Gwen Benwell and Arthur Waugh, *Sea Enchantress: The Tale of the Mermaid and her Kin*, (reference book—The Citadel Press, 1965)

The Mermaid Reader, ed. Helen O'cleary (anthology—Franklin Watts Inc., 1964)

W. B. Yeats, *Fairy and Folk Tales of Ireland*, (collection—Walter Scott, London, 1893)

Katherine Briggs, *An Encyclopedia of Fairies*, (reference book—Pantheon, 1976)

Richard Carrington, *Mermaids and Mastodons*, (reference book—Holt, Rinehart and Winston, 1957)

SHORT STORIES

Brian W. Aldiss, "A Kind of Artistry," *Best of F&SF, 12th Series*.

Hans Christian Andersen, "The Little Mermaid," *The Mermaid Reader*.

Poul Anderson, "Homo Aquaticus," *Amazing*, Sept. 1963.

—————, "The Merman's Children," *Flashing Swords! #1*.

Lloyd Biggle, "First Love," *A Galaxy of Strangers*.

James Blish and Norman L. Knight, "The Shipwrecked Hotel," *Galaxy*, Aug. 1965.

Robert Bloch, "Mr. Margate's Mermaids, Inc.," *Imaginative Tales*, Mar. 1955.

Ray Bradbury, "The Shoreline at Sunset," *Medicine for Melancholy*.

Fredric Brown, "Fish Story," *Nightmares and Geezenstacks*.

T. Crofton Croker, "Flory Cantillon's Funeral," *Fairy and Folk Tales of Ireland*.

——————, "The Lady of Gollerus," *Ibid*.

——————, "The Wonderful Tune," *The Mermaid Reader*.

Avram Davidson, "The Case of the Mother-In-Law of Pearl," *The Enquiries of Doctor Eszterhazy*.

Elispeth Davis, "Geological Episode," *The Night of the Funny Hats*.

L. Sprague de Camp, "The Merman," *The Best of L. Sprague de Camp*.

Lord Dunsany, "Mrs. Jorkens," *Tall Short Stories*.

E. M. Forster, "The Story of the Siren," *Anchor Book of Stories*.

Mr. and Mrs. S. C. Hall, "John O'Glin," *The Mermaid Reader*.

Herman Hesse, "The Merman," *Pictor's Metamorphoses and Other Fantasies*.

Geoffrey Household, "The Pejmuller," *The Europe That Was*.

Edward Jesby, "Sea Wrack," *World's Best Science Fiction, First Series*.

R. A. Lafferty, "The Ultimate Creature," *Does Anyone Else Have Something Further to Add?*

Sterling Lanier, "The Kings of the Sea," *F&SF*, Nov. 1968.

Fritz Leiber, "Pipe Dream," *A Pailful of Air*.

——————, "The Mer-She," *Heroes and Horrors*.

——————, "When the Sea-King's Away," *Swords in the Mist*.

Eric Linklater, "Sealskin Trousers," *F&SF*, April 1952.

John Masefield, "The Sealman," *A Decade of F&SF*.

Peter Redgrove, "Mr. Waterman," *9th Annual Year's Best SF*.

Keith Robers, "The Deeps," *The Passing of the Dragons*.

Victor Rosseau, "The Seal-Maiden," *A. Merritt Fantasies*, Feb. 1950.

Eric St. Clair, "Olsen and the Gull," *Best of F&SF, 14th Series*.

Bruce Sterling, "Telliamed," *F&SF*, Sept. 1984.

Theodore Sturgeon, "Cargo," *Not Without Sorcery*.

Thomas Burnett Swann, "The Dolphin and the Deep," *The Dolphin and the Deep*.

Lisa Tuttle, "Till Human Voices Wake Us," *Clarion III*.

Evangaline Walton, "Above Ker-Is," *Year's Best Fantasy, Vol. 5*

Oscar Wilde, "The Fisherman and His Soul," *The Mermaid Reader*.

Jane Yolen, "Greyling," *Neptune Rising*.

_____, "The Malaysian Mer," *Ibid*.

_____, "One Old Man, With Seals," *Ibid*.

_____, "The River Maid," *Ibid*.

_____, "Sule Skerry," *Ibid*.

_____, "The Undine," *Ibid*.

About the Editors

GARDNER DOZOIS was born and raised in Salem, Massachusetts, and now lives in Philadelphia. He is the author or editor of sixteen books, including the novel *Strangers* and the collection *The Visible Man*. He is the editor of *Isaac Asimov's Science Fiction Magazine*; he also edits the annual series *The Year's Best Science Fiction*. His short fiction has appeared in *Playboy, Penthouse, Omni*, and most of the leading magazines and anthologies. He has won two Nebula Awards for his short fiction, and he has many times been a finalist for other Hugo and Nebula Awards. His critical work has appeared in *Writer's Digest, Starship, Thrust, Writing and Selling Science Fiction, The Writer's Handbook*, and *Science Fiction Writers*, and he is the author of the critical chapbook *The Fiction of James Tiptree, Jr.* He has been a judge for The World Fantasy Award and has served several times on the Nebula Awards Jury. His most recent books are *The Year's Best Science Fiction, Second Annual Collection;* and *Magicats!* and *Bestiary!*, two anthologies edited in collaboration with Jack Dann. He is currently at work on another novel, *Nottamun Town*.

JACK DANN is the author or editor of fifteen books, including the novels *Junction* and *Starhiker*, and the collection *Timetipping*. He is the editor of the anthology *Wandering Stars*, one of the most acclaimed anthologies of the 1970's, and several other well-known anthologies, including the recently published *More Wandering Stars*. His short fiction has appeared in *Playboy, Penthouse, Omni*, and most of the leading SF magazines and anthologies. He has been a Nebula Award finalist ten times, as well as a finalist for the World Fantasy Award and the British Science Fiction Association Award. His critical work has appeared in *The Washington Post, Starship, Nickelodeon, The Bulletin of the Science Fiction Writers of America, Empire, Future Life,* and *The Fiction Writer's Handbook,* and he is the author of the chapbook, *Christs and Other Poems.* His most recent books are *The Man Who Melted,* a novel; and *Magicats!* and *Bestiary!,* two anthologies edited in collaboration with Gardner Dozois. He has just sold a new novel, *Counting Coup.* Dann lives with his family in Binghamton, New York.